The Legacy of a Fool

By: L. J. Henderson

The Legacy of a Fool

Revised Edition: 2025

ISBN: 979-8-9920298-3-3

To my dedicated wife and best friend Elizabeth.
Without you, this book would have never become a reality.
And to my late grandmother, who never stopped believing in
me.

Table of Contents

Table of Contents

Prologue

To Mr. and Mrs. Skye

Monday, March 16th, 2048

Dear Mr. and Mrs. Skye,

My name is Laura Simpson. I am your son's guidance counselor at T. I. Kellerman. I hope this letter finds you both doing well. The reason for this correspondence is to let you know about some recent changes in Devin's behavior that I and other members of the faculty have been growing very concerned about.

For the past few months or so, we've noticed that Devin has been rapidly falling behind in his classes, and he hasn't been attending his scheduled courses regularly. When he does show up, he is generally inattentive and obnoxious. On the surface, it seems like he's more interested in impressing his friends with crude jokes and rude behavior than he is in getting a proper education. Unfortunately, every time an attempt is made to address these issues, he becomes argumentative and lashes out. As a result, many of the students have reached out to me and other members of the faculty to express their frustration and annoyance, citing that Devin's disruptive behavior is affecting their ability to stay focused while in the classroom. Subsequently, a number of their parents have also contacted the school in the hopes of finding a solution.

I'm not sure if you're aware of this, but his continued unexcused absenteeism is not just bad for his academic record, it can result in his expulsion from the school. In a worst-case scenario, it could also mean legal trouble for you, as truancy carries the potential to be treated as a criminal offense if left unchecked.

Mr. and Mrs. Skye, it is not my intention to burden you with undue worry regarding your son, however, his behavioral issues don't seem to stop with the above-mentioned items. Just last week, his recklessness resulted in a minor explosion in the science lab. Apparently, he thought it would amuse his classmates if he created a dangerous, pyrotechnic display by lobbing a chunk of potassium into a tub of water while the teacher was away from the classroom. As impressive as it might be that he had a strong enough understanding of chemistry to pull off a stunt like this, the potential risk of physical harm he subjected himself and his classmates to cannot be overlooked.

Because of this latest mishap, my own credentials as a guidance counselor have come under scrutiny by both my coworkers and my superiors. After all, Devin has been meeting with me each week for the past month and a half, and that's supposed to make a difference. Just the other day, the principal, whom I consider to be a close friend, jokingly teased me, saying that I had better get a handle on his wild antics before he goes out into society and "blows up the world." Even though I'm sure this jest was meant to be tongue-in-cheek, I could sense a hint of real concern beneath it.

To sum things up, many of the faculty members are getting annoyed with Devin's misbehavior, and the school's environment is beginning to suffer for it. For example, some of the younger students on campus now look up to him for all of the wrong reasons – they seem to think he is "cool." A number of them are even trying to mimic his ways, which is obviously creating problems in their own respective classrooms. So I'm sure you can understand when I tell you that something really needs to be done!

As you already know, your son used to be one of the top students in his class. He has always been extremely bright, and underneath his childish antics, I know he has a heart of gold. I'm just not sure what has gotten into him lately. Nonetheless, I firmly believe that this news must be as concerning to you as it is to me.

With that being said, I would like to schedule a meeting with you so that, together, we can take a closer look at these negative changes and lay out an appropriate plan of action to get him back on the right track. Here at T. I. Kellerman, we realize that it's not unusual for a kid of his age to act out, as the overwhelming need to be accepted by one's peers can often result in these types of situations, but we also know that things can turn around if the proper amount of care and support is given.

Please contact me so that we can discuss how to best approach this situation in person. I look forward to hearing back from you soon!

Sincerely,

Laura Simpson
Guidance Counselor
T. I. Kellerman
LauraSimpson@TIKellerman.com

Chapter 1

Holograms and Hovercars

Year: 2054
Location: Highland City, Earth 2.79

Devin Skye was in a funk. He had just turned away from the brightly lit holo-display in front of him to gaze out the window to his left when he noticed that the sun was quickly sinking behind the tall skyscrapers in the distance. Throwing his headset down on the desk with a loud clang, he jumped up and began racing around his tiny apartment, pushing and kicking clothes and other random objects to the side, frantically searching for something nice and clean to wear. He cursed himself out loud for not watching the clock and, instead, allowing himself to get carried away with *Dungeon Destroyers*, a computer game that he had become hopelessly addicted to. Right at that moment, he was supposed to be with his best friend Erick helping him to throw a house party, however, as things stood, he was already running at least an hour behind schedule.

Under normal circumstances, he wouldn't have been in the least bit concerned about arriving late to any kind of party or social engagement, let alone one of Erick's casual get-togethers, but this night was different. If everything went according to plan, there was a chance that he might finally hook up with Tonya Mitchell, a cute twenty-year-old with long, wavy brunette hair and smoky brown eyes who worked at an Atlantean diner across the street from his place of employment.

Chapter 1

Just a couple of days prior, he had bumped into her on his way to the hoverbus landing, and she cheerfully asked him if he was going to be at Erick's big party. It wasn't exactly an invitation for a date, but in Devin's mind, it was close enough. Truth be told, up until that point, she hadn't taken much interest in him at all, and his attempts to "woo" her hadn't exactly been successful. However, inwardly, he believed that she was finally falling under the spell of his unique brand of charisma and charm. Yes, it would only be a matter of time before she realized that he was the man she had always been looking for.

Finally, Devin mused to himself as he attempted to shake out the wrinkles in a well-worn pair of blue jeans. *Tonight's the night that it's gonna happen. I can feel it.*

He turned to face a disorganized shelf and located a can of Intense Vibes, a cheap body spray he had scooped up from the bargain rack at a local pharmacy. After removing the plastic lid with a pop, he began to spray the jeans down profusely in an attempt to mask a faint moldy odor that seemed to emanate from the fading denim.

When he finished, he quickly pulled the jeans on and began scanning his bedroom floor for a decent shirt that might be hiding in plain sight. However, having no such luck, he moved on to scavenging through a messy heap of clothes lying next to the foot of his bed. As he neared the bottom of the pile, he managed to fish out an olive-green sweater that didn't appear overly dirty.

Perfect, he thought to himself as he held it up and examined it at arm's length. He then flattened it out on his bed and promptly emptied the last of the body spray onto it. Within a matter of seconds, the thick, vaporous fumes filled the small room like a cloud, and he found himself hunched over in a violent fit of sneezing and coughing.

"Good lord, man!" he exclaimed with a wheeze as he straightened up and took a moment to catch his breath. *Maybe I'm overdoing it?* However, he quickly shrugged away the thought and concluded, *Nah... The scent is bound to wear off long before I get to the party.*

After throwing on a pair of brown leather shoes that were a mix of casual and dress and finding a belt to match, he took a moment to assess himself in the dusty mirror hanging on the wall near his computer desk. With shaggy locks hanging down over his ears and wavy bangs dangling in a mess just above his pale blue eyes, his tousled light-brown hair was in serious need of a trim. He also hadn't shaved in nearly a week, which did nothing to improve his unkempt appearance. Try as he might, he just couldn't convince himself that this new "starving artist" look he was sporting was going to do much in the way of catching Tonya's eye. Nonetheless, he mentally reassured himself that his stellar wit and magnetic charm would more than make up for it.

Taking another look at himself, he said out loud, "You've got this, man."

At that moment, he caught sight of the reflection of the digital wall clock hanging behind him and began to panic. It was nearly seven o'clock! Time was running out, and he needed to hurry if he was going to make the hoverbus on time. He then made a sincere but futile attempt to arrange the mop on his head with his hands. After coming to the bleak realization that there was nothing more that could be done about his appearance, he hastily turned away from the mirror and raced over to his bed, where he found his phone, wallet, and key card lying in a small pile on the cluttered nightstand. Scooping them up, he swung around and made a beeline for the door.

Unfortunately, his apartment was on the top floor of a ten-story high-rise, and this was only going to slow him down. To make matters worse, upon exiting his room, he spotted one of his neighbors entering the elevator down the hallway to his left just as its sliding doors were beginning to close.

"Dang it!" he whispered under his breath. "I don't have time for this!"

Slamming his apartment door shut, he bolted in the opposite direction towards a broad white door with the word *STAIRS* stamped across its center in bold black letters. Thrusting the door open, he lunged forward at breakneck speed and proceeded to leap wildly down each flight of stairs, two and three steps at a time. About halfway down, he stumbled face-forward on an untied shoelace but caught hold of the metal railing just in the nick of time, saving himself from what surely would have been a medical emergency. He briefly stopped to tie his shoe and then swiftly continued his mad downward descent.

All was going well, with only two flights of stairs to go, when a startling realization stopped him dead in his tracks – he had left his bus pass lying next to his computer! And, just like that, his vigor and energy vanished with the speed of a flipped light switch.

"You've got to be kidding me!" he abruptly shouted before bending over and placing his hands on his sides, huffing, puffing, and trying to catch his breath. He then lifted his head and scolded himself in an exasperated whisper, "Devin, you idiot! Now, what are you going to do?!"

Chapter 1

Wiping the sweat that was pouring from his brow and looking utterly defeated, he proceeded to slowly saunter down the next flight of stairs – there was no use in hurrying now, the hoverbus he had planned on catching would be long gone by the time he arrived at the landing. He would just have to cut his losses and hop on the next available shuttle at 7:30 pm.

The trip down to the lobby, over to the elevator, back up to his apartment, and then back down again cost Devin another fifteen minutes. To say that the evening was off to a bad start was an understatement. By the time he reached the double glass doors that led out of the building, the sun had disappeared behind the skyscrapers, and it was beginning to get dark.

As he shoved the doors open, a gust of chilly autumn air whipped through the entryway along with a small whirlwind of orange and brown leaves. The crisp evening breeze sent slight shivers up and down his body, which prompted him to tightly fold his arms together in an attempt to stay warm. He briefly paused and wondered if he should go back upstairs and grab a jacket before heading out but, after glancing at the time on his phone, decided that this was definitely out of the question. Turning to face the wind, he began making his way down the long stretch of sidewalk that bent around the building and led towards the hoverbus landing two blocks away.

Outside of the gusty breeze wafting in and out of the shadowy walkways that ran between the tall buildings lining the quiet street, the trip to the hoverbus landing was actually quite pleasant, and Devin probably would have enjoyed it had he not been hung up on thoughts of Tonya and what he was going to say and do when he got to the party.

Chapter 1

In the sky, directly above him, delivery drones, surveillance drones, and communications drones quickly whizzed by, traveling in every conceivable direction. Their intermittent flashes of luminous reds, yellows, and greens made them resemble large alien fireflies flitting to and fro through the night. Further in the distance, floating just above the city's glowing skyline, a handful of passenger zeppelins that had been outfitted with festive rainbow-colored lights could be clearly seen as they drifted across the sky like great ships navigating a vast electric ocean. And, adding to the evening's surreal tranquility, the air around him was permeated by the sound of a type of soothing meditative music that always played in and around the busy urban centers, an effect achieved via the small speakers attached to the trees and color-changing LED lamps that lined the city streets. At that particular moment, the street lamps were glowing with a calming lemon-yellow iridescence, which made everything look and feel like a video game dreamland.

Yes, Highland City at night was truly a sight to behold, and Devin knew it. Nonetheless, he wasn't really in the mood to pay attention to it, appreciate it, or even give it much thought at all. So lost was he in his own world, he didn't even notice the surveillance drone that was silently hovering just a few feet above his head as it scanned and recorded his every last feature and movement. He also didn't notice the long, cylindrical transport craft that was drifting away from the landing at the end of the block. No, his mind was on one thing and one thing alone: the brunette beauty waiting for him at Erick's house.

Devin approached the landing just in time to spot the taillights of hoverbus #3 fading into the distance, getting smaller and smaller as the shuttle quickly accelerated from view. Not understanding, he checked the time on his phone. It was nearly 7:30 pm, the time when the transport was normally scheduled to arrive. Something wasn't right. Scratching his head, he began to ponder his dilemma. A minute or so passed before it finally hit him – it was Sunday, which meant that all of the shuttles were running on an alternate weekend schedule! He immediately began to wonder how he could have overlooked such an obvious detail when he made his plans with Erick. As things stood, there wouldn't be another hoverbus arriving for another twenty minutes or so. With a loud sigh, he threw his hands up in disgust.

What a mess! he thought to himself as he checked the time on his phone once more, a bitter scowl sweeping across his features.

Having nothing left to do and no other travel options, he shuffled over to a steel bench positioned near a lamppost that had been indiscriminately decorated with stickers, graffiti, and local advertisements. In an attempt to ward off the chill night air, he folded his arms together and began circling the lamppost while he perused over the ads, a habit he had fallen into after the first five or six times he had missed his shuttle.

After taking some time to traverse through the sketchy realm of guerrilla marketing and street art on display before him, he noticed a small flier flapping in the breeze that featured one of his favorite bands of all time, Dream Demons. Apparently, they were going to be in the city the following Friday night to play a free show at The Angry Bean, a coffee house and music venue that a lot of the local bands frequented. It was the first place they had ever given a live performance,

Chapter 1

long before they had grown to become a major force in the underground thrash-funk scene.

For a brief moment, Devin was overcome with excitement and forgot all about the evening's setbacks. Lifting up his cell phone, he zeroed in on the flier and took a quick snap of it, his plan being to post the picture on *Holo-Life*, the go-to social media app that all the people his age were using. He quickly sat down on the nearby bench and began contemplating how he might go about asking Tonya to accompany him to the show.

Tilting his head back, he closed his eyes and imagined introducing the girl of his dreams to one of the greatest thrash-funk bands to have ever come out of Highland City. A lazy smile crept across his face. He would find a table near the stage, buy her a drink, and let the magic happen. It would truly be a night to remember, the best part of it all being that it wouldn't cost him anything more than a few cups of coffee! It really couldn't get much better than that.

Suddenly, his whimsical daydream was interrupted by the low hum of electricity emanating from a long cigar-shaped transport that had drifted into the landing, hoverbus #27. Devin's eyes popped open, and his head snapped forward just as an automated female voice came across a loud speaker located to the left of the oval-shaped entrance: "Passengers, please form a single file line to the right side of the entryway. Do not attempt to board the shuttle until all previous passengers have disembarked and the red light above the entryway has turned green."

The oval-shaped door slid open with a whoosh, and a small staircase unfolded from the opening, lowering itself to the ground. The hoverbus hung perfectly still, floating about two feet above the pavement. A circular light above the entrance was currently glowing a bright shade of red.

As Devin stood outside the entryway and waited for any passengers to disembark, he took a moment to gaze back and forth, peering into the long row of circular windows that ran down the length of the metal tube to make sure his favorite spot near the back hadn't been taken. There only appeared to be a small handful of individuals on board, and they were all sitting near the front. No one was disembarking.

Perfect! he thought to himself as he removed his bus pass from his wallet.

A moment later, the automated voice came across the speaker again: "Passengers, please have your bus passes out and ready for scanning. Only one passenger may board at a time. Please remember to use caution as you climb the entryway steps." The light above the entrance turned green, and the voice continued, "You may now proceed with the boarding process."

Devin straightened up and climbed the steps. As he passed through the entryway, a bright beam of blue light swept up and down the full length of his six-foot frame. It disappeared with a small beep, indicating that his bus pass had been detected and that it matched the biometric data it had accrued from his person during the scan.

Immediately, the automated female voice came across the front interior speakers: "Welcome aboard, Mr. Skye. Please take your seat."

Half ignoring the chipper voice, Devin brushed his messy bangs away from his eyes and coolly shuffled down the narrow walkway towards the back of the hoverbus, nodding and smiling at a young couple, who glanced up at him casually as he passed by. A few rows behind them, to his right, he noticed a middle-aged woman staring intently at the display of a brightly lit laptop, seemingly transfixed by whatever it was she was looking at. She had dark gray hair that was pulled back with a headband, and she was dressed in business-friendly attire, a black blazer over a silken white blouse and black dress pants.

As he approached, she suddenly snapped up from her computer with a startled expression and gave him a sharp look. Wincing her eyes, which had begun to swell and water profusely, she crinkled her nose and covered her mouth with her hand. The second he passed by, she broke out into a tumultuous fit of sneezing. Eyes wide open in embarrassment, he thought of the body spray he was wearing and quickened his step, all the while hoping and praying that the cheap scent would tone down before he arrived at the party.

After he found his spot, a well-worn, leather-cushioned bench to his left that sat three rows from the back, he plopped down and slid over to the window. He then forced his hands into the crease formed between the back and the seat and felt around until he managed to locate the seat belt that had been shoved in between. With a short tug, he yanked it out and slid it behind him, snapping it into the connector to his left. This trick he discovered would fool the sensors into registering that he was buckled up.

After getting comfortably situated, he sat back and stared out the window, thinking about Tonya and the upcoming party. Unfortunately, he found it hard to focus, as his thoughts were repeatedly interrupted by the sound of the woman in front of him blowing her nose into a handkerchief in between short bouts of sneezes and sniffles.

Chapter 1

Finally, a loud beep came across the interior speakers that was followed by a message from the automated female voice: "Passengers, please fasten your safety belts and make sure that all personal items have been properly stored and secured. Travel will commence in exactly two minutes. We will be arriving at landing number nine on the corner of Grant Street and Stone Avenue at 8:10 pm. As always, thank you for using Highland City Shuttles!"

At this, Devin picked up his cell phone, which had been lying beside him, and began to scroll through his text messages and notifications. The interior lights of the hoverbus dimmed from a bright white to a mellow orange-yellow. A moment later, the automated systems took over. A slight shifting sensation could be felt as the shuttle lifted and started drifting towards the corner of the landing. After making a sharp turn, it began to accelerate down the long street that ran towards an entrance ramp to the hoverway, an eight-lane thoroughfare that circled the whole of Highland City. With exits and entrances that adjoined to every major street throughout the sprawling municipality, the hoverway was, quite literally, the only practical way to get from one side of the city to the next.

Seeing that there was nothing interesting on his phone, he gazed out the window while the hoverbus quickly gained momentum. It wasn't long until the shuttle was flying down the hoverway at 150 miles per hour, the maximum speed limit that all public transportation vehicles were required to adhere to. In the adjacent lanes, he watched as one hovercar after another zipped by, flying at speeds that had to be at least two to three times faster than his own. In his mind, the sensation of speeding down the hoverway would never get old, and soon,

Chapter 1

he was lost in a daydream, in which he was cruising around the city in his very own hovercar, the Polaritron 360X.

His thoughts began to drift, *If only my parents were even half as reasonable as Erick's parents or any of the other adults in my life, for that matter, I wouldn't have to catch rides on this stupid shuttle. Why they're making me save up my own money to buy a hovercar is beyond me. It's not like they can't afford to help me out. It's ridiculous. They're so outdated and old-fashioned.* The daydreaming smile on his face morphed into a frustrated frown.

I don't need to be taught a financial lesson. What I need is the ability to get around this city when and where I want to! At this, he huffed and physically crossed his arms. *If they really want me to make something of myself, I need the freedom to do so, and this stupid bus is only holding me back!* Rolling his eyes, he let out a disappointed sigh. *I swear they act like we're living in the 1900s or something.*

All of a sudden, the notification alert went off on his phone. With a slow shake of his head, he forced his personal resentments aside and swiped up to see what it was. A new video had been posted on *Holo-Life* by Erick. *Holo-Life* was short for *Holographic Life*, the star feature of the social media app being that it gave its users the ability to post and share three-dimensional, holographic videos at lightning-fast speeds.

Laying his phone flat on the palm of his outstretched left hand, he pushed the play button with the other. A quick burst of light shot up about six inches from the screen and morphed into a full-color, three-dimensional display, complete with sound. Not wanting to distract the other passengers on board, he quickly adjusted the phone's volume to a lower setting.

Chapter 1

It was a video of the party, and everyone in attendance seemed to be having a great time. Apparently, Erick had decided that an oldies theme would be the order of the night, this being made apparent by the old school decorum that had been hastily taped to the ceilings and walls and the bass-thumping music from the 2020s that could be heard blasting through a home stereo system in the background.

In the living room, some of the partygoers had gathered around a beer-pong table and were laughing hysterically at a match between two girls that had gone awry. Close by, a group of others could be seen loitering and chatting around the bar that separated the living area from the kitchen. They were all sipping on mixed drinks from martini glasses that glowed in various shades of blue, red, and yellow, an effect created by the luminescent strands of black lights that swooped down in wide arcs from the ceiling. Standing at separate corners of the three-dimensional display, Erick and three of his buddies could be seen simultaneously recording the party, their individual videos having been uploaded to *Holo-Life* at the same time so that the program's artificial intelligence system could extrapolate the data needed for the creation of the holo-vid currently being watched.

As Devin spun his phone around to get a better view of the party, he spotted Tonya strolling out of a darkened hallway near the kitchen. Immediately, he could feel the elevated beating of his heart as it thumped in his chest and sent a rush of blood to course throughout his body. Dressed in black high heels and a shimmery, form-fitting jumper that gave off a slight neon-blue iridescence beneath the black lights, she looked more beautiful than ever. Her dark brown hair was parted down the middle and had been styled in large, wavy curls that hung loosely around her lightly tanned face. A sparkling jeweled necklace that sharply refracted the glow of the party lights traipsed down across her chest, and a pair of matching bracelets adorned each of her wrists. He had never seen her dressed in anything so alluring before and could hardly believe that she might be doing all of this for him.

As he intently watched her saunter across the kitchen floor, glowing drink in hand and crooked smile on her pouty lips, the video came to a stop. Closing out the display, he added a comment below the post: *Looks like a great party, bro. I'm on my way!*

Chapter 2

How Devin Went Viral

The remainder of the trip flew by without incident, and Devin arrived at the hoverbus landing on the corner of Grant Street and Stone Avenue at exactly 8:10 pm, just as scheduled. After disembarking, it only took him another ten minutes or so of brisk walking to make his way down Stone Avenue, hook a left on Canterbury Lane, and then veer right onto Becket Court. Erick's party wasn't easy to miss, as nearly every window was lit up in his parent's two-story brick house that stood proudly at the end of the cul-de-sac.

Upon drawing closer, he noticed that the party was much bigger than anything Erick had thrown together in the past. A cluster of hovercars filled the driveway in front of his parent's three-bay garage and spilled out onto the street, forming two lines that ran up and down both sides of the block. Normally, Erick didn't throw parties that involved more than just a handful of close friends, and he almost never hosted them on Sunday nights, due to the fact that people had normal lives to return to on Monday morning. But this night was different, as the classes he was enrolled in at the local university had been temporarily suspended after a main waterline broke and flooded the campus. Coincidentally, both of his parents also happened to be away on business outside of the city and wouldn't be returning for a few days. There would literally never be a better or more opportune time to take advantage of their big, empty house. If everything went according to plan, they'd return home and never know that anything out of the ordinary had taken place.

Chapter 2

As Devin strolled up the front sidewalk that led to the house, the thumping of a loud kick drum accompanied by a funky bassline grew louder and louder. When he approached the stairs that climbed the front porch, he could hear the muffled sounds of chatter and laughter coming from inside. Smiling inwardly, he thought to himself, *This is gonna be awesome!*

Picking up the pace, he began to climb the staircase towards a big oaken door that was brightly lit on each side by two antique-style wall lamps. Suddenly, from out of nowhere, a wet snapping sensation burst across his forehead, leaving his face and chest drenched in an icy cold liquid. A split second later, a colorful barrage of water balloons came rocketing down from the sky, exploding on him and all around him, sending frigid shocks to course up and down his body from head to toe.

Abruptly ducking and covering his head with his arms, he swung around and dashed for cover behind some nearby bushes. Unfortunately, he tripped on an untied shoelace before he got there and fell, arms sprawling, right into the dense foliage. The sound of young boys laughing hysterically came from somewhere above. Rolling over and peering up from the ground, he spotted one of Erick's younger brothers, Finn, and a handful of his friends pointing and jeering from the second-story balcony.

"Are you freaking serious?!" Devin hollered as he forced himself up and wiped his drenched hair away from his eyes.

"Got ya, sucker!" Finn retorted before swinging around and scampering indoors with his buddies.

Chapter 2

Devin was officially ticked off. Soaked from head to toe and shivering, he made a vain attempt to wipe the dirt, leaves, and dead grass off of his soiled clothes before reluctantly heading back towards the stairs. Each step forward produced a squishy noise that left a sopping wet footprint behind. After reaching the porch, he removed his shoes along with his socks and placed them in a small pile near the door.

Sighing, he peered down woefully at his bare feet and thought, *I guess this is how it's gonna be*. He then shook his head with an angry frown and whispered, "What a disaster!" before reaching out to turn the aged brass door handle.

A wave of bright yellow light beaming down from the crystal chandelier hanging in the middle of the foyer hit him full in the face as he opened the door and caused him to squint. Almost immediately, a petite, blonde-haired girl in a pink knit sweater, blue jeans, and tennis shoes came scurrying down the foyer staircase, her golden ponytail and glasses bouncing as she held out her arms to greet him. It was none other than Penny Nylund, Devin's childhood neighbor and backyard playmate, who later became one of his closest friends.

"Devin! I'm so glad you made it!" she exclaimed.

Devin took a step back and held his hands up in warning before she reached him. "You don't want to hug me, Penny. I'm dirty and completely soaked!"

Stopping at the bottom of the stairs, she put her hand over her mouth and gasped, "Oh my gosh! What on earth happened to you?!" She proceeded to march forward.

"One of Erick's little brothers and some of his buddies ambushed me when I got to the front porch," Devin replied with a scowl as he crossed his arms to ward off the cold.

"Oh, no," Penny said sympathetically. "You must be freezing to death! It'll be okay though." She quickly brightened up. "At least you're here! I was so worried you weren't going to make it."

Unfolding his arms, he forced a laugh. "Yeah, I'm here, alright." His teeth began to clatter.

"Clarissa was also supposed to be here, but she bailed on me after she found out that her new boyfriend wouldn't be working tonight. I was actually going to leave – I mean, this isn't exactly my crowd." She briefly glanced towards the living room before continuing, "But then, I saw your message on Erick's post and decided that I just had to stick around!"

Her blue eyes twinkled as she stepped forward to grab Devin's arm and pull him through the doorway. Suddenly, she halted. "Pew wee, Devin! Were you attacked with cheap cologne as well?!" She quickly took a step back and covered her nose. "That's awful!"

He hung his head and sighed, "No... That was all me."

Raising an exaggerated brow, she playfully giggled and said, "What on earth were you thinking!? You smell like a sweaty stripper or something!"

Lifting his head with a chuckle, he bantered back, "And I guess you would know all about that, wouldn't you, Penny?!"

Penny put her hands on her sides, cocked her head, and rolled her eyes. She then pulled him through the entryway and into the warmth of the house before quickly shutting the door behind them. Changing the subject, she asked, "So did you hear that the Dream Demons are coming to town next week?"

Devin lit up at this, however, inwardly, his thoughts were already racing to Tonya. He quickly averted his gaze away from Penny and towards the crowd gathered in the living room at the end of the hallway. "Yeah, I did. It's pretty cool, right?"

"Yeah, it is. So I was thinking –"

He abruptly cut her off, "Hey, Penny, I need to talk to Erick for a minute. Do you know where he's at?"

"Oh, he's been hanging out by the bar with one of his friends from the university, some guy named Darin, I think."

"Oh, right on." Devin slightly bit on his lip. "Listen, I want to talk about the concert with you a little bit later, but I'm going to find Erick before this party gets too out of hand. Is that alright?"

"Yeah… Sure… I guess," Penny stammered. "What's your deal anyway?"

"It's nothing. I just feel bad for getting here late. I was supposed to help him set things up, you know?" His gaze darted back and forth as he reached up to scratch the back of his head.

"Oh, I see," Penny said, her voice tinged with a trace of disappointment.

"I'll find you in a bit," Devin said as he forced a smile. He then peered up the stairwell to avoid her eyes and threw in a quick, "I promise," before swiftly turning away and shuffling down the hallway towards the living room.

Penny shook her head as she moped over to the staircase and slumped down on the bottom step. With a sigh, she began to scroll through a feed on her phone.

When Devin reached the living room, some of the partygoers stopped what they were doing to glance over and see who the newcomer was, however, no one bothered to greet him. A couple of guys near the beer-pong table looked him up and down and exchanged skeptical glances when they noticed his muddy clothes. Smirking, they turned away and focused their attention back on the game in front of them. A few of the girls standing near the back wall began to giggle and whisper when he caught sight of them staring and pointing at his bare feet. His eyes lowered, and his heart sank into his stomach.

Shaking his head in frustration, he silently reprimanded himself, *What on earth am I doing?! Everyone here is dressed to impress. Meanwhile, here I am, sweaty, dirty, wet, and walking around with bare feet. What a catastrophe!*

He had just about decided to call the whole night off and was turning around to find Penny when Erick suddenly appeared at the end of the hallway by the kitchen and shouted, "Devin, my man! You finally made it! Ha ha!"

Devin's eyes lit up when he saw his buddy briskly strolling towards him in a red Highland City University hoodie and a pair of black jogging pants. Almost immediately, he was able to tune out the crowd of "snobs" all around him. He quickly called back, "I'm going to kill your little brother the next time I see him!"

Erick began to laugh but stopped when he reached the entryway where Devin was standing. Looking his friend up and down incredulously, he said, "Yeesh! What did you do to yourself? Did you slip and fall in a mud puddle on your way here or something?!"

Devin shook his head. "Not exactly. I'm so sorry for showing up like this, man. When I got to your front porch, Finn and his gang launched about twenty water balloons at me, and well… Things got a little crazy after that."

Chapter 2

Erick cocked his head and shot Devin a mischievous smile. "They kind of remind you of us back in the day, don't they?"

Devin responded with a laugh, "Yeah, I guess you're right. Someone really should have put us in our place back then, right?"

"Nah, that's just the way it goes, bro," Erick replied, a cool smile on his face. Suddenly, he crinkled his nose and began sniffing at the air. "Is that you?!" Leaning back, he shot Devin a sharp look from beneath a raised brow.

With a slight shake of his head, Devin sighed and cast his gaze towards the floor.

Erick leaned forward and, in a quieter tone, said, "Hey, listen, I don't know if you realize this, but that cheap body spray you're wearing reeks, man. That's not gonna work. Why don't you let me run upstairs and see if I can find you something clean to wear, alright?"

Glancing back up, Devin shrugged and said, "Thanks, man. I really appreciate it."

"No worries, bro!" Erick returned as he reached out and gave Devin a quick pat on the shoulder. He then squeezed past his old friend to make his way towards the foyer.

However, just as he began heading down the hall, Devin stopped him. "Hey, Erick, I was just wondering if Tonya Mitchell was still here, by any chance?"

"Yeah, she's around here somewhere. Why do you ask?"

"It's nothing. She just asked me if I was going to be at the party the other day, and I was hoping I'd run into her."

"Right on, bro. No worries! I'm sure you'll run into her. But you probably don't want her seeing you like this, right? Let me head upstairs now so we can get this party started!"

Erick spun back around and jogged towards the staircase. Penny, who was still perched on the bottom step, abruptly stood up and got out of the way. Devin, briefly glancing in her direction, noticed that she was glaring at him with eyes that did nothing to hide her disappointment. Acting as if he didn't notice, he abruptly shifted his focus back to the party.

Now that Erick had sort of indirectly introduced him to everyone, the tension in the air seemed to lighten up a bit. Breathing a sigh of relief, he coolly shuffled past the partygoers and made his way to an overstuffed white chair that was located in a far corner of the room, away from the crowd. Ignoring the fact that it probably wasn't a good idea to sit on a clean white chair in his current wet and muddied state, he plopped down and took a moment to see if there was anyone there that he actually recognized.

After a quick scan of the living room, bar, and kitchen, he didn't see any familiar faces and figured that nearly everyone in attendance was somehow associated with the Highland City University crowd, as many of them were proudly wearing the school's signature red hoodies, sweaters, or jackets that bore the insignia of a fierce bald eagle's head with the letters *HCU* stamped underneath. This triggered his mind to wander back to his parents and the situation they had put him in.

His parents had made the decision that they weren't going to pay for him to enroll in classes at the university, citing that his grades didn't warrant it. However, as a compromise, they promised he could attend later if he proved he could get his grades up at the local community college. HCU also happened to be where Tonya went to school.

How much different things might be if my parents weren't so lame? he thought to himself as he shook his head. *But it's no use; they just can't be reasoned with. Instead, I have to take night classes, part-time, at a crappy budget school while simultaneously holding down a dead-end job. It's completely ludicrous!*

Devin sat back in the comfy chair with a frown and began to run this conundrum over in his mind when, all of a sudden, his train of thought came to a screeching halt. It was Tonya. She had just appeared at the entrance of the dark hallway near the kitchen with one of her friends, a tall girl in a black party dress with almond-colored eyes and long, silky blonde hair. Sitting up straight, he zeroed in on the situation. Someone or something had clearly caught their attention. Turning to her friend, Tonya gestured towards the bar and whispered something in her ear. Her friend nodded with a sultry, mischievous smile and then turned away to walk back down the darkened hall. Meanwhile, Tonya made her way towards the bar.

As Devin intently watched the girl of his dreams saunter across the kitchen floor, hips swaying, his eyes began to widen. She was moving in the direction of a tall, sharply dressed guy with styled dark-brown hair and an athletic build, who appeared to be a few years older than everyone else. He was sitting casually on a stool near the end of the bar while leaning forward so that he could better listen to one of his buddies, who was in the middle of telling a story just a few feet further down.

Devin's jaw dropped in stunned astonishment as he watched Tonya slowly sneak up on him from behind and startle him with a kiss on the cheek. She then wrapped her slender arms around his broad shoulders and whispered something in his ear. Almost immediately, his eyes broadened, and a look of pleasant surprise overtook his features. Grabbing his hand, she beckoned for him to stand up. For a brief moment, they gazed into each other's eyes. He then downed the drink that had been sitting in front of him and pushed himself away from the bar. All of the color drained from Devin's face as he watched them make their way, hand in hand, towards the hallway and disappear into the shadows within.

Right then and there, Devin's heart fell out of his chest and splattered all over the floor. He felt like someone had crept up from behind, stuck him with a knife, and left him there to die. Without a single rational thought left in his mind, he forced himself out of his chair and proceeded to march across the living room and towards the kitchen hallway. What he was going to do or say when he caught up with them, he didn't know, but he just couldn't believe his eyes, and he had to find out what they were up to, even if it meant sacrificing what little was left of his crumbling pride and dilapidated dignity.

After entering the darkened hallway, he began making his way towards the far end, where dim yellow lighting filtered through a set of frosted window panels on each side of a door that led out to an enclosed deck. With just a few steps left to take, he suddenly heard someone call out his name.

Halting and turning around, he spotted a familiar face under a mop of curly, shaggy red hair poking out of a stream of bright light that was pouring into the hallway from an open doorway to his right. It was one of the students from the community college, a guy he had taken a couple of classes with named Jared.

"Devin! I thought that was you," Jared said as his face lit up with a cheesy grin. "What are you up to, buddy?"

For a moment, Devin didn't know what to do. Feeling caught between making an utter fool of himself and crying, he just stood in the hallway in a state of stunned silence.

Jared's expression quickly transformed from one of mirth to one of concern. "Are you alright, man?"

Devin stammered, "Yeah... Yeah, I'm alright." He paused to think for a second. "I was just going to check out the back deck to see if Erick had the hot tub going."

Jared smiled slyly. "Oh, dude, trust me, you don't want to go out there right now. It's *full*. You know what I mean?" He arched his eyebrows a couple of times and giggled mischievously.

"Oh... I... I see," Devin stuttered. "I didn't know."

"It's all good, buddy. Why don't you come in here and hang with us? We've got something special if you're feeling up to it?" Jared's eyes darted towards the room, as if to indicate that he was hiding a naughty secret.

Devin hesitated and briefly looked over his shoulder at the back door before reluctantly turning back and quietly responding, "That sounds cool, I guess."

With a quick motion of his hand, Jared beckoned him forward. "C'mon man! You look like you could use some cheering up, and I think I've got just what you need."

For a brief moment, Devin somehow regained a small part of his sanity, if only just enough to compel him to walk away from the back deck and towards the open doorway.

Chapter 2

When he entered the room, a small home office, Jared was standing beside a shady-looking character who was casually leaning back in a desk chair. Wearing black combat boots, torn blue jeans, and a denim jacket with a handful of biker-themed patches sewn on the front, the stranger had both of his hands crossed on the back of his shaved head, partially covering a garish tattoo of a snake that slithered back from his left temple, down behind his ear, and coiled around his neck. In stark contrast, Jared was dressed in a pair of black and gray cross-trainers, a red HCU basketball jersey, and shimmery gray jogging pants. Right behind them, Devin spotted a row of shot glasses and a large plastic bottle of cheap vodka lined up on the computer desk.

"So what are you guys up to?" Devin asked nervously as he eyed the stranger up and down with suspicion.

"Oh, you know, just hanging out and messing around on the computer," Jared replied nonchalantly. He nodded towards the holo-display sitting beside him and produced a sleazy grin.

Devin glanced over at a three-dimensional image of supermodel and exotic beauty, Corina Yvette, wearing a skimpy bathing suit and crouching down on all fours in an erotic pose. "Does Erick know you guys are back here?"

"Nah, but it's all good, brother," Jared replied with a chuckle. "We're not doing anything wrong. And, besides, what Erick doesn't know isn't going to hurt Erick. Am I right?" He casually glanced over at the bottle of vodka.

Jared's friend snickered and spun his chair around to face the desk. He then unscrewed the bottle cap and poured out three shots.

Chapter 2

Meanwhile, Devin poked his head through the doorway and desperately tried to see or hear if anything was happening out on the deck. A lithe shadow briefly obscured the dim light emanating from the window panels. Turning around, he asked, "What's going on back there?"

Jared shook his head and chuckled as he paced forward. Firmly grasping Devin's shoulder, he pulled him into the office and shut the door with a click. Immediately, the sound of the music and the party taking place in the living room dropped to a muffle.

He stared at Devin curiously. "Why do you ask? Does it have something to do with that smoking hot brunette who just walked by with some older dude a few minutes ago?"

Devin shot an uneasy glance at the closed door behind him before cautiously nodding his head.

"You don't need to worry about it, man. They're probably just having a little *fun*. You know what I mean?"

Stiffening up, Devin sharply retorted, "No, Jared, I don't know what you mean!"

Jared threw his hands up defensively. "Hey, whoa, man! You need to tone it down a bit! What's your problem, anyway? Is she your girlfriend or something?"

Devin lowered his eyes and slowly shook his head.

"Oh, okay. Then why are you so worried about it? They're grown adults, and they can do whatever they want. It ain't none of your business."

Not responding, Devin continued to stare at the floor, a look of defeat and worry sweeping over his features.

Upon seeing this, Jared rolled his eyes and, in a calmer tone of voice, said, "Look, bro, I don't know what they're doing back there, nor do I really care. But, if they're having some alone time, why should someone like you barge in and ruin things? That's just uncool."

He shuffled back over to the shot glasses sitting on the desk and picked one up. "Besides, if it makes you feel any better, I'm pretty sure that they're *not* alone. I watched a blonde girl, some other couple, and a cute ginger walk back there earlier." After swiftly guzzling down its contents, he picked up another and held it out towards Devin. "Here, take a shot. It'll help calm your nerves."

Sighing, Devin took the shot glass from his outstretched hand and slowly raised it to his lips. He briefly hesitated before tipping it up and pouring the foul-tasting liquid down his throat. Almost instantly, the vaporous smell and astringent aftertaste of grain alcohol permeated his nasal cavities and flamed up in his chest, causing him to cough, sputter, and wince.

Jared's buddy snickered out loud at this and began pouring Devin another shot. He took one for himself as well.

Devin gazed down at the clear liquid and swished it around in his tiny glass, wondering just what it was he thought he was doing. A brief, tense moment passed by then, with a shrug, he pushed away his nagging thoughts, lifted the glass, and chugged it down like a champion; this time it tasted a little smoother.

Jared casually sat down in another desk chair beside his friend and cast a hard stare at Devin. Then, leaning back, he half-asked and half-stated, "Now, that's a lot better, isn't it?"

Devin allowed himself to crack a guarded smile as he shuffled over and sat his empty glass back down on the desk. "Yeah, I guess so."

"So do you want to party, or what?"

Devin cocked his head. "What do you mean? Isn't that what we're doing?"

At this, Jared's buddy snickered out loud and turned to pour a few more shots.

Leaning forward, Jared clasped his hands together and shook his head. He then responded with a toothy grin, "No, Devin. Not yet. We're just getting warmed up."

Turning towards his buddy, he motioned at a front pocket on the denim jacket he was wearing. His buddy grinned broadly, exposing a missing front tooth, and nodded in understanding. Reaching down into his pocket, he produced a plastic bag full of little blue pills.

Jared shifted his gaze back towards Devin and pointed at the bag. "Do you want one?"

The effect of the vodka was starting to kick in, and Devin's inhibitions were beginning to loosen. He glanced suspiciously at the bag and responded with a couple of questions, "What are they? Are they safe?"

Jared laughed out loud, "Ha ha ha! We just call them *baby blues,* and they're about as *safe* as anything else. You know what I mean?" Chuckling, he turned towards his buddy. "Am I right?"

His buddy gave him a short nod and snickered; a sly smile crept across his features. He then opened the bag, carefully removed three pills, and proceeded to pass them out.

"One for each of us," Jared said as he popped a pill in his mouth and swiftly washed it down with a swig of cheap liquor. Following Jared's lead, his buddy picked up a glass, made a silent toast, and proceeded to do the same.

Jared then handed a fresh shot to Devin. "Bottoms up, buddy!"

Seeing that his new companions had each taken a pill, Devin threw all caution to the wind and decided that he might as well follow suit. After all, what did he really have to lose? His whole night was already an epic failure. What harm could it do? He took a deep breath and slowly placed the pill on his tongue. For a hesitant second, he once again considered the consequences of his actions. Then, with a resigned shrug, he tipped his shot glass up and washed it down.

Jared promptly stood up, shuffled over to Devin, and gave him a firm and hearty slap on the shoulder, which caused him to cough and sputter. "Now, that's what I'm talking about!" Chuckling, he grinned broadly from ear to ear.

Another twenty minutes or so passed by, and soon, Devin, Jared, and the guy, whose name turned out to be Jimmy, were joking and laughing like they were long-lost buddies, even though this was far from the actual reality of the situation. And, like a man who had fallen under a spell born of some deep, dark, and evil magic, Devin completely forgot all about Tonya, his muddy clothes, his bare feet, Penny, and even his best friend Erick. He felt like he was soaring through a whimsical twilight zone on a topsy-turvy cloud, and he was loving every last minute of it!

Before he knew what had come over him, Devin found himself by the beer-pong table, swaying back and forth and bobbing his head erratically to the loud music while simultaneously attempting to swig down a bottle of beer. He wasn't sure how he got there, and he really didn't care. The party had become his personal playground, and he was there to have a good time. In fact, he had become so oblivious to his surroundings that he didn't even notice that almost everyone in the room had backed away from him for one reason or another. As he glanced around, he came to the fuzzy realization that his new buddies were nowhere to be seen.

Oh, so that's how it's gonna be, he thought to himself as a woozy smile traced across his lips. *That's okay. I've totally got this.*

Dropping his empty beer bottle on the floor, he abruptly shouted out, "My parents told me that I just needed to say no to drugs! Well, you know what I told them?! I said, 'Yeah,'" he stammered, "I said, 'Oh, yeah... Well, if I'm talking to my drugs, then I've already said yes!' Ha ha ha!" He laughed hysterically.

The crowd gathered in the living room looked on in stunned disbelief. Outside of some quiet sneering and hushed snickering, no one was really laughing – at least not at Devin's joke. A few of the partygoers pulled out their cell phones and began to record the train wreck that was unfolding in front of them. Meanwhile, someone near the back of the room crept over to the stereo and turned the music down. Regardless, Devin didn't notice any of this and kept bobbing and bouncing his head to the music that was, somehow, still playing in his mind.

Finally, he picked up where he left off, "I've got another one for you! And, this time, it's a good one! I promise!" He thrust the face of his palm out in front of him as he bobbed his head and laughed wildly. "How do you make an archaeologist really uncomfortable?!" He peered around the room, which had begun to spin, and said, "You hand him your girl's used tampon and ask him which period it came from! Am I right?! Ha ha ha!"

Chapter 2

At this, Penny, who had been nervously standing in the foyer entryway with her hand cupped over her mouth, decided that she couldn't bear to watch Devin do this to himself anymore. Shaking her head and fighting back her tears, she turned and stomped away. A loud, clattery bang echoed down the hallway as she slammed the front door shut behind her.

Meanwhile, Devin's delirious mirth had rapidly morphed into an absurd form of anger, and he began to lash out, "Why aren't any of you laughing at my jokes?! That's some funny stuff! I don't care who you are!"

He spun around and pointed to see if anyone was laughing, which no one was. Just then, he spotted Tonya standing beside her new man in the kitchen. She was holding her cell phone up and recording everything, her pretty face contorted in shock, astonishment, and disgust.

Upon seeing this, he completely lost it. Half-jerking and half-spinning himself around in a circle, his bare foot slipped on the empty beer bottle he had dropped earlier, and he tumbled headfirst towards the beer-pong table. As he crashed into it, the table cracked in half and sent a slew of bottles, glasses, and half-empty drinks to fly across the room. Horrified partygoers yelled, ducked, and wildly ran for cover.

He then rolled himself off of the wreckage with a loud groan and began crawling on his hands and knees towards an end table that he planned on using to hoist himself back up. However, by some cruel trick of fate, his palm landed directly on the stereo remote that had been lying near the table's edge. As he exerted the downward pressure needed to push himself up, he mashed the volume button down and unleashed an ear-shattering explosion of electronic music that shook the walls in every corner of the house. Covering both his ears with his hands, he closed his eyes, fell over, and let out a dazed moan.

Suddenly, a sharp wave of nausea caused him to rapidly jerk upright and spew projectile vomit all over the place, which included the furniture and walls beside him and the clothes worn by those who were unfortunate enough to be standing nearby. Needless to say, the party was officially over.

A fuming, mad Erick had been standing near the back of the kitchen with his arms crossed the entire time. Upon seeing this, he swiftly rushed over to the blaring stereo and yanked the plug out of the wall. He then carefully picked his way across the destruction that had formerly been his parent's living room and made his way towards Devin. As he approached his best friend, who was now lying prostrate on the floor, he shook his head in serious disapproval and motioned for all of the onlookers to stay calm with a quick wave of his hands.

Leaning over, he helped pull Devin back to his feet, and then, with a look that was one part angry confusion and two parts genuine concern, he said, "Listen, bro. I think it's time to call it a night. I'm not sure what just came over you, but this isn't good – this isn't good at all."

Trembling, Devin stared back at his friend with teary, bloodshot eyes. "I'm so sorry, Erick. I have no idea what just happened." Feeling completely broken, he hung his head in abject humility, not wanting to make eye contact with anyone else in the room.

Sighing, Erick placed a hesitant hand on his old friend's shoulder. "We'll talk about this later, but right now, I'm going to get you a ride home."

Chapter 3

Rita Parker's Journal
Sunday, September 20th, 2054 – Evening

If I'm being honest with myself, I have to admit that there are times when I just feel like caving in to the pressure and throwing it all away. This job – the supposed "dream job" I spent years training both in and out of school for – is becoming far more trouble than it's worth. The organizational and structural changes that corporate is forcing me to make are not only causing me a lot of undeserved heartache and stress, but they also aren't sitting well with the people who've been here for years, people who've come to think of this place as a second home.

Everyday, I walk down the hallways of our small building, and I can see, hear, and feel it all around me, the nervous glances, the hushed whispers, and the looks that seem to ask, "Am I next?" Most of the time, I'm able to put on my professional face and pretend like everything's okay, however, there are days, like today, when I just can't keep up the facade, and I end up locking myself in my office to avoid it all. And it's not because I don't care – it's because I care too much.

I knew we had reached the point of no return when I was informed that corporate wanted the last of our "outdated" studio cameras replaced by new and improved robotic cameras. It was almost more than I could bear to handle when I had to let two of our veteran camera operators go. Both of them had been with the station for nearly twenty years. I'll never forget the looks of panic and distress they gave me when they found out that their skill sets would no longer be needed.

What did they ever do to deserve that? Why should they be replaced by robots?

To make matters worse, most of our technical media operators still aren't quite up to speed with their new job responsibilities, as only one or two of them seem to fully understand how to program the new robots to function as needed. The people in corporate seem to think that the two months of training sessions they paid for were more than enough to make the transition, but they're ignoring the fact that no one currently working in the production center was required to have an extensive background in coding or even information technology upon being hired. Up until this point, our on-the-job training programs have always been more than sufficient for keeping things running smoothly. But not anymore; it would seem that those days are gone forever.

I realize that our small television station has been operating on an outdated model for far longer than anyone thought possible, but has it really hurt anything? It's always been the number one source for news in the Highland City viewing area, and our old-fashioned way of doing things has never impeded upon our ability to find and retain advertisers – not in the least bit. As a matter of fact, I personally know that many of our long-term clients fell in love with the idea of doing business with a company that still valued people over profits, and we wouldn't be where we are today without them. Shouldn't that count for something?

No one knows it yet, but there will be even more job cuts in the near future. Just the other day, I was informed, via a cold and impersonal video call, that corporate wants to turn over even more production duties to the new computer systems. This time it's the script writers who will be out of a job, as the artificial intelligence programs they're being replaced with can "supposedly" outpace and outperform even the most talented of human personnel in this capacity. Whether I agree with this decision or not, the sad fact remains that it's cheaper to replace workers with machines. By doing so, the station saves a lot of money, which, of course, helps us to maintain our competitive edge in the modern marketplace.

All the same, I can't imagine that this new move will result in anything different than what I had to personally deal with in the business office over the past year when artificial intelligence put nearly half of the folks I spent years working alongside out of a job almost overnight. At this rate, it won't be long until I'm left with nothing more than a skeleton crew to run the entire station with!

I guess, when it comes right down to it, I always knew that automation would eventually take over, but still, I couldn't stop myself from hoping that, somehow, we would buck the trend and go on doing things like they've always been done. Now looking back, I realize that was foolish of me.

And this brings me to my biggest problem of all, Devin Patrick Skye. I honestly believed I was doing the right thing when I hired him. After all, his father and mother are both really good people, and it didn't seem like such a big deal to repay the kindness I was once shown when they provided me with room and board during college. I just wanted to give them a helping hand by providing their son with something productive to do that didn't involve playing video games all day long, to teach him how to take on some adult responsibility and guide him as he adjusts to life in the real world. But what do I get for my kindness and concern? A chronic headache and a stomach ulcer!

Chapter 3

I mean, where do I even begin? He's habitually late for work, he doesn't fit in with his coworkers, he's argumentative, and he doesn't understand how to properly use half of the equipment in the studio. To make matters worse, he actively avoids taking any responsibility for his own mistakes, and when he's confronted with these issues, he has the audacity to become quarrelsome to the point of agony. As if all of that isn't enough, he rarely dresses for the job. I swear that he just grabs random, dirty shirts from off the floor and douses them in cheap cologne. Half the time, he smells like an old locker room!

When I first took over the station, I never imagined that I would have to deal with someone like Devin on a regular basis. Truth be told, if I had been given my own way, I would have gladly let him go in place of one of the camera operators that were laid off. Unfortunately, he's a low-paid intern, the kind of person that corporate isn't in such a hurry to get rid of. So until he quits or really messes something up, it looks like I'm stuck with him.

I seriously don't get paid enough to put up with this.

Well, tomorrow is a big day for Channel 12. It's hard to say why I still care, but I've come this far, and there's no point in looking back now. I guess I had better get some sleep if I'm going to be of any use to anyone.

Chapter 4

The Hobo and the Holo-vid

A shrill, broken-sounding ping could be heard repetitively screeching and bouncing off the walls near Devin's bed. Groggily rolling over, he forced open one crust-filled, bloodshot eye to stare at the source of the noise, an alarm clock that was lying on the floor about three feet away. It wasn't just any old alarm clock, it was special. It had been fashioned from the finest of low-grade plastic with the cheapest of 3D printing technology to resemble a ferocious gray dragon with outstretched wings that was holding a round speaker in one clawed hand and a touchscreen display in the other, just one of a slew of cheaply made novelties that were regularly shipped in from distant countries like Taured or Atlantis to be sold in gift shops and bargain centers everywhere. It was just the kind of treasure that a guy like Devin didn't mind dropping a few extra bucks on.

Barely able to move, he proceeded to roll off the small bed and land face-first on the ground with a loud thud. He then engaged in a fierce battle with the dragon clock, in which he was clearly outmatched, and spent much longer than he should have just trying to shut it off. When the horrid screeching finally fell silent, he rubbed the sleep from his sore eyes and glanced at the time. It was half past seven, and he was running late. Just at that moment, an agonizing, pounding sensation began to pulse through his head, the start of an excruciating, painful hangover that threatened to bring him to tears.

Still partially drunk and reeling from his drug-fueled meltdown the night before, he pushed himself up and half-stumbled towards the edge of his bed, stubbing his big toe on an unknown something in the process. He let out a loud yelp that morphed into a wail and bounced around on one foot for a bit before finally managing to limp over to the pile of clothes that was now haphazardly strewn across the middle of the floor.

Quickly sifting through them, he found a pair of wrinkled gray pants and a well-worn button-up shirt that was patterned in vertical stripes of red, gold, and gray. He then attempted to locate a pair of dress shoes and matching socks in the disheveled mess but ended up having to settle for a dirty pair of white sneakers and discolored tube socks that had been carelessly tossed in the corner near his computer desk a few days earlier.

In a reckless attempt to complement the curious ensemble, he found a faded forest-green tie that had been lazily draped over the back of his desk chair and wrapped it around his collar in a hasty knot that left the skinny back end dangling down awkwardly an inch or so below the fat front-facing end. He knew better than to go to work looking like this, as he owned much nicer things, but on this particular Monday morning, he didn't really care because he had to get to work on time at all costs. One more absence or tardiness violation, and he was sure to be fired, he just knew it.

Devin's position, working as an intern at the local news station, Channel 12 – Highland City Broadcast News, was perfect for someone with a strong lack of motivation and a heavy predilection for laziness. Outside of the very rare occasion in which he might be handed an important task or serious assignment due to one or more of the veteran technical media operators being unavailable, he wasn't given a great deal of responsibility.

Chapter 4

His coworkers had long ago given up on entrusting him with tasks that carried any real weight of importance, for fear of the disasters that would inevitably ensue and be broadcast across live television. So, most of the time, he spent his days hiding out in the master control room, playing video games and doing his absolute best to accomplish the bare minimum amount of work that needed to be done for him to keep his job. Somehow, despite all of this, the news station still saw fit to give him a paycheck each week that allowed him to lead a semi-comfortable lifestyle. However, none of this prevented him from inwardly believing that he deserved more out of life.

After hurriedly prepping for work, he took the elevator down to the first floor, made a swift exit through the front doors, and dashed down the sidewalk towards the hoverbus landing two blocks away. He accidentally ran into an elderly woman in his haste but couldn't be bothered to do more than shout out a rushed apology as he sped on by. Privately, he hoped the Universe would forgive a man whose job was on the line. Nonetheless, despite his best effort, the shuttle he had planned on catching was already drifting down the road towards the hoverway by the time he arrived at the landing. Shaking his throbbing head in agony and throwing up his hands in defeat, he plopped himself down on the cold steel bench and stared out vacantly across the street.

At that moment, his eyes caught hold of something that was highly unusual for the neighborhood. An old bearded man, wearing an orange beanie and muddy coveralls that were speckled about with small rips and tears, was staring directly at him with sharp, penetrating brown eyes. In his hands was a large piece of torn cardboard that displayed an ominous message, *The End Is Near. Wake Up and Leave Your Hollow Life Behind.*

Something about the old man's unflinching gaze sent cold shivers flying up and down Devin's spine. With a shudder, he quickly averted his attention to the lamppost and pretended to take an interest in something he saw hanging there. A minute went by, two minutes, and then five. Finally, he risked turning his head, ever so slightly, to see if the situation had changed. However, to his horror, the stranger hadn't moved an inch. Standing across the street, still as a statue, he held his sign aloft, silently drilling holes into Devin's soul with his eyes.

Feeling completely unnerved, Devin abruptly stood up and paced over to the lamppost, where he proceeded to fake interest in an advertisement for free kittens while keeping a cautious eye on his surroundings. In this manner, he read through a number of help-wanted ads, a political poster that detailed all of the reasons he shouldn't vote in favor of Proposition 86, and a homemade flier announcing the date for an upcoming warehouse party in old town.

A painstaking ten minutes dredged by before the next hoverbus finally arrived. After hurriedly boarding the shuttle and settling into his usual spot near the back, he risked glancing out the window to see if the hobo was still standing there. Thankfully, he was gone.

Phew... That was kind of creepy, Devin thought to himself as he breathed a short sigh of relief. *The city really needs to do something about all of these vagrants clogging up the streets.*

A minute or so passed before a shifting sensation was felt, indicating that the hoverbus had begun moving. Out of habit, Devin leaned back and tilted his head to take in the passing scenery through the circular window. The sun was out, and the sky was a cool shade of blue. Everything seemed to be back to normal.

When the shuttle rounded the corner at the edge of the landing, the stranger reappeared, this time standing beside the road directly in Devin's line of sight. Holding his sign aloft with one hand, he lifted his other and began to slowly wave goodbye. As the shuttle drifted by, he never once took his eyes off of Devin, who was now visibly panicked.

The second he faded from view, Devin jerked away from the window and cast his eyes on the phone lying in his lap. Feeling frightened and not knowing quite how to process what he had just witnessed, he sat there, staring at the black screen in complete, dumbfounded silence. In the background, the faint mechanical sounds of the hoverbus blended in with occasional chitchat between passengers. For all intents and purposes, it was as if nothing out of the ordinary had taken place.

A few minutes passed by in this manner before he finally got control of his feelings and picked up his phone to check his notifications; he had to do something to take his mind off of the weirdness that had just transpired. Within a few seconds, he spotted a message stating that he had been tagged in a video posted on *Holo-Life*. His scrambled thoughts immediately raced back to the events from the night before.

Oh, dear God, no, he thought to himself as the last of the color drained from his already sallow face. *It couldn't be, could it?* Taking in a deep breath, he pressed his index finger down on the notification panel and opened up the app.

Chapter 4

Nothing could have prepared Devin for what came next. Rising up from the screen in all of its lifelike, holographic glory was truly one of the most cringe-inducing displays he had ever laid eyes on. It was a holo-vid of him behaving like an out-of-control lunatic. Everything was there, from the bad jokes to the broken beer-pong table. As he watched the three-dimensional horror show play out before his eyes in real time, his heart dipped into his stomach, and his pounding head began to swoon. How was he ever going to outlive this? How could he ever show his face around Tonya again? How many people would potentially see this? The questions came sweeping in like a tidal wave, paralyzing him with fear, guilt, and panic. As the video came to an end, he continued to stare at the frozen holographic display with his jaw dropped open in stunned disbelief.

All of a sudden, his phone beeped, stirring him from his trance. It was a voice message from Erick. With delayed effort, he closed out the video and opened it up. Holding the phone up to his ear, he heard, "Hey, man. I've been worried about you. I seriously hope you're okay. I don't know if you've seen it yet, but there's a video of you on *Holo-Life,* and it's gone viral! I don't know what you're gonna do, bro. According to the comments, some of the guys from the party aren't too happy about what happened, and they're threatening to teach you a lesson the next time they see you. We really need to talk, okay?"

Just then, a rare moment of clarity made its way into Devin's unusually foggy mind, and he thought, *What in the world am I doing with my life?* However, he didn't have much time to ponder the question further, as the shuttle was coming to a stop at the landing near the news station.

With a defeated sigh, he slowly shook his head and thought to himself, *Well, what's done is done. There's not a dang thing I can do about it now*. He then brushed a greasy hand across his forehead and wiped away the sweat that had begun to bead and drip down the sides of his cheeks. Curiously, his mind had wandered back to the strange old man and his ominous sign.

It was at this point that an automated female voice came across the interior speakers, announcing that the shuttle had arrived at its scheduled destination. Trying his best to calm his frazzled nerves, he took a deep breath in through his nose and exhaled slowly out of his mouth. He then pocketed his phone and proceeded to disembark.

As Devin forced his achy body down the sidewalk, the news station came into view. Standing only a couple of stories tall, it wasn't a large building of modern design that the average person might picture when visualizing what a television station should look like. The original owner hadn't planned on using the property as a broadcast center when the structure was first erected, so outside of the adjacent lot containing two tall signal towers and a handful of satellite receiver dishes, there was very little to set it apart from any random storehouse one might run across in the city. Nonetheless, the station's owners did their best to spruce up the place by planting small trees and shrubbery around its exterior and hanging a rectangular sign of medium size above the front door that featured the station's logo painted on a dark-blue backdrop in bold white letters, *Channel 12 – Highland City Broadcast News*.

Despite its modest appearance, this was a place where big things happened, and Devin knew it. Being the station that the majority of people in Highland City turned to for important information, weather bulletins, local updates, and emergency broadcasts, some of the city's most influential people were, by default, attached to the company in one way or another.

When Devin finally arrived at the front entrance, he briefly paused to glance across the street at Plato's Platter, the Atlantean diner where Tonya worked part-time as a waitress. Almost instantly, an image of Tonya's face, wrought with shock and disgust, flashed before his mind's eye. As the tragically embarrassing scene from the night before began to play itself out all over again, his shoulders slumped down, and his head fell forward in humiliation and defeat. The damage was done – he could never set foot in Plato's Platter again.

Slowly turning away, he thought, *How could I have been so completely and utterly stupid?*

He then proceeded to remove his security pass from his wallet and pass it in front of a scanner attached to the outer wall beside the front door. The scanner beeped, and the door unlocked with a click. Woefully, he made his way into the lobby.

Almost immediately, he was met by the station's general manager, Rita Parker. Dressed to impress, she was wearing a mid-length navy-blue dress along with matching high heels and fine gold jewelry. Her long red hair, which she normally pulled away from her face with a headband or a ponytail, had also been put up and styled. Upon seeing this, Devin swiftly came under the impression that something important was taking place. Straightening himself up, he made a speedy but futile attempt to smooth out the wrinkles in his shirt and pants.

Chapter 4

"Devin, you're late!" she said in a harsh tone as she assessed his messy attire through frustrated hazel-green eyes. "What on earth have you done with yourself?!"

Devin glanced down at his feet and noticed that his shoes were untied. Shaking his head apologetically, he responded, "I'm so sorry, Rita. The hoverbus showed up late for some reason, and my alarm didn't go off." He then began to nervously fidget with a button on his shirt that was unfastened.

Rita, not being the kind of woman who was easily taken for a fool, shook her head and sighed, "We'll deal with that later. Right now, I need you to grab the on-site recording gear and get prepared to head over to Jakob Salverson Military Complex. There's no time to waste!"

Devin abruptly looked up and asked, "Really? That's where my dad works. What's going on over there?"

"We're doing a special report on their new weapons testing facility." She forced a smile that quickly snapped into a frown after a second assessment of his tousled, mismatched attire. "Normally, I would let Adriana work a story as important as this one, but she's stuck in traffic on the other side of town."

"Stuck in traffic? Seriously?" Devin was genuinely curious, as this sort of thing was rarely ever known to happen on the hoverway.

"Would you believe it? A hoverbus disengaged right in the middle of 200 mph traffic. It crashed into the pavement and caused a twenty-five vehicle pile up!"

Devin's bloodshot eyes widened as he jerked his head back and stiffened his posture. "Whoa! How is that even possible?!"

"Authorities are speculating that it might be another hacker attack from terrorists, but nothing is definite yet. I'm just thankful that Adriana wasn't hurt." She stared at a blank spot on the wall, a look of consternation consuming her features, and then quickly snapped back, "But this really has nothing to do with you, now does it? Go get your equipment and meet me out in the parking bay!"

Not wanting to agitate his boss any further, Devin half-jogged over to the storage room and grabbed the camera gear that was reserved for on-site filming. He then jaunted towards the exit at the rear of the building while trying his best to ignore the disapproving glares that his co-workers were throwing in his direction.

When he arrived at the parking bay, Rita was already in front of the news station's dark-blue hovervan waiting for him. Standing next to her was a tall, dark, and handsome man with wavy brown hair that was styled and perfectly parted on one side. He had a red handkerchief neatly folded in the breast pocket of his charcoal-gray pinstripe suit, and he carried a black leather briefcase that matched his freshly shined shoes. It was Mateo Florez, the station's top field reporter.

"Ah, Devin!" he said through a cold and very fake smile. "I had no idea we would be working together again." He shot a quick sideways glance at Rita that said, "You can't be serious?" He then turned his attention to the time on his phone and whispered under his breath, "You better not ruin this, you little punk."

"Ha ha! Yep. I can't wait to get started," Devin politely quipped as he made a beeline for the back of the vehicle.

Doing his best to avoid further conversation, he busied himself with loading the camera gear into the back of the hovervan while Rita and Mateo climbed into the driver and passenger seats, respectively. After they were all seated, Rita typed the address of Jakob Salverson Military Complex into the dashboard console while Mateo flossed his perfect white teeth in front of the passenger-side vanity mirror.

A few seconds later, a polite female voice came across the hovervan audio system: "Destination: Jakob Salverson Military Complex. Estimated time of arrival: fifteen minutes. Enjoy your trip!"

As the vehicle lifted from the ground, Rita sat back in her seat, straightened out the wrinkles and folds in her dress, and began to thumb through her phone. Mateo stopped what he was doing and turned on some music that he apparently enjoyed. An artist with a deep baritone voice began singing about lost love on the river of dreams to a backdrop of jazzy salsa. Devin had never felt more out of place in his life. He only wished that he could be back at the station, sitting in front of a holo-display and playing a video game. Wearily, he tried to shake off the drunken grogginess and headache he had been battling all morning long.

A short while later, Rita put her phone down and, turning to face Devin, said, "I'm not sure if you're aware of this, but the special report we're conducting today is a rare opportunity for the news station, so it's vitally important that we get everything right. There's not going to be any room for silly mistakes."

Startled, he popped out of his stupor and replied with a short nod, "No worries, Rita. I've got this."

At this, she raised her eyebrows and continued, "Let's hope so."

Chapter 4

Mateo suddenly interjected, "Yeah, we wouldn't want another incident like last time."

"Hey, that wasn't my fault!" Devin quickly snapped back while rolling his eyes. "Do you think I really knew that I was filming the entire broadcast in black and white? I mean, what's the point of enabling a filter like that on a news camera anyway?"

Mateo sighed. "You know what, kid? That's your problem. You never take responsibility for anything you do. You always have an excuse."

Devin gritted his teeth and shifted around in his seat to stare out the window.

Mateo slowly shook his head and continued, "You're just really lucky that we were filming a historical special and were able to play the whole thing off as being purposeful for nostalgic effect." He then turned to face Devin with a look of derision and added, "Who knows? Maybe next time we'll all get lucky, and the folks in corporate will figure out a way to replace *you* with a robot."

"Yeah… Well, I told you I was sorry, Mateo. Why don't you try giving me a break? It's not like you've never done anything wrong." Devin huffed and tightly crossed his arms.

Rita interjected, "Both of you need to knock it off! We're nearly at the facility. So are you ready to hear the plan?"

They simultaneously replied, "Yes."

She continued, "Okay, Mateo, so the first interview you're going to do is with Colonel Gundersen. He's going to show you around the launch room and walk you through the safety procedures that the soldiers are trained to adhere to when working in that particular area."

She paused to make sure they were both paying attention. "I was given security passes that you will both need to keep on you at all times. Without them, you won't be able to get into most of the areas in the installation. And, Devin, I can't stress it enough that you cannot, under any circumstances, lose this security card. Do you understand?"

"Yes, mam." He rolled his eyes.

"After we've finished interviewing the colonel, we'll meet back here at the hovervan to discuss what we're doing next. Sound good?" She glanced back and forth at the two of them to make sure they understood. "Okay, we're here."

From a mirrored window, high up on a steel-beamed observation tower, the dark-blue hovervan, with its bold white station logo stamped across its side panels, could be seen coming to a stop in front of the tall metal gates just outside of the base. A soldier working the post spoke to the passengers through a microphone, which transmitted to the speakers inside the vehicle, "Please have your security clearance passes and personal identification cards ready. An escort will be with you shortly."

Chapter 5

A *Highland City Sentinel* News Excerpt
Friday, September 18th, 2054
Live Television Broadcast Planned in Wake of
Military's Turkey Farm Fiasco
By Joanna Schwartz

The New Scandinavia Home Guard has long played an integral role in defending New Scandinavia from threats both inside and outside of the nation's borders. However, in the wake of a recent weapons testing fiasco involving a large turkey farm on the outskirts of Highland City, many people are now wondering if the real threat to homeland peace and security is to be found within the uniformed ranks of this time-honored branch of the armed forces.

On Thursday afternoon, Edwin McDonald, owner and CEO of Talking Turkey Inc., had his entire world turned upside down after two misfired rockets hit one of his farms, killing hundreds of turkeys and critically injuring three of his employees. We were able to contact Mr. McDonald shortly afterward.

Regarding his initial reaction to learning that his farm had been hit with rockets, he had this to say: "It was like nothing I had ever experienced in my entire life. I mean, what do you do when you get a phone call informing you that your farm has just been decimated by live rocket fire? The first thing that ran through my mind was that we were under attack from a foreign nation, and war was breaking out! There was no one more surprised than me when I found out that our own military was responsible. Never, in all my years, did I imagine that anything like this would ever happen, especially not in my own backyard! To be perfectly honest, I still don't know what to make of it. The whole ordeal has left my head spinning."

When asked about the extent of damage done to his property, Mr. McDonald wasn't able to give us any exact details, as a thorough damage assessment had not yet been completed. However, he did let us know his personal sentiments on the matter: "The worst part of it all is the fact that three good people were injured and possibly maimed for life. What did they ever do to deserve that? What do I tell their families? The destruction of my property and the untimely deaths of a few hundred turkeys, I can handle, but make no mistake, if any of the good people who work for me had been killed, we'd be having a much different conversation right now."

Officials from Jakob Salverson Military Complex immediately took responsibility for the incident, claiming that a malfunction in an automated weapons deployment system was to blame. They were also quick to state that new safeguards were immediately being put into place that would prevent anything like this from ever happening again.

An official spokesperson from the complex, Lieutenant Akira Masuno, went on record later in the evening with the following statement: "The New Scandinavia Home Guard deeply regrets what happened and is prepared to fully compensate Mr. Edwin McDonald and his employees for any damages that have been incurred by this unfortunate accident."

As it regards the weapons deployment system malfunction, we reached out to Lieutenant Masuno to request more information. She informed us that a live television broadcast had been scheduled with Channel 12 – HCBN, for

Chapter 5

Monday morning, September 21st, and that it would help to clear up any questions and concerns the general public might have concerning the incident. When pressed for more details, she declined to comment any further.

Chapter 6

Cosmic Energy

The Channel 12 hovervan hung perfectly still in front of the military installation for around five minutes or so before the escort could finally be seen coming down the road in the distance. Devin, who was now battling blurry vision, motion sickness, and an upset stomach, closed his eyes and rubbed his achy belly in agony. Without even realizing it, he belched very loudly.

"That's disgusting!" exclaimed Mateo, who jerked around to stare at Devin with a look of contempt. "You smell like sauerkraut and rotten milk. Yuck!"

Rita attempted to calmly intercede, "Devin, I would suggest that you stay in the background and focus on your job during this interview. And I swear, if we weren't working such an important assignment, you and I would be having a talk right now." Despite her attempt to remain cool and collected, her annoyance was more than obvious.

Not feeling confident that he could say anything to defend himself, Devin looked away and slumped down in his seat. He then thought to himself, *I wonder if they have a vending machine with energy drinks in this place? That just might help.*

At that moment, the huge metal gates slid apart, and a soldier, mounted on a black hovercycle, drifted towards them. Coasting to the driver's side of the hovervan, he motioned for Rita to lower the window with his hand. As soon as she did, he said, "Mam, please state the purpose for your visit, and while you're at it, I need to see your personal identification cards and security passes."

Chapter 6

"Yes, of course. We're here from Channel 12 – Highland City Broadcast News. We have an interview scheduled with Colonel Gundersen this morning. We were also told that we would get to tour the facility later on." Rita smiled and handed him the requested items.

The soldier produced a tablet-like device from a holster attached to his belt and proceeded to scan each card with it. Within a few seconds, a green light flashed from the screen, and a message popped up: *Clearance granted*.

"Okay, mam. Please put your vehicle into manual mode and follow me. I'll take you to the visitor's area."

The soldier handed the cards back to Rita and navigated his hovercycle to the front of the news van. With a wave of his hand, he directed them to pull forward. Rita shifted the vehicle into manual mode and began to slowly follow the escort to their destination.

Once they drifted through the gates, Devin made a real effort to take in his surroundings, as he had never actually set foot inside of the military complex before. Even though his father was employed there as a research scientist, friends and family were not typically permitted to visit, so getting to see the inside of the place was kind of a rare treat.

Through the passenger-side window, he watched as soldiers engaged in various training routines. Some were equipped with flight suits and were hovering in the air while shooting short-range laser pistols at moving targets, and others were busily engaged in physical exercises, such as jogging, push-ups, and jumping jacks. Behind them, he observed row after row of hovertanks, mobile missile launchers, and various cargo transports silhouetted against the pale blue sky. He then shifted forward in his seat to gaze out the front window and noticed that the path they were traveling down led to a miniature skyline made up of tall metal buildings capped with satellite receivers, radio towers, and other wireless transmission devices.

Breaking the silence, Rita turned to Mateo and popped a question, "Do you know what all of this high-tech weaponry makes me think of?"

Mateo cocked his head with mild interest and replied, "No, not really. What were you thinking about?"

"It reminds me of all the flying saucer stories we covered over the past year."

Mateo chuckled lightly and said with a playful smile, "I think I know where you're going with this. You think all those reports and stories are somehow related to the military, don't you?"

Rita laughed, "Of course I do. Don't you? I mean, what else could they be?"

Mateo nodded his head in agreement. "Yeah, I'm pretty sure you're right, Rita. I don't claim to know a lot of things, but one thing I do know is that there's no such thing as aliens."

Taking a sudden interest, Devin interjected, "You can't prove that, man. What makes you so sure?"

Mateo twisted around and shot Devin a condescending look. "Are you freaking serious right now?"

Devin folded his arms defensively. "Yeah, I am. So what of it?"

Shaking his head in disbelief, Mateo turned to face the front window and threw his hands up in disgust. He then half-muttered what he was thinking, "I don't even know where to begin with you," and, in a much louder tone, said, "You really need to grow up and get your head out of the clouds, kid. Or maybe you'd like to tell us all about Santa Clause and the Easter Bunny while you're at it?"

Rita sharply cut in, "Are we really going to do this again?!"

Leaning back in his seat, Mateo folded his arms stiffly and stared out the front window at the buildings rising up before them, a look of frustration contorting his normally calm and confident demeanor. Devin didn't bother to offer a response, as he really didn't have the physical energy or the presence of mind to argue back and figured it was probably just a waste of time to even try.

A few short minutes quietly crept by before they arrived at a circular-shaped parking lot dotted with glowing orange lights. Pulling into the middle of the circle, they waited for the military's automated systems to take control of the hovervan. As soon as this happened, the craft lowered itself to the ground, and the doors slid open. Rita and Mateo exited the vehicle while Devin gathered up the camera equipment and unloaded it through the rear doors.

After they were all outside and everything had been unloaded, Rita issued a voice command that let the automated systems know they had finished disembarking. Upon her command, the doors slid shut, and the vehicle proceeded to lift off the ground. It then drifted over to an empty parking space. As they stood, patiently waiting for the escort to lead them inside the building, a mild, autumn breeze whipped around them.

"Mateo, do you need to look over your interview questions one last time before we get started?" Rita asked as she glanced up at the tall building in front of them.

Chapter 6

"No, I think I'm ready, Rita," came his quick reply, along with a smile that exuded confidence.

"Good," she said with a nod. She then shifted towards Devin and, in a much different tone, said, "Devin, please try to keep it together while we're in here. It's completely obvious that you're hungover." She sniffed at the air a couple of times. "And, by the way, you smell awful. Did you even bother to shower today?" She glared into his bloodshot eyes, fully expecting a response.

"I'm so sorry, Rita. I swear, if I had known what we were going to be doing, none of this would have happened." He hung his head and examined the pavement below.

After Rita and Mateo turned away, he stole a quick whiff of his shirt sleeve. *Wow, that really is awful. What in the world are you doing with yourself, man?* The unfinished thought from earlier that morning returned as he shook his pounding head and fought off a fresh wave of nausea.

At that moment, the military escort walked up to them and asked if they were all set. They nodded, and he proceeded to usher them towards the big glass doors at the entrance of the building.

Rita was just beginning to think that things would start to smooth themselves out and was allowing herself to relax a little bit when a series of clanking, crashing sounds and a painful "Ouch!" stopped her dead in her tracks. Swiftly swinging around, she saw Devin lying flat on the parking lot, surrounded by a handful of dropped equipment bags, one having popped open upon impact, its fragile contents scattered across the pavement.

After forcing himself up with a slight struggle, he threw his hands out in front of him and said, "Sorry, I tripped on my shoelace." He then began wiping gravel and dirt off of a scraped knee that was now fully exposed through a fresh rip in his pants.

"You've got to be kidding me," Rita muttered as she turned her back on him and resumed trekking forward. "Devin, I swear there better not be a single thing broken back there!"

Mateo, who had also stopped to see what happened, shook his head and smirked before turning to follow Rita's lead.

Meanwhile, Devin, ignoring his coworkers, focused his attention on gathering up his bags and cleaning up the mess he had just made. After making sure that nothing was broken and everything was in its proper place, he slung the equipment bags over his shoulder and jogged up the long stretch of sidewalk that led towards the building. Huffing and puffing, he caught up with everyone just as they were arriving at the entrance.

When they passed through the glass doors, Devin, now woozy and winded, spotted what he had been hoping to find – a vending machine standing against a wall across from the receptionist's desk. Fully stocked with candy, soda, and a wide variety of snacks, almost anything he could have wanted was there. Nonetheless, it was the shiny silver can that featured a stylized diagram of an atom with electrons revolving around its nucleus and the words *Cosmic Energy* emblazoned across its center that really caught his eye.

Yes! That's just what I need right now, he thought to himself as he followed Rita and Mateo towards the desk. *The amount of caffeine, herbs, and vitamins in those things can keep a person going strong all day and night. If there's anything that can get me through this rotten hangover, that's gotta be it!*

The receptionist, an eager young woman in her early twenties with curly blonde hair put up in a frizzy bun, looked up at them from behind eyeglasses with cherry-red frames and greeted them with a bright smile, "Welcome to Jakob Salverson! How may I help you?"

"Thank you," Rita replied in a warm but professional manner. "We're here from Channel 12. We're scheduled to do an interview with Colonel Gundersen today."

"Ah, yes. I was informed that you would be arriving. Please have a seat in the lobby, and the colonel will be with you shortly."

With that, the trio sauntered over to a row of cushy chairs upholstered in a shimmery, maroon-colored fabric. Rita and Mateo sat down and opened up their phones to check their messages while Devin placed the equipment bags on the floor beside them. He then excused himself to grab a drink from the vending machine.

On his way over to the machine, he took a moment to observe his surroundings. They weren't at all cold, bleak, or uninviting, like what he expected to see in a military installation. Instead, he was pleasantly surprised to see that the whole place had been decorated with exotic hanging plants, paintings of quaint countrysides, and various art pieces. Although, in stark contrast, he noticed that a dark movie about the destruction of the planet and a handful of survivors fighting to stay alive was quietly playing on a large holo-display near the receptionist's desk. Devin had seen the film before and found it to be rather depressing, if not completely unbelievable.

Chapter 6

It seems like filmmakers can't produce anything other than pure trash these days, he thought to himself as he stopped to check it out with arms folded in derision. *What a mess! I really wish I could get those two hours of my life back.* He shook his head, uncrossed his arms, and ran a hand through his greasy hair before resuming his trek across the lobby.

Arriving at the vending machine, he inserted his currency card. After scanning the numbers and letters displayed next to the drinks, he proceeded to push the letter *B* and the number *12*. The buzzing sounds of churning gears greeted him, and with a clunk, his favorite drink landed on the holding tray at the bottom of the machine.

As he pulled back the tab and cracked open the king-sized can of "life-saving medicine," a fizzy hiss and a loud snap echoed throughout the quiet lobby. Briefly startled, everyone looked up from what they were doing. Disregarding their stares, Devin tipped the can up to his lips and proceeded to swallow a large gulp.

"Ahhh, that's much better," he quietly whispered as he rubbed his belly, struggling to contain the gas that was rapidly building up inside.

"Sir?" came the chipper voice of the receptionist. "Sir?"

"Yeah, what's up?" he called back, trying to play it cool.

"Sir, I'm sorry, but you'll need to finish that drink before the colonel arrives. There's no food or drink allowed in the sensitive areas you'll be visiting." Devin thought he heard a slight hint of disapproval in her tone. She pointed with an ink pen towards a recycling bin on the other side of the lobby before turning back to her computer and resuming her work.

Chapter 6

"Okay. Thank you!" Devin called back. He then thought to himself, *I'll just have to hide this in my bag. There's no way I'm throwing away a perfectly good can of Cosmic Energy.* After taking another sip, he coolly shuffled back to the others, who were still busy playing on their phones.

A few minutes later, a large brute of a man, who was wearing a neatly-ironed black dress uniform that had been decorated with shiny medals and rows of colorful bars, appeared at the entrance to the hallway leading out of the lobby. He had light gray hair that was cropped closely to his head and sharp hazel-brown eyes. He strolled briskly towards the news team with an outstretched hand and greeted them in a loud, booming voice, "Hello, I'm Colonel Gundersen. Welcome to Jakob Salverson!"

A big smile lit up Rita's face as she stood and stretched out her hand to return the colonel's firm handshake. "Thank you for having us, Colonel Gundersen. We're honored to be here."

"We're glad to have you," the colonel said, returning her smile. "If you'll just walk with me, we'll get started." He warmly ushered them forward with both of his hands.

As soon as the colonel and the receptionist weren't looking, Devin slipped his open drink into an inner side pocket in one of the smaller bags he was carrying. Noticing that it didn't fit very well, he carefully held the bag steady by his side in an attempt to prevent the drink from sloshing around and making a mess while he walked.

Colonel Gundersen, a no-nonsense, matter-of-fact kind of guy, didn't have a lot to say as he led them down a handful of various plain hallways that were lined with wooden doors. The hallways intersected with other hallways at odd intervals, making the newcomers feel as if they were lost in some kind of bizarre office maze. Aside from the gold placards hanging on each door that indicated which offices they led into and the numbered tiles that adorned the walls at each cross-section, there weren't many objects that could be used to distinguish one hallway from the next. The warmth of the lobby had truly been nothing more than a facade; this area definitely felt more like a military installation.

After a few more minutes of walking, they arrived at a windowless metal door standing tall at the end of the hallway. A red light bulb glowed from within a small cylindrical cage right above it. The colonel asked for each of them to produce their security clearance cards before entering, as only one person could go through the door at a time. If any more than that attempted to enter, an alarm would be set off.

Mateo volunteered to go first. He strolled up to the door and waved his security pass in front of a metal panel next to the handle. A green light flashed in the middle of the handle, and a small click was heard. The red bulb flickered off and back on again as he turned the handle and pulled the heavy door open. Behind it, a long staircase descended to a lower level. A soldier, dressed in black combat gear and holding a laser rifle to her shoulder, was patiently waiting at the bottom of the stairs. She waved her hand and beckoned Mateo forward. After passing through the door, it shut behind him with a loud clang. Rita went next, Devin came after her, and Colonel Gundersen followed closely behind.

While carefully treading down the staircase, Devin began to feel dizzy and nearly lost his balance. Apparently, the energy drink he had started on earlier still hadn't quite kicked in. *I can't believe this*, he thought to himself. *What on earth was I thinking last night?* He stopped walking about halfway down the stairs to steady himself on the railing and thought, *You need to try to act normal!*

The colonel, noticing that Devin was having trouble keeping his balance, was overcome with suspicion. By the time they all reached the bottom of the stairs, he walked up to Rita and asked in a quiet whisper, "Is he alright?"

Rita nervously explained that he was just a bit clumsy and shot a burning look at Devin that could have cut through thick steel. Devin shuffled back and forth on his feet and fidgeted with his phone before straightening up the equipment bags that hung over his shoulder. He then woefully stared down at the floor to avoid her condemning gaze.

The colonel scrutinized Devin for a few seconds longer before directing the soldier, who was now firmly standing at attention, to take them to the launch room.

With a salute, she replied, "Yes, sir!" and proceeded to lead them down a winding stone hallway that was lit from above with bright fluorescent tube lights.

As the crew followed her, they passed by a small handful of metal doors that led into top-secret areas before finally coming to a standstill in front of another large metal door. The procedure for this door was exactly the same as it had been for the first one. Each member of the group, with the exception of the soldier, passed through the door and descended yet another stairway that took them even deeper underground.

When they reached the bottom, they found themselves in a large command center that was lined with computers, servers, holo-displays, and various control panels. Men and women, clad in ashen-gray dress uniforms, were all busy working at each of their respective stations, writing code, deciphering code, analyzing stats, and evaluating data. At the far end of the room, a gigantic digital map of the world was on full display.

Taking a sudden yet unexpected interest in the map, Devin observed that many of the major countries were highlighted with bright, bold colors. New Scandinavia was rose-red, Tierra del Pueblo, an ancient desert country located to the southwest, was lemon-yellow, and Darkovia, a massive woodland nation in the far north, was shamrock-green. Across the ocean to the east, Atlantis was highlighted in amethyst-purple, and Taured, a tiny but powerful nation-state located near the Great Persian Sea, was lit up in aquamarine-blue.

Upon further examination, he also noticed that there were a handful of blinking orange lights scattered across the map; one of them happened to be right in the location of Highland City. *This is so interesting*, he thought to himself. *I wonder what each light represents? Different military bases, maybe? Or are they special operations facilities, like this one?* He absently stroked at the stubble growing on his chin as he pondered the possibilities.

Meanwhile, Colonel Gundersen politely asked the news team to stay put for a few minutes while he got everything prepared. He then strode across the room, where a high-ranking female officer stood waiting for him. The two of them proceeded to engage in a private conversation, using hushed tones that were indecipherable from far away.

All of a sudden, a loud, angry scream and a wave of heavily distorted guitar ripped across the command center. "I'll do what I want 'cause I don't give a damn! Life's too short, and I just wanna jam!"

In an instant, the low-key hustle and bustle of the launch room came to a sharp halt, and every eye in the room fell on Devin, who was fumbling around in a mad panic while frantically trying to shut off his phone. Apparently, he had forgotten to switch it over to silent mode, and Erick was trying to get a hold of him.

When he finally accomplished the task, the sound of a pin drop could have been heard. Both Rita and Mateo looked utterly mortified. Devin's eyes were the size of silver dollars, and his face had turned three shades of red. The stark silence lasted for a few long seconds before being disrupted by a loud and distinct "Hmph!" that came from the colonel.

"Mam, if you're ready, I think it would be best if we got this interview over with," Colonel Gundersen stated in a matter-of-fact tone. He then briskly paced back across the room towards Rita.

"Yes, of course. Ugh… Ahem." Rita cleared her throat. "Devin, please set the cameras up."

Devin nodded and began removing the recording equipment from his bags. When he was finished, he decided that it would be best to keep the small bag containing the energy drink close to him, as this would prevent Rita or Mateo from discovering it if either of them needed to sift through the bags for fresh batteries, extra microphones, makeup, and so forth.

It's better to be safe than sorry, he thought to himself as he gently placed the small bag over his shoulder and adjusted the strap, taking extra care not to spill the drink hidden inside.

A short while later, he was standing behind a camera that was focused on Mateo and the colonel, who had just started going over the safety procedures involved with launching missiles. He explained how nothing was left to chance when it came to launching missiles during an armed conflict as he walked Mateo over to a console that featured a big red button and a key protruding from an ignition switch that looked much like the kind used in motor vehicles in the old days, before the advent of hovertech. A soldier sitting in front of the console was staring intently at a flat-screen monitor that featured a graphic identical to the giant map at the far end of the room.

"You see," said the colonel, "In order to launch a missile, a weapons technician has to manually turn this key, which connects the circuitry to the launch mechanisms, otherwise, the big red button won't work. It's a two-step process that is carefully maintained by soldiers, like this one, who are highly disciplined." Devin aimed the camera at the soldier, who maintained his stern and controlled demeanor.

"This safety mechanism ensures that our systems can never be hacked from the outside. As an added bonus, it also ensures that our missiles can never be accidentally launched." Colonel Gundersen was beaming with pride.

Rita motioned for Devin to move in closer to the launch console to get a good closeup of everything. He nodded, gave a quick thumbs up, and carefully began to inch the camera forward.

Suddenly, by some trick of gravity or Devin's negligence, the hidden energy drink tipped over and slipped out of an open zipper on the side of the small bag hanging at his side. Hitting the concrete floor with a loud smack, the can spun around like a top and began profusely spewing carbonated bursts of liquid all over the place. The colonel, Rita, and Mateo were nothing short of dumbstruck.

Without thinking, Devin completely freaked out and haphazardly jerked himself down to grab the can. However, upon doing so, his foot hit a slick spot on the floor and flew out from underneath him, causing him to knock the camera across the room. Unable to regain his balance, he began hurtling headfirst towards the soldier sitting in front of the launch console with the force of an angry, charging bull.

The soldier, having no time to think, spun around in his chair and braced himself for impact. As Devin collided with him in mid-spin, his elbow knocked the launch key into the *on* position. At the exact same time, Devin threw both of his arms out in front of him in an attempt to steady himself and smashed into the big red button with the palm of his hand. A few seconds of dead silence filled the air, and then, like the first crack of earthshaking thunder before an intense storm, security alarms began to sound everywhere.

Colonel Gundersen, eyes wide open in panic, focused a bewildered, desperate gaze on Devin and cried out, "My god, boy! What have you done?!"

Devin didn't know it, as the colonel had purposely avoided mentioning it during the interview, but that particular button's only purpose was to launch a plethora of New Scandinavia's nuclear missiles at neighboring countries. If the process wasn't reversed, the world would never be the same.

The chaos that followed soon thereafter was very real. If a lunatic had broken into the facility and set a pack of rabid dogs loose, the results wouldn't have been much different. Soldiers were running to and fro in a crazed panic as Colonel Gundersen barked out futile orders in a vain attempt to regain some semblance of control. Rita was on her phone frantically seeking some sort of help from the news station while Mateo, like a man who had completely given up, just sat helplessly on the ground, shoulders slumped and head propped back against a computer station. All around, blaring alarms continued to resound throughout the complex.

As a storm of fear and confusion unfurled around him, Devin stood frozen in place, stupefied and barely able to think, having been overcome with a rush of shock and horror at what had just happened. The fact that he was personally responsible for the scene playing out in front of him was just too much for his quickly sobering mind to fully comprehend.

Just then, a young soldier briskly approached the colonel with a phone and said, "Sir, it's the president. He has new orders for you."

"Give me that!" barked the colonel as he yanked the phone away. "Hello, Mr. President. Colonel Gundersen speaking, sir."

A deep, controlled, and oddly calm voice came across the line, "Colonel Gundersen, please try not to panic. Simply turn the launch key back to its original position. General Fletcher has informed me that there's a small window of opportunity to act before the missiles actually launch."

"Yes, sir! I'll get right on it!"

After setting the phone down, the colonel dashed over to the console and attempted to turn the key back to its original position. However, to his extreme frustration and utter dismay, he found that it was bent and jammed in place. Still, he prodded, pulled, and twisted at the key, but to no avail. Finally, in a last ditch effort, he summoned every last bit of strength he had into making it budge. Sweat poured from his face, and loud grunting noises came from the deepest part of his belly. All of a sudden, he felt the key turn!

A wave of relief washed over his soaking wet face as he lowered his head to peer down closer at the console, and then, like the arrival of a fresh tidal wave, his relief morphed into sheer terror. The key had turned, but that was only because he had somehow managed to twist it into the shape of a corkscrew. There was no coming back now. It was definitely all over.

Beaten and defeated, he slowly backed away from the console. Retrieving the phone, he said in a gravelly voice, "I'm sorry, sir. I've failed both you and this country. Please forgive me." Before the president had a chance to respond, he dropped the phone on the ground and began making his way towards the exit.

Right at that moment, the exit door burst open at the top of the stairs, and an older man wearing a white lab coat and a pair of thick, round glasses came rushing in. He had graying brown hair, a full beard, and a mustache that curled up at both ends. Devin came out of his daze and immediately took notice. It was his father!

"Dad!" Devin yelled across the room. "What's going on?!"

"Devin, I heard you were here! Follow me quickly!" the old man called back. "There's no time to waste!" He quickly motioned for his son to follow.

Devin darted past the colonel and headed up the stairs, straight for the door. His father then led him back into the long, winding hallway he had come from. When they were about halfway down it, he stopped in front of one of the metal doors the news team had passed by earlier and proceeded to open it using a security pass.

He then turned towards Devin and said, "Hurry inside! We have to be quick!"

"What just happened?!" Devin asked in a confused and exasperated tone.

His father shook his head. "You just launched about a hundred nuclear missiles at various countries all around the world!"

Devin froze in place, legs wobbling and head swooning, as a wave of panic sent his heart rate soaring.

"It won't be long until all of those countries retaliate by launching their own nuclear arsenals back at us. It's called mutually assured destruction!"

Devin felt sick but managed to force himself to snap back into reality before bolting behind his father into the chamber. Once inside, he spotted a bullet-shaped rail car at the far end of the room that was sitting on a set of tracks that led into a dark, narrow tunnel.

He glanced at his dad nervously. "What is this? What are we doing?"

"It's not what we're doing. It's what you're going to do. You're going to take that security pass you have, climb into this car, and ride it until you reach its final destination."

"What are you talking about? Why?! I want to stay here with you!"

"I'm sorry, Devin." He looked at his son with sympathy. "This is the best that I can do."

"What do you mean?!"

Ignoring Devin's frustration, he calmly went on, "Listen to me. When the rail car stops, you will find yourself in front of a doorway leading into a steep cliff wall. Use your security card to enter. Once inside, you will see a sleep-chamber that resembles a glass coffin positioned against the back wall. Climb inside of it, pull the lid down, and press the black button on the metal panel inside. The rest will take care of itself."

"Dad, I don't want to leave you!" Devin exclaimed in fright. "What about Mom?!"

Tears began to well up in his father's eyes. "I'll explain later! Just please do as I told you! You have to trust me – it's the only way you'll be safe. I love you!"

With those final words, Devin's father hurried him across the chamber and forced him into the rail car. As soon as he was inside, the door on the right-hand side of the vehicle slid shut. His father then quickly rushed over to a small control panel on the left-hand side of the chamber and began typing on the keypad. Within seconds, a low hum of electricity could be heard as it coursed through the rails. A half-second later, the rail car bolted away like lightning.

Devin was violently jerked back against his seat, and he tried to brace himself as he raced forward at a speed that was unlike anything he had ever experienced in waking reality. A few agonizing minutes of terror flew by, and then he shot out of the dark tunnel like a rocket. As the bright daylight poured in through the front window, it was all he could do to keep his wincing, watery eyes open. From what he could gather, he seemed to be darting down the steep slope of a mountain. Within mere seconds, the car reached the bottom of the incline, and to Devin's total horror and sheer dismay, it appeared as if the rails in front of him were about to come to an abrupt end. Shutting his eyes and gripping the edge of his seat, he fought off a wave of nausea and prepared himself for the worst.

All of a sudden, the rail car screeched to a complete stop, jerking him back to reality. The right-hand door slid open, and a tall steel door that seemingly led into a steep cliff face could be seen just a few yards away. Head spinning and hands shaking, he frantically dug the security pass out of his front pocket and then stumbled out of the vehicle and fell to the ground. Almost immediately, he picked himself back up and sprinted as fast as he could towards the entrance.

When he arrived, he waved his security pass in front of a metal panel positioned next to the door in the same manner as he had done with the doors in the military complex. With a whoosh, it slid open in elevator-like fashion. After stepping inside the entryway, he found himself staring at a darkened room. All was quiet except for a low hum of electricity that faintly buzzed in the background.

The smooth cement walls were lined with mechanical devices and electronic systems that resembled massive servers. Near the center of the room, a large computer station sat all by itself. Against the back wall, shrouded in a soft yellow fluorescence, he spotted what appeared to be the sleep-chamber, as it was the only thing in the room that resembled a coffin made of glass. Directly behind it, he noticed a series of tubes and wires running along the floor that were connected to the various mechanisms lining the room's exterior.

With no time to waste on further observation, Devin hurriedly made his way inside. As he did so, the steel door swiftly slid shut behind him, leaving him in a shadowy space that was faintly lit by the dim glow of various lights flickering from the buttons and display panels on the machines housed within. Outside of the low hum of electricity, all was completely silent. Next, he did the only thing his frazzled mind could think of to do: he obeyed his father.

Pacing over to the sleep-chamber, he cautiously stretched out a hand and pressed down on the soft padding that lined the bottom of the glass box. It appeared that there was just enough room inside for him to lay down comfortably. Briefly pausing in hesitation, he considered the absurdity and potential danger of what he was about to do. However, nothing came to mind that could convince him that he had any other choice in the matter. So, taking a deep breath, he forced himself to fully climb inside.

After quietly muttering a desperate plea for help and forgiveness to God above, he proceeded to reach up and pull the lid down. He then lifted his hand and pressed the black button that was centered in a metal panel beside him. The faint yellow lighting that enveloped the sleep-chamber began to flicker rapidly as the lid sealed itself shut with a sharp hiss.

In an instant, the interior of the chamber was flooded with an odorless, icy mist that stung his eyes and forced him to tightly close them. Within seconds, all of his limbs went completely numb. However, before he could fully comprehend what was happening, his body involuntarily succumbed to an overwhelming weariness and weakness that swiftly shut off his mind and silently stole him away to a world of deep, dark, and dreamless sleep.

Chapter 7

A Selection from Aydin Culpepper's Notes – A Brief History of the Great Firefall

In regards to the earth-shattering event that has come to be known as the Great Firefall, there is so much to say and yet, sadly, so very little. When the final explosions had shaken the planet to its core and the last of the ashen dust had finally settled, those who were left standing were very few and far between. There were even fewer still who managed to outlive the horrid disasters that came hurtling in afterwards, such as plague, famine, and starvation. As a result, the accounts of what took place during that tragic time are just as scattered and varied as those who lived long enough to give them.

Being a historian, I've spent a great deal of time and effort collecting as many details as I possibly could about what happened during that dark period. Unfortunately, the scarce resources I've stumbled across over the years have, at best, left me with a fragmented picture that hardly does the truth any real justice. Though it pains me to write this, as things stand, we may never know the full extent of what happened back then or what it was that actually caused it.

That being said, the following is a description I pieced together using the few written accounts I was able to scavenge during my travels and the stories that have been passed down from one generation to the next by word of mouth.

It would seem that the Great Firefall began with blinding flashes of light that streaked across the skies from one corner of the planet to the next. These were directly followed by massive explosions that could be seen, heard, and felt from hundreds of miles away; eyewitness accounts likened their appearance to giant, mushroom-shaped clouds with long stems that rose up like great pillars on the distant horizons. As the explosions increased in intensity, mass hysteria swept throughout the lands like a tsunami. This prompted a worldwide war to break out, in which the mightiest of nations used terrible weapons of every shape and description to obliterate each other into nonexistence.

Unfortunately, billions of terrified, innocent people were caught in the crossfire, which caused many of them to lose their sanity and turn on each other in a panic-fueled craze. In less than a day, most of civilization had digressed into a state of chaos that was more barbaric and brutal than anything previously recorded in history.

Major cities and tiny towns crumbled and disintegrated into ashes and dust as devices of devastating destruction rained down from above, emaciating entire geographic regions all at once. The tranquil blues of the natural skies were transformed into deep, dark shades of crimson, and the air became a thick miasma of hot ash, burning vapor, and choking smoke. At night, the moon and the stars were blotted out by dark, churning clouds that hazily reflected back the hellish orange glow of forests set ablaze and fiery cities torn asunder. The infernos raged on until massive portions of the planet were reduced to little more than ashen deserts of silent darkness.

Sometime in the middle of the pandemonium, a curious sight appeared in the sky near the mountainous region east of the once great metropolis known as Highland City, a mysterious conical tower standing erect on a floating, island-like chunk of earth. Most people had no idea where it came from, nor did they care, as they were preoccupied with fleeing the chaos and destruction unfolding around them at the time of its appearance. However, in later years, rumors began to circulate among survivors that seemed to suggest that it rose up near the mountains just as the first explosions took place.

Concerning those who survived, it's safe to say that they fell into one of three groups. The first group consisted of people, like my ancestors, who were fortunate enough to have access to underground shelters that were specifically designed to handle a crisis such as this. The second group was made up of people who lived in rural areas that were so distant and remote they were able to, more or less, avoid the direct impact of the terrible explosions. The third group was composed of those who, somehow, managed to escape the destruction by hiding within deep underground caverns or abandoned mine shafts and the like. It almost goes without saying that there were far fewer survivors within this last group, as many of them would later be taken by starvation and disease.

Sadly, no one, regardless of locale or level of shelter, was safe from or completely immune to the mysterious poison left behind in the wake of the destruction, an invisible substance our ancestors called nuclear radiation. Nearly everything it came into contact with, human, plant, and beast alike, succumbed to a form of rot and decay that would slowly sap the life from its victims. Those who had enough food, medicine, supplies, and survival skills somehow endured through it all, but the rest (the vast majority) suffered cruel, bitter, and agonizing deaths.

It would be many long years before small handfuls of survivors would cautiously emerge from hiding to explore the decimated wastelands that had once been fertile farms and flourishing cities, and it would be many years more before anyone attempted to resettle them. How humanity managed to outlive the horrors unleashed upon the world during that dark time is a mystery that still confounds even the wisest among us. Most have been forced to settle with the inescapable conclusion that it was either luck or divine intervention. Personally, I've never been a big believer in luck. Nonetheless, regardless of one's philosophical persuasion, new life did, in fact, manage to force itself free from the wreckage and devastation, and civilization began a slow and perilous journey towards rebuilding itself.

As it regards the mysterious tower that suddenly appeared in the middle of the cataclysm, it never did come down from the sky. To this very day, it can still be seen drifting near the ancient ruins of Highland City. Until a time comes in which we have the necessary means to discover its true origin and purpose, I believe it is best viewed as a symbol of the great evil that befell our world so long ago, a stark reminder that, one day, it could all happen again.

Chapter 8

Chance and Happenstance

It had been 300 years since the first missile found its mark and ushered in the cataclysmic event that came to be known as the Great Firefall. During that time, the world took shape again and slowly came back to life, but nearly everything had changed. The governments, societal establishments, and technological advancements of old had become nothing more than a distant and hazy memory from a long bygone era, and the small communities that sprung up afterwards were made up of the descendants of those who had, somehow, survived the unfathomable horrors of the past.

These people were not weak by any stretch of the term, and their history was not a pretty one, embellished by stories of political intrigue, heroic military campaigns, or the rise and fall of family dynasties. No, these were a people who spent most of their time fighting tooth and nail just to survive, often living more like savage barbarians than patrons of good society.

And, just as the structure of society had been forever altered, the entire planet had also morphed into a deadly and more sinister version of its former self. Radiation and chemically induced genetic mutations led to the rise of thousands of new species of plants, animals, insects, and fungi, and they soon began to overtake and dominate the permanently changed environments and landscapes. Many of these mutated creatures were nothing more than grotesque, bloodthirsty monsters that harbored insatiable cravings for all forms of flesh, including that of humans. Subsequently, it was only the foolish or unwise who left the confines of their homes and shelters without taking precautions to counter such threats.

In addition to these changes, mysterious abilities that could almost be likened to magic began to gradually manifest themselves among certain humans. Whether this happened as a result of the many years of exposure to various forms of radiation and chemicals or because people had grown more in touch with their spirits and nature, the fact remained that there were a handful of special individuals who had developed powers resembling those spoken of in the fairytales and legends of old, such as enhanced sensory perception, telekinesis, and the ability to communicate telepathically. Some were even able to manipulate the elements around them and bring about healing or harm by drawing energy out of nothing more than thin air. Needless to say, it was the individuals with these miraculous gifts that usually rose up to become the leaders in their various communities, as they typically used their capabilities and insights to better the lives of those around them; however, not everyone who possessed such powers chose to be so kind with them.

It was during this period of violent rebirth and radical transformation that Devin Skye finally woke up. When he opened his misty, bleary eyes, the first thing he saw was a glowing ceiling panel that cast a dim yellow light all around him. As he slowly rolled his head over and shifted his gaze to take in his surroundings, a trembling wave of confusion and panic washed over his body from head to toe. His mind was completely blank – he had no recollection of anything. He didn't know who he was, what time it was, or what he was doing. And, try as he might, he just couldn't figure out why he was lying on his back in a large glass box inside a strange, dark room.

The lid to the glass container was wide open, so he decided that his next move would be to lift himself up and climb out of it. All was going well until he swung his legs over the side of the enclosure and placed his feet down on the floor beside it. At that moment, a series of unpleasant, prickly sensations began to race up and down the entire length of his body, similar to the kind felt after sitting or standing in one place for too long in an awkward position. He only came to the realization that he couldn't fully support his own weight when he forced himself to stand up and his legs buckled of their own accord, sending him tumbling headfirst into a somersault that ended with him banging his head against a computer station in the center of the room. Wincing in pain, he propped himself up on his elbows and abruptly succumbed to a fit of coughing and gagging, as a cloud of ancient dust had made its way into his nose and mouth.

When he finally caught his breath and the dust began to settle, he spun his head around and examined the strange room precariously. There appeared to be a number of machines and electronic devices lined up along its exterior walls, but it was hard to make out much more than that. A thick blanket of dust had settled over everything, significantly dimming the light that came from their glowing buttons and display panels. All around him, a low hum of electricity filled the air.

Sensing some of the life returning to his limbs, he decided that he would try to get up again. However, at that moment, a pounding sensation began to pulsate near the top of his head, which caused him to lift a hand reflexively and place it near the source of the pain. Feeling something sticky and wet, he jerked his hand back and noticed blood on his fingers.

It was at this point when the amnesic fog lifted from his mind like a quickly dissipating cloud, the blow to his head having triggered the subsequent neural response. Within seconds, his mind was flooded with vivid images of panicky soldiers running to and fro in confusion, a pretty but angry woman in a navy-blue dress, and an old man in a white lab coat with tears in his eyes. His heart began to beat rapidly, and sweat began to stream profusely down the sides of his cheeks. Suddenly, the memory of who he was and what he had done came rushing back to him with the force of a bullet train. However, it was all too much to take at once – in a mere instant, his entire body went numb, and everything went pitch black.

Meanwhile, just outside the chamber, Chance Whitley, a young man from the nearby village of Iron Cove, had been curiously poking around the area in boredom when a loud crash and a series of strange noises that sounded like moaning and sneezing came from the other side of the steel door. The unusual sounds stopped him dead in his tracks and caused his big green eyes to widen and his ears to perk up. He ran his hands back through his curly sandy-blonde hair, pushing it away from his ears, and leaned in closer to the door to make sure that what he heard wasn't just a trick of his imagination. If what he thought he had heard turned out to be real, it would be big news. After all, the mysterious, impenetrable metal door on the side of the mountain behind the village had been an object of suspicion and concern for far longer than he had been alive. It was the kind of thing the kids in the village talked about when they wanted to spook each other at night with tales of spirits and the like. He stood by the door motionless, straining to hear anything else. Finally, he decided that it would be best to go back home and inform the village guide of what had just happened.

A short while later, he was standing in the middle of the quaint but comfortable living area of a cozy stone cottage that sat near the center of the village, busily engaging in a frantic discussion with a distinguished older man named Leo Watts. The village guide, Iron Cove's equivalent to an elder or a mayor, was a bit perturbed by the unexpected visit, as he had just put on his comfy smoky-blue robe and furry house shoes and had been preparing to settle in and enjoy a quiet cup of herbal tea by the warmth of the fire.

"So what you're telling me is that you think you heard a ghost from behind the door in the side of the cliff?" Leo asked as he cast a scrutinizing gaze at the young man from beneath his bushy eyebrows and stroked the length of his long salt and pepper goatee. "You do realize how foolish that sounds, don't you?"

Chance shifted back and forth on his feet, stared up at the ceiling, and nervously played with his hands before responding, "I know it sounds crazy, sir, but I'm not making things up this time." A slight tinge of desperation could be heard in his voice. "I realize that I've been known to play a prank or two on the village kids, and the folks around here might not always take me seriously, but this is definitely no joke!"

Steadying himself with one hand on a shiny black cane and the other on the arm of his favorite comfy chair, the guide lifted himself from where he had been sitting and straightened up. He then cleared his throat and said, "Chance, it's not that I don't want to believe you, but if what you're saying turns out to be true…" He stared hard into Chance's green eyes. "Well… I think this is a matter that would be best resolved with Aydin."

A look of relief flitted across Chance's face.

"I want you to travel to Aydin's place and tell him everything you just told me. He'll know what to do."

"So, you believe me?"

Leo paused for a moment, looking the young man up and down, then, in a gravelly voice, replied, "Your father was a good man, Chance. I spent a lot of time with him when he was younger, and I can see some of him in you – at times, anyway." He lightly chuckled, and his cynical gaze softened. "I believe in you just like I believed in him, but you better not make me look like a fool."

Chance nodded. "That's not my intention, sir. I promise!"

"Good… Good… Well, off with you then, boy!" With a jerk, he poked and waved his cane towards the entrance of his cottage. "There's no time to waste!"

"Yes, sir!" Chance exclaimed before turning around and excitedly making his way out the front door, leaving it wide open behind him.

Shaking his head, Leo leaned over on his cane with both hands and watched the young man leave. "Ah, to be young again," he said with a sigh. He then closed the door and sauntered back towards his chair to finish his herbal tea in front of the small fire.

Chapter 9

The Final Farewell

About an hour or so passed by before Devin finally began to stir from his fainting spell. He opened his eyes and laid perfectly still, trying his best not to let the reality of his situation overwhelm him. As he gazed up at the shadowy ceiling, he began to smack his lips together and noticed that his mouth had become painfully dry. Making matters worse, his stomach also felt twisted and knotted up.

Grunting loudly, he pushed himself up from the floor and stood upright. Thankfully, it seemed that his strength was returning. He then began to look around for a receptacle of some kind that might be housing some form of nourishment, all the while hoping and praying that someone had actually taken the time to stock the chamber with provisions. After a minute or two, he spotted what appeared to be a small fridge sitting on the floor between two of the computer stations.

He shuffled over to it and firmly tugged on the handle near the top of the door. With a pop and a hiss, it swung open. It wasn't a fridge but, rather, a vacuum-sealed storage compartment. Inside were three metal canisters and a handful of silver foil packages. White labels that simply read *H2O* were attached to each of the canisters, and the silver packages had the word *Nutrimeal* printed across them in bold black letters.

Ha! Just what I was looking for, Devin thought to himself as a slight smile cracked across his dry lips.

He hastily unscrewed a tightly sealed lid from one of the canisters, spilling some of the water in the process, and proceeded to drink what was left, all at once, which probably wasn't the smartest thing to do in a survival-type situation. Next, he ripped open one of the packages of Nutrimeal. Inside, he discovered a large helping of bite-sized, grainy clusters that were made of some kind of dehydrated substance. They didn't look good, and after stuffing a handful of them into his mouth, he discovered that they didn't taste good either. Stale cardboard with a dash of salt immediately came to mind. Nonetheless, the food and water helped to ease the cramping pains in his stomach.

It was at this point that he began feeling a strong urge to relieve himself, as the food and water seemed to be running right through him.

"Please tell me there's a bathroom in here," he muttered as he twisted and turned, trying to spot one.

Glancing back towards the far end of the room, he noticed that the dim yellow light shining down from the ceiling was also illuminating a tall panel a few feet to the left of the sleep-chamber. It had an embossed icon of a toilet in its center, and it looked to be just large enough for one person to enter or exit. He quickly paced over to the panel and spotted a red button glowing beside it. As he pressed the button, the panel slid open to reveal a small rectangular space with a hole in the center of the floor. Next to the hole was a metal slot with yellowed brittle paper sticking out of it.

Leaning over and staring down woefully, he thought to himself, *Well, it's not exactly luxury, but I guess it'll have to do.*

A short while later, he found himself back by the storage compartment, eating another package of Nutrimeal and guzzling down another canister of water. As he was finishing the last grainy cluster of salty cardboard delight, the memories of everything he had just been through began to punctuate his thoughts. This time he didn't try to fight them but, instead, curled up into a ball on the floor and had a good cry.

It might have been hours before he finally got tired of hearing the sound of his own whimpers and gave up out of sheer exhaustion. At that point, all was silent, save for the low hum of electricity and the strained sounds of his own labored breathing. While he lay there, absently watching the flickering shadows as they bounced around the walls, the dark ambiance of the room began to weigh down on him like a thick cloud, and a dreadful sense of anxiety and claustrophobia began to overpower his psyche.

Finding that he couldn't take much more, he forced himself to stand up and search for a real source of light. First, he inspected the exterior walls but wasn't able to locate anything resembling a light switch. Next, he decided to check out the computer station in the center of the room, where he had hit his head, figuring that the lighting in the chamber might be controlled through some kind of graphical user interface.

After wiping the dust from a display attached to it and fumbling around for a few minutes with the various buttons that ran along its surface, he managed to turn it on. The screen blinked on and off a couple of times, and then, to his complete and total surprise, an image of his father flashed into place. As he stood there, staring at the monitor in a shocked stupor, the brightness of the screen stung and burned his eyes.

Suddenly, his father began to speak, "Son, if you're viewing this video, it means that you've survived, and everything worked out the way that I hoped it would. I guess the first thing I need to tell you is that I never wanted any of this for you. Things weren't supposed to work out this way. However, before you assume that I'm referring to your accident, please understand that I'm not. Though it pains me to say this, a day like this was bound to come, sooner or later. You just happened to speed the process up a bit." A hint of a defeated smile traced across the scientist's anguished features that faded into a sad and somber expression.

"You see, the world had been heading towards a bad end for quite some time. Not many knew it, except for me, some of my colleagues, and the high-ranking military officials we worked alongside. As the details of our projects were highly classified, the most an overcurious person might have ever discovered would have been through the various conspiracy theory sites on the internet. Of course, the military wasn't too worried about this because nearly all of those sites were scrupulously monitored by both human personnel and artificial intelligence systems, and the general public never really believed anything posted on them anyway.

In short, international relations had begun to take a violent turn for the worse, and our government's top leaders were anticipating the threat of nuclear war. In preparation for that time, they contracted scientists, like myself, to work out all of the details regarding their future survival. They also tasked us with the development of weapons that would help them to maintain their dominance over the world once the dust had settled, so to speak.

I wasn't happy about any of this, and I always felt like there had to be a better way to solve the world's problems. But, regardless of my personal feelings, I was forced to continue my work under their careful guidance and close oversight – people in my position never have a choice in the matter."

At this, Devin's father stopped and let out a brief sigh. "Son, I tried my hardest to avert disaster in my own way. I really did… I wasn't alone in this endeavor either. A few of my colleagues and I secretly worked on ways to keep the worst from happening. At times, it seemed like our efforts to maintain peace were going somewhere, however, when all was said and done, we would always end up feeling like we had taken one step forward and two steps back.

One of the last big projects we were tasked with working on was a military installation in the form of a flying tower that could house weapons of a strength and magnitude the world had never seen before, the idea being that the military could use the weapons stored within to completely subjugate any and all opposition to their rule after a nuclear disaster broke out. If my calculations are correct, it should be hovering in the sky around the mountains near Highland City, even as you view this video.

After the tower was completed, we were instructed to design survival-chambers for the highest-ranking officers in our military so that they could escape the inevitable horrors that a nuclear catastrophe would bring upon the world and humanity. We were also directed to build chambers for ourselves, as they figured that they might still have need of our expertise in the future. The chamber you are sitting in is the result of our work. However, others were also built, and as much as I hate to tell you this, some of those chambers may be occupied."

He briefly paused in silence. "Son, I don't have a lot of time, so I'm going to speed this up. By my calculations, you should have been asleep for exactly 300 years. The chamber you've been housed in was designed to slow all of your metabolic processes down to near zero while still keeping you alive. It's a complicated matter that I can't fully explain right now, but if you're watching this video, it means that it worked. It also means that the crystals used to energize the mechanisms that kept you alive are just as powerful as my colleagues and I anticipated – I'll explain more on this in a bit.

Within the tower, there are genetically enhanced super soldiers that have been housed in similar chambers. These creatures are half-human and half-machine, and they were programmed to carry out one task and one task alone, to use the weapons housed within to subjugate any and all opposition. Son, if they are awakened, they will stop at nothing to accomplish this mission." At this, the old scientist grew quiet and shook his head.

Without blinking, Devin stared intently into his father's wise, old eyes, feeling for a brief moment like he was still alive and standing in the room right in front of him. Tears began to stream down his cheeks.

The message continued, "The good news is that they can't wake up without the tower being fully activated. The idea behind this decision was that it would give the military personnel on the ground extra time to assess the situation around them. If they found that the weapons in the tower wouldn't be needed, they could postpone activation and approach global dominance from a different vantage point. However, if things on the ground proved to be *complicated*, the tower's activation would ensure a swift victory over anyone or anything standing in their way."

Chapter 9

Devin's father gazed straight into the camera, a serious expression overtaking his demeanor. "Son, I don't know what kind of world you're going to find yourself in when you exit the survival-chamber. I don't know if it will be a peaceful one, a war-torn wasteland, or if there will even be a world left, but I feel it's important that you know that the floating tower cannot, under any circumstances, be activated. If it is, the world you find yourself in, good or bad, will be completely overthrown."

He tried to fight back a wave of emotion. "I'm so sorry." Removing his glasses, he wiped the tears that had begun to well up in his eyes. "Devin, there is a silver lining to all of this. My colleagues and I created a self-destruct mechanism within the tower that the military was not aware of. We had to be very careful about it, at the risk of being imprisoned or worse, had our plans been discovered.

The fully activated tower is designed to run on a new form of energy that is generated by using three powerful crystalline orbs that were discovered during an archaeological dig at an Indigenous burial site near Highland City. The orbs were found hidden in a series of underground chambers among a treasure trove of strange energy-producing crystals.

Scientists, who had been authorized to work alongside the archaeologists on the project, discovered that the crystals could be used to power everything from simple alarm clocks to massive hover-tanks. After running a series of experiments and tests, they found that the three crystalline orbs were more powerful than all of the smaller energy crystals combined. It wasn't long before they came to the conclusion that the new technology would go a long way in helping to fix the planet's energy crises. However, as things like that usually go, the government forced them to keep the underground chambers, the energy crystals, and the orbs a secret. The technology was used, instead, to build powerful new weapons."

He glanced around for a moment and collected his thoughts. "To sum things up, the three orbs, when used together, can generate enough energy to power weapons more destructive than anything the world has ever seen, and the tower was constructed to house these weapons.

As I mentioned earlier, a self-destruct mechanism was installed in the tower. It's activated by placing all three of the orbs in a special compartment that's hidden within the tower's innermost chamber. Unfortunately, Devin, they have to be disposed of in this manner, as there doesn't seem to be any other way to destroy them. Unlike the simpler energy crystals that were discovered alongside them, they cannot be split, cracked, or cut with normal tools. Their bizarre chemical makeup and complex crystalline structures have rendered them nearly impervious to damage.

Anyway, shortly after the tower's completion, my colleagues and I secretly hid the crystalline orbs in various caves around the region you're currently located in. They've each been sealed in secure containers behind doors that function just like the one you came through when you entered the survival-chamber. If the world hasn't been decimated to the point of no return and the landscape hasn't been altered to a state that's unrecognizable, they should all still be where we left them. I've granted you access to the chambers, so all you'll need is your security clearance card to retrieve them. You'll also need to use your card to access the hidden compartment in the tower's innermost chamber."

Chapter 9

His features were suddenly overcome with a look of worry. "Devin, as much as I hate to say this, I fear that you won't be the only one after the orbs, as the military needs them to fully activate the tower. Nonetheless, you cannot, under any circumstances, let them fall into the wrong hands. If they do, the world you are living in will be decimated and overthrown, and whatever is left of humanity will be permanently enslaved."

Straightening up, he took a deep breath. "Well, there's not much time left, as the first missiles will be hitting the ground any minute now. I want you to know that I'm not expecting you to stop the destruction that the tower might bring, but I'd be doing you a great disservice if I didn't inform you of what's to come. What you decide to do with this knowledge is your choice.

Son, all I ever wanted for you was a life of peace. I never wanted any of this to happen to you, your mother, or anyone else, and I'm ashamed that I ever got involved with any of it. If I could go back and change things, I would. Unfortunately, even if I could go back, I'm not sure that it would make much of a difference. I don't feel like I have the right to ask you this, but if you could, please try to forgive me." The old scientist covered his face with his hands and broke down in tears.

A brief moment passed before he was able to compose himself and look back into the camera. Choking back his emotions, he finished his message, "The exit door should now be fully functional. I don't know if you tried to open it yet, but it was programmed not to open until after this message had been accessed. There's also a powerful weapon and a supply of rations stored within the chamber. Be sure to find them and take them with you before you leave.

I guess, at this point, the best I can do is send up a prayer for your survival. In saying that, I hope you end up in a better world than the one you left behind. I want you to know that I always tried my best. I love you, Devin." With those last words, the screen went dark.

Numb with shock and overcome by grief, Devin just stood there and stared wide-eyed at the black screen while one agonizing, soul-crushing thought after another ran through his mind. Everyone he ever loved was dead, everything he ever cared about was gone, and he had no one to blame but himself. The weight of his thoughts and the oppressive darkness of the room began to sweep in and bear down on his mind, threatening to break him completely when, all of a sudden, a loud beep and a series of clicking and buzzing sounds brought him back to reality. Lowering his eyes to stare at the source of the noise, he saw what looked like an image of a map slowly inching its way onto the outstretched holding tray of a printer.

Chapter 10

Aydin's Letter to Oren Mendel

Tuesday, September 21ˢᵗ, 2354

Dear Oren,

    I hope this message finds you and yours well. I also hope that it has reached you safely and swiftly, as I believe you'll find its contents to be of great interest.

    Something most unusual has happened in my part of the wild lands. A young man from Iron Cove, Chance Whitley, showed up on my doorstep with a strange story, but it wasn't just any story. He told me that he heard something stirring from behind the sealed metal door located near the hidden back entrance to the village.

    Now, before you think I've grown old and foolish, please hear me out. I wouldn't run the risk of using my best carrier pigeon to deliver a letter to you over wild rumors and hearsay.

    You see, Oren, as of late, my sleep has been troubled by a strange recurring dream. In it, I'm standing outside my home and watching the night sky when, all of a sudden, the mysterious tower floating near the ruins of Highland City begins to descend upon the earth. Loud and thunderous explosions are happening all around me, and the sky is filled with blinding flashes of light that span the entire spectrum. When I turn around to take cover, the dream shifts, and I'm instantly transported to the front of the sealed door behind Iron Cove. I sense that something is stirring on the other side, and just as I am sure that the door will open of its own accord, I wake up.

Chapter 10

This isn't just an ordinary dream. It feels much too real, and it has been happening far too often. At this point, I'm beginning to wonder if it's a message from the divine, and I can't help but feel that I should keep my eyes open and stay alert.

For some time now, I've been troubled over the meaning of this vision, but I haven't been able to ascertain any clear understanding. So when Chance showed up at my door just to tell me that he had heard something coming from behind the metal door, I felt deep in my heart that it was more than just a ghost story or some wild animal shuffling around. I believe that the village guide must be feeling the same way, or else he wouldn't have sent Chance on such an errand.

Oren, I know that you are wise in the esoteric ways of old, and I have not forgotten how our visions and insights have often run parallel to each other, irrespective of the great distances between us or the large spans of time that have traversed between our physical meetings. In saying that, I must know if the unseen energies have revealed anything about this to you. Could it be that the Darkovian prophecies regarding the tower are actually true?

I refuse to assume anything about these matters just yet, as there is still much that I must learn. In the meantime, I have asked Chance to keep a watchful eye on the sealed door. He is to report back to me if anything unusual happens, and I trust that he will.

Regardless of how strange this may sound, I feel like a great, sweeping change is on the horizon. If I'm wrong about this, I ask that you'll forgive me, as my old age and this hard life may finally be taking their toll on me. However, something has begun to stir inside of me, something unsettling and worrisome, and you know as well as I do that it is unwise, if not downright foolish, to ignore a strong premonition, no matter how fantastical it may seem.

It has been well over a year since our last visit, and I sincerely apologize for that. However, if I'm reading the signs correctly, it seems that future events could very well bring us together once again. Until then, best regards.

– Aydin

Chapter 11

Sarina's Diary
Tuesday, September 21st, 2354 – Evening

Dear Diary,

I'm really starting to get concerned. It seems like everyone in the village has been talking about Chance behind his back, and I think it would crush him if he heard some of the things that have been said. I'm not going to pretend like he didn't bring it all on himself, but I'm worried for him, just the same.

Apparently, sometime this morning, he heard a series of strange noises coming from the other side of the old sealed door behind the village, but instead of keeping it to himself, he went straight to my grandpa and told him all about it. At the very least, he could have come to me first. I might have been able to convince him to handle things differently. It's bad enough that he already has a reputation for acting like a fool, and this latest stunt certainly isn't going to help his case.

I just don't understand why he won't settle down and be the man I know him to truly be. The people around here don't see what I see in him – a bold dreamer with a heart as big as the sun. No, they just see a troublemaker who has been too slow to take on any real responsibilities. It's absolutely frustrating!

First, it was the incident involving some of the gate guards and what was supposed to be a "friendly" game of Darkovian poker. Whatever it was that convinced Chance that he could defend himself against three men in a fist fight all by himself is beyond me. I suppose, when it comes right down to it, he wasn't given much of a choice, but I still think he should have had enough sense to walk away before it got to that point.

Shortly after that, he and a couple of his friends were caught trying to sneak melons out of Ted Crane's garden. When Ted discovered that the whole ordeal was intended to be a harmless prank, he backed off and let the matter go (as he should have), but the way that everything played out was nothing short of embarrassing. To this day, I'm still running into people who are convinced that Chance is some sort of petty melon thief.

Finally, there was the accident at The Pumara's Den. On the evening that Leandra first started serving her new and improved beer recipe, Chance made sure he was one of the first in line to try it out. The night started out harmless enough, just a casual get-together with a few friends, and then one drink turned into two drinks, two drinks turned into three, and three turned into four. After that, things rapidly went south. You'd think the humiliation that comes from falling off of a table and nearly breaking your arm after giving a slurred speech about "progress" in front of everyone in the tavern would be more than enough to slow a person down. But not Chance; he just doesn't know when to give it up.

At this rate, I don't know that I'll ever be able to take him seriously, but what am I supposed to do? I know deep in my heart that he's better than this, and I'm not going to stop caring about him just because he's made a few silly errors in judgment.

And, speaking of errors in judgment, I'm not really sure what my grandpa is thinking right now. It turns out that, after hearing Chance's story, he immediately sent him off to meet with Aydin Culpepper. I just can't understand why he would ever do such a thing. Everyone knows that there's no real mystery behind the sealed door, at least not any kind that matters. After all, I've been hearing ghost stories and tall tales about it since I was a little girl, and both my mother and my grandmother grew up listening to the same stories as me. At some point, you just have to let go of childhood nonsense and grow up.

If you ask me, he needs to step down from his position as the village guide. Here lately, he's been acting old and senile, and the fact that he would take Chance's story at face value proves it. I love my grandpa and all – he's one of the sweetest and most caring people in the entire world – but it breaks my heart to see him being played for a fool. If you ask me, the Watts family name doesn't need to be dragged through the mud by all of this, and more importantly, my grandpa doesn't deserve it!

I swear, the next time I see Chance, I'm going to let him know how I really feel. I don't care if he doesn't want to listen to me, his erratic behavior has got to stop. Enough is enough!

Meanwhile, on a different note, Kalob Spear came by my mother's shop again today. For some reason, she wouldn't quit going on about him. I had to hear about his promotion, his plans for the future, and, last but not least, about how much he likes me. The whole time I just wanted to plug my ears and walk away. I honestly don't get what it is that she sees in him.

I think Kalob is an alright guy, but he's just so boring and predictable, and the way he constantly plays with his hair is maddening. To make matters worse, he never talks about anyone or anything other than himself. I swear he thinks that just because he's been given a job as a gatekeeper all of the women in the village are suddenly going to throw themselves at him. Well, maybe Phoebe would – she's absolutely shameless.

But, seriously, I can't believe that, after all this time, he thinks I'm going to start taking an interest in him. It's not as if I don't go out of my way to ignore him every time he comes around. A more sensible guy would get the hint and stop trying.

Thankfully, it doesn't look like I'll have to worry about seeing him for a while. Just before he left the shop, he told my mother that he would be on guard duty at the Stone Ridge Tunnel gate in the northern end of the valley for the next two weeks. That was the first bit of good news I'd heard all day. Now, maybe I'll finally be able to focus and get some actual work done.

Well, it's getting late. I should probably stop writing and get ready for bed. Chance is supposed to be arriving back in the village any time now. I pray that he returns safely, as the pumaras are out in large numbers this time of year, and it's not safe to travel alone.

Chapter 12

Devin's Logbook

Entry 1:

My dad used to tell me that I should write things down – my future plans, my goals, my thoughts. He claimed that it was a good habit to get into because it would help me to be successful in life. Of course, I didn't take his advice. It was just one of the many things he tried to teach me that went in one ear and right out the other. I mean, I hated being forced to write papers in school. Why would I ever willingly choose to write in my own free time? Back then, it didn't make much sense to me.

But now, I find myself sitting here and writing, and I don't even know why. Maybe it's because I'm feeling guilty? Or maybe it's just a way for me to make sense of my scattered thoughts and the hopeless situation I'm in? I can't really say for sure. All I know is that putting these thoughts on paper somehow makes me feel a little more sane, which, at this point, is really saying something.

It's cold and dark in here, and there's nothing to do. I searched the room, top to bottom, looking for anything that might be of use to me. Unfortunately, outside of this daily logbook, a handful of machine schematics, and the pencil I'm currently using, all I found was a strange-looking dagger lying in a drawer near the food compartment – I'm guessing it's the weapon that my dad referred to in his message.

I'm pretty sure that this place was intended to be stocked with more, as there are a number of empty storage bins lined up along the walls. However, from the looks of things, it doesn't seem like the military was anticipating that the apocalypse would happen so soon. I guess there's no way they could have predicted that someone like me would randomly come along and push the big red button. Even as I write it down, it seems so mindbogglingly stupid and utterly bizarre – it feels like it shouldn't even be real. If I'm honest with myself, I'm still having trouble believing that I actually did it. How on earth could I have been so reckless? What could I have possibly been thinking? I swear there's something seriously wrong with me.

As if my situation couldn't get any worse, I reached into my back pocket to pull out my wallet and discovered it was missing. I spent about twenty minutes or so scanning the floor and searching for it but came up empty-handed. When I fell earlier, I'm guessing that it must have flew out of my pocket and slid underneath one of the machines that line the walls in this place. If I could just find a decent source of light, I'm sure I could locate it. However, as things stand, the only real source of light I have is coming from the dim yellow ceiling panel above the sleep-chamber, which barely illuminates the back of the room, let alone anything else.

I'm not sure why I'm letting this upset me so much, considering that everything in my wallet would most likely be useless in the outside world. Nonetheless, it's just one more thing that I can add to a long list of things that have gone wrong.

On a more positive note, I still have my security clearance card, as I'd shoved it in my front pocket, right behind my phone, shortly after I entered this place. According to my dad, I'll need it to get into the chambers where the crystalline orbs are kept. He also said that I'll need it to access the hidden compartment within the floating tower. So I cannot, under any circumstances, lose it, no matter what.

As far as my phone is concerned, it's dead and completely useless. I've been debating whether or not I should even bother keeping it, considering that it's highly unlikely that the battery is still functional. Speaking of the battery, I have absolutely no way of recharging it. I mean, it's not like I brought a charging cable with me when I came in here. At this point, it just seems like extra, useless baggage that I should probably leave behind. All the same, if I could get it working again, the calculator, the camera, and the flashlight would definitely come in handy. I think I'm going to hold on to it – just in case.

The dagger I found is one of the coolest things I've ever laid eyes on. The more I think about it, calling it an ordinary dagger doesn't seem quite right, as there seems to be more to it than that. It's about a foot and a half long with a double-edged blade that glistens like a polished mirror. In the center of the crossguard, there's an inset of a bluish-green crystal, streaked about with dark-blue swirls. The crystal is roughly the size of a marble. Just below it, there's a small silver switch. There's also a vertical lever on one side of the black leather grip handle.

I found that the lever can be squeezed and functions just like a brake handle on an antique bicycle. I'm not sure what it's for, but it almost seems like it might be some kind of trigger button. I tried flipping the small switch, but nothing happened. I also tried out various combinations of flipping the switch and squeezing the handle at the same time but got the same results. Now that I think about it, that's probably a good thing, as I'm indoors and might have blown something up.

Chapter 12

Good lord! What was I thinking?!

Anyway, I'm guessing that it's missing something, or it's possible that I'm doing something wrong. Maybe it just needs to be charged like a cell phone? I'm not really sure. I'll have to mess around with it some more after I leave this place.

I also spent some time looking at the map that my father left for me. It's printed on strange, plastic-like material. I guess he had the foresight to know that regular printer paper wouldn't hold up very well over such a long period of time. He was so smart when it came to things like that.

The map accurately details the mountainous regions surrounding Highland City and shows the locations of a number of caves, rivers, and valleys. Some of these areas are marked with bold dots. According to the legend, these indicate where the crystalline orbs are located. In addition to the dots, there are also two bold stars. One is in a stretch of the mountains northeast of Highland City, and it indicates the location of the archaeological dig site where the energy crystals were first discovered. The other is on the eastern outskirts of the city, and it marks the entrance to the floating tower. The map also includes a diagram of the tower that details the exact location of the innermost chamber where the self-destruct mechanism can be accessed.

Despite how accurate the map is, I'm having my doubts as to how helpful it will be, considering that the world outside might not even look the same. And this brings me to another point – I have absolutely no idea what it's going to be like out there. I don't know if it's going to be safe or if I'm getting ready to walk into a decimated wasteland. The water could be poisoned. The air might be toxic. What am I going to do if I walk out of this place and discover that I'm the only person left alive on the entire planet? I can't even begin to imagine what that might mean, and I honestly don't want to think about it. Still, I can't help myself, as there are just too many questions that need answers. Unfortunately, I won't be able to answer any of them until I leave this survival-chamber behind, and I just can't bring myself to do that right now.

If I'm being honest with myself, it's because I'm scared. Leaving this place means facing the cold, hard truth, and I'm not sure if I'm ready for that. I realize that I can't stay in here forever, but I'm worried sick about what awaits me on the other side of that door.

Entry 2:

Well, here I am, writing again. I've been kicking myself for eating most of the Nutrimeal and drinking most of the water. How could I have been so careless? Now, I'm at serious risk of starving to death. To make matters worse, my stomach is bloated and cramping from eating too much at once. Whether I like it or not, I'm going to have to leave the safety of this room behind, but I still can't bring myself to open the door.

In an effort to get my mind off of things, I tried to turn the monitor in the center of the room back on, but all I got was a black screen covered in line after line of indecipherable code. At this point, I'm really wishing I would have paid more attention during those computer science courses I took in college. Honestly, I'm wishing I would have done a lot of things differently.

I've been trying my best not to overthink things, but I can't help but feel like my entire life has been one huge mistake. Everything that led up to me pushing that button seems like such a waste. I honestly hate myself right now, and I don't know that I'll find anything that resembles inner peace ever again.

My father, my mother, my friends, Rita, and even Mateo are all dead because of me. I can't imagine a single scenario in which they lived. I really can't. But, even if it turns out that I'm wrong, what kind of world did they survive to live in? I remember enough from school to know that a nuclear disaster would change everything for the worse. God, I'm such an idiot! What on earth have I done?!

Entry 3:

I just woke up from a nap. Outside of worrying about what lies behind the door, there's really nothing else to do in here. Against my better judgment, I caved in and helped myself to some more water and a few clusters of Nutrimeal. The stomach cramps have finally gone away. Physically, I feel better than I have in a while. However, I seriously can't stand the smell of myself. In the words of the late, great Mateo Florez, I smell like sauerkraut and rotten milk. I really do. When I think about it, he really wasn't such a bad guy. I mean, I probably would have acted just like him if I had to put up with someone like me. As much as I hate to admit it, that's the truth.

I don't know how much time has passed in this place since I first woke up. I'm thinking it's been at least a day, but it could be longer. There's no way to tell. I searched the room, high and low, but I couldn't find a single clock anywhere. I thought about turning on one of the computers to check the time but soon gave up on that idea, as I don't have the passwords needed to access them. Of course, the one in the center of the room seems to be out of order, and as far as fixing it is concerned, I wouldn't even know where to begin. I'm so worried that if I mess around with things in here too much, I'll end up shutting down the life-support systems that keep this place habitable. Nope, there's no more button pushing for this guy.

For some reason, I'm feeling really drowsy again. It seems like the darkness, the flashing machine lights, and the low hum of electricity are having a hypnotic effect on me. What I wouldn't give for a warm blanket and a soft pillow right now.

Entry 4:

Well, I'm awake again. Nothing has changed, except for the fact that I want to gag every time I catch a whiff of myself. I know that I can't stay in here forever, and truth be told, I've had enough of this cold, dark chamber. So, for better or worse, I'm going to do it. I'm going to walk right out that door and take whatever is coming to me. If a quick and painful death awaits me on the other side, then so be it. I honestly can't say that I deserve anything less. So I guess this is it.

Chapter 13

Leo's Request for Assistance

Wednesday, September 22nd, 2354

Greetings Aydin,

It's been quite a while since you last spent any time here in Iron Cove. I know I'm not alone when I say that you've been missed. All the same, I hope life out in your neck of the woods has been treating you well. As far as life here in the village is concerned, things have been going much better than expected, especially considering the unusual and precarious times we've been living through.

I'm happy to say that the summer was good to us. Our hunters were able to bring in an abundance of wild game, which we were in desperate need of, as our supplies of fur and leather were beginning to dwindle. Of course, it almost goes without saying that the excess meat will make the upcoming winter months much easier to endure.

I think you'll be happy to hear that the blue onions you suggested we plant in the spring were recently harvested, and the farmers couldn't be happier with the quality and abundance of their crops. It also appears that the last of the beet, turnip, carrot, radish, and cabbage crops will all be just as plentiful. You can rest assured that as soon as the harvest has been brought in, a portion will be sent your way.

Recently, I had a chance to taste the blue onions, and let me just say this, Aydin, you're in for a real treat! My granddaughter used one to flavor a pumara steak that she prepared for me, and it was one of the best dishes I'd tasted in a long time. It also seemed to produce a burst of energy within me along with a kind of boost that worked to clear the haze from my mind. I don't know if you were already aware that the onions possessed these latent medicinal properties? I have no doubt that the villagers will greatly benefit from their use.

Yes, it does my heart a lot of good to know that we will have coats and blankets to keep us warm and more than enough food to keep our bellies full. I only hope that we never have to endure another winter like the one we barely survived back in 2306. I haven't forgotten how you brought me back from the brink of death; your knowledge of herbs and their healing properties is truly a gift from above. But I'm rambling on again and getting away from why I felt the need to write you.

Despite our good fortunes, it appears that we have a most unusual situation on our hands, and I'm not quite sure if I'm handling it properly. As you already know, Chance Whitley claimed that he heard something stirring behind the old sealed door behind the village. At first, I was hesitant to take him at his word. After all, it's old Gavin's boy we're talking about, and just like the much younger version of his father I once knew so well, he still has more than a few wild oats to sow – and that's putting it nicely! Nonetheless, I couldn't shake the strange, nagging feeling that I needed to listen to him.

Well, for once, it turns out that the boy was right. At this very moment, it would seem that I am housing a ghost from the very, very distant past. I realize that this probably doesn't make any sense to you, but I really don't know how else to put it. I guess I should start from the beginning to catch you up to speed.

Chapter 13

Last night, right after Chance got back from your house, he stopped by my place to let me know that he was going to camp out near the sealed door in order to keep a better eye on it. The thought that he might be taking things a little too far briefly crossed my mind, but it was easy to see that his mind was already made up, and there wasn't going to be any talking him out of it. So I let the matter be and went off to bed, figuring that he'd eventually get bored and give up after the initial excitement of the whole affair had worn off. Little did I know that I was about to wake up to the surprise of my life.

When Chance wildly burst into my house this morning, throwing the front door open without so much as a single knock, I had half a mind to beat him with my cane and toss him out – the boy has no manners! Instead, I scolded him and asked him for the meaning behind his rash behavior. After a whole slew of apologies, he told me that he had been standing outside of the sealed door when it opened of its own accord. A moment later, a ghoulish-looking creature, maybe a mutant, came walking right out into the morning sun.

At this point, he began to get panicky and fidget, so I prompted him to calm down and finish his story. He then told me that the door behind the mutant hit a jam as it began to close, which created a violent jarring motion that, somehow, sparked a small avalanche. Apparently, just as the mountain came crashing down around the door, the mutant hurled itself in his direction. Chance, having fallen under the impression that he was being attacked, abruptly turned tail and ran away.

I quickly explained to him that the mutant was probably just trying to save itself from being smashed under a rock slide. Foolish boy!

Chapter 13

So picture this, the mountainside is crumbling down around the sealed door, which is causing a loud rumble that can be heard all throughout the village, and Chance is scampering down the street, raising alarm and shouting out panicked warnings in a state of hysteria. By the time the mutant found its way through the hidden back entrance of the village wall, frightened mothers were scooping up their children and fleeing indoors in a complete frenzy as a group of watchmen, now on high alert, readied their weapons and prepared to rush in his direction.

It was at this point that our terrified mutant helplessly dropped its belongings and fell over in a dead faint right in the middle of the street. The sight of our village's bravest and strongest approaching with blades drawn must have scared it senseless. When the watchmen saw this, they lowered their weapons and scurried over to where it was lying. After binding it up, one of them thought it might be a good idea to stick it in the arm with a sleeping dart as a precautionary measure and, without waiting for a second opinion, proceeded to do just that. Unfortunately, I discovered all of these details after the fact.

As all of this was taking place, I was in the middle of demanding that Chance straighten up and lead me in the direction of the mutant. After all, being the village guide, I needed to know what was really going on. However, right at that moment, two of the watchmen, Cyrus and Tristam, showed up at my door holding our now comatose "mutant" before me in their arms.

I'll spare you the rest of the details, as they don't really matter. The long and short of it all is that I could clearly see it was not a mutant or some kind of monster that they had captured. No, it was just a pale and sickly young man dressed in strange attire who appeared to be malnourished and in desperate need of a bath. Oh, the smell, Aydin! It's hard to put into words. The closest thing that comes to mind is a moldy mix of bad eggs, pumara dung, and pig vomit!

After taking just one look at him, I could tell that he was in desperate need of care, so I directed the men to take him to the washroom and clean him up. Afterwards, I had them dress him in fresh clothes and lay him down in my spare bedroom, where he slept until about noon.

This brings me to the present. He's finally up and around, and he seems to be doing okay. I spent some time trying to get to know more about him but couldn't get him to reveal anything more than his name, which, by the way, is Devin Skye. Aside from that, he's been a bit on the quiet side and, altogether, just seems more or less lost. However, I happen to know that he hasn't been completely forthcoming with me about the true nature of his past, as he's been trying to convince me that he hit his head and is suffering from some kind of memory loss.

What he doesn't realize is that I know more than I've let on. When the watchmen brought him to my doorstep, they carried with them the items that he had dropped in the street, a curious-looking dagger and what appears to be an ancient map of the region. Also, after they had finished cleaning and dressing him, they checked the pockets in his dirty clothes and discovered a leather-bound journal, a strange object that resembles one of the mysterious communication devices of old, and a small rectangular card with the words *Jakob Salverson Military Complex* stamped on it.

Chapter 13

Naturally, I took some time to look through the journal while he was sleeping, and what I discovered shook me to the core. As absurd as this may sound, everything I read seemed to imply that our mysterious visitor arrived here from the distant past after escaping a worldwide disaster of cataclysmic proportions. But how could that even be possible? I obviously don't need to tell you, of all people, that there hasn't been a catastrophe of that nature since the time of the Great Firefall. Even as I write it down, I'm having trouble believing it, yet no other interpretation makes sense. All I can say is that you'll understand what I mean after you've seen the evidence for yourself.

As soon as I was finished with the journal, I decided to examine his personal belongings a second time. As it turns out, every single item in his possession also seems to suggest that he really might not be from this timeline. For example, I've never seen a dagger like the one he was carrying in my entire life. It's beautifully designed, it's in mint condition, and it's fashioned from materials that I'm not sure I can even put a name to. In the center of the crossguard, there's a small blueish-green crystal that almost shines with its own quiet light. It's truly a marvelous and curious item, indeed.

Also, there's the ancient communication device. Although I've never seen one in person, I'm fairly certain that what he carries is one. He called it a *phone* in his journal. Reading that word out loud and looking at the strange object brought a long forgotten memory back to me from my childhood. My grandfather showed me a picture of a similar-looking object when I was still quite small. It was in an ancient manuscript, what they used to call a *magazine*, that somehow survived the Great Firefall. He told me that it was called a phone and that people used them to communicate with one another over great distances, even all the way around the world! I remember thinking at the time that it was almost like magic.

As far as the map he was carrying is concerned, I have no doubt that it's a map of this region, but the cities and locations marked on it haven't been around since before the Great Firefall! I don't think I need to tell you that, outside of myself, you, and maybe a small handful of scholars, there aren't many people left who even remember their existence, let alone their original locations. The map also contains an intricate layout of what looks to be a tower. Its design is unlike anything I've ever laid eyes on.

Aydin, I am at a complete loss of what to do. Never in all my years did I imagine that I would end up dealing with anything as confounding yet remarkable as this. It's amazing, frightening, and puzzling all at the same time. I do feel, at the moment, that I should keep the young man close to me, as I'm only too sure that, in his current state, he wouldn't last a week if I set him loose to roam the wild lands on his own. And, obviously, there is still much that I need to learn from him.

Under normal circumstances, I wouldn't ask this of you, but I am truly hoping that you will see fit to come and stay in Iron Cove for a while. I asked Chance to personally deliver this letter to you in the hopes that you would accompany him on his return trip to the village.

For better or worse, I feel in my heart of hearts that the appearance of this young man may change everything, and I'm not sure that I can handle what may come with those changes on my own. As things stand, the people in the village are nervous and a bit on edge, and they're demanding answers to questions that I have no good way of answering. I could go on, but I think you get the picture.

I hope this message finds you well, Aydin. I'm looking forward to seeing you soon!

– Leo

Chapter 14

Breakfast and Bad News

The sharp rays of the glaring morning sun shot through the small round window on the eastern side of the little bedroom Devin was sleeping in and hit him right in the eyes. As he groggily rolled over to avoid the painful light, a delicious aroma coming from the kitchen drifted into the room. However, before he could even begin to wonder what was cooking, his attention was overtaken by the muffled sounds of yelling and shouting that seemed to be coming from just outside of the cottage.

What on earth is going on?! he wondered as he propped himself up and wiped the sleep from his eyes.

He then proceeded to get out of bed and make his way across the wooden plank floor to a tall mirror with a rustic wooden frame that was hanging next to a dresser. As he stared at his reflection, he was overcome with strong feelings of relief. Aside from the curious outfit he was wearing, he looked, felt, and smelled like his old self again.

A slight smile crept across his face as he took a minute to assess his new attire, a style of dress resembling something he might have seen in an old medieval-based fantasy film. He was wearing a long-sleeved cream-colored linen shirt that buttoned up in the front along with a pair of light brown trousers that were made of a thicker version of the same material. He also had on a pair of comfortable gray woolen socks. Behind him, a brown leather vest and a matching leather belt were draped over the bedpost, and lying on the floor beneath them was a well-worn pair of brown leather boots.

With a light chuckle, he thought to himself, *You really should have been an actor or something. This rugged woodsman look really suits you.*

Just then, the bedroom door swung open, and Leo shuffled through the doorway, leaning on his shiny black cane for support. Dressed in his favorite smoky-blue robe and a matching night cap that had a fuzzy white tassel toppled over to one side, his style of dress and the frown on his face gave him the appearance of a perturbed, old mage. Looking Devin up and down, he said, "I'm glad to see that you're doing better. How are you feeling?"

Turning away from the mirror, Devin replied, "I'm feeling a lot better." He then paused and added, "I really don't know how to thank you. When I saw those men charging at me in the street, I was sure I was done for."

Leo nodded his head in understanding. "Well, you're safe now, and you can rest assured that they wouldn't have done anything to you without going through *me* first."

A loud banging on the front door interrupted them. Leo stamped his cane on the floor in frustration and annoyance. "Speaking of being *done for*, my house is being surrounded by an angry mob as we speak, or maybe you hadn't noticed?"

"No, I noticed," Devin said with a look of worry. He then walked over to the window to see if he could catch a glimpse of the crowd, but it appeared that, at the moment, they were all staying near the front entrance to the cottage. "I take it this has something to do with me, doesn't it?"

Leo sighed. "I'm going to say that you're right." He then gazed hard into Devin's eyes and said, "I don't know what to do. Your sudden appearance has set the entire village on edge, and they want answers – answers that I can't give them."

Devin just stood in place and stared back blankly while nervously fidgeting with his hands.

Turning his head, the old guide momentarily let his eyes rest upon the logbook lying on the dresser next to Devin's things. "I think we both know that you haven't been completely honest with me about your past or what brought you here."

Devin stopped fidgeting and briefly glanced down at the ground. Then, looking back up, he began to slowly nod his head.

All of a sudden, a booming voice rose above the general clamor coming from outside: "We're not going anywhere, Leo! We'll wait out here all day if we have to. The sooner you open up your door and meet with us, the sooner this can all stop!" The sound of the crowd immediately grew louder, and angry shouts of agreement and approval could be heard clearly through it all.

At that moment, a young woman stepped through the doorway. Devin was completely taken back by both her sudden appearance and her astonishing beauty and tried his best to disguise his shock when he looked into her eyes. She had fair, smooth skin and long, silky dark-brown hair that was parted over to the side. Her lips were painted an alluring shade of plum-red that matched the long-sleeved gown she was wearing, and an expensive-looking gold chain hung loosely around her neck. However, it was her eyes that really caught him off guard. She had intense aqua-blue eyes that were accented by light streaks of sea-green. Never had he seen anything quite like them in his entire life.

Placing a hand on her hip, she briefly assessed the unexpected houseguest with a skeptical curiosity before averting her attention to Leo. "We really can't ignore them much longer. I swear they're going to beat the door down if we don't do something!"

Leo immediately shifted around on his cane and shook his head while nervously eyeing the front door. He then turned his attention back towards the young woman and Devin. "Sarina, this is Devin. Devin, this is my granddaughter, Sarina. She was kind enough to come over early this morning and prepare us a breakfast of fresh eggs and pumara sausage. I don't know about you, but I'm hungry, so why don't we make our way over to the dinner table?"

Devin responded with a quick nod of his head and said, "Give me just a minute or two to put my boots on, and I'll be right with you."

Sarina sauntered back to the kitchen to put the final touches on their morning meal, and Leo followed her, closing the bedroom door behind him. As soon as the door was shut, Devin scooped up the leather boots, the belt, and the vest and proceeded to finish dressing himself, all the while the shouts and grumblings of the villagers could be clearly heard coming through the cottage walls.

When he was finally seated at a circular wooden table in the dining room, he took a few minutes to observe his surroundings. Even though he had already spent a fair amount of time sitting in that very spot with Leo the day before, he hadn't been in the right frame of mind to take it all in.

The guide's home wasn't large, but it wasn't tiny either – it was just right. The walls were constructed from different materials. Some of them were made with plaster and ruddy-colored bricks, while others were made out of wood and stone. Next to each side of the front door, large round windows that were currently hidden behind brown leather drapes looked out upon the front yard. The walls were adorned with various hand-painted pictures that featured things like birds flying across open skies over jagged mountains or little farms set against pretty country landscapes. A stone fireplace had been built into the center of the back wall, opposite the front door, and above it, the huge head of a ferocious beast that resembled an oversized mountain lion could be seen gazing out across the living room, its mouth wide open in a growl, exposing long, curvy, shiny fangs that reflected the flickering firelight.

To the right of the fireplace, a set of shelves climbed up the wall, featuring a sizable collection of dusty books that appeared to be ancient. Sitting alongside them were a number of interesting trinkets and various odds and ends that included things like a large chunk of rose quartz, an exotic-looking turtle shell, and a wooden carving of a hawk with outstretched talons and great wings spread open in flight. To the left of the fireplace leaned a metal rack, piled high with freshly cut logs. A poker covered in black soot was casually propped up against it. In front of the fireplace, a braided rug, dirty-white in color, sprawled out across the plank flooring. The rug was circular in shape and featured an intricate design of an oak tree that had been carefully woven into its center with thick green and brown threads. Near the rug's edge, two comfy-looking cushioned chairs sat facing the fire. They were each upholstered in a fine fabric that resembled green velvet. A squat wooden table was centered between them.

The home was lit from within by a number of oil lamps that dangled down from time-stained brass hooks attached high up on the walls. Each of them cast a hazy golden orb of light down on the floor beneath them. A wooden chandelier that featured a handful of these same lamps also hung down over the center of the dining room table. The gentle amber glow of the oil lamps and the flickering orange-yellow light of the fireplace came together to give the whole place a kind of warm and sleepy ambiance.

As Devin continued to gaze around the house, his eyes drifted to the kitchen, where Sarina was busily filling their plates. Aside from the wood-burning stove that she was standing in front of, the only piece of furniture in the room was a narrow wooden table sitting against the wall that held a washbasin, a rack full of cookware, and a stack of bowls and plates.

Just then, Sarina turned away from the stove and began carrying the morning meal to the dining room table. Within a few minutes, they were each sitting in front of a plateful of fried eggs and pumara sausage.

Meanwhile, the noisy shouts and ramblings of the villagers outside grew in intensity. It sounded as if more people were joining the throng. Trying to ignore them, Devin glanced down at his plate, inwardly battling a confused mix of hunger and suspicion. When he noticed that both Leo and Sarina had stopped eating and were staring at him, he quickly made up his mind to scoop up a mouthful of the sausage, figuring that he had already caused enough problems – he didn't want to add insult to injury by turning his nose up at their food. To his great relief and pleasant surprise, he found the meat to be more than satisfying.

"Sarina sure is a good cook," Leo remarked as he cut up his eggs.

"She sure is," Devin agreed. "This might be some of the best sausage I've ever had in my entire life!"

Upon hearing this, Sarina's eyes lit up, and a hint of a self-satisfied smile flit across her face.

"Yeah, she takes after her grandma in that respect," Leo said as he glanced up from his meal and cast an approving glance at his granddaughter. "She was the best cook in all of Iron Cove."

"Yes, she was," said Sarina wistfully. "I sure do miss her."

Leo stopped eating and reached over to pat her on the back. "I do too... She'd be proud of the woman you've become, Sarina." A faint hint of tears welled up in the old man's eyes.

The three of them continued eating for a few more minutes, but the clamor and ruckus from outside made enjoying their meal difficult. Finally, Leo pushed his plate away, leaned back in his chair, and cast a penetrating gaze at Devin, who, with a fork halfway up to his mouth, had stopped eating and was currently shifting nervous eyes back and forth between the old guide and his granddaughter.

"Devin, don't you think it's about time that you told us what's really going on here?" he asked in a tone suggesting that he wasn't going to take *no* for an answer.

Devin laid his fork down, pushed his plate forward, and sighed as he cast his gaze down at the table. After a brief pause, he lifted his head and spoke, "The first thing I want you both to know is that I never meant for any of this to happen. I really didn't."

Leo and Sarina listened intently, not knowing quite what he meant.

He cast an uneasy glance at both of them. "You're not going to like what I'm about to say, and I'll be really surprised if you believe even half of it."

Leo interjected, "You just tell us what you know and let us decide what we think of your story."

Devin nodded his head. "Okay. Well, don't say that I didn't warn you." Taking in a deep breath, he began, "It all started 300 years ago on the day that I showed up late for work after a long night of drinking and partying." He then went on to relate to them his entire story, doing his best not to leave out any important details.

By the time he finished, Leo and Sarina were both sitting stone-cold silent in their chairs, looking nothing short of dumbstruck. Sarina's skin had turned a shade paler than a ghost. The tension in the air, thick and stifling, was only made worse by the hollering and general upheaval taking place just outside the front door.

Devin, feeling lost and not knowing what else to say, decided that he might as well end things with a bang. Looking directly into Leo's eyes, he said, "I know all of this probably sounds completely bizarre to you, but I promise you that I'm not making any of it up. Unfortunately, I haven't even told you the worst part yet."

This seemed to shake Leo out of his stupor. Stroking his salt and pepper goatee, he leaned forward to listen more closely. Sarina placed a hand over her mouth and sent a sharp, piercing glare in Devin's direction. It almost seemed to him as if the sea-green streaks in her eyes were glowing.

"Yes, through my clumsiness and careless stupidity, I inadvertently set off a chain of events that ended up destroying the entire world, and if that isn't bad enough... well... it may be getting ready to happen again." Devin nervously glanced back and forth at them. "There's a good chance that the floating tower I told you about is going to be activated soon, and when that happens, the creatures housed inside will use an arsenal unlike anything the world has ever seen before to subjugate and enslave anyone who stands in their way."

As soon as Devin finished the last sentence, Leo's jaw dropped open and Sarina tensed up while placing a trembling hand over her rapidly beating heart. They both sat frozen, still as statues.

"The only way to stop any of this from happening is to place the three crystalline orbs I was telling you about inside a hidden compartment within the tower. This will put the tower into self-destruct mode, and everything will be made safe again." Devin paused to take a deep breath and assess his audience. Seeing that they were icebound in a state of something like shock or disbelief, he threw his hands up and ended with, "There, I said it. I told you it was going to sound crazy, and I knew you wouldn't believe me. Now, please say something – anything!"

A series of booming knocks on the front door snapped everyone back to reality. Leo leaned back in his chair and rubbed his eyes while Sarina hurriedly picked up the plates and carried them into the kitchen. Devin continued to sit still, staring down at his half-eaten food, anxiously awaiting whatever was going to happen next.

Finally, Leo spoke up, "Son, I've never... not in all my years." He briefly shook his head. "I honestly don't even know how to respond to what you just told me. Who would? You basically just told us that you caused the Great Firefall!" He then sighed. "Nonetheless, if your story is true, we haven't a moment to waste."

Devin glanced up at Leo and woefully shook his head in regret. "As much as I would like to tell you differently, I can't. Every last thing I've said is completely true."

Using his cane as a support, Leo lifted himself up from the table and glanced over at the front door and then back at Devin. "Well, I guess that settles it then. You're just going to have to stay here with me until Aydin arrives. He'll know what we need to do. I'm sure of it. In the meantime, we need to do something about all of this ruckus and commotion. I've had about as much as I can stand!" He shook his head. "Devin, I think I have a plan. Follow me!"

Devin glanced down at the table and did his best to get control of his emotions before getting up from his chair to follow the old guide to the front door.

When they arrived, Leo spun around and gave him a quick wink. "Stay put until I give you the signal. Now, just follow my lead." He then proceeded to pull the door open.

As Leo took his first few steps outside, a sudden hush fell over the crowd of twenty-five or thirty people who had gathered in his yard. For the first time all morning, the sing-song chirping of birds could be heard in the distance. He continued to shuffle forward until he reached the edge of his covered porch, where a small flight of steps led down to a cobblestone walkway.

Straightening himself up, he gazed out at the frustrated faces staring up at him and exclaimed with a loud voice, "Never, in all my years, did I think I would live to see the day when an old man can't get a lick of peace in his own home!

Every single last one of you should be ashamed of yourselves!"

A few of the villagers cast worried and nervous glances back and forth at each other. Leo then toned his voice down a bit, "I think I know why you're all in an uproar, and to some degree, I can't blame you. The sealed door, which has been an object of suspicion for longer than I've been alive, is no longer sealed, and the stranger, who seemingly came through it, now resides among us. I'm sure that many of you are wondering what it all means, and you probably have a lot of questions."

Leo paused and stroked his salt and pepper goatee thoughtfully. "Is he a mutant? Is he a monster? Is he a ghost? What is it that he's doing here? Should we be concerned?"

He let his gaze drift from one side of the crowd to the other, making sure that his words were having their desired effect. "Believe me, I understand. I grew up hearing the same ghost stories and harboring the same fears and suspicions as all of you. I understand why you might be worried, but you can lay your fears to rest! The man who came out of the cave is not a monster, he's not a bloodthirsty mutant, and he's certainly not a ghost. He is, in fact, just a young man. Look and see for yourselves!" At this, he turned around and motioned for Devin to come forward.

As Devin stepped through the door, loud whispers erupted all around the front porch, causing an unexpected wave of anxiety to hit him. He paused in mid-step, shut his eyes, and tried his best to bury the rising emotions that were threatening to overwhelm him. After standing frozen in place for a short space of time that seemed much longer than it actually was, he mustered up the courage and resolve to push through it. Opening his eyes, he walked forward until he came to the edge of the porch to stand next to Leo. The crowd gazed upon him with eyes that conveyed everything from surprise and suspicion to confusion and fright.

Turning to face everyone, Leo spoke up, "My friends, I'd like to introduce you to Devin Skye. I know this may seem odd and unbelievable to most of you, but please hear me out. This young man traveled clear through the mountains in an effort to save his life. As it turns out, the sealed door behind the village was actually just an entrance to a series of caverns and tunnels that lead all the way to the lands surrounding Harstad Hollow."

As soon as he finished the last sentence, the aggravated mob erupted with startled shouts, questions, and confused mutterings. Leo, not wanting to lose control of his audience so quickly, lifted his cane into the air with one hand and waved it up and down erratically while motioning for everyone to quiet down with the other. He waited for a moment to see if the uproar would subside before moving on to his next plan, which was to loudly bang on the porch with the bottom of his cane. The second plan seemed to work, and the murmuring eased up a bit.

He then picked up where he left off, "This young man barely escaped a gang of cruel bandits within an inch of his life! Had he not discovered the entrance to the tunnel that led him here, he might not be alive right now! Thankfully, he was able to lose his pursuers in the dark caverns that run through the mountains, and by some stroke of luck or divine intervention, he managed to find his way out of them and ended up here."

Suddenly, the same loud and boisterous voice that had been the source of so many threats earlier in the morning thundered out, "How do we know he ain't lying!?" The voice belonged to a portly man with ruddy cheeks named Harlow Tub, a blusterous mischief-maker who had lived in Iron Cove all of his life.

Leo skillfully hid a trace of a smile when he saw who it was. Waving his hand, he beckoned for him to calm down and replied, "Harlow, I suppose the only way to prove he isn't lying would be to travel back through the tunnel to see where it leads. Unfortunately, the entrance has been buried in an avalanche, and there's no way to do that, now is there?"

Harlow cocked his head sideways and proceeded to scratch a large balding spot on the top of his head while squinting his eyes in consternation. "Well, I guess ya might have a point."

Leo slowly nodded in agreement. "Look at this young man. Does he look like a monster or a mutant to you? Does he really seem like any ghost you've ever heard about?" He cast a scrutinizing gaze at Harlow and briefly waited for him to answer, but Harlow just continued to stare back stupidly while using a finger to dig and scratch at something in his right ear.

Leo then turned towards Devin and gave him a sharp jab in the ribs with the bottom of his cane. Devin yelped as he grabbed his side with both hands and shot the village guide a look of alarm.

The old man grinned mischievously before shifting back towards the crowd and exclaiming, "You see! He's flesh and blood, just like you and me! He's no ghost. As it turns out, he's just an ordinary young man who ran into some trouble and is in desperate need of help."

Apparently, the theatrical stunt worked, as the heavy murmuring of the crowd began to take on a softer tone. All around the porch, concerned whispers and quiet remarks like, "That poor boy," and "Oh, my! How awful!" could be clearly heard.

Feeling that his objective was nearly accomplished, Leo decided that it would be best to wrap things up while he was still ahead. He gazed out at the crowd and said, "Just so you know, I'm bringing our new friend to The Pumara's Den this evening so that we can all get to know him a bit better. In the meantime, why don't we try to get on with our lives? I'm sure we've all got better things to do than to stand around in my yard looking silly."

Another half hour or so passed by before the last members of the crowd finally began to trail off in their own directions. Leo, exercising the patience of a saint, spent the majority of that time answering questions and quelling the concerns and suspicions of some of the more obstinate residents of the village.

However, before he could return indoors to the comfort of his chair in front of the fire, he had to settle a dispute with the last remaining person in his yard, Cyrus Gibbons, a giant hulk of a man who was as stubborn as he was strong. Broad-shouldered, muscular, and dark-skinned, Cyrus stood nearly seven feet tall and was widely considered by the locals to be the unofficial leader of the village watch. He also happened to be one of the two men who took on the task of carrying Devin to the guide's cottage soon after they found him passed out in the middle of the road.

Long story short, Cyrus wasn't buying the story about the mysterious visitor's origins. The strange items he had discovered on Devin's person the day before provided more than enough evidence to cast doubt on everything that he had just heard, and he intended to find out the truth, one way or another. Regardless of this, Leo stuck to his version of events, not bending an inch, and after a few minutes of heated deliberation, Cyrus was forced to let the matter be, at least for the time being.

Meanwhile, Devin, who had retreated indoors at the first possible chance, had been spending his time in a futile effort at making light conversation with Sarina. Unfortunately, her curt manner along with the short responses she chose to give him whenever he'd inquire about herself or life in Iron Cove made it painfully obvious that she didn't trust him. Nonetheless, it wasn't until she retreated into the washroom and never came back out that he fully got the message. Devin had always struggled with matters involving the opposite sex, and this was no exception.

When Leo shuffled back in through the front door, Devin was more than a little bit relieved to see him. Coincidentally, it was just at that moment that Sarina decided to come out of her hiding place. She ran up to the frazzled old guide and threw her arms around him. "Grandpa, you really are the best! The way you handled everyone out there was just perfect. I'm so proud of you!"

Upon hearing her words of adoration, a big smile brightened up his tired visage. He returned her hug and said, "One day, I fully expect that you'll be able to do the same."

He then focused his attention on Devin, who was now slumped down at the dining room table with his head propped up on one hand, and said, "Young man, you need to straighten up and listen to me. This goes for you as well, Sarina." He glanced at each of them in turn to make sure they were paying attention. "Outside of the three of us, no one else in the village knows the truth about what's really going on here, and until further notice, I intend on keeping it that way. I never tell lies for anyone, and I'm not feeling in the least bit comfortable about what just took place here." He then heaved and sighed. "Unfortunately, due to the unique circumstances we're dealing with, I don't think I was left with much of a choice."

They both nodded their heads in understanding.

Shifting his focus towards his granddaughter, he said, "Sarina, I don't want you peeping a word about any of this to anyone, not even your folks. If you need to talk about it, you know that I'm here, and you can come see me any time you like."

Turning his attention back to Devin, he continued, "And, young man, from this point forward, you fled here from Harstad Hollow. You were a farmhand who barely escaped a gang of bandits by fleeing into a nearby cave. You spent many days lost in the caverns beneath the mountains before finding your way back out through the old sealed door behind the village. That'll explain the sorry state you were in when we found you. Do you understand?"

Devin, suddenly feeling stressed and a little bit worried, replied, "Yes, sir. But, to be honest, I'm not really sure if anyone will believe me – I mean, I don't know the first thing about farming."

Leo chuckled lightly. "Well, there's no need to stew and fret about that. You can rest assured that I'll have you lined out before the day is through. When it comes to farming and surviving in the wild lands, I happen to be somewhat of an expert." He gave Devin a quick wink and shifted his attention to his granddaughter.

Chapter 14

"Sweetheart, I think it's best that you run on home now. I'll get a hold of you if I need anything." Pausing shortly, he added, "Just so you know, I don't think I would have handled things nearly as well if I hadn't eaten that delicious breakfast you cooked up this morning. There's nothing quite like a belly full of good food to prepare an old man for a morning spent calming an angry mob."

At this, Sarina rolled her eyes and giggled. "That's crazy, and you know it!" She gave him a short hug and turned away to head out the front door. "I guess I'll see you tonight at the tavern!"

Leo spent the rest of the day guiding Devin through a crash course on farming in the wild lands. He talked about the kinds of crops that were common, explaining when they were planted and how they were harvested. He went over things like how many people a crop of fall cabbage might feed during a good year. He lectured him on the best ways to keep hungry critters from eating all of the melons before they were fully ripened and described how to make effective barriers out of various strong herbs and spices that worked to keep bugs and other pests away from the leafy greens. He told stories about the struggles farmers had with the dangerous beasts that roamed the area – most of which Devin had never heard of – and explained how, over the years, this led to the widely held belief that farmers were generally handy with a bow and arrow. The list went on and on.

Though Devin tried his best to memorize everything and keep up, he found the challenge to be daunting, if not impossible. Being a city boy who had never cultivated a living thing in his entire life proved to be a real disadvantage in this regard. Nonetheless, he gave it his absolute best.

Chapter 14

The agriculture and history lessons lasted well into the late afternoon, and by the time Leo finally ran out of things to say, the sun was just beginning to sink into an early evening sky. Devin, who had all but given up on cramming his brain with a lifetime of farming knowledge, was on the verge of passing out from fatigue. Upon seeing this, Leo quietly chuckled to himself and strolled over to the front window to take a look outside. After realizing what time it was, he suggested that they call it a day and head over to The Pumara's Den.

Chapter 15

The Pumara's Den

As Devin and Leo trekked along the crumbling cobblestone street, a crisp evening breeze drifted in from the north. The fresh air brought new life to Devin's spirit and helped to clear the haze from his weary mind. The scenery that unfolded around him was like nothing he had ever experienced while growing up in the city. Lone pines stood beside quaint stone cottages that were sectioned off with rustic wooden fences. Along these, colorful flower gardens grew that featured sunflower, mum, goldenrod, crocus, and a number of exotic-looking varieties that he couldn't put a name to. Even though many of their petals were beginning to close with the day's fading light, they were still a sight to behold. In the sky above, a few trails of wispy clouds drifted by as a flock of geese soared over the distant mountains in a giant v-shaped pattern. It was almost picture-perfect.

A bit of daylight was still left when Devin casually glanced up and caught sight of something altogether unexpected that stopped him dead in his tracks. It was the one thing he had been dreading to see ever since leaving the survival-chamber behind. Just above the thick orange horizon line running behind the jagged mountains to his west, the dark silhouette of a levitating island with a great conical tower rising out of its center could be seen hovering in the distance between two towering peaks. In that moment, the fairy tale world around him began to fade, and the tower was all that existed.

All of a sudden, the full weight of the task ahead began to bear down upon him, and pervasive thoughts of helplessness and heavy feelings of worthlessness began to wreak havoc on his mind. Without even realizing it, he spoke out loud, "I don't think I can do this."

Just then, he felt a warm hand on his shoulder, and the world around him slowly came back into focus. Leo, wearing a look that conveyed a kind of empathy that can only come from one who has lived a long time and experienced many painful things, gently patted his back and said, "You're not alone, Devin."

In that moment, something inside of Devin began to change, and he gazed back at the old guide with gratitude, humility, and maybe a touch of sadness. There was nothing more that needed to be said. In the background, the katydids and crickets were just beginning to play the leading notes of their night songs, and the first stars were beginning to twinkle in the sky above. The two of them set their eyes on the path ahead and continued to walk on.

The Pumara's Den rose up at the end of the cobblestone path like a rustic beacon of warmth and safety. Balmy golden glows poured out from the large square windows that lined each side of the two-story tavern and lodge, and the cheerful reverberations of laughter, chatter, and jovial-sounding music drifted through the double doors that marked its entrance. Leo held on to Devin's arm as the two of them ascended a staircase that led to a wide covered porch that surrounded the entire building.

As they stepped through the big double doors, they were met with a wave of warmth and good cheer. The delicious aroma of hot food and fresh brew filled the air around them, and a slurry of random greetings rang out from every corner of the tavern. Having never experienced anything quite like this in his entire life, Devin gazed around in a state of fascination.

To his left, a long bar, lined with round wooden stools, stretched the entire length of the dining hall. Against the back wall, a blazing fire roared within the mouth of a giant stone fireplace, illuminating a number of rectangular tables and wooden benches that were staged in front of it. On the right-hand side of the hall, opposite the bar, a raised platform had been constructed, which was currently occupied by a band of local musicians. They had stringed instruments, wind instruments, drums, and musical devices that Devin had never seen or heard before. The folksy music they were creating seemed to add an extra layer of mirth and magic to the atmosphere. For a moment, he was swept away by it and felt as if he could listen to them perform all night long.

The bar was already filling up with its usual patrons, and many of the tables in the middle of the room were occupied by folks who decided to show up after hearing the news that the mysterious stranger from the sealed cave would be making an appearance that night.

While Devin stood inside the entrance, awestruck and mesmerized by the atmosphere and music, Leo took the opportunity to search for a place to sit down. After a brief moment, he spotted a table near the fireplace that wasn't occupied. Tapping Devin's foot with his cane, he stirred him from his trance and then proceeded to lead him across the hall. As they shuffled along, more than a handful of villagers shifted completely around in their seats to get a good look at the mysterious stranger they had been hearing so much about. It was a bit uncomfortable and awkward to deal with, but Leo had a way of dispelling the worst of it with a simple smile and a nod.

After getting comfortably seated, a tall, handsome woman with big brown eyes and long, wavy blonde hair approached the table. She carried a wooden tray under her right arm and wore a white apron over a plain blue dress.

"It's so good to see you, Leo!" she said with a bright smile as she curiously glanced back and forth between the guide and Devin. "It's been a while since you were last over this way."

"It's good to see you, too, Leandra," Leo returned her smile. "You know I'd come here more often if I could, but it's beginning to be quite the trip for an old graybeard like me."

She playfully shot back, "Nonsense! Aren't you the one who is always telling me that age is just a state of mind?"

He lightly chuckled and responded with a wink and a grin.

She then casually glanced over at Devin. "I take it this is the mysterious visitor that everyone's been talking about?"

"This is him in the flesh. But, if you ask me, he's not really that mysterious. He's just a young farmhand from Harstad Hollow who was fortunate enough to happen upon our little village during a time of need." He glanced over at Devin and proceeded to make his introductions, "Leandra, this is Devin Skye, and Devin, this is Leandra Gibbons, the owner of this fine establishment."

Standing up, Devin politely reached out his hand to complete the introduction. "It's nice to meet you, Leandra."

She returned his handshake and laughed, "There's no need to be so formal around here, sweetie!" She then thoughtfully added, "I heard about how my husband and the other watchmen came at you when you first arrived. I hope they didn't frighten you too badly. We just don't get many strangers in this neck of the woods, and the way you showed up was quite a shock to all of us. We do apologize."

Devin nodded his head in understanding and said, "I can't really say that I blame them. I'm sure the folks I grew up around would have done the same thing. You can't be too careful these days." He sat back down and noticed Leo quietly nodding his head in approval.

She then shifted her attention back to Leo. "Well, I'm just glad that everything seems to be getting back to normal now. So I take it that you two will be eating tonight?"

"Of course!" came Leo's eager reply. "Are you still serving that fried mushroom dish I like so well?"

A big smile swept across her face. "I don't think the folks around here would have it any other way!"

"That sounds good then, and we'll each have a mug of your finest."

"Okay, two plates of fried mushrooms and two beers coming right up!" She nodded and proceeded to move on to another patron who had caught her attention.

For the next hour or so, things went on in the same pleasant manner. Leo and Devin tried their best to enjoy their meal in between satisfying the curiosities or warding off the suspicions of villagers who would meander over to their table to introduce themselves. Some inquired about what life was like in Harstad Hollow, some asked what it felt like to be lost in a cave, and others simply made small talk about life in Iron Cove. Devin did his best to play along with the ruse but struggled on some of the finer points of history and geography.

Nonetheless, Leo was always quick to intercede when it seemed like Devin was getting cornered in a bad spot.

About halfway into the evening, Sarina showed up with her parents. Upon seeing them walk through the door, Leo waved them over to his table. He then introduced Devin to his son Garret and his son's wife Olivia. Garret looked a lot like a younger version of Leo, only he was clean-shaven, and his brown hair hadn't begun to gray yet. Olivia could have easily passed for Sarina's older sister with her dark hair, fair skin, and bright blue eyes. They both warmly welcomed him to their village and even went so far as to tell him that their home was always open if he ever needed anything.

Sarina played along but didn't go out of her way to encourage her parents in their kind offers of hospitality, especially as it regarded their home. After she felt that enough had been said, she managed to talk both of them into sitting closer to the platform and further away from her grandpa and Devin, as the band had just begun to perform one of her favorite songs.

A short while later, Leandra's husband Cyrus, the gruff watchman who had been giving Leo a hard time earlier that morning, strolled up to the table with two of his companions and apologized for his rude behavior. Leo told him not to worry about it and invited them all to sit down. Soon afterward, they got caught up in a discussion about the recent troubles that local farmers had been having with wild beasts in the region.

It was during this part of the evening that Harlow Tub, having drank one too many, decided that it would be a good idea to climb up the platform and apologize to Leo. With slurred words and a dizzy shuffle, he began, "Leooo, we've known eesh other for a loooong time." He stumbled forward a bit but then quickly steadied himself. "I don' know wash I wash... theenkin." At this, he wobbled forward a little too closely to the edge of the platform. A sweeping hiss of gasps echoed across the hall. Leo glanced over at Devin with a raised eyebrow before staring down at his mug of beer and shaking his head.

Suddenly, he threw his hands up in the air and declared, "Leo, I don' care wash they shay about ya... Yerrr... a good man!" And just as the word *man* left his lips, he tipped forward and flopped off the platform, arms flailing wildly. A loud thunk echoed across the dining hall as he crashed onto the wooden floor below. Immediately, Cyrus and his companions leaped up from the table and rushed over to help him to his feet. Loud muttering and murmuring swept through the crowd as they proceeded to carry Harlow, face bruised and nose bloodied, towards the exit.

As Devin watched the embarrassing scene play out before him, he was caught off guard by a flashback of his own drunken behavior on the night prior to the big accident. Sitting there, totally transfixed and still as a statue, he quietly thought about how stupid and foolish he must have looked to everyone around him. He softly shook his head as his spirit began to sink with regret.

Just then, the big double doors at the far end of the dining hall swung wide open, and two figures cloaked in forest green stepped inside. Devin snapped out of his stupor and glanced over to see who the new arrivals were. As they pulled back their hoods, he noticed that one was a young man with a full head of curly sandy-blonde hair, a big smile, and glistening green eyes. The other was a much older man who had long silver hair, a lengthy silver beard, and bushy eyebrows that stuck out over his dark gray eyes.

From across the room, Sarina gleefully exclaimed, "It's Chance!"

The newcomers quickly stepped aside, making room for Cyrus and company to pass by.

"It's good to see you again, Aydin," Cyrus said with a short nod as he approached the exit.

Aydin returned the nod and, in an amused tone, remarked, "I can see that not much has changed around here."

Cyrus' hardened features lit up at this, and a hint of a smile surfaced above his bushy beard. "Nope, just the same old, same old."

After the heavy wooden doors swung shut behind them, Aydin's gaze slowly drifted across the large crowd, searching for the man he had come to see. Within a few seconds, he spotted Leo, who had just stood up in an effort to catch his eye. His face brightened up, and he and Chance proceeded to make their way towards the table near the fireplace. As they passed by Sarina's table, Chance made it a point to smile back at the girl, whose dazzled blue-green eyes and glowing expression weren't about to let him get away without any kind of acknowledgment.

When they finally reached Leo's table, Devin joined the guide and stood up to greet them. Leo wasted no time in embracing his old friend warmly. "It's so good to see you again, Aydin. It's been too long."

"Yes, it really has," Aydin returned. "You're still looking well and feeling just as well, I assume?"

"I'm looking and feeling about as good as anyone my age could ever hope too, friend," Leo chuckled. "And I assume you're doing well yourself?"

Aydin nodded. "As well as I can, I suppose."

Aydin then turned his attention to Devin. "I take it this is the young man I've been hearing so much about?"

"Yes, this is him in the flesh," Leo replied with a short nod of his head. He then formally introduced the two men to each other and went on to explain Devin's situation in brief, "Apparently, he was attacked by a gang of bandits while working the fields near Harstad Hollow but managed to escape to safety by fleeing into a nearby tunnel. As fortune would have it, the exit on the other end just happened to be the sealed door behind our village. Can you believe it?"

"I see…" came Aydin's slow response. Lost in thought, he stood there for a moment, stroking the curls in his silver beard. He then abruptly came out of his trance, looked Devin in the eyes, and said, "I'm glad you were able to find "refuge" here." A faint hint of a smile traced across his wizened, old visage.

Devin nodded shortly. "I feel very lucky to be here. Honestly, it's hard to say what would have become of me had I not managed to find my way out of that mess I was in." With a slow shake of his head, he gazed down at the table, trying his best to make it appear that he was troubled and shaken by the whole ordeal and was sincerely relieved to have found safety.

Suddenly, Leandra reappeared, wooden tray in hand. "Ah, if it isn't Aydin Culpepper! It's so good to have you back in Iron Cove. What's the special occasion?"

Aydin brightened up at her appearance and turned to greet her, "It's good to see you too, Leandra. I'm just here checking up on an old friend." He grinned and casually motioned towards Leo with an outstretched hand.

Leandra smiled. "Well, I'm sure that he appreciates it. So do you know what you'll be having tonight?"

Aydin glanced down at the empty plates and half-drunk mugs on the table and replied, "I think we'll have what they had." He turned towards Chance. "Does that sound alright?"

"Sounds good to me!" Chance replied with a grin.

"Okay, then." Aydin nodded. "Would you mind bringing a fresh round of drinks for everyone as well?"

"That'll be no problem at all. Two plates of fried mushrooms and a fresh round coming right up!" Leandra flashed them a bright smile and swung around to make her way back towards the bar and kitchen area.

Aydin and Chance both took a seat at the table directly across from Leo and Devin. Upon doing so, Chance stretched out a hand towards Devin. "I'm Chance."

Devin nodded and returned the handshake. "I'm Devin. Nice to meet you."

All of a sudden, Leo glanced over Chance's shoulders, as he had spotted his granddaughter creeping up from behind, fully prepared to surprise him. Chance, seeing the quick motion of his eyes, quickly jerked around to find Sarina's beaming face staring back at him.

Straightening up, she placed both hands on her hips and pouted, "Grandpa! Why'd you have to ruin it?!"

Leo chuckled and said, "Sweetie, why don't you sit down. I'm sure that Chance – I mean, we – would love the company."

Aydin softly grinned in mild amusement. He then directed his attention back to Leo and said, "It seems we have a lot to discuss."

"Indeed, we do, old friend." Leo tipped back his mug and finished the last of his beer.

A few minutes passed, and Leandra returned with two steaming plates of fried mushrooms and a fresh round of drinks. Both Leo and Aydin politely thanked her and then proceeded to engage in small talk. Meanwhile, Chance and Sarina got caught up in an important conversation of their own. Devin, feeling awkward and left out, silently listened in as he sipped on his drink and attempted to soak up the ambiance.

A short while later, the folksy music that had been playing in the background came to a halt, and Leandra ascended the raised platform to take center stage. With a loud and cheery voice, she beckoned for everyone's attention, "Hey, everyone! I hope you've been having a good time tonight!"

A handful of hollers and elated cheers rang out across the hall.

"So, as most of you already know, we've had a traveling merchant from the northern lands of Darkovia here in the village for the past week or so, a man by the name of Raul Rostova." The energy of the crowd quickly morphed from jubilant to teetering on the side of awkward.

Taking notice, Leandra cleared her throat and promptly added, "Well, he came up to me earlier and asked if he could perform a song he wrote, and I told him that we would love to hear it. After all, it's not that often that we get to hear music from that part of the world. So let's give him a warm round of applause!"

Chapter 15

A halfhearted smattering of clapping flitted across the hall as Raul arose from the dark, shadowy corner of the tavern he had been quietly occupying. He was an older man with dark brown eyes, bushy eyebrows, and long graying hair. A thick curlicue mustache spread across his sunken cheeks, and a stiff, pointy goatee dangled from his chin like an iron spike. Dressed in an ashen-gray hooded robe, his appearance was both strange and somewhat foreboding. As he strolled across the dining hall, he carried with him a guitar that was lavishly gilded in ornate spiral patterns that wound themselves around the sound hole and branched out across the face of the instrument's body.

The crowd grew silent as he took the stage and sat down on a wooden stool. After carefully positioning the guitar in his lap, he coolly gazed out at everyone from beneath a hood that served to darken most of his features and began to pluck a haunting yet strangely enchanting melody that slowly but surely wormed its way into the ears and minds of an audience that wasn't quite sure how to take it. As the exotic-sounding notes undulated and swayed back and forth in a hypnotic rhythm, he started to sing:

From high atop your mighty tower,
You hear us in our darkest hour.
The land cries out in rage and pain.
You promise us your healing rain.

We pray to you throughout the day.
We plea for you to light our night.
We wait for you to shine our way.
We look to you to fix our sight.

Chapter 15

Oh, Kanthis eternal, defender of light,
Lend us your strength and show us your might.
Teach us your truth and vision of justice.
Purge us of shame and lead us to fight.

With passion divine and riches untold,
A brand new world will surely unfold.
The earth below will quake with laughter,
And sacred truth will rule thereafter.

Oh, Kanthis divine, destroyer of night,
Lend us your strength, and show us your might.
Teach us your plan and purpose for living.
Reign from above with power and light.

As the last notes of the strange hymn echoed throughout the hall, the dining hall fell ominously quiet. The uneasy crowd sat at their tables, still as statues, only barely moving their heads to cast unsettled glances at one another. Raul, wearing a furtive grin that was partially hidden beneath the long shadows thrown down from his mustache and hood, remained perched upon the stool, reposing behind his gaudy instrument in quiet amusement.

Finally, the deafening silence was broken by the hard click-clack of footsteps echoing off the wood floor as Leandra briskly strode towards the platform. Before even climbing the stairs, she started in, "Well, that sure was something, wasn't it?" She nervously laughed.

Upon seeing her approach, Raul rose up from the stool, nodded, and moved aside so that she could take his place.

When she reached center stage, she acknowledged the old merchant by forcing a polite smile and a quick thank-you and then turned to the crowd and said, "Let's all have a nice round of applause for Raul."

The crowd responded with bemused murmurs that were mixed with a few halfhearted claps. Raul bowed deeply and stretched out a long arm in front of him in a grand, sweeping gesture. He then promptly made his way off the stage.

Leandra continued talking, a slight hint of frustration in her tone, "Well, I don't know about all of you, but I think it's about time to wrap things up here at the den and call it a night." As she fully expected, her announcement was met by a handful of disappointed moans and groans, but much to her surprise, it also appeared that many of the patrons were already busy making preparations to leave. Figuring that it probably had something to do with Raul's unsettling performance, she added, "Thank you so much for dropping in!" and then promptly made her way towards the bar.

The old merchant, who had already found his way to the exit, peered back over his shoulder one last time before disappearing into the darkness beyond.

Aydin, who had never taken his eyes off of the merchant, quickly focused his attention back on the others sitting with him at the table and, in a serious tone, said, "I'm getting a room here. I realize that it's getting late, but I think it would be for the best if we all meet there before parting ways." He glanced around at each of them to get their approval and then turned to face Leo. "It seems that change is upon us, old friend."

Chapter 16

A Midnight Meeting

The little room that Aydin acquired was located on the second story of the tavern. Though sparse in its furnishings, it was cozy enough. It featured a simple feather bed, a wooden table with four chairs, a squat bookshelf, and a small wood burning stove that sat by itself in a corner. Near the bed, long red drapes were tied back on each side of a large rectangular window that looked out past the village wall and into the forest beyond. In the center of the table, a tall white candle gave off a dim flickering light that softly coalesced with the warm orange glow of embers roasting in the wood stove.

Upon entering the room, Aydin loosened the drapes and pulled them across the window. "It's better that we don't take a chance on anyone getting too curious."

Leo nodded in approval as he, Sarina, and Devin stepped inside and found a spot at the small table. Chance, following from behind, plopped down on the floor next to the door to listen for anyone coming up or down the hallway outside.

As soon as everyone was settled in, Aydin reached into a pocket within his cloak and pulled out a long reed and a hand-carved pipe. He then proceeded to ignite the end of the reed in the wood stove and used it to spark up a fragrant medicinal herb that was packed inside the pipe's bowl. After taking a couple of puffs, he whispered, "Ah, that's much better," and shuffled over to the table to sit with the others.

All around them, everything was quiet. The last of the tavern regulars had vacated the vicinity, and even Leandra and the cooks had seemingly decided to retire for the night.

Leo was the first to break the silence, "That was quite a performance the old merchant put on for us tonight."

"Indeed, it was." Aydin replied in a far-off tone. "I haven't told you this yet, but Draken, an old associate of mine, contacted me telepathically right before Chance arrived at my place. He informed me that there was a lot of unusual excitement stirring in Darkovia and warned me to keep my eyes and ears open. I started to ask him what he meant, but our mind link was, somehow, broken. Unfortunately, I've not been able to restore our connection to get any more details."

Leo leaned in closer. "Darkovia, huh? Isn't that where the old merchant is from?"

Sarina piped in, "Yes, it is. He's been here all week trading lantern oil for the lavender pearls our hunters harvested from the slime shifters."

Meanwhile, Devin's head was spinning in confusion. *Did I really just hear Aydin say what I thought he did? That couldn't be right.* Feeling baffled and wholly tired of being left out from all of the conversations, he jerked around to face Aydin. "Did I just hear you say that you were contacted telepathically?!"

Caught completely off guard, Aydin wrinkled his brow as he paused to deliberate an answer. However, before he could respond, Devin shifted his attention towards Sarina and asked another question, "And what are lavender pearls and slime shifters?"

Upon hearing this, Chance blurted out, "What are slime shifters?! You've got to be kidding me, right? I've never heard of a farmer that didn't know what a slime shifter was!"

Devin, immediately realizing his mistake, tried his best to save face. "I'm not a farmer. I just work on a farm, and we… um… don't deal with slime shifters… Or, well, we call them something else… I think." His mind drew a blank, and he worriedly twisted to face Leo, who was shaking his head in amusement and battling back a grin that had just begun to surface.

After clearing his throat and composing himself, Leo said, "Alright, I think that's about enough, Devin. The ruse is up, and you're beginning to sound like a babbling fool."

He glanced back at Chance and continued, "As I'm sure you've already figured out by now, our friend Devin is not from Harstad Hollow. As a matter of fact, he's from Highland City, at least in a manner of speaking."

Chance's eyes widened in astonishment. "Highland City? But how? That place is nothing more than a ruined wasteland, overrun with foul creatures and mutants." He shot an inquisitive look at Devin and then jerked his head to face Aydin, who had fully straightened himself up in his chair and was stroking the curls in his beard in contemplation.

A few silent seconds passed, and Aydin said, "I see… Hmmm… This is very interesting, indeed." He let his gaze rest upon a flushed Devin, who suddenly felt like he had been thrust center stage beneath a hot spotlight.

Leo peered over at Devin. "Son, I think I've said enough. Why don't you just go ahead and fill everyone in on the rest of the details."

Devin sat still for a brief moment, fumbling over his thoughts and fighting off a mild panic attack. After taking a deep breath, he shook off his feelings and told his story, starting with the events that led up to the accidental missile launch and ending with his departure from the survival-chamber. As he recounted all that took place, both Aydin and

Chapter 16

Chance listened intently, never taking their eyes off of him for even a second. When he finally finished, he glanced over to see Chance sitting cross-legged and hunched over, anxiously stroking at the stubble on his chin; he was clearly overcome with a mix of thoughts and emotions. Peering across the table, he observed that Aydin also appeared to be lost in thought. All was quiet, save for the faint hooting of an owl that could be heard coming through the window.

Finally, Aydin came out of his trance and spoke up, "This is all beginning to become clear to me, yet there is still more that I need to know." He took a long pull from his pipe and continued, "You mentioned a map that specifies the locations of special crystalline orbs in the region. If you don't mind, I would be very much interested in studying it?"

Leo quickly jumped in, "All of his belongings are stored in my cottage, and I'm sure that he'd be more than happy to let you take a look at his map." He glanced over at Devin and winked.

Devin, thinking that he didn't have much choice in the matter, reluctantly nodded his head in agreement. He then turned towards Aydin and said, "Yeah, and you also can look over my other things as well – that is, if you feel the need."

Seemingly pleased, Aydin said, "Very well then."

It was at this point that Chance stirred from his thoughts and decided to speak his mind, "So he says that he isn't from around here, and he also comes from a time when life was altogether different – correct me if I'm wrong?" He glanced over at Devin, who slowly nodded his head. He then directed his attention towards the old men. "If this is all true, I'm gonna assume that he wouldn't last more than a week in the wild lands out on his own. And, if this mission he speaks of is as urgent as he says it is, well, that's just not gonna work."

Upon hearing this, Devin leaned back and crossed his arms. "Look guys, I'm sitting right here in the room, and I can tell you right now that this *mission* I speak of is just as important as I say it is."

He then glared down at Chance in frustration and said, "And, no, I don't know the first thing about how I should go about any of it!"

The serious look on Chance's face suddenly transformed into a pert grin. "Well, no worries there, Devin. I've got you covered." Sarina, Leo, and Aydin honed in on Chance as he continued, "I can teach you how to shoot a bow, how to skin a pumara, how to catch a catfish, and how to cook a meal over an open fire in no time at all."

Sarina, having heard about as much as she wanted to, swiftly cut in, "I don't think that's a good idea, Chance!"

Chance immediately shot back, "Why not, Sarina?! Don't you have any faith in me?"

"Of course I have faith in you. It's him that I don't have faith in!" The sea-green streaks in her eyes began to flare up and glow as she threw a piercing glare at Devin that pinned him stiffly to the back of his chair. "One day, he waltzes into the village from out of nowhere. We know absolutely nothing about him or where he's from. All he has is this wild story about the floating tower and the Great Firefall, but instead of being cautious, everyone around me has done nothing but bend over backwards to meet his every need. And why? Why are we supposed to be going out of our way to help someone we barely know anything about? How do we know that what he says is even true? I don't like it, Chance. It's pure insanity!"

Before Chance could argue back, Aydin stepped in to intervene. "Sarina, I can see that you are angry, and I don't believe that it's without just cause. What is it that you sense? What is it that you feel? I see your eyes, and I know of your gift. What is it that you really want to say?" He peered into her eyes thoughtfully.

For a few seconds, the sea-green glow around her pupils intensified, and then, like the dimming of an empty oil lamp, the luminosity subsided, and her features began to soften. Her shoulders slumped down, and, in a subdued tone, she said, "I'm sorry, Aydin. I shouldn't have acted that way."

Her gaze drifted towards Devin, who was still troubled and taken back by everything that he had just heard. She briefly let her eyes rest upon him before refocusing her attention on Aydin. "I sense great danger, and I feel that he will lead anyone who follows him into a world of hurt and pain." Lowering her eyes to the table, she paused to collect her scattered thoughts and added, "I'm worried that something awful will happen to Chance if he chooses the company of this man." A single tear streamed down her cheek.

Aydin gazed back at her with empathy and said, "I understand, Sarina. That's not the kind of premonition that should be taken lightly by anyone, and there's no doubt in my mind that what you speak is true." He reflected for a moment before continuing, "I want you to know that I can sense things too. So, as much as it pains me to say this, what must be done, must be done. Even before hearing Devin's story, I was able to stumble upon certain insights that have led me to believe that the events surrounding his sudden appearance cannot and should not be ignored by any of us. If Chance chooses to play a role in all of this, it is his own choice to make."

Sarina cast a worried glance at Chance, who quickly averted his gaze and began staring at a blank spot on the wall in front of him.

Aydin then said, "Sarina, he has heard what you had to say. Now, it's up to him to decide what to do with that knowledge. Neither you nor I can make that choice for him."

As soon as the words left Aydin's mouth, Chance lifted himself from off the floor and said, "Look, I know my way around this part of the world just as well, if not better, than most of the hunters in the village. I'm not suggesting that he and I trek off into the great unknown on a crazy adventure or anything. I just want to take him out to the wind towers near Roaring River Falls and maybe teach him a few basic survival skills along the way, that's all."

Sarina shot him a sharp look. "Really?! Even after everything I just told you?" Her blue-green eyes pierced deep into his soul. "Chance, I'm not going to try to stop you. I know you well enough to know that you're going to do what you want, regardless of what I say, but I just don't like it. I don't like it at all! Doesn't that mean anything to you?"

At this, Chance succumbed to a fit of frustration and fired back, "Sarina, of course it means something to me! But you've gotta learn to trust me! I promise that I'll be okay. You need to realize that I'm a grown man, and I can take care of myself."

She shook her head in irritation and stared back at him with a look of longing and sadness before turning away to cast her gaze at the small flame flickering atop the candle.

Leo, who had been trying to remain quiet, decided that it might be a good idea to step in. "Well, I hate to be the one to state the obvious, but I really do think we should call it a night." He glanced around at everyone in the room. "We're all tired right now, and our emotions are running high. I'm sure we'll see things a lot clearer in the light of day, after we've had a good night's rest."

Aydin, stifling a yawn, slowly nodded his head in approval. "That sounds like wise counsel, old friend. We can continue where we left off tomorrow – at your place."

Leo grinned. "Then my place it is!"

As no one in the room really felt like arguing with the notion and everyone was beginning to get sleepy, they all decided to pick themselves up, say their farewells, and go their separate ways.

A short while later, two elongated shadows lazily drifted in and out of the hazy orange glow of a street lamp as Leo and Devin trekked down the old cobblestone street that led to the guide's cottage. A chilly breeze blew in and whipped around them, nipping at the tips of their noses and hinting at the change of seasons. Along the way, Devin silently wondered to himself why no one had bothered to explain what a slime shifter was.

Chapter 17

Daggers in the Dark

On the northern side of Iron Woods, near the edge of the valley, a dim light shone out from an open window in the little wooden guardhouse that stood near the entrance to Stone Ridge Tunnel. The guardhouse, occupied, both day and night, by a small crew of watchmen who took turns traveling out to the location to work the post for a week or two at a time, was constructed to house the mechanisms that raised and lowered a heavy iron portcullis that had been installed within the entrance of the tunnel. For as long as anyone living in the region could remember, the gate had effectively worked to keep both unwanted visitors and unwelcome intruders out of the valley.

Since the job of guarding the gate at night was typically regarded as a mindless, boring task that no one really wanted to do, the older and more experienced daytime watchmen thought that it would be humorous to retire to bed much earlier than usual and let the newbies work an extended shift. Consequently, the newbies, Kalob Spear and Zephyr Pratt, not wanting to be outdone, thought it would be just as amusing if they kept themselves "busy" by working on two bottles of an exotic wine that they had secretly managed to smuggle in via a small group of traveling merchants who just happened to be passing through earlier that evening. As soon as they were sure that the daytime guards were fast asleep, they popped the corks, and the fun began.

Meanwhile, a slender, shadowy figure shot across the open yard that stretched out in front of the building. Dressed from head to toe in black form-fitting attire that included a black hood and a black mask that covered the bottom half of her face, she stealthily hid in the dark shadows cast by a nearby copse of trees and listened intently for anything that might give her away. Upon hearing muffled sounds of stifled laughter, she carefully prowled her way to the front of the building. From there, she slowly inched her way towards the open window from which the sounds were emerging. Remaining hidden in the shadows of the greenery that had grown up along the base of the wall, she crouched just beneath the dim lantern light spilling out of the opening and quietly spied in on two young men casually seated across from each other at a round wooden table who were in the process of drinking themselves into oblivion.

"I'll tell you what, Kalob, you've really outdone yourself this time," Zephyr said before belching and raising a half-drunk bottle of wine to his lips. "I knew that talking my dad into giving you this job was the right move."

Kalob grinned and took a large swig from his own bottle. "I have a feeling we're gonna have some good times out here, Zeph."

"I'll make a toast to that!" Zephyr stretched his drink out in front of him with a wobbly arm. "To good times!"

They raucously clanked their bottles together, accidentally sending a high-pitched ring to reverberate throughout the room. Almost instantly, the snoring in the room adjacent to them came to a sharp halt and was replaced by the sounds of shifting bodies and ruffling covers. The young men cupped their mouths, trying their hardest to keep from laughing out loud. When the snoring finally resumed, they were both giddy and shaking from the adrenaline rush that had just been triggered by nearly getting caught.

Chapter 17

"Phew! That was a close call," Kalob whispered as he attempted to stifle a giggle.

"You can say… that again," came his buddy's woozy reply, followed by a fit of wheezy chuckling.

As the young men stared at each other through bloodshot, watery eyes, they suddenly realized how intoxicated they were and slipped into a bout of uncontrollable laughter that ended in a fit of shaking convulsions as they struggled to contain the noise.

After they finally managed to calm down, Zephyr took a heavy swig from his bottle and grinned mischievously at his friend. "So have you put the moves on Sarina yet?"

Kalob glanced back slyly. "Not yet, but it's only a matter of time." He briefly paused. "I'm pretty sure that I've just about got her where I want her."

Shaking his head in disbelief, Zephyr chuckled jovially. "Yeah, you wish, man. I'll believe it when I see it."

"Then prepare to be a believer!" Kalob shot back. "I put in a little practice with Phoebe just last week, and I didn't hear her complaining none." He coolly ran a hand back through his wavy brown hair. "Sarina's not gonna be any different." An arrogant, toothy smile spread across his face from cheek to cheek as he leaned back in his chair, puffed out his chest, and guzzled down another drink.

"You're full of it, man! Phoebe ain't nowhere near the same league as Sarina, and you ain't even thinking about that slime shifter, Chance, she's been fooling around with. What do you suppose you're gonna do about him?" Zephyr looked at his friend incredulously before draining the rest of his bottle and belching loudly.

Kalob's lips curled into a snarl, and a kind of darkness flit across his eyes. "Hmph! I hate that guy. He really thinks he's something, doesn't he?" He downed the rest of his bottle, wiped his lips, and sat it down on the table. "All I've got to say is he better never let me catch him out in the woods alone."

Zephyr raised a brow and shot his friend a skeptical look. "That's a bit extreme, don't ya think? You're not gonna go rogue on me right after I got ya this job, are ya?"

Kalob lowered his gaze to stare at the surface of the table. For a moment, it seemed as if he had completely lost himself in a dark cloud. Finally, he glanced back up and, with a half-smile, said, "I'm just messing around, Zeph, but seriously, that guy needs to be taught a lesson. He needs to learn about a little thing called respect."

A few moments of empty silence trailed by as the two men sat at the table and woefully stared down at their empty bottles.

All of a sudden, Zephyr clutched at his stomach tightly. "Hey, man, are you feeling alright?" He let out a painful groan. "I'm not feeling so great."

"We probably just drank too much too quickly," Kalob replied as he eyed his empty bottle with suspicion. The color in his face was quickly beginning to diminish. "Maybe we ought to pace ourselves next time, huh?" He tried to force a chuckle and smiled weakly, as his own stomach had begun to cramp as well.

"Yeah… I think maybe you're right." Zephyr said as he rubbed his belly and glanced down at his empty bottle with a look of worry.

All of a sudden, Kalob began to panic. "Ugh! I think... I'm gonna... puke." He abruptly doubled over and threw up all over the floor.

Zephyr quickly sprang up and exclaimed in a frightened whisper, "Are you okay?!"

"No... No, I'm not." Kalob abruptly tumbled out of his chair while clutching at his gut and landed with a splat in his own vomit.

Just then, Zephyr spotted a shadowy figure climbing in through the open window. With a loud gasp, he cried out, "Kalob, look! Someone's in here!"

The dark figure swiftly stood erect and then, with a soft, teasing voice, mocked, "Having a bit of trouble, boys?"

A hint of a sadistic smile seemed to surface as her cheeks lifted behind her mask and her brows furrowed above intense, cat-like green eyes. With a quick flick of the wrist, she sent a sharp blade flying straight into Zephyr's jugular. Gasping and gurgling, he clutched at his throat and crumpled to the floor. Two seconds later, she was on top of Kalob, running a second blade across his neck.

In the adjacent room, the snoring came to an abrupt halt, and the hard thud of feet hitting the floor echoed throughout the vicinity. The assassin wasted no time in standing around. With lightning-fast reflexes, she darted over to Zephyr's body and jerked the dagger out of his throat and then dashed across the room and stood by the open doorway, where she silently waited in the shadows.

A moment later, a scruffy old man with a tangled mop of gray hair and a matching scraggly beard came shuffling out in nothing but his underpants. His big brown eyes grew wide with horror as he turned to see the two young men lying in a pool of puke and blood. However, before he could let out a cry of alarm, a slender hand came up from behind him and cupped his mouth. A split second later, the razor-sharp edge of her dagger was buried deep inside his neck.

Letting his body topple to the floor, she bolted into the dark room he had emerged from. The other guard had just lifted himself from his bunk and was in the process of putting his feet on the floor when he felt the sharp point of cold steel puncture his chest. Crying out in pain, he helplessly clutched at the dagger's hilt and fell backwards on the mattress. A moment later, all was silent.

The assassin quickly spun around to assess the situation. It appeared that she had successfully dispatched everyone in the guardhouse. After retrieving her blade from the dead guard's chest, she knelt on one knee, raised a closed fist to her forehead, and whispered a soft prayer.

Promptly standing up, she proceeded to pace back into the room with the open window. After glancing at her victim's bodies one last time, a self-satisfied smile traced across her lips. Her work was finished. The gate barring entry into the valley would remain tightly shut, at least for the time being. Knowing the urgency and time-sensitive nature of her mission, she made a quick exit and darted down Old Hunter's Path.

Chapter 18

Sarina's Diary
Friday, September 24th, 2354 – Evening

Dear Diary,

I couldn't be more upset right now if I wanted to. I just told the love of my life that he was getting ready to put himself in serious danger, and he all but ignored me. I'm beginning to wonder why I even bother trying.

It's not that I want to believe that what I'm feeling is true. I really don't. Nonetheless, I see things, and I sense things, and whether I like it or not, my insights have rarely ever been wrong. My whole life I've been told that I was given a valuable gift, but there are times, like right now, when it feels more like a curse.

Regardless, I managed to push my personal feelings aside just long enough to send Chance and his new "friend" out on their merry way. My father offered to loan out two of his best spiral-horns for the journey, but Chance insisted that they'd get far more out of the trip without them. He kept going on about the value of "taking it all in" and "learning how to rough it." Of course, Devin, not knowing any better, didn't bother to object to any of the survivalist nonsense that was gushing out of his mouth.

As far as all of the mystery surrounding Devin's sudden arrival is concerned, I know deep in my heart that there's probably something to it, but I just don't want to think about what that could possibly mean right now.

Earlier in the day, I helped pack their bags and made sure that they each had enough food and water for the journey. Chance kept insisting that they'd hunt and fish for their food, however, I managed to talk some sense into him on this point and ended up giving each of them a bag of dried pumara meat and veggies along with a pouch of medicinal herbs from my mother's shop. Devin actually seemed to be grateful for this – as he should have been! There's so much that can go wrong out there, and they could both die from any number of things. It's not just the dangerous creatures roaming the woods that I worry about, it's also the fact that the entire forest is overrun with poisonous insects and plants. To me, this whole trip just seems like one big accident waiting to happen.

It was nearly mid-afternoon when Chance and Devin finally headed out the front gate and began hiking up Old Hunter's Path. Grandpa, Aydin, and my parents were all there to see them off. I can't imagine that I'll be seeing Chance again for at least another three or four days, as he insisted that they were going to travel all the way out to Roaring River Falls, of all places. So, in the meantime, I'm just going to keep busy at the shop, as it always seems to help pass the time.

It's getting late again, so I had probably better call it a night.

Dear God, please keep Chance safe.

Chapter 19

Old Hunter's Path

As Devin and Chance strolled down the middle of the hoof-beaten trail, a light breeze drifted through the trees that was permeated by the scent of pine needles and fallen leaves. In the background, the raucous chatter of chirping birds blended with the noisy trills, rattles, and buzzing sounds of insects, and overhead, the autumnal hues of leafy limbs stretching out across the path contrasted starkly with the perfect blue sky. The combination of sights, sounds, and smells created a kind of rustic woodland ambiance that both enlivened Devin's spirit and sharpened his senses, and it wasn't long before he found himself wondering why he had never taken even a single day to appreciate the natural beauty of the landscape he grew up around.

Suddenly, Chance interrupted his thoughts with a simple question, "So what do you think?"

Devin shook his head as he came back to the present. "I really like it, Chance. It's amazing."

"It really is," Chance said with a grin. "Just wait until we get further in. You're gonna love it!"

"I'm sure I will, but I have a question." Devin adjusted the heavy pack and the long wooden bow and quiver of arrows that were strapped to his back. "Do you think there's any chance that we can find a place to sit down?"

Chance raised an eyebrow as he stopped to turn and look at his new friend, who was clearly beginning to struggle. "Are you alright, man? We've only been walking for about an hour."

Chapter 19

Stopping dead in his tracks, Devin stared back at Chance with a blank expression, not knowing quite how he should respond.

Chance shook his head and teasingly laughed. "I knew I was right about you. If you were out here with the village hunters, they'd never let you hear the end of it!"

Feeling more than a little bit embarrassed, Devin shrugged and nodded his head humbly. "I'm okay, man. I've just never done anything like this before. In my old world, most of the guys I grew up around spent more time indoors playing video games than they did doing anything physical, and honestly, I think they would have been put to shame by any number of the men I've run into while spending time in your village." The full reality and truth of this insight caused him to feel a little bit uneasy.

Chance cocked his head in curiosity. "What are video games?"

Devin started to answer but immediately stopped himself upon realizing that he didn't have a clue as to how he should go about describing a video game to someone who had never even seen a holo-display. After taking a minute to think it over, he came up with an analogy that seemed to make sense (at least, in his own mind) and began to explain, "Video games were basically a form of entertainment in the old days. They were kind of like adventures or storybooks that you could take part in right from the comfort of your home. All you had to do was press a button on a machine, and a whole adventure would come to life right before your eyes."

Not seeming to fully comprehend, Chance began to scratch at the back of his head.

Chapter 19

Devin attempted a better explanation, "I guess you could say that playing a video game was kind of like stepping inside of a painting in which everything seemed real and lifelike. The painting was like a whole new world that you could interact with in various ways. For example, if you were hiking through the woods and you discovered a lake, you could swim in it. If you happened to encounter a vicious beast while exploring an area near the lake, you could draw a weapon and kill it. Pretty cool, right?"

Chance nodded his head but still looked just as perplexed.

Devin went on, "The different things you could do really just depended on the type of video game you were playing. Some games were puzzles, some were mysteries, and others made you feel like you were living a whole other life in a fantasy world. Truthfully, there were so many different types of games that I don't think I could list them all even if I wanted to." He briefly paused and thought about what else he could say but decided to give up, figuring that Chance probably found his vague description to be just as baffling as it sounded.

Chance squinted his eyes and tried his best to create a mental image of everything he had just heard. After a brief moment, he shook his head and said, "I don't know, man. I'm honestly having trouble even imagining something like that. It all sounds amazing but kind of crazy at the same time, almost like magic or something."

"Yeah, I guess I can see why you would think that." Devin's features were suddenly vexed with frustration. "But, to be honest with you, I don't think very many of us really appreciated what we had. At least, I know I didn't. I mean, I never fully realized, until this very moment, what kind of a world I was actually living in."

"What do you mean by that?"

Devin stared up the trail with a far-off look in his eyes. "Well, we had all of these incredible inventions that made life easier, but no matter how much society progressed, it never seemed to be enough. Even though we were surrounded by an entire world full of beauty and mystery that we could explore and enjoy any time we wanted to, very few of us ever really took advantage of it. Maybe it's because we just didn't realize how good we had it?" He shrugged. "I don't know. But, whatever the reason, it seems like somewhere along the way we lost touch."

"Wow… That's really something," Chance said wistfully.

Devin merely nodded in agreement, as he had lost all desire to delve into the subject any further.

Suddenly, Chance perked up and said, "Well, you're here now, and what better time than the present to catch up on everything you missed out on, right?"

"I suppose you've got a point," Devin replied as he brushed the bangs away from his eyes. Then, feeling a surge of new energy, he straightened up his heavy pack and resolved within himself to tough it out and keep walking.

Unfortunately, it only took another hour or so for Devin to lose both his energy and his newfound resolve. The muscles in his legs had begun to ache and burn, he was sweating profusely, and a sharp pain had begun to shoot up and down his back. Feeling completely defeated, he tossed what was left of his pride to the side of the trail and plopped himself down right where he stood.

Chapter 19

Chance, fully lost in the sights, sounds, and smells of the forest around him, kept marching forward, oblivious to his companion's agony. A minute or so went by before he came to the realization that he was only hearing one set of footsteps, his own. Coming to a standstill, he swiftly swung around to see Devin lying flat on his back in the middle of the path about twenty yards back, his bow, quiver, and pack carelessly tossed to the side. The sight was pathetic, if not a bit humorous.

"You've got to be kidding me!" he exclaimed with a jeering laugh. "That does it. I guess we'll take a break." He quickly paced back towards Devin while quietly wondering if bringing this newcomer into the woods was really such a good idea.

Devin propped himself up on one elbow and wiped the sweat from his brow before managing to fully sit up. "I'm sorry, Chance. I just might not be cut out for this."

Forcing his private concerns aside, Chance reached down to help Devin to his feet and said, "You're fine, man. You're just not used to it." He then glanced around for a decent spot to bivouac and spotted a shady clearing about ten yards away from the side of the path. "Let's go over there and rest for a bit. It's probably not the best idea to just sit here in the middle of the trail."

Overcome with relief, Devin hurriedly gathered his things and followed Chance towards the small clearing. When they arrived, he tossed his bow and quiver to the side and sat down next to an enormous oak tree. He then reached into his pack and pulled out the leather-bound canteen of water he had brought along for the journey and began to guzzle it down voraciously.

Chapter 19

"Whoa, Devin! You need to slow down, or you'll make yourself sick," Chance said as he cocked an eyebrow in disbelief. "You really have no idea what you're doing, do you?"

Devin lowered the canteen from his lips and wiped his mouth. "I'm sorry, Chance. I'm just so thirsty."

"Yeah, I get that, but we've got to be careful with the water out here. We're still quite a ways from Roaring River, and you're probably gonna want another drink before then." Chance removed the cork from his own canteen and took a more conservative sip. "This is the wild lands, Devin, and anything can happen. Eating all of your food and drinking all of your water at the beginning of a journey is a surefire way to land yourself in a disaster."

"Disaster? What do you mean?" Devin twisted his head to stare into the woods sprawling out around him.

"I mean that this place is crawling with wild beasts and other atrocities that won't hesitate for a second to end your life if given half a chance. Not to mention that even some of the plants growing around here are flesh-hungry blood suckers."

Upon hearing these words, Devin's eyes grew to the size of silver dollars. "Flesh-hungry blood suckers?"

"Heh heh! Yeah, you're sitting about three feet from one right now." Chance pointed and glanced over to Devin's left-hand side.

Devin's ruddy complexion suddenly changed to a ghostly shade of white as he slowly began to inch his head around to look at what Chance was referring to. Right where Chance had been staring, he spotted a thick green vine covered in dark blotches and prickly red thorns that wound itself around the trunk of an elm tree. It had little round leaves and reddish-violet blossoms that were traced about with bulbous lines resembling thick, spidery veins.

All of a sudden, a large dragonfly whizzed past Devin's field of vision, causing him to jolt back in alarm. A split second later, one of the blossoms shot out from the vine like a frog's tongue and enveloped the dragonfly in mid-flight. It then sprung back into place with the speed of a rubber band, its petals cinched tightly around its prey. Wiggling and twitching from within, the dragonfly struggled to break free. After a brief moment, the movement ceased completely. As the flower opened back up, a fresh bulge appeared along the vine beneath it.

Devin sat perfectly still in a befuddled state of terror and panic, not knowing whether he should make a quick break for the forest path or whether he should attempt to move at all. However, his hysteria was quickly put to rest by the sound of unconstrained laughter coming from his amused travel guide, who was doubled over and trying to regain his composure.

Devin carefully scooted himself further away from the vine before jumping up and exclaiming, "What's so funny! That thing could have killed me!"

"Ha ha ha!" Chance laughed. "I highly doubt it. That thing's just a baby! It's the bigger ones that you have to worry about." He grinned and shot Devin a quick wink.

"Bigger ones!?"

"Yep. If you go deeper into the woods, there are similar vines, flowers, and even mushrooms that you'll want to steer completely clear of, but these little guys are actually okay, as far as I'm concerned. They do a good job of culling the neck biter population." Chance stroked the stubble on his chin thoughtfully.

"Neck biters? What are those?"

"Neck biters are kind of like a cross between a housefly and a mosquito, only they attack in swarms, and they go straight for a person's neck. Once one gets a taste of your blood, the rest of the swarm quickly joins in. If you don't get help quickly – well, you're pretty much done for."

"Oh, so do they look like houseflies?"

"Yeah, kind of, but they each have a long, spiky tube protruding from their mouths that they use for sucking blood. They're also bigger, fatter, and a whole lot meaner."

"Man, I'm not trying to sound like a pansy, but you're really freaking me out." Devin's eyes darted back and forth and all around the clearing.

"There's no need to worry! They're easy to spot. If any kind of light hits them at all, it brightly reflects off their backs, making them easy to see from a distance. They're armored in a mirrored carapace that reflects sunlight, firelight, and even moonlight, so a swarm kind of looks like a sparkly ball of light – trust me, they're really hard to miss. If for some reason you can't see them, you can still hear the loud buzzing of their wings from far away."

Chance's confident reassurances didn't seem to be helping, as Devin was still nervously twitching around and examining every inch of his surroundings in a state of intense paranoia.

Chance calmly reached over and patted him on the shoulder. "I didn't plan on bringing you out here to get you killed, Devin. You'll be alright – you're just gonna have to trust me. These are the kinds of things I was worried about when I first heard your story back at the den, and that's why we're here now."

Devin forced himself to calm down, if only just a little bit. "I trust you, Chance. I guess I just need to man up, huh?" He smiled nervously.

"Yeah, to say the least." Chance briefly glanced around the small clearing. "I know you don't want to, but I think we had better get back on the trail if we want to reach the campsite before dark. Are you okay?"

Devin took in a deep breath and said, "I guess I'm about as *okay* as I'll ever be." Oddly enough, the fright and the adrenaline rush that accompanied it served to reinvigorate his out-of-shape body, and the aches and pains he had previously been battling weren't bothering him as much anymore. He quickly strapped his pack, bow, and quiver of arrows onto his back and followed Chance out to the path.

They hiked along the trail for another hour or so without incident. Outside of passing by the occasional smaller path that would branch off the main road and dive into depths of the forest, the scenery didn't change that much, however, the lighting around them was beginning to fade. It was at this point that Chance stopped to observe his surroundings. After a brief moment, he spotted a small travel-worn footpath that skittered off the east side of the main road and into the woods.

He motioned for Devin to stand beside him and said, "That's the path we want to take. I'm assuming you don't know the first thing about using that bow strapped to your back, so it would be best if you stay right behind me. Got it?"

Devin nodded his head and asked, "Is it dangerous?"

Chance lightly chuckled. "No, it's not *that* dangerous – at least not for someone who knows what they're doing, like me." He grinned playfully. "But, for a guy like you, I don't really know. I guess we'll see."

Devin shook his head and looked down at the ground, feeling even more pathetic than usual.

"Relax, man! I'm just messing with you!" Chance laughed out loud. "You've really gotta lighten up!"

Devin quickly retorted, "That's easy for you to say, but I'm feeling like a level one hunter who just took a wrong turn and ended up in a level twenty danger zone, and it's not looking good."

Chance's mouth dropped open as he looked at his companion in confusion. "Devin, I have absolutely no idea what you're talking about. You've really got to stop." He then shook his head and proceeded to lead the way forward.

The two men followed the path as it wound through the dense undergrowth of the forest. The already fading daylight was made that much dimmer by the thick cover of trees, and even Chance seemed to have trouble staying on the trail as they plodded along. All around them, the sounds of chirping birds started to dwindle, and soon the air was filled with the new sounds of crickets, locusts, and nameless flying insects that buzzed loudly as they whizzed by. The faint howl of a wolf traveled through the air, sending shivers up and down Devin's back.

Devin suddenly spoke up, "Um, Chance, are we nearly there?"

Chance broke his stride and gazed around. "Yeah, I think so. It's been quite a while since I last camped at this spot. Normally, we would spend the night at a well-used campsite that's further up Old Hunter's Path, but we got started on this journey a little too late in the day to make it before dark."

"Oh, I see," Devin said as he nervously glanced around in every direction.

Chapter 19

"Relax, buddy. I've got this." Chance looked back reassuringly. "This isn't my first trip into the dark, scary forest." He lightly chuckled.

"That's not funny."

Chance laughed again and proceeded to lead them forward.

The sun had completely set behind them, and the first stars were just beginning to light up the sky alongside a waxing crescent moon by the time they reached a large clearing that opened up at the end of the path. There was just enough twilight left to see that the entire clearing was surrounded by the same species of carnivorous vines that they had encountered earlier, only these were much bigger, and they grew up much taller and fuller around the surrounding trees. Devin gazed all around with a look of severe unease.

Chance piped up, "Believe it or not, those vines are the reason that this is such a good spot."

"What do you mean?"

"Well, do you remember the neck biters I was telling you about earlier? They won't come anywhere near this place. Those vines would make short work of them, and they know it."

"Ah, I see." A wave of relief washed over Devin's face.

"In the meantime, we need to build a fire. It's starting to get cold." Chance strolled towards a large pile of brush and fallen limbs that the previous campers had left behind and said, "The hunters try to take care of each other out here. Whenever one of these piles starts to run low, it's expected that whoever depletes the supply will take the time to replenish it with fresh wood for the next person who comes along. It's kind of an unspoken rule among the hunters here in Iron

Woods." He smiled in pride. "Do you mind giving me a hand?"

Devin quickly set his things down and proceeded to help out with the gathering of logs and kindling material for the fire. By the time they were done, it was completely dark. Chance retrieved a tinderbox from his pack and used the flint and fire steel contained within to strike up a small patch of flames beneath the pile.

Devin watched in amazement, as he had never seen anyone start a fire in this manner before. "Wow, that's really impressive. Where did you learn to do that?"

Chance laughed. "What do you mean? That's the only way I know of to start a fire." He then cocked his head and asked, " Is there something I'm missing?"

"No, I guess not." Devin shrugged. "However, in the old world, we had these things called lighters. You just pushed a button and you instantly had fire."

"Really? That's incredible."

"Yeah, I guess it's one of those inventions that we all just kind of took for granted. I never really thought much about it until I watched you start a fire using nothing but metal and stone."

A few more minutes passed, and the little fire slowly began to grow in intensity as Chance added small sticks, leaves, and twigs to it and then expertly positioned bigger logs and sticks around the rising flames. Within fifteen minutes or so, the two of them were comfortably sitting and warming themselves in front of the toasty, warm glow of a full-fledged campfire.

Chance opened up his pack and produced a bag of dried pumara meat and veggies. "I guess it's a good thing that

Sarina had enough sense to send these along with us, otherwise, I think we'd be going to bed hungry tonight." He let out a nervous chuckle as he passed a piece of the meat over to Devin.

Devin ripped off a mouthful and happily chewed on it before remarking, "You know, this is really good! It kind of reminds me of the beef jerky that I used to get from the vending machine at work."

Chance cocked his head and raised an eyebrow. "Yeah, it is really good. Sarina's a good cook. But, Devin, once again, you're talking about things that I've never heard of. I mean, what's a vending machine?"

"Yeah, sorry about that, man," Devin said with a slight chuckle. "A vending machine was a large container full of snacks and drinks that you could access anytime you wanted to. All you had to do was put some money in one, and you could have any snack you wanted with just the push of a button."

Chance shook his head in wonder. "You really did come from a different kind of world, didn't you?"

"Yeah, I guess I really did," Devin replied, a wistful tone in his voice and a faraway look in his eyes. A silent moment passed, and then, in a somber tone, he added, "And I destroyed all of it."

Chance softly shook his head and quietly gazed into the fire. "I can't imagine what it must feel like living with that kind of a burden."

"Honestly, I've been trying not to think about it too much because it seems like every time I do, I start to fall apart. I mean, when it comes right down to it, I don't even feel like I deserve to be alive. All of my friends, my family, and everyone

I ever knew is gone, and it's all because of me." He winced as he tried to hold back the tears that were beginning to form.

"I'm sorry, man." Chance looked at his companion with empathy. "I don't think there's anything I can say or do that'll make that any easier for you to deal with, but I really am sorry."

The two of them sat in silence for a while, watching the orange-yellow flames dance around small logs that popped, sizzled, and crackled as they burned.

Finally, Devin spoke up, "You know, the worst part of it all is that the damage I've caused isn't over and done with. If I don't do something to deactivate that tower, it's all going to happen again, and I don't have a clue as to how I'm supposed to go about it."

Chance looked up from the fire. "I'm not sure if this will make you feel any better, but my dad always used to say, 'Where there's a will, there's a way.' Over the years, I've come to believe that he was right."

Devin stared back at him and listened intently.

"I think it was just his way of reminding me that I should never give up on anything important that I try to accomplish in life when things get tough because even the worst of situations can be turned around if I choose to keep pushing forward." He thought for a moment then added, "I guess it's that belief and faith that's kept all of us pressing on out here in the wild lands. Truth be told, I don't think any of us would have made it this far without believing in that simple magic that comes to life just when you need it the most." He returned his gaze to the campfire. "Maybe that helps."

Chapter 19

Seemingly lost in thought, Devin, too, stared back into the flames. The sound of a wolf howling somewhere in the distance could once again be heard.

Glancing up at the night sky, Chance said, "We had probably better get some rest now, especially if we want to get an early start tomorrow."

Devin nodded his head in agreement as he tried to stifle a yawn. "So I take it we're sleeping on the ground?"

"Well, I don't see a bed around here, do you?" Chance rolled his eyes and shook his head as he proceeded to unfold the blankets that were attached to his pack and lay them out next to the fire. Devin, following his example, did the same.

"I'm thinking we should have dressed a bit warmer," Devin said as he tightly wrapped a blanket around himself in an attempt to ward off the chill night air that was hitting his back.

"Yeah, maybe."

A few silent minutes passed, and the two of them, completely worn out from the long hike, fell into a deep sleep.

The next morning came quickly. The air was cooler than it had been the day before, and the blue sky that had kept things cheerful during the first part of their journey was now overshadowed by menacing dark gray clouds. Chance was already awake and packing up his things when Devin rolled over, moaning and groaning from the stiffness and pain that had overtaken his entire body.

"You're finally up. It's about time," Chance teased as he looked over at his companion, who was looking pretty rough, to say the least.

Devin forced himself up and groggily wiped the sleep from his eyes. "I feel like I've been run over by a hoverbus, and I really need a bath."

Chance rolled his eyes and ran his hands back through the messy curls in his sandy-blonde hair. "I guess you can take a swim in the river when we get there. It's near the campsite I was telling you about last night, about a third of the way to our final destination." Glancing up at the darkened sky, he added, "Although Mother Nature might be planning to give us a bath much sooner."

All of a sudden, Devin was overcome with worry and anxiety as he thought about the things in his backpack that could get ruined in the rain, which included his phone, logbook, security pass, and the map his father had given him. He was originally supposed to leave his personal belongings behind with Aydin for further research, but something deep inside of him warned him not to, as the information printed on the map alone was much too important to risk leaving with a complete stranger, no matter what anyone else said or thought. Bearing this in mind, he immediately got busy wrapping everything up as tightly as he could in the blankets he had been sleeping on, being extra careful to safeguard his most important possessions by burying them as deeply in his pack as possible.

When he was satisfied with his work, he joined Chance for a quick breakfast of dried meat and veggies. After they finished eating, they shouldered their belongings and headed back towards the main path. The walk back seemed to be much easier than it had been the night before.

By the time they reached their destination, the first drops of cold rain began to patter down around them. A few minutes later, a bright flash of lightning streaked across the sky that was immediately followed by a deafening thunderclap. All at once, the wind picked up and the clouds burst open in a torrential downpour. Devin pulled his pack around him tightly and tucked his head down towards his chest in a useless attempt to keep the biting, whipping rain out of his eyes. Chance, resilient to the end, continued marching forward with his head held high.

As they trudged along, the storm only seemed to intensify. Soon, wild streaks of lightning were splintering off in every direction as crashing booms of thunder shook and rattled the ground like an earthquake. Overhead, huge trees were swaying back and forth violently as cold, bitter gusts of wind stripped away their dying leaves and branches and haphazardly flung them all over the place.

Eventually, the going began to get really rough. The dirt path, which was solid only minutes prior, had morphed into a flowing river of slick mud. The two companions tried to keep moving forward by navigating over to the side of the path where the tall weeds and bushes created a natural barrier between the downpour and the stable ground below, but this soon proved to be just as futile, as some of the bushes were just too thick to navigate through.

Suddenly, Chance swung around and shouted, "We need to take cover! It's useless trying to go any further right now!"

Devin, who was clearly at his wit's end, frantically shouted back, "You think!?"

Chance pointed into the woods. "Follow me!" He then made a sharp left turn and bolted into the treeline on the western side of the path. Devin did his best to pick up the pace and dashed into the woods, following closely behind.

The intense swaying, rustling, and creaking of the trees all around them made it sound as if the whole forest was on the verge of being wiped out by a raging tornado. Devin's body trembled and shook as he silently battled the overwhelming fear that his life was about to come to an abrupt end. The rain falling through the trees wasn't quite as intense, but it did little to bring calm to a seemingly out of control situation.

Chance plodded forward, using a long dagger to swipe and cut at the weeds, vines, and bushes that barred the path in front of them. Devin, suddenly remembering his own dagger tucked away in his pack, stopped to retrieve it so that he could help. Between the two of them, they managed to cut a path into the forest that, by some stroke of luck or divine intervention, led them into a small area where a thick tangle of branches arching overhead managed to give them a bit of relief from the storm that was raging all around them.

The little wooded alcove wasn't perfect, but it was a hundred times better than what they had just come out of. The ground was wet in places, but it wasn't completely soaked, and the trees grew so close together that they formed a kind of wooden wall around the little space. The two men, soaked, cold, and exhausted, plopped down on the ground with their backs against the tree trunks.

After spending a few minutes catching their breath and regaining their composure, Chance looked over at Devin with a grin and said, "Well, I can honestly say that I didn't see that coming."

Chapter 19

In a move that was completely out of character, Devin glanced back at Chance and began to laugh, despite himself. He was soaking wet, sore, and scared out of his mind, but something inside of him had changed. Whether it was the feeling of accomplishment that came from barely escaping certain disaster or it was Chance's infectious confidence and optimism that had somehow rubbed off on him, something was definitely different. He then added, "Yeah, that was completely ridiculous! I honestly thought we were about to get killed out there!"

"You and me both!" Chance joined in the laughter.

The two of them probably looked and sounded like wild madmen of the woods, but they didn't care. In that moment, they were heroes who had battled and overcome the fury of Mother Nature, and nothing else in the world mattered.

A couple of hours passed by before the rumbling thunder finally started to recede and the shaking and creaking of the woods around them began to decrease in intensity. Strapping on their backpacks, they left the wooded alcove behind and proceeded to make their way back towards the main path.

Everything seemed to be going well until Chance came to an abrupt halt. Raising an outstretched hand, he swung around and motioned for Devin to stop. Then, with a finger lifted to his lips, he whispered, "I don't think we're alone."

As Devin stopped to listen, he heard a heavy rustling in the weeds and bushes just a short distance away to the right of their makeshift trail. In a whisper that was barely audible, he asked, "What is it?"

Chance held a finger up to his lips once more and then proceeded to unstrap his bow and nock an arrow onto the bowstring. Both of the men stood perfectly still, waiting, watching, and listening.

Suddenly, a monstrosity of a beast came crashing through the thicket. Devin, overcome with shock and terror, leaped backwards, nearly tripping and falling in the process. The creature looked like a cross between a gigantic mountain lion and a gorilla. It stood at least six feet tall on two legs and roared violently in their direction.

Almost immediately, it dropped on all fours and came charging at them like a raging bull. Without a second of hesitation, Chance drew back his bowstring and let the arrow fly. In an instant, it found its mark, and the awful beast fell over, roaring wildly as it ripped and tore at its chest with huge barbarous claws. Straightaway, he loosed another arrow that buried itself right beside the first one. The beast fiercely kicked at the air before letting out one final roar that ended in a gasp and a gurgle.

Lowering his bow, he took a deep breath and exhaled slowly. "That was close – a little too close."

Just then, Devin came up from behind. "What on earth is that!?" He gazed down at the creature in disbelief.

Chance calmly replied, "That, my friend, is a pumara, the scourge of Iron Woods, and there's plenty more where he came from."

Devin glanced around nervously. "We've got to get out of here!"

"Yeah, I agree. That was definitely cutting it a bit too close for my comfort." Chance strapped the bow on his back. "I normally prefer to hunt pumara from a distance."

"Are there more coming?"

"Maybe."

Chapter 19

"What should we do?!"

With a wave of his hands, Chance motioned for Devin to calm down. "There's no need to worry. It's highly unusual for a pumara to come this close to people in broad daylight. They tend to do most of their hunting in the evening and at night. More than likely, we invaded its territory when we cut a path through the woods." He briefly paused and rubbed the stubble on his chin. "After we get back on the main trail, we should be fine."

"How can you be sure?"

"You can never be completely sure, but if another one comes our way, it'll meet the same fate as this one – you can count on it." Chance dropped his serious expression and replaced it with a confident grin.

Devin nodded but, inwardly, wasn't feeling nearly as optimistic.

The two men then resumed their trek back to the main trail. As they were leaving, Devin turned his head to get one last glimpse of the pumara. With a tan coat of fur, it had the head and overall appearance of a mountain lion, but its body structure, long, muscular, and bulky, was more like that of a gorilla. The sight of its sharp fangs protruding from its open mouth and its glassy yellow eyes staring back at him caused him to shudder.

By the time they reached Old Hunter's Path, the rainfall had come to a complete stop, and a few scattered patches of blue could be seen peeking out from behind the dark clouds that slowly drifted by. Unfortunately, the trail had been transformed into a long, winding stretch of thick, sludgy mud.

Chapter 19

Momentarily stopping to assess the situation, Chance turned to face Devin with a grin and said, "Well, we survived a raging thunderstorm and a pumara attack all in less than a day. I'd say the worst is behind us."

Devin looked back at his friend with skeptical eyes but nodded his head just the same. With their sites set on the trail ahead, the two men began trudging forward.

Chapter 20

Darkovian Hospitality

The going was slow and cumbersome as Chance and Devin made their way down the rain-soaked path. Every bit of forward progress resulted in the thick accumulation of sludgy mud around their boots that made each new step feel heavier than the last. As a result, the two men often found themselves stopping off on the side of the trail to rest while they scraped the weighty muck from off their boots. The fact that they were already burdened down with backpacks and clothes that were soaking wet didn't help matters at all. They carried on like this, moving forward at a snail's pace, well into the late afternoon until, finally, Chance decided that it was time for a new course of action.

"Devin, this isn't gonna work," he remarked as he wiped a glop of rocks and mud from off of his dagger. "At this rate, we'll wear ourselves out long before nightfall. I think it might be for the best if we stop at the campsite near the river that I was telling you about yesterday. Once we're there, we can attempt to build a fire and let our clothes dry out. Plus, that ought to give the trail some time to dry out before we continue to venture forward."

Devin plopped himself down on a semi-dry bush and sat there huffing and puffing as he wiped the dirty sweat from his flushed cheeks. Looking back at Chance, he said, "You'll get no argument from me."

"I didn't think so. We're almost at the campsite. Can you handle this for just a bit longer?"

Devin rolled his eyes and shook his head. "Do I really have a choice?"

"I'm sorry, man. It's not like I had any idea that this would happen." He scraped a glop of gunk from off his boot. "Try to look at it this way, it's good practice for the road ahead. Just imagine all of the troubles we might run into when we leave the valley to search for a way into the floating tower."

At this, Devin cocked his head. "We? I didn't know that you were planning on coming along with me."

Chance grinned broadly. "Of course! Do you really think I'd let someone like *you* attempt something as important as saving the entire planet alone? I don't mean any harm when I say this, but you wouldn't last two days out on your own, and I'd never be able to live with myself knowing that I just sat back and watched as you raced off towards certain disaster." He paused briefly and then added, "Nope, Devin, I'm afraid you're stuck with me."

Upon hearing this, a trace of a smile crept across Devin's tired face. With a slight shake of his head, he said, "Chance, I really don't think you know what you're getting yourself into."

"Well, that might be true, but you obviously don't either, and I can't just sit back and let you do this all on your own. Besides, what kind of a person would that make me?" He stared back at Devin with a look that was more serious than usual. "You're not getting rid of me, Devin." He then glanced down at the dagger that Devin had been using to remove the mud from his boots and said, "That's a beautiful blade. Where did you get it?"

Devin held it up, admiring the bluish-green crystal that was set in the crossguard. "It was stored in the survival-chamber. My father told me to take it with me."

Chance moved in closer to examine it. "I've never seen anything quite like it before."

"Yeah, it's definitely strange. I still haven't figured out how to use it, but I'm guessing that it needs to be charged up or something to unlock its full potential." At this, he turned the blade over in his hand and held it out in the sunlight. He then handed it over to Chance.

Chance took a minute to look it up and down, twisting the blade and watching as the sunlight streaked across its surface with a lustrous shine. He then tightly gripped the hilt and jabbed it into the air in front of him before flipping it over and handing it back to Devin. "What do you mean by *charging it up*?"

"What I'm saying is that it needs electricity to function." Devin pointed the blade forward and depressed the trigger. "It obviously needs some sort of power source in order to work. I mean, why else would it have a trigger?" Holding the dagger upright again, he toggled the small silver switch located below the crystal with his thumb. "It's just a guess, but it would make sense, considering the kind of technology my dad was working on for so long."

Chance listened intently and then shook his head. "I wish I could help you, man, but I really don't have a clue what you're talking about. It all sounds like more magic talk to me."

Devin shrugged and nodded before placing the blade back in his pack. He then stood up and stretched. "Well, we probably better get back on the path, right?"

"Absolutely!" Chance stood up and arched his back while stretching out his arms as wide as possible. "You know, we need to find a sheath for that dagger. A backpack is no place for such a beautiful weapon."

Devin quietly nodded in agreement as he adjusted the straps on his heavy pack.

This time around, the going was slightly easier. The sun had been out for awhile, and the mud was beginning to thicken up a bit. It only took another half hour or so to spot the well-used campsite that Chance had described to Devin the night before, as a thick column of white smoke seemed to be rising from the general area. Upon drawing closer, they noticed that the air was permeated by the delicious aroma of meat roasting over an open fire. In the distance, the sound of Roaring River could be faintly heard as it swiftly rushed by.

Stopping in the middle of the trail, Chance sniffed at the air and remarked, "It smells like something's cooking."

Devin's eyes lit up. "I know. It smells so good!"

Chance caught another heavy whiff of the scent, and his mouth began to water. "I don't know about you, but I'm starving!"

"Yeah, you and me both!"

"I bet you that some of the hunters from Iron Cove stopped here before the storm hit, and they're making camp until everything dries out. We should hurry up so that we can join the feast!"

"Do you think they'll mind?"

A bright smile lit up Chance's face. "Of course they won't! Like I told you, we all take care of each other out here."

Devin suddenly perked up. "Alright, then. Let's do it!"

They both picked up their pace and pressed forward. However, when they were about fifty yards out, Chance swiftly threw a hand up and motioned for Devin to stop walking. He then put his finger up to his lips and darted over to a shady recess in the treeline running along the western side of the trail. Devin ducked down and quickly followed suit.

Once they were out of eyesight, Chance whispered, "Devin, whoever is camping up there isn't one of our own. Did you see the striped tents, the black horses, and the large covered wagon?"

"Yeah, there were three tents altogether – I think."

"Uh huh, and those aren't the kinds of tents that we use out here. They look like they might be Darkovian."

Devin cocked his head and asked, "Darkovian?"

"Do you remember the merchant who sang at the tavern last night? He was from Darkovia."

Devin nodded his head in understanding. "So what's the big deal?"

Chance squinted his eyes and began to rub his chin. "Well, I don't know how things were back in your time, but nowadays, the people of Darkovia aren't completely trustworthy. We do business with them once in a while, as they provide us with essential supplies, like lamp oil, flint, and fire steel, but they have some very *different* ideas about living that don't exactly mesh with the Iron Cove way of life."

Devin wrinkled a brow. "What do you mean?"

"Well, to begin with, they're notorious for making unfair deals, and they've been caught overcharging people in the village for their goods on more than one occasion. Even worse than that, there have been rumors floating around that suggest that some of them are involved in the slave trade." Pausing, Chance took a moment to scratch a spot on the back of his head and brush a tangle of hair away from his face. "A lot of them also seem to be infatuated with a strange religion that's based around some kind of goddess who is supposedly living in the floating tower. I obviously don't need to tell *you* that it's all a complete lie. They're just not the kind of people you want to get very close to."

Devin shifted his position to catch a glimpse of the smoke rising up from the campfire behind his friend. The delicious scent of roasting meat was stronger than ever, and it was beginning to make his belly grumble.

Chance pursed his lips and glanced at the campsite again. He seemed to be running something over in his mind. Finally, he spoke up, "Okay, here's the plan. We're gonna drop in and check things out, but we need to be extra careful and stay on our guard. We can't afford to be too careless out here so far from the village."

Devin nodded his head.

Chance continued, "When we get there, just follow my lead. If I think that we need to keep moving on up the path, I'll give you a signal."

"Okay, what's the signal?"

Chance rubbed his chin and squinted his eyes in thought before responding, "If I offer you a drink of water and toss you my canteen, you'll know that we need to make our exit. Will that work?"

Devin nodded his head again. "Yeah, that sounds good."

After a few more minutes of carefully scoping out the campsite, they left their hiding spot and began making their way towards the potential of warmth, safety, and a freshly cooked meal.

The campsite lay to the west of the path in a large clearing surrounded by tall oaks, pines, and elms. The same strange vines that covered the trees at the previous campsite were crawling up the exposed lengths of their trunks. Near the middle of the clearing, a cozy campfire was roaring in front of three round tents that were patterned in vertical stripes of white and gold. A plump rabbit was slowly roasting on a metal skewer positioned over the campfire, and a man with a darkly tanned complexion and long, curly black hair sat cross-legged and hunched over watching it. He had a long mustache and goatee that was carefully braided and tied off at the end with shiny silver beads. He wore a dark blue cloak, and around his neck hung a golden chain that had a ruby-like gemstone dangling from its center. The finely cut jewel caught the flickering glow of the flames and reflected it back in all different directions, making it seem as if it were imbued with some kind of mystical energy.

Just as the two men appeared at the edge of the clearing, he picked himself up from the ground and waved at them with a bright white smile and then, in a loud voice, called out, "Ah, we have visitors!"

A moment later, two young women appeared from behind the curtained entrance of a tent that was positioned directly behind the fire. As they ventured forward to stand beside him, both Devin and Chance were taken back by their alluring beauty. They were each dressed in silky long-sleeved gowns that were fashioned in such a way as to accent their natural curves.

One woman wore a midnight blue gown that was complemented by a sky blue scarf interwoven with silver floral patterns. She had bright blue eyes, fair skin, and wavy blonde hair parted over to the side that draped down loosely over the folds of the scarf that lay wrapped around her neck and shoulders. Around her forehead, she wore a thin silver circlet with a sparkling white jewel set in its center.

The other woman was dressed in a similarly fashioned gown, only it was dark red. She also wore a scarf, but it was a shimmery white and featured a row of fuzzy tassels that dangled loosely from end to end. As it was chilly outside, she had it pulled tightly around her shoulders. She had a smooth chocolate-brown complexion and long, curly black hair that was put up with shiny silver pins, exposing a set of sparkling diamond earrings that dangled down on each side of her slender face. However, her most stunning feature was her cat-like green eyes that almost seemed to glow with their own energy. Like her companion, she was also adorned in a thin silver circlet that featured a white jewel of similar cut and design.

When Chance and Devin saw the two women come out to stand next to the man by the fire, they both came to an abrupt halt. Regardless of the fact that both men came from completely different backgrounds and time periods, they were each thinking the exact same thing – these women were stunningly gorgeous.

Smiling, Chance straightened up his shoulders, adjusted his pack, and proceeded to confidently march forward. Devin, quietly wondering how this was all going to turn out, slowly shook his head and followed along.

As they approached, the man wearing the cloak extended his outstretched arms with palms facing upward and bowed. He then lifted his head and said with a smile, "Welcome to our humble camp, travelers."

Chance, having a limited knowledge of Darkovian culture, put one hand over his belly, dropped the other to his side, and politely bowed before the stranger. He then returned the greeting with, "Thank you for having us, friend. My name is Chance, and this is my companion, Devin." He motioned over to Devin, who seemed to be transfixed by the whole scene that was playing out in front of him. Caught off guard, he swiftly came out of his daze and attempted an awkward bow.

Chance continued, "We were out traveling when we were waylaid by the storm that passed through earlier."

The man, seeming pleased, if not slightly amused, by their clumsy attempt at good manners, responded with, "I am Drake Thorne, and these two lovely women are Rowanne and Kysa." He turned and stretched a hand out towards them. "Please come and sit down by the fire. Dry and warm yourselves." He then motioned with another outstretched hand to a bare spot of dry ground near where he had been sitting. The two women continued to stand silently beside him, wearing just a trace of a smile on their faces as they coolly observed Chance and Devin with piercing eyes.

Chance lit up and said, "Thank you so much, friend." After unstrapping his bow, quiver, and pack, he proceeded to set down in front of the fire just a few feet away from the man. Devin found a spot a few feet away from Chance and wasted no time in doing the same.

After they were both comfortably seated, Drake turned towards the two women and gave them instructions, "Ladies, please run into my tent and fetch our guests something warm and dry to wear. We can't have them sitting out here cold and wet." With a wink, he added, "That is not the Darkovian way."

Both of the women smiled politely and bowed before making their way back into the tent from which they had come. As soon as they departed, he shuffled over to the fire and turned the skewer that the rabbit was roasting on. He then glanced over at the newcomers and said, "It is good fortune that you stumbled upon our camp, for we were warned that another round of stormy weather might be heading this way, possibly arriving as soon as tomorrow."

Chance looked up at Drake and said, "Well, we really appreciate that you're willing to let us stay here for a while. I think I speak for the both of us," he turned to glance at Devin, "when I say that neither one of us is in a hurry to weather another storm like the one that just came through." Devin nodded in agreement.

A big grin appeared on Drake's face. "Good, then it's settled. We shall have you here for the evening or even longer if necessary." Turning around, he shuffled over to his place in front of the fire.

As soon as Drake's back was turned, Devin swiftly glanced over at Chance with raised eyebrows as if to ask, "Are you sure about this?"

Raising his hand, Chance shot back with a look that said, "No worries. I've got this."

Devin reluctantly turned his gaze away from his friend and stared into the bright glow of the fire, not quite sure what to make of everything.

As soon as Drake sat back down, the two young women returned, each carrying a bundle of fresh clothes and shoes. Glancing up, he said, "Ah, very good. Please give them to our guests."

Rowanne, the woman wearing the midnight blue gown and the sky blue scarf, walked over to Devin and handed him her bundle. She flashed him an alluring smile, being sure to make eye contact, before returning to stand slightly behind Drake on his right-hand side. Kysa, the woman with the cat eyes, diamond earrings, and dark red gown, traipsed over to Chance and proceeded to do the same.

As soon as the women had completed their task, Drake shifted around to look up at them and asked if they would return to their tents while their guests changed into the dry clothes. He then directed Chance and Devin to an area behind the tents near the horses and the covered wagon where they could have some privacy.

After peeling off their wet clothes and changing into the long white robes and soft leather slippers that Drake had lent them, the two men stared at each other with stupid grins on their faces.

Chance was the first to speak up, "Please tell me that I don't look as ridiculous as you do right now?"

Devin replied with a chuckle, "I can't. But, hey, at least we're dry!" Looking himself up and down, he added, "Who knows, maybe the women of Darkovia really go for this sort of thing?"

Chance rolled his eyes and shook his head. "You have to swear to me that no one back home ever hears a word of this!"

"I'll try my best, but I can't make you any promises." Devin laughed and threw his hands up in mock uncertainty.

"I mean it, Devin!"

The two men, freshly dressed and mostly dry, made their way back to the front of the tents to find their packs neatly arranged and drying out by the fire. When Drake saw them, he smiled and exclaimed, "Ah! You two look good in Darkovian fashion, and I'm sure you feel better as well, yes?"

Chapter 20

Devin and Chance each nodded and expressed their appreciation and gratitude before finding their spots and settling back down.

Drake then called out to Rowanne and Kysa, "Ladies, you can come out now, and please bring a bottle of wine with you. I'm sure our guests are thirsty after their long journey." Turning back towards the men, he continued, "Since you will be staying with us until tomorrow, I think we should make the most of it, don't you?"

Chance glanced at Devin to get his thoughts, but Devin only lifted his hands and shrugged, as he wasn't in the least bit familiar with Darkovian custom.

Returning his attention to their host, Chance replied, "I think that sounds like a great idea."

Drake called out to the ladies again, "Please bring the plates with you as well. The rabbit is nearly finished."

A few moments later, the women arrived at the fire bearing a large bottle of red wine, two clay mugs, and five plates. Rowanne handed Chance and Devin each a mug while Kysa uncorked the bottle and filled them to the brim. Afterwards, Rowanne held the plates while Kysa, using a set of tongs and a knife, removed choice cuts of meat from the skewer and filled them with it. After the plates had been passed around, the women took theirs back to Rowanne's tent and left the newcomers to enjoy their meal.

The rabbit tasted just as delicious as it smelled, and Chance and Devin wasted no time in
devouring it as quickly as they could, their manners clearly taking a backseat to their hunger.

About halfway through the meal, Devin, who had remained mostly silent for the biggest share of the evening, finally decided to break the silence with a question, "Drake, I noticed that the women are not eating with us. I hope I'm not being rude by asking, but is there a reason for this?"

Wearing a furtive grin, Drake glanced up from his plate and said, "It is against Darkovian custom for servants to eat with their masters."

Devin's eyes widened in a mix of shock and surprise. "Oh... I apologize... I... I didn't know," he stammered. "It's just that I've never spent any time with anyone from Darkovia, and I was just... curious." His eyes darted over to Chance, who shook his head slightly and shrugged his shoulders, seeming to be just as perplexed by the situation.

Almost immediately, Chance interceded with a question of his own, "This wine is fantastic, Drake. Why aren't you drinking any of it with us?"

Drake shifted his gaze away from Devin and chuckled. "I had my fill of wine last night. Today, I must cleanse myself with water." He raised a leather-bound canteen into the air. "But please feel free to drink as much as you want. It does my heart good to see my guests happy." He then stared off into the distance, as if distracted by some quiet, nagging thought, before abruptly smiling again and returning his attention to the plate of rabbit meat in front of him.

Sensing that the conversation was teetering on the edge of awkward, Chance decided to hold off on asking any more questions, thinking that it might be for the best if he just focused on enjoying his meal. Devin, perceiving the same thing, followed his lead.

Another ten minutes or so passed by before they were all finished eating. With the exception of the soft crackling and popping noises coming from the fire and the roar of the river rushing by in the distance, all was still and quiet.

At this point, Drake casually glanced over at the men's empty plates and called out to the women, "Rowanne! Kysa! Please come and get these plates!"

Rowanne came out of her tent carrying the half-empty bottle of wine and proceeded to fill both of their mugs up to the brim. Meanwhile, Kysa busied herself with gathering up the empty plates.

As they were turning to leave, Drake called out again, "Could you please bring me my guitar, Kysa? I'm sure that our guests would enjoy some music with their wine."

She smiled and bowed her head. "As you wish."

A few minutes later, both of the women returned, Kysa carrying with her a guitar that was fashioned in a manner similar to the instrument Raul had been playing at The Pumara's Den. Handing it over to Drake, she asked, "Would you like us to dance for you and your guests while you play?"

He took the guitar into his lap, glanced over at the two men, who were beginning to seem more relaxed as they sat and watched the fire in contentment, and replied, "Let them have another drink first. Come nightfall, we will enjoy your dance." He then turned and nodded at the men.

Chance and Devin both sat by the fire, eagerly anticipating what the night might bring. Wine, music, and dancing? What was this all leading up to? The strong drink, the good food, and the warm glow of the fire had loosened them up, and both of them felt their previous inhibitions begin to slip away.

Just then, Drake struck the first chord of an unusual-sounding Darkovian composition. Dark, sultry, rhythmic, and exotic, it had a similar sound and feel to the music that the men previously heard Raul perform at the tavern. As he skillfully plucked the strings, he lowered his eyes to the fretboard of his guitar, letting himself become fully entranced in the music. Meanwhile, the women each retreated into their separate tents.

Devin took the opportunity to get Chance's attention and whispered, "Chance, what do you think of all of this? Are Darkovians normally this hospitable?"

Chance looked at his friend and whispered back, "I don't know. It's all kind of strange to me. I'm wondering if we should get out of here. How about you?"

Devin thought for a moment before responding, "I'm not sure. I get the feeling that if we leave right now, it might not go over very well."

Chance lowered his head and stared into his half-empty mug. "Yeah, I think that maybe you're right. I guess it wouldn't hurt to stay a little while longer."

"It's probably only right that we do. After all, he fed us and gave us clothes. We don't want to be rude, do we?"

Chance gazed down into his half-empty mug again. "Okay, we'll wait awhile longer. Just don't forget about the signal we discussed earlier. I'm not too sure that we won't have to use it."

Devin nodded his head but tried to change the subject, "At least our things are drying out. That's good, right?"

Chance surveyed the backpacks, the wet clothes, and the weapons drying out by the fire and shrugged. "Yeah, I'm not exactly in a hurry to put those wet clothes back on or anything."

Devin grinned in acknowledgment and began bobbing his head to the music. Suddenly, he tilted his mug back and chugged down what was left of his wine.

Upon seeing this, Chance chuckled and gave a playful warning, "You might want to go easy on that Devin. It's really strong." However, in defiance of his own advice, he lifted his drink to his lips and proceeded to finish what was left of it as well.

A short while later, Drake glanced up from his guitar. Seeing the men smiling and laughing, he ended his song and called for Rowanne to bring out more drinks. A moment later, she came out of her tent carrying an ornate bottle of something different than wine. The young men both brightened up at her appearance and thanked her as she poured a dark liqueur that had a heavy perfume-like scent into each of their mugs. Before she turned to leave, she took a moment to softly gaze at each of them, pausing just a bit longer when her eyes met Devin's. In the background, Drake had already begun to work on a fresh tune.

It didn't seem like much time had passed when Chance looked up at the sky and said, "Look, Devin. It's getting dark. Does it really feel like we've been sitting here that long to you?"

Devin gazed up at the sky with a chuckle and then, in a jubilant tone, said, "No, not at all." He raised his mug in a toast, "Cheers, buddy! To good friends and good times!"

Chance downed what was left of his drink and said, "Wow, you really *are* drunk!"

"I know, right!?"

Chance was, in fact, feeling woozy, but he hadn't lost complete control of his wits yet. He wasn't sure if he could say the same for Devin. As he gazed into his empty mug, the thought occurred to him that something might be off, but before he could ponder the thought any further, Kysa appeared next to him and immediately began filling it back up with the same strange intoxicant. As she tipped the bottle up, she gazed deeply into his eyes and gave him a sensual smile that quickly dissipated any thought he might have had about sobering up. He glanced over at Devin and noticed that Rowanne was refilling his drink as well.

All of a sudden, the music came to an abrupt stop. The two men glanced up and noticed that Drake had laid his guitar down and was shuffling towards a large pile of logs stacked beneath a leather tarp just a short distance from where he had been sitting. Picking them up, two at a time, he tossed them on the fire. He did this until the blaze grew to be nearly three times its original size. As soon as he was finished, he turned towards the men and asked, "Are you warm enough?"

Chance shifted around to get Devin's input and noticed that he had already scooted a few feet away from the intense blaze and was currently using one hand to wipe away giant beads of sweat that were dripping from his face. He noticed that both of the women had backed away from the heat as well. He then called back to Drake, "Yeah, I'm pretty sure that'll work!"

Upon hearing this, a big, wide grin appeared on his face. He then directed his attention towards the women and said, "Ladies! I think we're ready to see your dance!"

Rowanne spun around and curtsied and then, with a mischievous smile, said, "I was thinking you'd never ask," before traipsing back towards her tent.

Chapter 20

Kysa gazed into Drake's eyes and flashed a playful smile before turning to follow Rowanne. Still grinning, Drake glanced over at the two men and winked before setting back down to strum out a new tune.

The melody he played this time around was much more vibrant than anything they had heard all evening. The exotic-sounding chords he strummed and the complementary notes he plucked weaved together to create a smoky, sensual ambiance that was lively yet strangely mesmeric. The two men couldn't help but bob their heads up and down and tap their feet to the undulating rhythm.

Shortly thereafter, the young women appeared again, each wearing a new outfit. Rowanne had replaced her silky gown with a shimmery black top that only covered the lower half of her bosom, exposing both a great deal of cleavage and most of her belly. A golden choker with a sparkling ruby pendant set in its center was clasped tightly around her neck. To complement her top, she wore a matching pair of shimmery panties that were partially hidden behind a black sheer sarong knotted around her waist.

Kysa's outfit was slightly more conservative but no less enticing. She had replaced her gown with a similar top to that of Rowanne's, only it was fashioned from silk that had been dyed a rich shade of purple and was decorated with golden paisley swirls. A pashmina shawl of the same color lay folded and ruffled around her neck, and to match her top, she wore a fitted pair of silken purple pants with a golden waistband that hugged her hips well below her exposed naval.

As Drake continued to play his exotic melody, the women gracefully swayed and shimmied to the undulating rhythm and slowly made their way towards the fire. As they danced barefoot around the growing orange blaze, both Devin and Chance watched intently with a mixture of excitement and wonder, neither one of them having experienced anything quite like it before.

Devin, now fully intoxicated, playfully bobbed his head to the music and sipped on his drink, fully losing himself in the bliss and exhilaration of the moment. In his mind, he was convinced that he had stumbled upon a wild gypsy harem, and he wasn't about to let the experience slip away from him. As he gazed at the slender bodies of Rowanne and Kysa swaying and twirling in the firelight, all he could do was imagine taking the both of them into one of the tents and losing himself in a night of sensual pleasure beyond compare.

Chance wasn't in much better shape, however, due to some inborn higher tolerance to the effects of alcohol, he still hadn't quite lost all of his wits. As he gazed upon the two women dancing, he felt his mind being prodded, pulled, and dragged into a place that was just as dark and sensual as the one that Devin was already lost to. It wasn't that he didn't have the same thoughts and desires as other men his age, but he just couldn't shake the thought of Sarina, worried and waiting for him to come home.

Finally, in a moment of clarity that was on the verge of slipping away forever, he forced himself to stand up and stumble over to his backpack. Leaning over, he reached inside and dug out a leather-bound canteen of water. Upon raising back up, he saw that Rowanne had made her way into Devin's lap, had draped a slender arm around his neck, and was running a hand through his tousled hair.

Uh oh… We're in trouble, he thought to himself as he abruptly began to shuffle in their direction, feeling the sudden urge to end the madness before things got any more out of control.

When Devin saw him approach, he briefly glanced away from Rowanne, who was in the process of strapping her legs around his waist and kissing his neck, and shouted, "Are you having a good time?!"

Chance tried to force a smile but shook his head. He held the canteen up in the air, struggling to think of a good way to toss it in Devin's direction without striking Rowanne in the back.

Upon spotting the canteen, Devin laughed and raised his mug in celebration. "No worries! I'm good, man!" He then tipped it back and took a big swig. Rowanne suddenly threw her hand out, gripped his wrist, and gently lowered it back down. As she did this, Devin turned his head to face her and, closing his eyes, lost himself in a rush of pleasure.

Upon witnessing this, Chance hung his head and let the canteen slip from his hands. Just as he did so, he felt a soft, warm hand slip into his own. Looking back up, he saw Kysa smiling back at him, her cat-like eyes gently reflecting the orange glow of firelight and tempting him as they pierced deep into his soul. She then grabbed his other hand and swayed back and forth with the music that still hadn't stopped. With barely a tug and pull, she compelled him to sit down. Feeling drunk and defeated, he didn't even try to fight back.

After he was seated, she jumped up and skittered to the other side of the fire. It only seemed like a few seconds had passed before she returned, carrying with her a fresh bottle of liqueur. At this point, Chance was too befuddled and bedazzled to even wonder where it had come from. Uncorking the bottle, she dropped to her knees, held it up to his lips, and softly whispered, "Take another sip. I promise it'll make you feel so much better."

As he allowed her to pour the rich liqueur into his mouth, he noticed something strange about the taste, but being too drunk to care and quickly falling under the young woman's spell, he swallowed the perfumy intoxicant and sent the last of his reservations drifting off into the cold, dark of night. Kysa then gingerly lowered the bottle from his lips and crawled into his lap while running her long fingers through his blonde curls. He smiled warmly as his eyes wandered from her exposed cleavage to her glowing green eyes. Slowly, she let the tips of her fingers traipse down the side of his cheek, never once loosing him from the intense grip of her seductive gaze. In the background, the sultry music that filled the air began to take on an ethereal quality, the notes almost seeming to melt into one another, and within the span of a fleeting moment, his eyelids began to droop and the world around him faded to black.

Chapter 21

Dread and Daring in the Dead of Night

As Sarina stepped out the back door, a cool night breeze whipped around her, sending a wave of goosebumps to race up and down her slender arms. Shaking off the chill, she tightly wrapped her forest-green cloak around her shoulders and pulled the fur-trimmed hood up over her head. She then slung her backpack on and proceeded to quietly make her way towards the stables behind the house.

Opaque darkness covered everything like a thick blanket, a wall of clouds having moved in to overshadow the light of a nearly perfect half moon. The dim illumination of starlight did little to make up for its absence. Stopping just outside the stables to make some quick adjustments to the straps on her backpack, Sarina took a moment to gaze into an unobscured portion of the night sky. It almost seemed as if she could see forever into the black expanse of outer space. Briefly overcome with wonder, she began to imagine what else might be out there – other worlds, other creatures, or other civilizations completely different from her own. As she continued to gaze outward, a shooting star streaked across her field of vision, burning brightly before it disappeared behind some nearby clouds. Standing mesmerized, her mind continued to wander for just a few seconds longer.

Suddenly, the tranquility of the night was interrupted by the sound of a lone wolf howling somewhere in the distance. Within a matter of seconds, a number of other wolves returned its call from seemingly different locations. Startled from her trance, Sarina's thoughts raced back to the terrible premonition that had awoken her from a dead sleep and compelled her to be outside in the first place – a vision of Chance struggling in a dark place, helpless and scared. As the wolves continued howling, she was overcome by an overwhelming sense of foreboding and fear. In an attempt to gain inner peace, she whispered a silent prayer for Chance's well-being as well as her own and sent it drifting into the heavens above.

Stepping into the shadows of the horse stables, a strong scent of hay and manure permeated the air around her. She tried her best to ignore the overpowering odor and swiftly made her way to Valoria's stable. Smiling, she patted her old friend's back and traipsed a hand over the small, spiral-shaped horns that protruded just above her perky ears. She then ran her fingers through her thick, flaxen mane and whispered, "I hope you're ready for this, girl. I'm going to need all of the help you can lend me."

Since she knew where all of the riding equipment had been stored by heart, she was able to have the palomino spiral-horn saddled and ready for travel in no time at all, even in the dark of night. After locating one of her father's unlit lanterns and carefully storing it in a saddlebag, she led the horse towards the cobblestone road that ran in front of her house.

A short while later, Sarina arrived at the hidden back entrance to the village, a gaping crack in the southern wall that was partially shrouded by overgrown shrubs and long, dangling vines. Before leaving the house, she had decided against exiting through the front gate to avoid running the risk of getting caught and interrogated by the night watch. Alternatively, the path just beyond the back entrance would give her the perfect cover of darkness to quietly leave the village behind without being seen. Winding itself around the western half of the village wall and running parallel to the steep mountain cliffs that surrounded the southern end of Iron Cove, it wasn't wide enough or used often enough for more than two people to walk abreast on it at the same time, but it was perfect for a daring middle of the night escape, like the one she was currently attempting.

Stopping to glance around, Sarina took a moment to make sure that she hadn't been spotted or followed by anyone. The eerie howling in the distance had ceased, and all was quiet, save for the sound of the steady breeze sweeping across the grass and rustling through the trees. Seeing and hearing nothing out of the ordinary, she cast her eyes forward and led Valoria through the wide fissure and onto the hidden trail.

The overhanging shadows created by the steep mountain cliffs to her west and the tall stone wall to her east worked together to shroud the old footpath in a blanket of pitch-black darkness. For a hesitant moment, she began to have second thoughts about what she was getting ready to do. If she couldn't muster up enough courage to travel just outside of the village wall by herself in the dark of night, how would she ever manage to make her way through the vast, shadowy expanse of Iron Woods?

Shaking her head, she thought to herself, *If only I could light the lantern that I brought along with me.*

Unfortunately, she knew that the glow of the lantern would just draw unwanted attention, and she couldn't risk it. Lowering her hand to a sheath hanging down from her belt and grasping the hilt of the long hunting knife she had brought along with her for protection, she whispered, "I sure hope I don't have to use this." She then took a deep breath and found the inner resolve to bury her fear and carry on.

Chapter 21

As she quietly led her horse down the old, beaten path, her eyes began to slowly adjust to the darkness. Eventually, she was able to see just a short distance in front of her, if only in the darkest shades of gray. The fact that she could see anything at all brought a little bit of comfort where, previously, there had been none. Fortunately, the trip to the northern face of the village wall where Old Hunter's Path merged with West Valley Trail was quiet and uneventful. The sound of the brisk breeze blowing down the pathway, the chirping of crickets, and an occasional owl hooting in the distance were the only things to be heard. As she rounded the northwestern corner of the village wall, she immediately left the beaten path behind and led her horse in a northeasterly direction towards the treeline just up ahead while doing her best to avoid the wandering eyes of guardsmen who were surely keeping watch over the road near the front gate.

By the time she reached the first line of tall pine trees towering up into the sky above, the full scope and weight of what she was about to do came crashing down upon her. Sure, she had safely escaped the confines of the village, but that paled in comparison to the real challenge that was now staring her straight in the face. Gazing into the thick forest, all she could see was wall after wall of dark shadow.

Suddenly, her heart began to beat rapidly, and strong feelings of fear and uncertainty threatened to overpower her will to carry on. If it hadn't been for the unrelenting premonition concerning Chance that still weighed heavily upon her heart, she probably would have called off the whole search right then and there. However, after taking a minute to remind herself of why she was standing there in the first place, she dug deep within her soul and summoned the strength and courage needed to push aside her misgivings and take her first few steps forward.

The trees grew close together and towered high above her, blocking out all but the faintest traces of starlight that, somehow, still managed to find its way down to the forest floor. It wasn't much illumination to navigate by, but it was enough to allow Sarina to guide her horse forward in somewhat of a straight line without getting disoriented. She figured that she would cut across a small corner of the forest and make her way onto the main trail, where it began to curve away from the village, thus giving her the freedom to ignite her lantern without drawing any unwanted attention from the night watch. At that point, she could also mount her horse and venture up the trail at a much quicker pace.

As she guided Valoria through the outer hedge, the open-air sounds she had grown accustomed to hearing were gradually muted and replaced by the sounds of trees rustling in the wind and the incessant chatter of nameless insects. Above her, twisted branches could be heard creaking and cracking as various creatures of the dark made their way across tangled limbs. Beneath her, the forest floor was draped in a thick, foreboding haze. Even the air itself seemed different. Though it remained chilly, it was pervaded by a dank, heavy dampness that clung to everything it came into contact with.

The going was rough and slow, and she had to be extremely careful about the amount of noise she was making. She also had to keep a watchful eye out for anything in front of her that might trip her up or bar the way forward. Each step she took led her further and further into what felt like a vast maze of darkness. All around her, the drone and buzz of the forest increased in intensity, and her senses, already on overload, heightened themselves to a state of acute paranoia. Try as she might, she just couldn't shake the uneasy feeling that leering, invisible eyes were watching her every step and stalking her every move. Nonetheless, she continued to cautiously plod onward, tightly gripping the leather-wrapped hilt of her hunting knife with one hand while clenching Valoria's reins with the other.

Another grueling hour or so passed by in this same manner before she finally found the confidence to lower her guard and relax a little bit. Maybe fortune was smiling upon her, and she would make it to the main trail without incident after all, or maybe the dark stories of the dangers lurking in the forest she had heard the locals recount while spending time at The Pumara's Den were nothing more than tall tales created to keep the younger generations in line. She smiled inwardly at the thought of Chance telling a few tall tales of his own.

Suddenly, her arm was yanked back by Valoria, who, coming to a sharp halt, had violently jerked on her reins while snorting and stamping her hoofs down in front of her. Sarina's blood ran cold, and her heart nearly fell out of her chest. Drawing her knife, she swiftly peered down at the ground and then up and all around her.

Within seconds, she spotted a long and slithery shade stalker, a grotesque, poisonous creature that looked like a cross between a viper and a giant centipede. It was hanging down and descending from a tree limb directly in her path. About a third of its thick black body was still draped and coiled around the low hanging branch where it had been resting, tiny legs undulating like the fidgety tentacles of a squid, but the rest of it was already on the forest floor, shimmying, swaying, and crawling in her direction with its snake-like head lifted and poised to strike. Having no time to think, she did the only thing that came to her frightened mind: she pulled on Valoria's reins and bolted as fast as her legs would carry her into the deep of the forest.

Never in her life had she run so fast. Small tree limbs, thorny vines, and prickly bushes whipped back and lashed at her arms and face as she darted away in a terrified panic, nearly tripping twenty times over when her foot would catch upon a stray root or a stretch of tangled undergrowth. Still, she ran and ran until, suddenly, a loud, squishy crunch beneath her foot brought her mad dash to a stumbling halt.

Huffing and puffing, she cautiously reached down a hand to examine what it was she had just stepped on. As her fingers sunk into a thick layer of warm, slimy goop, a wave of nausea washed over her. Her left boot was completely enveloped in the remains of an oversized slime shifter. Turning towards Valoria, she frantically threw her arms around the old mare's neck and buried her sweaty, scratched-up face in its soft flaxen mane, drying the tears that had begun to form and stream down her cheeks.

She stayed in that position for a few minutes, panting heavily, as she tried to calm herself down and regain her wits. Finally, she pulled away and forced herself to straighten up. Removing her backpack, she dug a leather canteen of water from within and took a long, refreshing drink. Then, while staring up at the night sky through an opening in the branches overhead, she noticed that most of the cloud cover had begun to dissipate, and it wasn't quite as dark as it had been. Seeing this caused her to smile, as she knew that she wouldn't have to worry about using the lantern after all.

Chapter 21

A little more time passed before she was ready to resume her journey towards the main path. She wasn't completely sure where she was, but the dim hint of daylight coming from the east gave her an idea of which direction she needed to travel. After putting the leather canteen back in her pack and using an old rag stored in Valoria's saddlebag to wipe the blood and sweat from her face and clean off her boot, she slung her backpack over her shoulders and began trekking through the woods once again.

It only took another ten or fifteen minutes for Sarina to make her way out of the forest and onto the main road. As she and Valoria exited the line of trees growing near the trail's edge, the weighty burden of anxiety and fear that had been her constant companion throughout the night finally began to lessen. It was much brighter outside than it had been when she first entered the forest, and it seemed like the coming dawn was bringing with it fresh energy and renewed hope.

Turning to face the north, she made the decision to continue her search on the main road, figuring it was the likely route that Chance and Devin would have taken to get to the falls. She had been around Chance long enough to know that he wouldn't have used any kind of shortcut to reach their final destination, such as one of the hunting trails that ran near Aydin's place. No, he would want to keep Devin out in the forest for as long as possible, which meant that they would probably travel north across Roaring River to Star Road, a well-used trade route that intersected with Old Hunter's Path on the other side.

From there, the two of them would journey west until they came to a crossroads near the edge of Iron Woods, and then, turning south, they would make their way down River

Basin Way, which would eventually bring them to the wind towers near the falls. Though there was no way to be completely sure that this was the exact route Chance would choose to take, she reasoned that it was still her best shot at finding him. So with her mind made up, she mounted her horse and proceeded to head up the trail.

As Sarina traveled north, the last few remaining stars disappeared, and all around her, the morning sky began to grow brighter and brighter. Soon, the dark indigo hues hanging overhead began to lighten, and the horizon began to glow in shades of azure, lavender, and peach. Though she couldn't see through the trees, she knew that the sun was just peeking over the eastern horizon. It wouldn't be long until the sky morphed into a pale shade of morning blue. As the morning sun continued to rise, so did her hopes of finding Chance. It was at this point that a fresh burst of invigorating energy welled up within her and prompted her to stir Valoria into a quick but steady gallop.

It didn't take her long to come upon a stretch of the path that immediately caught her attention. Running along its western side, she spotted two sets of footprints that sank down deeply into the mud. Quickly remembering that a heavy storm had swept through the day before, she slowed her horse down to a trot and thought, *I wonder if these belong to Chance and Devin?*

Pondering the possibility, she guided Valoria over to a spot near the side of the trail where she could get a closer look. After dismounting, she examined the size, shape, and direction that the footprints were pointing. They definitely appeared to be heading north, and they also seemed fresh, as the distinct imprints left behind by the soles of the boots that made them were still intact; the heavy rain would have quickly diminished markings such as these had they been made prior to the storm.

As it became clear that the prints might have been left behind by Chance and Devin, her heart began to swell with joy. Since she was riding on horseback, she knew that she had to be traveling at least two to three times the speed they were, and it wouldn't be long until she overtook them. With her heart full of hope, she quickly mounted Valoria and proceeded to follow the tracks further north.

It didn't seem like much time had passed when she noticed a column of white smoke rising up on the horizon. Stirring her horse to a full gallop, she sped forward, thinking that maybe Chance and Devin had built a fire at the campsite near the river. However, as she drew closer, a sudden gut feeling prompted her to slow down and pull over to the side of the trail.

Dismounting from her horse, she thought to herself, *Something's not right.* Almost immediately, the light of hope she had previously been holding on to was diminished by an overwhelming sense of dread, the same kind of dread that had accompanied her strange vision from earlier in the morning.

Sighing, she quickly made up her mind to tie Valoria to a tree just a short distance from the trail and sneak up on the campsite. She would use the shadows of the forest as cover so that she could spy in on the camp and get a good idea of what was going on, as opposed to walking straight into what could potentially be a dangerous situation. If there was anything she had learned during her short time on earth, it was that ignoring her gut feelings never ended well.

Gripping Valoria's reins, she guided her past the treeline on the western side of the path and led her over to a tall maple standing behind a dense thicket of bushes about fifteen yards away. She swiftly leashed her to the trunk and whispered, "Hang tight, girl. I promise that I'll be back soon." She then gently stroked the old mare's soft mane and patted her back before turning to make her way towards the campsite.

Once again, she was traveling through the thick of the forest in the same manner as she had earlier that morning, only it wasn't nearly as threatening in the light of day. All the same, she kept her guard up and slowly crept forward, staying focused and using caution with every step. Soon, the smell of something strange cooking over a campfire came drifting in through the woods. There was something very off-putting about it, but Sarina couldn't quite put her finger on what it was. Taking extra precaution to remain unseen, she ducked down low and began to dart from tree to tree, making sure that she stayed well-hidden behind the cover of the tall bushes and dense undergrowth that carpeted the forest floor.

Finally, after a fair amount of effort, she came to a spot where she could see through a gap in the treeline surrounding the campsite. Ever so carefully, she crept and crawled forward until she came upon a shadowy patch behind a boulder that was overgrown with thick vines. Positioning herself behind it, she found that she could comfortably spy in on the camp without being noticed. As she gazed out, she spotted a large covered wagon, two black horses, and three striped tents with a blazing campfire centered in front of them. Without even having to think about it, she immediately knew that the tents were of Darkovian design.

Sitting as still as a statue and as silent as the stone in front of her, she waited for anything to happen that might give her a clue about what was going on. A few uneventful minutes slowly crept by when, all of a sudden, a tall, dark-haired man, wearing a long dark blue cloak and a dazzling pendant necklace, appeared from behind a set of silk drapes that were lazily hanging over the entrance to the tent erected in the center of the camp. Carrying with him a plate, he casually shuffled over to the campfire and used his free hand to rotate a metal skewer that had what looked to be a young shade stalker coiled around its center.

So that's what that awful smell is, Sarina thought as she frowned and scrunched up her nose. In her mind, there were some things that should never be eaten, and shade stalker was one of them.

After removing a small portion and finding it to his liking, the man called out with a loud voice, "Rowanne! Kysa! Breakfast is ready!" He then helped himself to a fat slice and sat down by the fire.

Shortly thereafter, two women came sauntering out from the other tents positioned near the fire, each one carrying a plate. One had fair skin and wavy blonde hair, and she was dressed in an expensive-looking blue gown that shimmered in the sunlight and flowed down around her feet, which were adorned in matching blue slippers. The other woman had brown skin and curly black hair, and she was wearing plain riding clothes that consisted of a pair of light brown trousers, a loose-fitting cream-colored top, a pair of travel-worn boots, and a hooded cloak that was the same shade of brown as her pants. Sarina happened to notice that both of the women were wearing matching jeweled circlets around their foreheads.

Turning towards the woman dressed in riding clothes, the man said, "Kysa, I've decided that I want you to take the letter I wrote earlier and deliver it to Zandria Volkov in

Starview as soon as you are finished eating. I cannot stress it enough that there is very little time to waste as it regards this matter."

Bowing her head, she said, "It will be done according to your desire, my lord." She then turned and helped herself to a fresh cut from the roasted shade stalker before returning to her tent.

Meanwhile, Sarina, now smitten with curiosity, strained her ears to hear anything else that might be said.

As the other woman sauntered over to the skewer, the man turned his attention towards her and asked, "How are the prisoners faring this morning, Rowanne?"

Looking up from the shade stalker, she said, "They seem to be doing well, my lord, although it's hard to say since all three of them are gagged and cannot speak." Her brows furrowed, and a hint of a sadistic smile formed on her lips.

The man nodded approvingly. "Very good." He then looked her up and down salaciously and said, "I want you to know that Zandria will be proud of what we accomplished back in Stone Ridge, and you should consider yourself honored to have played a role in all of it. I'm sure the reward that awaits us for returning her little troublemaker will be lucrative, indeed."

At this, she smiled and bowed her head in humble gratitude. Then, lifting her head back up, she asked, "My lord, I don't mean to speak out of line, but shouldn't we be concerned about the possibility that someone will come to the realization that the men we captured last night have gone missing?"

The man stroked the braid in his long goatee and stared back at her for a moment. "There's no need for you to concern yourself with such things, Rowanne. The storm has passed, and soon we'll be back on the trail that leads to Starview. By the time anyone realizes that they've gone missing, we'll be long gone from this accursed valley." He paused to spit. "The only thing you need to concern yourself with is making sure that they don't escape. I have a feeling they're going to fetch a high price at the market."

Rowanne submissively lowered her head and said, "Yes, my lord." She then helped herself to a slice of shade stalker and returned to her tent.

After she disappeared, the man focused his attention on his plate and began to eat voraciously. Sarina, fully transfixed and thoroughly disgusted by everything she was witnessing, continued to watch on in silence from the shadows.

Finally, laying his plate to the side, the man picked himself up from where he had been sitting and let out a huge yawn while stretching both of his arms towards the sky. As he did so, Sarina caught sight of a bright jewel glistening in the crossguard of a dagger that hung down from his belt in a plain leather sheath.

Peering in closer, she realized that she had seen it somewhere before. *It couldn't be, could it? But it has to be! That small bluish-green crystal and the lever running alongside the hilt are dead giveaways. That's Devin's dagger! The men they captured last night are Chance and Devin!*

Sarina's heart began to pound rapidly as a pulsing wave of panic coursed throughout her body. How was she going to rescue them? What could she possibly hope to do on her own? How could this even be happening, and why were they captured so easily? What was this disgusting man planning to do to them? And did she hear right? Was there a third prisoner? The questions began to race through her mind faster than she could ever hope to answer them.

Nonetheless, one thing was for certain: she needed help, and she needed it fast. As much as she would have liked to believe that she could create a diversion and formulate a daring rescue on her own, she knew better – there was absolutely no way that she could hope to save Chance and Devin by herself. She may have had a few rash moments in her life, but she wasn't stupid.

Though it pained her to do so, she turned away from the campsite and quietly crept back in the direction from which she had come. Her only reasonable course of action was to get back to the village as quickly as possible before any more time ran out.

Chapter 22

Drake Thorne's Message to Zandria Volkov

Sunday, September 26th, 2354

Lady Zandria,

    I am pleased to inform you that your little runaway has been caught and is now in my careful safekeeping. I found her just where you said I would, hiding out in the small trading hub of Stone Ridge. Apparently, a local merchant had been letting her stay in a spare room in the back of his shop in return for her "services." Unfortunately, after we politely informed him of who she was, he grew obstinate and refused to hand her over, demanding that we show him proof of our claim. Left with no other choice, I drew my blade and swiftly gave him all the proof he would ever need.

    After recovering the girl, my small group and I immediately fled the village, knowing that it would only be a matter of time before the unlucky merchant was discovered and someone was commissioned to hunt us down. We had no other viable choice but to escape via Stone Ridge Tunnel. Thankfully, we were able to gain entry into the valley without any trouble, as the young guardsmen working the post didn't even bother to check the contents of our wagon. It would seem that they've grown so accustomed to trading with the merchants of Darkovia that they just assumed our unexpected arrival was little more than business as usual.

    Before leaving, we gifted the young guards with two bottles of an exotic wine laced with wild acidia berry extract. As I'm sure you're already aware, it only takes a small dose of this potent tranquilizer to incapacitate a full-grown man. In heavier doses, it can even be fatal. My hope was that they would drink the wine, thus making our assassin's job much easier.

After traveling down the path a short distance, I covertly dropped Kysa off in a patch of nearby woods so that she could keep a close eye on the guardhouse until an opportune time to strike made itself apparent. Fortune must have been smiling on us because the young men drank the wine and my servant was able to carry out her mission with unusual ease. I am happy to report that the iron gate barring entry into the valley is now firmly closed with no one alive and present to open it back up; you can rest assured that we will not be pursued anytime soon.

Currently, we are camped out near Roaring River, as we were forced to take shelter from a violent storm that quickly swept in and prevented any further travel. Unfortunately, it appears that another round of inclement weather may be forming on the northern horizon. As soon as it passes, we will resume our journey. My hope is to arrive in Starview within a week or so. I am graciously looking forward to our future meeting.

Kanthis be praised!

Drake Thorne

Chapter 23

Rescue Impromptu

By the time Sarina was back in the saddle and riding south, the morning sun was climbing high in the sky and well on its way towards ushering in the noon hour. She raced forth like the wind, hoping and praying that nothing ill would befall Chance and Devin during the span of time it would take her to get back to the village and return with a rescue party. However, after rounding a sharp bend in the trail, she spotted two figures on horseback who were hurriedly traveling in her direction.

Slowing her horse's brisk gallop down to a canter and then to a trot, she strained her eyes to see who they could possibly be and mentally prepared herself for a frantic escape into the woods. For all she knew, they could easily be in league with the Darkovians. But, as they drew closer, her worries and fears quickly gave way to strong feelings of relief and renewed hope. The two riders appeared to be none other than Cyrus Gibbons and Tristam Kolbeck.

Of all the men in the village, none could easily be mistaken for Cyrus. His towering height, his massive build, and the makeshift chain mail he wore were all dead giveaways, even from a distance. Sarina also noticed that he had armed himself with a massive spiked club that hung at his right-hand side and swung back and forth loosely with the rhythmic motion of his galloping horse.

Traveling beside him was Tristam, tall and lanky with long, dark hair flowing behind him in the wind. Wearing traditional leather armor and a dark brown cloak, he also appeared to be outfitted for battle. However, it was the

228

signature x-pattern created by the two thick bandoliers crisscrossing his chest that gave his identity away. One of them would usually feature a mid-length bamboo pole running across his back that worked as both a blowgun and a melee weapon. The other was typically lined with a long row of blow-darts and short throwing knives.

When Sarina realized who the two men were, she immediately began thinking that maybe they could all work together to save Chance and Devin before any more time had passed. Stirring Valoria into a full sprint, she raced ahead to meet them as quickly as possible.

As they approached each other, Cyrus called out with a loud, booming voice, "Sarina! Thank God we've found you!"

Sarina swiftly drew her horse up in front of them and said, "Cyrus! Tristam! I'm so glad you're here!"

Tristam, not appearing the least bit happy, cut in and scolded, "Sarina, what on earth do you think you're doing!? The entire village watch went on high alert after it was discovered that you were missing. Don't you know you could have gotten yourself killed out here?"

Overcome with remorse, Sarina briefly cast her gaze towards the ground in front of her. She then lifted her head and said, "I know, Tristam, and I'm so sorry, but there's really no time to explain. Chance and Devin are in serious trouble."

Cyrus' eyes suddenly widened in alarm. "Trouble? What kind of trouble?"

Sarina's voice took on a worried tone, "I know this may sound unbelievable, but I think they've been captured by a small band of Darkovian slavers who've set up camp near Roaring River."

Both the men seemed to tense up, sitting up a little bit straighter and briefly exchanging concerned glances.

Turning back towards Sarina, Cyrus asked, "Are you sure? How did you discover this?"

"I secretly spied in on their camp and overheard them talking about some prisoners that they had captured last night. At first, I wasn't sure if it was Chance and Devin that they were referring to, but after I spotted Devin's unique dagger hanging from their leader's belt, I just knew it had to be them."

Reaching up to stroke the length of his bristly beard, Cyrus said, "I remember the weapon clearly. Our mysterious visitor was carrying it with him on the day that Tristam and I found him passed out in the middle of the road. If I recall correctly, it had a small bluish-green crystal set in the crossguard and a strange lever that ran the length of its hilt. It didn't look like anything I'd ever seen before." He glanced over at his companion and related an unspoken thought.

Sarina quickly nodded her head. "Yes, that's the dagger I'm talking about! So you have to know that I'm telling the truth, right?!"

Raising his hand, Cyrus calmly responded, "No worries, Sarina. We believe you. However, if this is all true, we need to figure out a way to rescue them, and that means we're going to need to know more about what we're getting ourselves into. What else can you tell us?"

Shifting around to stare at the trail behind her, Sarina tried to recall everything that she had witnessed. Then, after a brief moment, she turned back and replied, "Well, from what I could see, it appeared that there were only three people at the camp, one man and two women. I'm pretty sure that the two women were servants, or maybe even slaves. As of right now,

I'm guessing that only the man and one of his servants are still at the campsite, as I overheard him commanding his other servant to journey to Starview and deliver a letter to a woman named Zandria Volkov. I could be wrong, but his tone of voice seemed to indicate a sense of urgency as it regarded the matter. I would imagine that she traveled north across the river and headed west on Star Road, as that's the most obvious route to Starview from here."

With a disappointed shake of his head, Tristam glanced over at Cyrus and remarked, "This is ridiculous. How on earth did those two ever manage to get captured by one man and a couple of servant girls? There has to be more to this story."

Cyrus glanced back at his friend and calmly nodded his head. "I'm sure you're right, Tristam, but on the bright side, at least we know they're outmatched, which means we can take them in a fight if that's what it comes to."

"Yeah, I suppose that's true, but still…" Tristam curled his upper lip in a scowl and briefly glanced down at the ground. Then, looking back up, he said, "I don't understand why any of this would be happening. Up until this point, even the worst of our Darkovian neighbors would never dare to ply the slave trade in this region. They've always understood that to do so would bring a quick end to any dealings we have with them, business or otherwise. It just doesn't make sense."

Cyrus shook his head with a sigh. "No, it sure doesn't. However, right at the moment, we need to figure out how we're going to rescue Chance and Devin while we still have an opportunity to do so."

With that, the three of them proceeded to exchange ideas in the middle of the trail, which, eventually, led to the formulation of a plan that seemed like it might work. Cyrus and Sarina would enter the campsite while pretending to be travelers who were seeking news of the road ahead. Meanwhile, Tristam would sneak up on the camp through the forest using the same route that Sarina had taken earlier that morning. Then, using his blowgun and a couple of darts laced with a sleep-inducing tranquilizer, he would dispatch the leader and the servant girl from a distance as soon as the right moment presented itself. At that point, they would rescue the prisoners and make a quick getaway. If for some reason things took a turn for the worse, Tristam agreed that he would secretly slip away and return to the village to round up more help. As soon as all of the details were worked out, they pointed their horses north and made for the Roaring River campsite.

The sun was hanging in the middle of the sky and shining brightly by the time they reached the spot where Sarina had entered the forest earlier that morning. However, in stark contrast, it appeared that a thick wall of dark clouds was beginning to form in the distant north, threatening to bring a swift end to the mild weather they were currently experiencing. Tristam guided his chestnut spiral-horn past the treeline and tied it to a sturdy maple growing behind a dense thicket of bushes. As soon as he was finished, Sarina and Cyrus bid him farewell and casually trotted their horses up the trail towards the campsite. He then proceeded to follow along using the alternate path Sarina had laid out for him.

When they arrived at the site, everything looked exactly as it had during Sarina's previous visit, with one exception, the shade stalker roasting on the metal skewer had been replaced by a young rabbit. Sitting cross-legged next to the fire, the dark-haired man with the pendant necklace gazed intently into the flames, seemingly lost in deep thought.

As Cyrus and Sarina dismounted from their horses and began to walk in his direction, he suddenly jerked his head up, a look of puzzlement sweeping across his features. Quickly rising to his feet, he called out, "Rowanne, we have guests!"

Almost immediately, Rowanne appeared at the entrance of her tent. She briefly glanced over her shoulder at something behind her before turning to make her way towards the fire to stand beside her master.

Meanwhile, Tristam quietly crept up behind the vine-covered boulder Sarina had described to him while keeping a watchful eye on everything that was taking place. Ever so carefully, he removed his blowgun from the strap on his back and loaded it with a fresh sleeping dart. Crouching down low, he made himself ready to attack.

As Cyrus and Sarina drew nearer, the man bowed down with a sweeping gesture of his outstretched hand and said, "Welcome to my humble camp, travelers. I am Drake Thorne, a merchant of Darkovia. How may I be of service to you on this glorious day?" He then gazed up at the newcomers, a toothy grin spread across his cheeks.

Cyrus straightened up his posture, took the lead, and marched forward with his head held high. "Pleased to meet you, Drake. I'm Cyrus, and this is Sarina." He gestured towards her with a short wave of his hand. "We're on our way to Stone Ridge. We had planned on stopping at this very spot for a short rest when we noticed that it was already occupied. I hope you don't mind the intrusion. We were just hoping we could give our horses a break from the road before continuing our journey north?"

Still smiling, Drake replied, "It's no intrusion at all. We're always happy to have guests." At this, he turned towards Rowanne, who smiled and nodded her head. "Please feel free to tie your horses up and warm yourselves beside the fire."

Cyrus, doing his best to feign politeness, returned the smile and said, "Thank you, Drake. That's really kind of you." He then directed Sarina to guide the horses over to a hitching post that was staked into the ground near the covered wagon.

As Sarina led the horses away, Cyrus plopped himself down by the fire. After getting comfortably seated, he turned towards Drake and asked, "So what brings you to this neck of the woods, Drake? We don't often get many visitors in these parts this time of year."

Drake shifted his attention to Rowanne and bade her to return to her tent. As she turned to leave, he sat down in front of the rabbit roasting on the skewer. An awkward moment of silence passed while he quietly devised a convenient story. He then abruptly looked away from the fire and replied to Cyrus' inquiry, "I apologize. I did not mean to ignore you. Rowanne and I are on our way to deliver some of the finest wine in all of Darkovia to a tavern in the village of Iron Cove, The Pumara's Den. Maybe you've heard of it?"

"Ah, I see," Cyrus replied, trying to appear genuinely interested. "I've spent a fair amount of time in The Pumara's Den. It's a fine establishment."

"Oh, splendid!" Drake exclaimed. "Perhaps I could convince you and your companion to stay awhile and sample a bottle from the shipment? Being a merchant of fine wines and artisan liqueurs, I would love to hear your personal feedback as it regards my latest offering."

Cyrus smiled politely and raised his hand to decline. "As much as we hate to turn down such a tempting invitation, my companion and I still have a lot of trail to travel if we hope to reach Stone Ridge Tunnel before nightfall. Unfortunately, I'm afraid our stay here will have to be a short one."

"I see... Well, that is very unfortunate, but I do understand. There is little time for life's simpler pleasures when a man has more pressing matters to attend to." At this, Drake clasped both of his hands together and rested his chin on them. A moment later, he lifted his head and pointed at the skewer. "As you can see, we have a fresh young rabbit that is nearly roasted to perfection. Would you care to stay and eat before you leave?"

Once again, Cyrus politely declined. "Again, I do appreciate your kind offer, but as soon as our horses are rested, we'll be back out on the trail. We would hate to eat and run."

At that moment, Sarina approached the fire. Glancing at Cyrus, she said, "Well, the horses are resting and should be ready to mount again soon." She then turned and smiled at Drake courteously. "Thank you so much for allowing our horses a bit of respite. They don't often journey this far into the forest, and I'm sure the break will do them both a lot of good."

Drake nodded with a grin while Sarina sat down next to Cyrus. He then lifted himself from the ground and began to rotate the metal skewer. As he did so, Sarina and Cyrus both took notice of the glistening bluish-green jewel centered in the crossguard of the dagger he was wearing. The strange vertical lever on the side of the black leather bound hilt was also visible. There could be no doubt – it was most definitely Devin's.

Behind the large boulder, Tristam sat perfectly still, like a hungry cat carefully stalking its prey. He wasn't quite feeling like it was time to strike, but he knew that the moment would come soon enough. Slowly lifting the bamboo pole to his lips, he skillfully targeted an exposed patch of skin on the left side of Drake's neck and waited. It would be any minute now.

All of a sudden, Drake looked away from the rabbit and cocked his head as if he had just stumbled upon the hidden solution to a complex problem he had been struggling to work out in the back of his mind. With a loud voice, he called out, "Rowanne, our guests will not be staying for very much longer! They have decided to travel *north*! Would you be so kind as to bring out a fresh bottle of our finest wine to send along with them as a parting gift?"

It seemed to both Cyrus and Sarina that Drake put an unnecessarily strong inflection on the word *north*. This was no accident, nor was it a trick of their imagination. Upon hearing it, they both turned to glance at each other with suspicion.

At that moment, Rowanne jumped out from behind the drapes of her tent with a crossbow, cocked, loaded, and aimed directly at Cyrus' head. Simultaneously, another man appeared within the entrance to the tent opposite of hers. He also had a loaded crossbow, and it was pointed directly at Sarina.

Reveling in what appeared to be another easy capture, Drake leered at his "guests" with a nasty smirk upon his face and mocked, "Well, I guess it looks like you'll be staying for a while after all." He then turned towards the stranger with an outstretched hand and said, "Perhaps you've met my associate Raul? From what I've heard, he's spent quite a bit of time in your humble village. He claims it's a really nice place."

At this, Raul, wearing a cruel smile beneath his thick, curlicue mustache, stepped out from the tent and began to slowly creep in closer to Sarina. Rowanne, following his example, began to step forward as well. The companions both threw their hands up as they trembled in shock and fear. Cyrus cautiously glanced over at Sarina from out of the corner of his eye and noticed that the sea-green streaks around her pupils were glowing with a fierce luminescence.

Tristam was now completely at a loss for what to do. Nervously sweating and trying his hardest to control the tempo of his accelerating heart rate, his mind raced forward in search of the next best possible move. He hadn't counted on dealing with three armed Darkovians, and he definitely didn't foresee his friends being thrown into such a precarious situation. Nonetheless, he never took his eyes off of the merchants. He wasn't about to give up hope – not yet.

Glaring down at Cyrus and Sarina from beneath furrowed brows, Drake mocked, "I really wish we could have taken a little time to get to know each other better and, maybe, shared a bottle of wine – you know, before it came to this. I can assure you that it would have been a much better experience." He then swung around and strode inside his tent while Rowanne and Raul kept their crossbows carefully trained on their targets.

A moment later, Drake returned carrying a load of heavy chains, padlocks, and filthy rags. With a loud voice, he commanded, "On your faces, scum! Hands and feet together! Make one wrong move, and it's over!"

Having no other choice, they gritted their teeth and obeyed.

Chapter 23

Cyrus' thoughts raced forward in a panic, *Where's Tristam? What's he thinking? This was definitely not part of the plan!*

After Cyrus and Sarina laid down and clasped their hands and feet together, Drake stood over them and bound their ankles and wrists with the iron chains. As soon as he was finished, he forced filthy rags into each of their mouths and violently tightened and tied them around the backs of their heads, causing both of them to choke and gag. He then commanded them to crawl towards Rowanne, who stood waiting to force them into her tent with the tip of her crossbow.

While all of this was taking place, Tristam sat quietly in the shadows of his hiding spot, patiently watching the merchants with the eyes of a hawk. He hadn't given up hope yet, and he hadn't abandoned the plan. He just knew that he had to wait until the absolute perfect moment if his next move was going to succeed. Lowering his blowgun, he loosened a short throwing knife from his bandolier, making it easier to access in a moment's notice. He then slowly raised the loaded blowgun to his lips and, once again, set his sights on the merchants.

As soon as Cyrus and Sarina disappeared into the dark confines of the tent, Raul lowered his crossbow and walked over to take a seat by the fire. Drake continued to stand and gaze at the tent for a moment longer before turning to join his companion. The two then sat silently as they waited for Rowanne to wrap things up.

Finally, she appeared at the entrance wearing a proud smile. Turning towards Drake, she bowed her head and said, "The prisoners are fully secured, my lord."

Chapter 23

Upon hearing this, both men glanced up at her and grinned.

Motioning towards the skewer, Drake said, "Rowanne, it appears that the rabbit is ready to be served. Please bring out some plates and a fresh bottle of wine. I believe this calls for a celebration." He turned and flashed a wide grin at Raul, who smiled back and nodded his head in agreement.

Bowing her head submissively, she said, "As you wish," before swinging around to fetch the plates, mugs, and a fresh bottle of Darkovia's finest.

It was at this point that Tristam knew his time had come. He had to act quickly if he was to have any chance at success. As soon as Rowanne reappeared at the entrance of her tent carrying the dishes, he took a deep breath and raised the blowgun up to his lips. He then set his sights on Raul's neck and prepared to strike.

One, two, three.

The projectile flew with the speed of a bullet and hit its mark with the accuracy of a laser-guided missile. Raul's eyes widened with shock as he grasped at the stinging sensation in his neck and felt the soft feathery shaft of Tristam's dart; only it was too late; the tip of the needle had buried itself deeply and the tranquilizer was already at work. Within a few short seconds, his entire body was stricken with paralysis. As his crossbow slipped from his numb hands, he toppled over like a limp sack of potatoes.

Upon seeing this, Drake sprung up from where he was sitting and started to run, but he wasn't fast enough. He only made it a few steps before an excruciating pain prompted him to look down. He was instantly overcome with debilitating horror – the leather-strapped hilt of a throwing knife was protruding from the center of his gut. Falling to his knees, he gasped for air as he helplessly clutched at the buried blade. Beside him, the sounds of dishes shattering on the ground resonated loudly within his pulsing ears. Shifting his eyes, he watched as Rowanne fled to take cover somewhere behind the tent. Unfortunately, that was the last thing he would ever see.

Meanwhile, Tristam was already in the process of loading a second sleeping dart into the barrel of his blowgun. Bolting from his hiding spot, he made a beeline towards Rowanne, who was frantically fleeing towards the back of the covered wagon. Realizing he had little time to act, he came to an abrupt stop and lifted the bamboo pole to his lips. A quick second later, the dart found its mark, hitting her squarely in the back. Within a few blinks, she was lying face-first on the ground with one arm stretched out in front of her and the other reaching behind.

Lowering the weapon from his mouth, he let out a quiet sigh and took a minute to catch his breath. All was silent. After observing his surroundings and coming to the conclusion that there weren't any more surprises waiting to pop out of the shadows, he made his way to the tent where his friends were being held captive. As he pulled back the silken drapes, a sharp beam of sunlight burst through the entrance and landed on the group of prisoners, who were all gagged, bound, and sitting next to each other in a big circle. After tying back the drapes, he proceeded to remove the gags from each member of the group, one by one, starting with his best friend.

Cyrus began to sputter and spit as the filthy rag came loose and fell from his mouth. Shaking his head in relief, he said, "I owe you one."

Tristam chuckled lightly. "Don't mention it!"

Next, he untied Sarina's rag and then quickly moved on to do the same for Chance and Devin. Finally, he came to a young woman with long, tangled light-brown hair and strange hazel-brown eyes that were outlined in rings of bright yellow. As he removed the filthy rag from her mouth, she gasped as if it were the first full breath of fresh air she had taken in days. Having grown too weak from thirst and hunger to even speak, it was all she could do to force a faint smile. She then closed her curious eyes and slumped her head down on her chest in sheer exhaustion.

About a half hour passed before everyone was completely free of their bonds. Things might have gone a bit smoother and a lot quicker had all the keys needed to finish the task been located in one place. However, Drake had used three different sets of keys to lock his prisoners up, and all of them were located in different areas of the camp. The first set required to free Sarina and Cyrus was stuffed in an inner pocket in Drake's cloak; the second set needed to loose Chance and Devin was lying on a crate in the back of the merchant's tent; and the third set that had been used to secure the young woman was hanging from a hook inside the covered wagon. After Tristam loosened the last set of chains from around the young woman's ankles, he helped her up to her feet and then half-carried her over to a spot near the fire.

In the meantime, just a few yards away, Chance and Sarina were reveling in a happy reunion, holding each other close as they gazed into each other's eyes. Chance had clearly been humbled by the whole experience of being captured and spent the first fifteen minutes of his newfound freedom throwing every line he could think of at Sarina in an attempt to let her know how glad he was to see her and how much she meant to him. Of course, she didn't need to hear any of his soppy apologies; all that mattered to her was that her one true love was alive, safe, and able to be with her in that moment.

On the other side of the campfire, Devin was sitting alone in a silent stupor. Shortly after the gag had been removed from his mouth, he made sure to go out of his way to let Tristam, Cyrus, and Sarina know how thankful he was that they had come to his rescue. However, deep down inside, he felt like a total failure. He just couldn't get over the fact that he had royally screwed everything up – again. Not only had he failed himself, but he had also failed his only real friend in the new world.

How could he have let himself get so carried away? How hard would it have been to remember the signal? What possessed him to believe, for even half a second, that he was some kind of suave lady's man? Was he really so naive that he couldn't see that he was being played for an ignorant fool by the merchant and his slave girls the entire time? His careless stupidity nearly got himself and Chance killed. Right then and there, he silently vowed that it would never happen again, and he was going to do whatever it took to make sure of it. As he stared into the flames, he pondered how to move forward. Unfortunately, there were no easy answers.

Right after Tristam laid the young woman down next to the campfire, Cyrus strolled over to see if there was anything that he could do to help. It was clear that she was in need of food, water, and medical attention, but the unfortunate truth was that all of those things were in short supply. With this in mind, he decided to give her what little food and water he had brought along with him for the journey, as the rabbit roasting on the skewer had long been burnt to a blackened crisp.

A short while later, Chance and Devin began searching the campsite for their original clothes and their other belongings, eventually finding that all of it had been piled in a messy heap in the back of Drake's tent. Fortunately, everything was still intact, and nothing important seemed to be missing.

Devin also made it a point to retrieve his dagger from Drake's corpse. As he examined the featureless leather sheath it was stored in, he cracked a smile and thought, *It isn't fancy, but it's a lot better than nothing*.

Meanwhile, Tristam and Cyrus used the locks and chains that had bound the prisoners to secure both Rowanne and Raul and carried each of them to the back of the covered wagon, where another set of chains was used to tie them up. After ensuring that there was no possible way for the prisoners to escape should they awaken during the trip home, the men proceeded to lay Drake's lifeless body right beside them.

Soon afterwards, everyone pitched in to help tear down the campsite, being sure to store anything of value alongside the prisoners in the back of the covered wagon. When they arrived back in Iron Cove, the two prisoners would be tried and sentenced, and Drake would be given a proper burial. Even though his actions had been evil, he was still a human being, and there wasn't any good reason to leave him lying on the ground like a dead animal for the neck biters and carrion birds to feast upon.

Just as everyone was preparing to get back on the trail, the mysterious young woman, who was now sitting in the front seat of the covered wagon next to Tristam, suddenly spoke up, "Wait! I need my pendant. I can't leave without it!"

Startled, Tristam turned towards her and asked, "What pendant? Where is it?"

"It's hanging around Drake's neck. I'm so sorry... Please... We can't leave without it."

Tristam laid the reins down, climbed to the ground, and jogged to the back of the wagon. Carefully lifting Drake's head, he unclasped the necklace and placed it in a pocket within his cloak. He then shouted back at the woman, "I found it!"

After settling back in the driver's seat, he snapped the reins and stirred the horses to a trot. Following the others, he steered the wagon away from the campsite and began traveling towards the spot where his own horse was still tied up and waiting for him. It wouldn't be long until they were all safely back in Iron Cove, where things still made sense and life could return to normal.

Chapter 24

Devin's Logbook

Entry 5:

    I have absolutely no idea how I'm still awake and functioning right now. From head to toe, I'm scraped, cut, battered, and bruised. My eyes feel like they're on fire, and my head is pounding from a severe lack of sleep and a massive hangover. I honestly can't think of a single time in my life in which I remember being this sore. It literally feels like my entire body is on the verge of giving up and shutting down.

    Maybe what I'm saying is a bit on the dramatic side, but that doesn't change the fact that I feel like I've been hit and run over by an out-of-control hoverbus. I know that if I could just get some rest, I'd probably feel somewhat better, but after coming within an inch of my life during a freak thunderstorm and narrowly avoiding being sold off as a slave the very next day, my mind won't seem to shut off long enough for me to fall asleep. So here I am, sitting alone in Leo's living room, writing by the dim light of the fireplace. I guess I'm hoping that it will help me to make sense of these scattered thoughts.

    It's kind of crazy to think that it's been almost a week since I last recorded anything in here. So much has taken place since I first stepped out of the survival-chamber and into this strange, post-apocalyptic version of reality, so much that I'm still trying to make sense of. It just feels like I've been on a nonstop roller coaster ride, and I haven't been able to find a moment's rest to clear my head, let alone write about anything I've been going through or how I actually feel about all of it.

Chapter 24

I mean, for starters, who are these people I've suddenly found myself surrounded by? I obviously realize that they're the descendants of those who survived the Great Firefall, but who are they, really? When it comes right down to it, I know next to nothing about any of them.

To begin with, there's Chance. From the first time I met him, he's been nothing but good to me. However, I still don't really know his story, like who his family is or what his past was like. Don't get me wrong, I couldn't be more grateful that he's been taking the time to show me how to survive out in the wild lands, but it just doesn't make any sense as to why he would. In the world I came from, people didn't trust each other so easily, and I was no exception to the rule. Yet here I am, putting my trust in a complete stranger who is seemingly doing the same for me. That's not to say that I don't know the reason why. It's simply because I don't have any other choice. I mean, my very survival depends on it. But why is he?

Then there's Sarina. I wish I could say more about her, but I really can't. She's been nothing but distant with me the entire time I've known her. And, now, after all of the trouble that Chance and I got into over the past couple of days, I can't really see how things are going to improve between us, at least not anytime soon. After all, every last thing she said about me at The Pumara's Den came true. She predicted that Chance would be putting himself in great danger if he associated with me, and that's exactly what happened. As much as I hate to admit this, if I were in her shoes, I don't think I'd trust me either.

Finally, there's everyone else: Aydin, Cyrus, Tristam, and even Leo. I haven't had the chance to get to know any of them like I should, so there's not a whole lot I can actually say, except that, on the surface, they all seem like really good people, the kind of people who would go above and beyond for those they truly care about. Nonetheless, I'm not too sure that their kindhearted natures are going to be enough to look past the horrible first impression I left them with. Truth be told, I'll be shocked if they ever take me seriously again.

But I guess none of that actually matters right now, as I'm getting away from the real reason I felt the urge to pull out this logbook and write in the first place, which has to do with the fact that I'm terrified of what the future may hold. I mean, after the events of this past week, the path forward seems more uncertain than ever. At this point, I can only guess as to what horrible atrocity may be lying in wait for me when I get around to leaving the safety of the village behind to search for the crystalline orbs. Every time I allow my mind to go there, I freeze up with anxiety.

Somehow, in some way, I need to figure out a way to get past these negative feelings; otherwise, this quest I'm supposed to be on is doomed for certain failure. Oddly enough, I've found that writing seems to help. It seems to give me a sense of calm and clarity that I didn't have before, even if all I can write about is the thoughts I'm having and, maybe, what I did throughout the day.

Unfortunately, it looks as though the fire is starting to die out, and it's getting harder and harder to see the words I've written on this page. It's also starting to get kind of chilly. I feel like there's so much more that I need to get off my chest, but my eyes are getting heavy and my thoughts are becoming a jumbled mess. I guess now would be a good time to wrap up and add a few more logs to the fire before I head off to bed.

Chapter 24

But, seriously, what on earth have I gotten myself into? How am I supposed to move forward after all of this? And, above all, why didn't I just do what I was told and throw that stupid energy drink in the recycling bin?!

Chapter 25

All Work and No Play

Huffing and puffing, Devin wiped the dirty sweat from his brow and carelessly tossed his ax to the ground. With a look of exasperation, he turned to face Chance and said, "This is the absolute worst."

Chance merely shook his head and sighed. Then, heaving back, he lifted his ax into the air and swiftly brought it down on a freshly cut log, splitting it into two perfect halves.

"I mean, how much longer is this going to last?" Devin groaned as he plopped himself down on top of an old tree stump. "First, we were forced to patch the holes in Leo's roof in the middle of a rainstorm. Next, we were put to work cleaning out the stables at Sarina's house. And, now, this." Doubling over, he used an arm to twist his head and stretch out a crick in his neck. "Not to mention that my back aches, my arms feel like they're about to fall off, and I have a splitting headache that won't seem to stop."

At this, Chance finally spoke up, "You sure do complain a lot." He scooped up the two halves and stacked them on a nearby pile. "You do realize that if you'd just stop griping and get back to work, we'd be done a whole lot sooner."

Rolling his eyes, Devin proceeded to yawn while stretching out both of his arms as wide as he could. Dropping them back down, he glanced up at Chance and flatly stated, "I'm done, Chance. I'm not splitting another single stinking, rotten log. We've spent the last three days out here, breaking our backs in this cold, wet forest from morning 'til night, and we've probably chopped enough firewood to keep half the village warm for the next month."

Chance shook his head. "I hate to tell you this, but this wood isn't going to last nearly as long as you seem to think it will."

"Regardless, don't you think this is a bit unfair?" Devin pleaded. "I mean, if you want my opinion, I'd say we've been punished long enough. At this point, it just feels like we're being taken advantage of."

Chance lifted his ax into the air and brought it down on a nearby tree stump, deeply burying its head in the flat, smooth surface. He then unscrewed the cap from the canteen hanging by his side and took a large swig. After wiping his mouth, he turned and said, "Maybe you're right, but that isn't to say that we haven't done anything to deserve it. We made some really stupid decisions, Devin, and other people ended up risking their lives to save us." Gazing up towards the treetops, he stretched out his arms and twisted and turned to release the tension in his back. "The truth of the matter is that we're probably never gonna hear the end of it – ever."

Devin slumped his shoulders and sighed. "Yeah, I suppose you're right." He waited for a few seconds and then, picking himself up from the stump, proceeded to press his case even further. "All the same, I feel like we're wasting a lot of time by doing this when we could be out hunting down the crystalline orbs. I'm not trying to make an excuse to get out of work, but the fate of the entire world, literally, depends on it."

Dropping his serious expression, Chance lightly chuckled. "Of all the excuses I've ever heard for getting out of a hard day's work, that one, by far, tops the list!" He shook his head and began to laugh heartily.

Devin grinned and quickly shot back, "It's not an excuse! It's the truth!" and began to laugh as well.

After their laughter subsided, Chance spoke up, "All joking aside, I think you're right. This is absolutely ridiculous, and I don't understand what Leo – or Aydin, for that matter – could possibly be thinking right now."

"Exactly! Surely they have to know that we can't keep putting things off. Sooner or later, someone is going to start looking for the orbs if they haven't already – my father said as much in his last message. Personally, I think we need to take a stand for ourselves and talk to them about it."

Chance nodded. "Okay, I agree. But, first, we have to finish what we started." He strolled towards the log pile and motioned for Devin to follow. "As soon as we finish stacking all of this firewood on the back of the wagon, we'll wrap things up and get out of here."

With an audible sigh, Devin rolled his eyes and reluctantly got back to work.

Chapter 26

Dear Diary,

I'm not even sure who I am anymore. I once saw myself as a caring, compassionate, and confident young woman who knew what she wanted out of life and just how to get it. However, after everything that took place tonight, all I feel is lost, confused, bitter, and sad. I've even found myself doubting my love for Chance, something that I never would have believed possible. It's so hard to find the right words to describe what I'm going through. All I can really say is that I've never felt this scared or vulnerable in my entire life.

Even though I know it's not right, I find myself wanting to blame everything on Devin. He acts as if he's Chance's new best friend, but he's really his worst enemy. If he was any kind of friend at all, he wouldn't be so quick to drag Chance into danger. He'd take a minute to think about the consequences of his actions and how this "mission" he's on might affect other people.

Apparently, earlier today, Devin managed to convince Chance to drop work so that they could start making preparations to leave the village behind and search for the crystalline orbs. When the two of them showed up together at my grandpa's house to boldly inform him of their latest plans, they hadn't counted on me being there. Upon hearing what they had to say, I about fainted from shock. I truly thought things were going to get better. I honestly believed that, after last weekend's incident, Chance was going to grow some sense and walk away from anything that had to do with Devin or the floating tower, but I couldn't have been more wrong.

I became so agitated that I lashed out at Chance and told him that running off with Devin into trouble and God only knows what else was one of the stupidest ideas I'd ever heard him come up with. At first, he was silent, and then he furrowed his brows with a look of disgust that he sometimes gets when I say or do something he doesn't agree with. I almost immediately regretted saying anything – not because I wasn't right – but rather because I knew there was going to be a fight.

First, he raised his voice and accused me of being jealous of Devin. Next, he told me that I didn't understand the value of friendship or how important it was for Devin to learn how to survive out in the wild lands. As if his words didn't already sting enough, he had the audacity to "remind" me that I wasn't the only person in his life. And, according to him, I just needed to learn how to deal with it.

When he was finished, his breathing slowed down, and he began to stare off at a wall behind me, just like he always does when he knows that he's said or done something wrong. Finally, he found the courage to look me in the eyes. I could instantly tell that he was overcome with guilt. When he saw the tears streaming down my cheeks, he frantically began to apologize.

The hurt and betrayal I felt is hard to put into words. Nonetheless, I just didn't have the heart or the will to keep on fighting. All I could do was remind him that I love him and tell him that I didn't want anything bad to happen to him. Still, my words weren't enough to change his mind – he insisted that he was going to leave anyway. After everything that I went through for him, after I, literally, put my life on the line to save his, he goes and does this! For the life of me, I just can't understand why?!

It was at this point that our argument was interrupted by a loud knocking on the front door. Grandpa glanced at both of us in frustration before shuffling away to answer it. It was Cyrus and Tristam. They had just arrived back in the village after traveling out to Stone Ridge Tunnel to investigate. Unfortunately, they returned with terrible news. It appeared that all of the watchmen stationed at the guardhouse had been brutally murdered, including Kalob Spear!

In that moment, I was speechless. I couldn't believe what I was hearing. How was that even possible? Why was any of this happening? What did Kalob or any of the other guards ever do to deserve such a fate? It just wasn't fair! The news hit me like an avalanche; the fact that I'd never see Kalob's smiling face again or have my day interrupted by one of his ridiculous attempts to catch my attention was more than my breaking heart could handle.

I suddenly found that I just wanted to scream or hit something, but instead, I burst into tears. Nothing my grandpa could say or do was going to help. Chance tried his best to console me but only ended up making things worse. As all of this was happening, I noticed that Devin was cowering down in his chair next to the fireplace, looking even more pathetic than usual.

Just when I was sure that things were about as bad as they could ever be, another knock was heard at the front door. This time it was Aydin and, standing next to him, a girl who appeared to be about my age. Dressed in a wine-colored gown and a pewter-gray, hooded cloak, she had long, straight light-brown hair that draped down loosely over her shoulders. Her skin was lightly tanned, and her eyes were a striking shade of hazel-brown. At first, I had no idea who she was, however, after taking a second look at her eyes, I realized that her irises were outlined in rings of bright yellow. All at once, it hit me – she was the mysterious girl that we had rescued along with Chance and Devin! She just looked so much different than when I first saw her.

As they stepped inside, I could see that Aydin had a troubled look upon his face; something wasn't right. Grandpa asked me to put a kettle of tea on the stove and invited the two of them to sit down at the table. I reluctantly got up from my seat and made my way into the kitchen.

While I prepared the tea, Aydin introduced the girl to everyone in the room. Her name was Alexis Volkov. Apparently, she was the daughter of a wealthy and powerful woman residing in Starview named Zandria Volkov. Hearing that name instantly rang a bell – it was the same name that I overheard the Darkovian slaver mention when he sent his servant girl away on a delivery.

After Alexis had been introduced, Aydin asked her to recount her story in her own words. I dropped what I was doing and listened intently. Apparently, she was the heiress to her mother's growing business empire, and as such, it was expected that she would soon start taking on more responsibility by helping out with the day-to-day operations. However, unbeknownst to her mother, she had long ago decided that she wanted nothing to do with the family business, as most of their wealth had been acquired through the slave trade, a practice she was vehemently opposed to.

Long story short, she had run away from home just a month prior by utilizing the help of a family friend named

Oren Mendel, a well-respected local historian who had been hired as her personal tutor when she was still just a small child. Secretly sharing her views on slavery, he empathized with her plight. So when she revealed to him her intention to run away, he agreed that he would help in any way that he could. Unfortunately, it was beginning to appear that he might have been caught after aiding her escape, as he was supposed to make contact with her soon after she reached Stone Ridge but never did. If what she feared turned out to be true, it would most likely mean that he had been imprisoned in her mother's private dungeon.

As soon as her story was finished, Aydin stepped in and informed all of us that Oren Mendel happened to be a longtime associate of his and was one of his closest friends. He then revealed that he had attempted to contact him almost a week and a half ago but still hadn't received any kind of response, which had left him with a growing sense of unease. In his opinion, Alexis' story seemed to explain the long delay in communication perfectly.

At this point, I was nothing short of dumbstruck and baffled. It literally felt like the entire world was conspiring against me. Within less than an hour, everyone in the room had come to the conclusion that Oren needed to be rescued, and all of the men, with the exception of my grandpa, agreed that they would accompany Aydin and Alexis on an expedition to Starview, their plan being to leave first thing in the morning.

That brings me to now. I'm sitting here alone in my bedroom, a confused and gloomy mess. No one knows it yet, but I've decided that I'm going with them. Regardless of whether they agree to have me along or not, there's no way under the sun that I'm letting Chance get away from me ever again. Still, I can't help but wonder why our love isn't enough to keep him in the village? Why am I not enough? Why doesn't my opinion or my feelings matter to the one person I want to give the rest of my life to? Deep down inside, I know that Chance hasn't found his definition of love, but I've found mine, and that's why I'm with him. Am I broken?

Chapter 27

Devin's Logbook

Entry 6:

I had the worst dream last night. I was back in Highland City, and I was playing a bizarre video game in which I had to race a miniature version of myself across a stone platform that was speckled about with hidden traps and pitfalls. On the surface, it seemed like it should have been a simple game, like something the kids might have played in the early 2000s, yet it was anything but that. No matter how hard I tried to get across the platform, the end result was always the same: I would end up falling down a hidden pitfall, or I would find myself cornered in a spot that I couldn't escape from. Every time my character would die, I heard Colonel Gundersen's terrified voice rise up in the background and condemn me, "My god, boy! What have you done?!"

I continued to play the game without much success, my level of frustration increasing with each new attempt, until, finally, I couldn't take it anymore. In a mad fit, I yanked the Holo-Vision headset from off my face and launched it across my apartment. I watched as it sailed through the air in slow motion and slammed into my front door in a surreal yet violent explosion. As the smoke cleared away and the dust began to settle, I could see that the door had been blown to pieces.

I immediately jumped up and ran through the singed hole that was left behind and, to my surprise, found that I was in the middle of Erick's living room. It seemed like everyone I knew had gathered around me in a big circle – my classmates, my coworkers, and even my parents. As I began to peer around the circle, the crowd vanished into thin air, leaving only Erick,

Chapter 27

Penny, Rita, and Mateo. They were each glaring at me with looks of contempt, anger, and sadness. When my eyes met Penny's, she turned away from me and paced over to the living room window. After pulling back the curtains, she began to stare off into the hazy orange and gray light that filtered through the foggy window panels. I stood motionless, watching her, when, suddenly, she spun around, looked me dead in the eyes, and asked, "Why?" Tears were streaming down her cheeks.

Feeling my heart break into a million pieces, I bolted across the room to comfort her. However, when I arrived at the window, she disappeared along with the house and everyone else. I quickly swung around to see that I was now standing in the middle of a ruinous city. Fires were raging everywhere, and a dark, choking smoke clouded my vision. All of a sudden, I had trouble breathing. Feeling helpless and completely bewildered, I began to twist and turn in a frightened panic, and then, in an instant, my eyes shot open and I woke up. My pillow was drenched with the sweat that was still dripping from my forehead and streaming down the sides of my cheeks.

That was about twenty minutes ago. I'm now sitting here, writing by the dim light of a candle, and I'm a complete mess. I just can't seem to get Penny's tortured expression out of my mind. She looked so heartbroken and horrified. Every time I picture it, I'm overwhelmed with anxiety and grief. I honestly don't know how I'm going to get past this – I'm alive, and everyone I ever knew or cared about isn't. In my heart of hearts, I know that I don't deserve to be here, and the guilt I feel is tearing me apart. I just wish there was some way I could go back and fix things – a second chance, a redo. But there isn't, and the sad fact is there never will be.

Though I could sit here and ponder the details of my dream all morning long, I think its meaning is more than obvious. Right now, I need to stop writing and finish packing my things. Leo will be getting up soon, and Chance is supposed to meet me here at sunrise. Last night, he stayed at the cottage well after everyone else had gone home. After Leo went to bed, we spent some time poring over the map that my father gave me, trying to figure out how we should go about retrieving the crystalline orbs. As it turns out, the first orb is in a cavern that appears to be just a short journey west of River Basin Way, one of the trails that Aydin plans on using to take us to Starview. The second orb is hidden in the same general region as Starview, and the third is located in a mountainous area east of Highland City.

I figure we can let Aydin know about the first location after we're out on the trail. I could be wrong, but I'm fairly certain that he won't mind taking a short detour to grab the orb. My only real concern is how I'm going to explain what we're doing to the others, namely Alexis, Tristam, and Cyrus. They still don't know the truth about who I am or why I'm here, and there's no telling how they'll handle it. If they're anything like Sarina was when she found out, things could be problematic. But what else can I do? It's not like I have any other choice.

Entry 7:

I've decided that now is a good time to write again, as no one outside of Aydin and Chance has bothered to say more than a few words to me all morning long. I'm going to assume it has something to do with the trouble that Chance and I got into last week. I mean, what else could it be? Nothing else makes much sense. It's obvious that they don't trust me.

I really wish Leo could have come along with us. Though I realize that his bad leg makes extended travel too difficult for him, there's no denying that his presence on this journey would have made a big difference. After all, he was the one person who showed me friendship and gave me a chance when most people would have turned their back on me. The fact of the matter is that I might be dead or worse right now if he hadn't stepped in to intervene in the crazy situation that I found myself in shortly after exiting the survival-chamber. I can only hope that in the future I find a way to repay his kindness, if that's even possible.

So far, the journey to Starview has been quiet and uneventful, not at all like what I experienced when I first trekked out into these woods with Chance. Aydin has been at the front of the line along with Alexis, guiding us up West Valley Trail towards River Basin Way. He says that we're due to arrive there sometime near the end of the day. From there, we'll travel north until we come to Star Road and then west until we reach our final destination. The whole trip should only take us three to four days, assuming nothing unexpected or out of the ordinary takes place.

Unfortunately, I still haven't found an opportunity to inform Aydin of the first orb's location. At this point, it's looking like I may have to wait until sometime later tonight after we've set up camp.

It would be really helpful if I could discuss all of this with Chance first, but I haven't been able to get him away from Sarina long enough to do so. She's been glued to his side ever since she unexpectedly showed up at Leo's house this morning to inform us that she was coming along for the journey. It's obvious that she's purposely keeping him away from me, as she seems to have convinced herself that I'm somehow to blame for everything that happened last week. Truth be told, I'm beginning to think that she'd like to see Chance and I end our friendship altogether. I just hope that this ridiculous state of affairs doesn't end up causing more trouble than it already has.

At the moment, we're bivouacking in a grassy glade just a short distance from the edge of the trail. We just finished eating a light lunch, and now we're giving the two horses that were brought along for the journey some time to rest. So far, it's been kind of quiet. Aydin and Alexis are sitting away from everyone, engaged in a private conversation; Tristam and Cyrus are silently pacing around the parameter, keeping watch on the path and the surrounding woods; and Sarina is having Chance go through the saddlebags to double-check our inventory. As for me, I'm just taking in the scenery – I mean, it's not like I have anything better to do.

Chapter 28

Crystal Energy

It was late in the afternoon when the rescue party finally emerged from the outer hedge of Iron Woods and stepped out into a wide expanse of open grassland that stretched into the distance for what seemed like miles. At the valley's western edge, just beyond the glade, steep, rocky cliffsides and dark, jagged mountains rose up sharply from the ground below, forming a natural barrier that trailed away both to the north and to the south. To the northwest, a series of rushing waterfalls could be seen spilling over the cliffsides and cascading down into a large basin below. Behind all of this, the sinking sun had set the sky ablaze in a vibrant array of fiery yellows and golden oranges that drifted up and melded into a sweeping canvas of hazy blues and dark indigo. For a moment, everyone stopped walking and gazed upon the picturesque scenery in a state of awe and wonder.

As Devin scanned the mountain range, he spotted something that he never expected to see. Staged along a high plateau that rose up on the far side of the waterfalls, a series of enormous towering poles were lined up next to each other in wide rows. All of them were completely overgrown with thick, leafy vines, and many of them had begun to lean and appeared as if they might fall over at any minute. As he squinted his eyes to bring them into clearer focus, he noticed that some of them were topped with giant propellers that were slowly spinning around in large circles in the mountain breeze.

I can't believe it, he thought to himself. *Wind turbines. I bet those are the wind towers that Chance wanted to show me last week.*

263

Chapter 28

A smile crept across his face as a long-forgotten memory from his childhood came back to him. For a brief moment, he was sitting in the back of his mom and dad's hovercar, staring out the side window at the scenery swiftly flying by. It was a lazy Sunday afternoon, and his father had decided to take him and his mother on a joyride through the country. Soon after they had left the city behind, they came upon a field lined with long rows of wind turbines that seemed to stretch alongside the highway for miles. It was the first time that he had ever seen a wind farm. His father, noticing the look of curiosity in his eyes, took the opportunity to teach him all about wind energy. As the happy memory continued to play out in his mind, he shed a quiet tear.

Just then, Chance came up from behind and patted him on the back. "What do you think, man?"

"I think it's pretty amazing," Devin said with a smile.

Chance nodded. "It really is." He then pointed towards the plateau and asked, "Did you happen to notice the wind towers over there?"

"I did. I was actually just checking them out." Devin shifted his gaze to scan the surrounding countryside.

With a slight shake of his head, Chance looked away from the wind turbines. "You know, I wish things would have worked out differently last week. I was really looking forward to exploring the area after we got here."

Devin started to grin and nod, but something sparkling in the corner of his eye abruptly stole his attention. As he jerked his head around to face the source of the distraction, he heard Cyrus shout out, "Neck biters!" A giant, sparkly swarm was hovering just above the glade to the south, and it appeared to be drifting in their direction.

With little time to spare, the group swiftly took action. Chance and Tristam scurried back towards the outer hedge and began gathering anything they could find that would easily burn while Alexis and Sarina led the horses to a nearby tree to tie them off. Devin, having no idea of what was going on, just stood frozen in place, shocked and stupefied.

As he twisted his head back and forth between the others and the large buzzing swarm that seemed to be getting closer, he began to sweat and panic and shouted out, "What do I do!?"

Tristam, looked up with a bitter scowl and angrily yelled back, "You can get over here and help, you idiot!"

Chance promptly intervened. "Here, Devin, you can help with these!" He pointed towards a pile of dead wood and kindling that he and Tristam had gathered.

Devin raced over to the pile and scooped up as much as he could carry. Chance and Tristam quickly followed suit. They then carried the wood over to Aydin and Cyrus, who immediately went to work using it to build a hasty campfire. As soon as the fire was burning brightly, Aydin removed a small brown bottle from an inner pocket in his cloak and began sprinkling small droplets of a dark, oily substance onto the flames. Everywhere the droplets landed, a thick, choking cloud of foul-smelling black smoke rose into the air and snaked off in every direction.

Aydin then shouted out for everyone to gather around the fire and stay close to the smoke. Within seconds, everyone was hunched down around the smoky blaze with their cloaks pulled up around their mouths and noses to keep from inhaling too many of the toxic fumes at once.

Chapter 28

In the background, a low, droning buzz could faintly be heard, slowly growing in volume and intensity as the swarm drew closer. The companions, paranoid and frightened, threw nervous glances at each other, privately debating whether or not it might be a good idea to run. A few apprehensive moments dredged by before the cacophonous noise finally peaked and began to trail off in the opposite direction.

As soon as it disappeared completely, Cyrus heaved an exasperated sigh of relief and blurted out, "Thank God that's over!"

Nodding his head in agreement, Aydin said, "Thank God, indeed." He then picked himself up from the ground and added, "I think we can all relax now. The concoction I used on the fire should keep the neck biters away from us for the rest of the night. We'll just need to add a few drops of it to the fire every hour or so." He paused in thought for a moment. "I think it would be for the best if we take turns keeping watch throughout the night. Does anyone want to volunteer to go first?"

Feeling a strong need to redeem himself from his previous blunder, Devin slowly raised his hand and said, "I will."

Almost immediately, Tristam objected, "You will?!" He curled his lips in disgust. "I'd just as soon sleep the night away with no watch than put my life in the hands of someone like you!"

Chance abruptly cut in, "Hey, man! That's not fair. What did he do to deserve that?!"

Standing up, Tristam threw his arms out. "What do you mean, what did he do?!" He spat into the fire. "Didn't you see him stand there like some kind of mindless dolt when he saw the neck biters? He obviously doesn't have any good sense!"

Shaking his head, Devin said, "Hey, Tristam! I've got more than enough good sense. I've just never had to deal with neck biters before. Why don't you try cutting me some slack!"

Tristam shot back, "Never dealt with neck biters before?! What do you mean you've never dealt with neck biters before?! Do you think I just fell off the turnip cart or something?!"

Immediately realizing his mistake, Devin spun a hasty lie, "I've never dealt with them because they don't exist in Harstad Hollow."

A sudden hush fell over the entire group. Tristam's jaw dropped in stunned disbelief.

As Devin glanced around at everyone's puzzled expressions, he could clearly tell that he had just said something ridiculous; however, it was Alexis' strange yellow-ringed eyes glistening in the firelight that really caught his attention. She not only seemed taken back but genuinely frightened as well. With a slow shake of his head, he thought to himself, *Oh great, now you've done it.*

Aydin finally broke the silence, "Devin, I know you don't realize what you've just said, but there isn't anyone sitting here who's going to buy it. You might as well have made the claim that houseflies don't exist." Then, sighing loudly, he added, "Maybe it's time that you tell them the truth?"

Both Cyrus and Tristam glanced at each other inquisitively. Alexis pulled her pewter-gray cloak around her shoulders and hunched over with her arms folded tightly as she stared intensely into the fire.

Devin was at a complete loss for what to do. This wasn't how things were supposed to play out. He needed a little more time to prepare himself. With an audible sigh, he took one last look at everyone, shrugged, and decided that he might as well go with it.

Gazing up at Tristam, he said, "Listen, I know you don't trust me, and it's obvious that you think there's something wrong with me. Well… The truth is you're not completely wrong to feel the way you do. However, you're not completely right either."

At this, Tristam cocked his head and raised an eyebrow. He then slowly sat down and waited to hear more.

Devin continued, "The truth of the matter is that I'm not from your timeline. Though this may sound impossible, I came here from the distant past."

Cyrus, Tristam, and Alexis all sat up stiffly and glared at Devin as if he had completely lost his mind.

Ignoring their stares, he went on, "It all started right before the Great Firefall. I had just woken up with a massive hangover after one of the worst nights of my life, and I was running late for work…" He then recounted his entire story, beginning with the incident at the military complex and ending with his departure from the survival-chamber.

By the time he finished, both Cyrus and Tristam were looking at him like he was some kind of an alien from another planet. Alexis, on the other hand, was gazing at him with unflinching eyes that conveyed a mix of wonder, confusion, and fear.

Tristam was the first to speak up, "You really expect us to believe all that? You must think we're a special kind of dumb, don't ya?" Sneering at Devin, he abruptly stood up in a huff. "I think I've heard just about enough of this nonsense. Why don't you go back to whatever hole you crawled out of and leave the rest of us out of your delusions!"

Aydin swiftly interjected, "Tristam, sit back down. He's not lying. I, personally, have great reason to believe that everything he just said is true."

Tristam shot Aydin a look of surprise. "You're kidding me, right?"

Aydin slowly shook his head. A few seconds of strained silence slowly ticked by. Finally, Tristam threw his hands up in the air in annoyance and plopped himself back down.

Aydin turned to face Devin. "I assume you brought your things with you? Maybe you should show them the proof of your past?"

Devin nodded and proceeded to empty the contents of his pack onto the ground in front of him. Everything was there – his phone, his map, his logbook, his dagger, and even his security clearance card. He then began to pass the items around in a circle while explaining each one in great detail.

When the dagger was handed to Alexis, she unsheathed it and gasped, "This is impossible! Where did you get this?!" She glared at Devin with an intensity that temporarily caused his mind to go blank. The yellow rings around her irises were glowing.

"Uh... Um..." Devin stammered. "It was stored in the survival-chamber. Why do you ask? I don't understand."

The rings in Alexis' eyes began to dim, and she replied in a softer tone, "I apologize. It's just that I've seen this blade before. However, up until this very moment, I was under the impression that there was only one in existence, the one my mother carries by her side as a symbol of her station."

Devin's eyes widened in surprise. "You mean to tell me that your mother has one, too?"

"Yes. It's called The Blade of Kanthis. It's a weapon of immense power that's been in my family for nearly 120 years." Alexis gazed into the fire. "My great-great-grandfather found it hidden in a cavern when he was a young man. It was stored alongside one of the fabled Goddess Stones."

Devin wrinkled a brow. "Goddess Stones? What on earth are those?"

"They're mysterious crystal orbs that are believed to contain powers so vast and so great that only those chosen by the Goddess herself are capable of controlling them."

At this point, everyone sitting around the campfire was completely silent, having become fully transfixed by what they were hearing.

Alexis went on, "Shortly after my great-great-grandfather made his discovery, he was visited by a mysterious oracle who told him that he had been specially chosen by Kanthis herself to safeguard her treasures. He promised him that the blessings of the Goddess would be upon our family for as long as the treasures remained unharmed, adding that a day would come when Kanthis would return to gather them again to herself in the sky tower. On that day, the greatness of her power would be fully revealed for all the world to see. Ever since then, the safeguarding of the Goddess Stone and The Blade of Kanthis has been treated as my family's sacred duty."

Glancing down at the dagger, she said, "This weapon you have is far more powerful than I think you realize."

Devin nodded his head in understanding. "My dad told me the same thing. However, I have no idea how to use it. Until I can figure out a way to activate it, it might as well just be a fancy-looking knife."

Alexis giggled at this, and her features softened. Turning the blade over in her hand, she unscrewed the bottom of the hilt and revealed an empty chamber. Devin's eyes widened in amazement.

Alexis grinned. "The reason your blade doesn't work is because it's missing a Kanthisian power gem." She pointed towards the empty chamber.

A look of astonishment swept across Devin's face. "So that's how it works. I knew it was missing something." He shook his head and momentarily gazed into the campfire. Suddenly, his eyes lit up. "I think I know what this all means now! What you call a Kanthisian power gem is what my father called an energy crystal, and the Goddess Stone your great-great-grandfather discovered must be one of the crystalline orbs that is needed to activate the tower. It all makes perfect sense!"

Alexis didn't respond but seemed troubled by his words. Standing up, she paced over to where he was sitting and handed the dagger back to him. She then reached up to her chest and began to unlatch the jewel from her pendant necklace. When she finished, she held out the bright red stone and said, "This is a Kanthisian power gem. Place it in the empty chamber of your dagger and twist the cap back on."

Devin reached up and took the gem from her outstretched hand. Holding it up, he watched as it glistened and sparkled in the orange glow of the firelight. He then placed it in the empty compartment at the bottom of the dagger's hilt and tightened the cap back on, just as instructed.

She then directed, "Now, flip the silver switch up below the crossguard."

As Devin did this, the bluish-green crystal set in the center of the crossguard began to glow. His eyes lit up in amazement. A series of surprised gasps circled around the campfire as everyone stood up to get a closer look.

Alexis gave an abrupt warning, "Whatever you do, don't point that at anyone when the switch is flipped!"

Overcome with excitement, Chance piped up, "Devin, you need to try it out on something!"

A look of worry flit across Sarina's eyes. "Chance! What are you saying? We don't know what it will do!"

With a short wave of her hands, Alexis motioned for both of them to calm down. "It's okay. No one will get hurt as long as we all stand back."

She then strolled over to the pile of dead wood that was lying nearby and removed one of the largest pieces. After carrying it over to a patch of grass about ten yards away from everyone, she thought to herself, *This ought to do,* and laid it down.

Pacing back to the others, she said, "Okay, Devin, when you're ready, just point your dagger at that piece of wood and squeeze the lever."

Devin was overwhelmed with nervous anticipation as he lifted himself from the ground and stepped a few feet away from the group. Raising the dagger out in front of him, he aimed it directly at the center of the wood. Looking over his shoulder one last time, he noticed Aydin nod in his direction.

He then focused his gaze on his target, inhaled deeply, and depressed the vertical lever that ran alongside the hilt.

The blade lit up in a flash of white, and a short beam of light shot out from its tip. A split second later, the dead log lit up in a blaze of fiery blue and exploded into a thousand smoldering pieces. Tristam yelled out in fright and jumped backwards, nearly knocking Cyrus off his feet; Sarina gasped and held a hand up to her mouth as the sea green streaks in her eyes flared up; and Chance leaped back three feet in wide-eyed astonishment. Aydin, however, stood, unmoving, stroking the curls in his beard as he looked on in fascination.

Devin, feeling both awestruck and amazed by the sheer power of his weapon, turned to face Alexis with a huge grin but noticed that she was wearing a pensive expression and the yellow rings around her irises were glowing.

Glancing back, she quietly said, "It's just as I had always feared. If everything you said about your past is true, it would mean that my family's legacy was built on a lie." Her eyes suddenly flashed with anger and a hint of sadness. "Do you care if I take a look at your map again?"

He nodded and strolled back towards his pack to retrieve it.

A few minutes passed by as Alexis scoured over the map by the light of the fire. Finally, she looked up and said, "I think you may be right about the Goddess Stones. The location marked on this map for one of the crystalline orbs just happens to be in the exact same area that the first Goddess Stone was discovered." She sighed and laid the map down beside her. "It would seem that my mother has one of the orbs you're looking for."

Chapter 28

Devin furrowed his brow and gazed into the campfire in contemplation. Everyone remained silent.

Suddenly, Chance spoke up, "So, Devin, do you want to tell everyone about the first orb location or should I?

Devin didn't immediately respond but thought to himself, *I can't believe this is actually happening*. Then, looking up with a grin, he ran his fingers back through his hair and said, "Let's tell them together."

Chapter 29

A Detour to Disaster

Morning came early for the companions, who were still shaken by Devin's startling revelations from the evening prior. Even though the decision to take a short detour away from the main path to retrieve the first orb had been unanimous, Oren's rescue was still the top priority. So in order to save time and not detract from their original mission too much, Aydin suggested that it would be best to get an early start. Heeding his advice, the group dismantled their makeshift camp and got back on the trail well before sunrise.

It was around mid-morning when they crossed over an old, rickety wooden bridge and stepped onto the northern bank of Roaring River. Up to that point, the weather had been mild and pleasant, and travel had been relatively swift. Unfortunately, the horses were in need of water, and the sleep-deprived rescue party was in need of rest, so Aydin made the decision to bring their march to a halt.

A short while later, everyone, with the exception of Alexis, found a comfortable seat along the riverbank and sat down to relax and enjoy a light snack. Meanwhile, Alexis, not feeling very hungry, decided to excuse herself and take a short stroll up the trail.

As she sauntered along, she gazed into the distance at the glistening waterfalls that plunged into the pristine river basin below. The majestic cascades were truly a sight to behold, and the enchanting scenery that spread out around her was no less mesmerizing. Regardless, all she could think about was how she was that much closer to returning to the one place she had done everything in her power to leave behind. In a mere instant, she was struck by a wave of anxiety that caused her to question everything she was doing.

Was she really making the right choice in coming back? Had she made a foolish decision in choosing to put so much trust in complete strangers? Could they really be relied upon to stand strong when the going got rough? And what about Devin and his strange, ominous tale? Could it really be true? Everything she had witnessed the night before seemed to indicate as much. But, if that were the case, what exactly were the odds that her own story would randomly intertwine with his?

The heavy questions caused her to tense up and shudder. She had to put them out of her mind and think about Oren. He was the reason she was doing all of this; he was the reason she was risking everything to go back.

"I'm so sorry, Oren," she softly whispered to herself. "This is all my fault."

Oren was the closest thing to a father she had ever known and the only person she was ever able to put her complete trust in. The possibility that he might be rotting away in her mother's foul dungeon was almost more than she could bear to think about, and the fact that it was all on her account was simply unacceptable. Deep in her heart, she already knew that she would do whatever it took to rescue him, even if that meant risking the very freedom she had struggled for so long to obtain. But, still, the thought of returning to a life she had spent years trying to escape filled her with a sense of dread that she just couldn't seem to shake.

Hiking further up the trail, she tried her best to bury the worst of her fears when, all of a sudden, it dawned on her that she had traveled much further than she had originally intended. Swiftly spinning around, she noticed that the others were already in the midst of making preparations to leave. Not wanting to be the reason for any more delays, she hurried back to join them.

The next leg of the trip flew by quickly. The lemon-yellow sun continued to shine brightly, and the mild breeze that drifted down from the north held steady. It was turning out to be a perfect day for traveling.

As Devin paced alongside Chance and Sarina, he found himself beginning to relax and enjoy himself. For the first time since the beginning of the journey, conversation among the three was lighthearted and, at times, even jovial. Despite the fact that the road ahead was sure to be fraught with peril and danger, the previous evening's revelations had sparked a childlike sense of wonder and adventure in each of them, and they all seemed to believe that things were finally looking up.

The party continued to hike north along River Basin Way in this manner for another hour or so before Aydin, once again, brought everyone to a halt. After carefully scanning the rocky cliffsides to the west, he turned towards Devin and asked, "Would you mind allowing me to look over your map?"

"Sure! No problem!" Devin cheerfully replied as he removed his pack and began digging through it.

However, a moment later, he let out a distressed gasp, "My map! It's missing!" His eyes widened in panic as he overturned his pack and emptied all of its contents into a messy heap on the ground. "Where on earth could it have gone?!" He frantically began to sift through the pile.

Chapter 29

As he did this, Tristam, with arms crossed and a snide smirk upon his face, strolled up coolly and stood beside him. "Did you lose something, boy?"

Devin glanced up in fear. "My map, it's nowhere to be found!" He wiped the sweat that had begun to bead upon his brow. "I don't understand. I could have sworn I put it back in my pack last night."

"Or perhaps you accidentally dropped it somewhere along the trail?" Tristam sarcastically offered. "I'm sure we won't lose much time if we turn around and look for it. I'd even be willing to bet that we could make it back to our old campsite by nightfall – if we hurry." He smirked and turned his head to spit on the ground.

Just then, Aydin interjected, "What's the meaning of this?! What do you mean you lost your map?!"

The companions all honed in on Devin, each of them visibly distressed.

"I don't know. I placed it back in my pack with my other things before I went to sleep last night, and now it's gone." A look of worry and defeat swept across Devin's already downcast features.

Glancing up, Aydin's gaze met Tristam's. It almost seemed as if the salty watchman was getting some sort of sick pleasure from the whole ordeal.

Aydin's eyes suddenly lit up in a flash of anger. "Tristam, is there something you find amusing about all of this? I'm failing to see the humor."

With a loud grunt and a shake of his head, Tristam spat on the ground and replied, "This is absolutely pathetic. To think that the future of humanity rests upon the shoulders of a careless dimwit."

Chapter 29

Reaching into his cloak, he produced a rolled-up plastic-like parchment. Then, glaring down at Devin, he said, "You'd do well to keep a better eye on your things, boy. I found this lying near the campfire long after you'd retired for the night. It's a wonder that it didn't catch a breeze and burn up." He hesitated briefly, battling back an urge to say something more, then reluctantly turned away and handed the map to Aydin.

Everyone stood still as Aydin perused over the map and plotted out the next leg of the journey. A few moments of silence slowly passed by before he finally glanced up and said, "It appears that this is where we get off the beaten path." Rolling the map back up, he held it out to Devin and, in a somber tone, said, "Keep it close and keep it safe. The future may very well depend upon it."

Devin nodded his head humbly as he retrieved the map from Aydin's outstretched hand. He then carefully placed it in his pack with his other things. The seriousness of the situation spoke for itself; there was nothing more that needed to be said.

The next stage of the trip should have been a breeze, but the tall, grassy terrain that looked easily accessible from a distance turned out to be concealing long, swathes of sludgy mud and mucky marshland. Apparently, the entire area had been flooded during the previous week's storms, and not enough time had passed for the ground to dry out. As the group pushed through the tall, woody reeds and picked their way around the patches of mud and water that barred the way forward, their progress nearly came to a standstill.

Fully frustrated and feeling the need to take matters into his own hands, Cyrus borrowed Sarina's horse and promptly led it to the front of the line. He then climbed into the saddle and peered out over the tall stalks of cattails that were previously blocking his view. "It appears that the ground begins to rise as we approach the cliffsides. If we travel just a little further north, I believe we can cut around this last stretch of marsh and get back on dry land."

"Then north it shall be," Aydin said. "It's been many years since I last traveled by foot through this kind of wilderness. In all reality, I should have known better."

"There's no way that any of us could have known," Cyrus replied. "These long stretches of muddy waste were completely hidden from the trail." Dismounting from the horse, he chuckled and added, "The good news is that we're nearly out of it."

"That's good news, indeed," Aydin returned with a grin. "I'm not sure these old legs can handle much more of this."

Following Cyrus' lead, the party began to hike north. Tristam walked beside Cyrus and used a long machete to cut down the wet foliage that barred their way forward. Aydin kept a step or two behind them, and Chance and Devin followed alongside him. In the rear of the line, Sarina and Alexis did their best to keep up while simultaneously dealing with two skittish horses that weren't used to traveling through boggy terrain. Fortunately, it wasn't long before the soppy marshland gave way to wide patches of thick mud and then, finally, dry dirt. It seemed that the worst of it was finally over.

It was at this point that Cyrus and Tristam came to a sharp stop. Swiftly turning around, Cyrus placed a finger up to his lips and motioned for everyone to stay quiet. Crouching beside him, Tristam went on full alert. With the tense posture of a cat, he peered into the tall grass in front of him, watching, waiting, and listening for some disturbance that remained unseen.

All of a sudden, just a few yards ahead, the weeds began to rustle, and a loud, raspy hissing noise erupted from within. Jumping back, Cyrus unbuckled his large, spiky club and held it out in front of him. Tristam crouched back, machete in hand, poised and ready to strike. At the same time, Aydin scurried back to stand beside the two women while Chance unslung his bow and Devin unsheathed his dagger.

A few tense seconds passed, and then, without warning, a giant, hissing serpent sprang up from the weeds directly in front of Cyrus. The suddenness of its appearance nearly caused Devin to pass out in fright. As the creature reared back its enormous head and whipped out its tail, nearly everyone in the party quaked and trembled in fear. Devin had never seen anything quite like it. It had a diamond-shaped head the size of a large pumpkin, and its brown, leathery body, thick as a tree trunk, could have been at least thirty feet long.

"My god! It's a river wyrm!" Cyrus shouted out as he leaned back with his club in hand, fully prepared to defend himself. "Everyone, take cover now!"

Suddenly, the snake began to advance in Cyrus' direction. As it did so, its fierce golden eyes seemed to flare up with their own fiery light. A split second later, it coiled itself around Cyrus' bulky frame and began to squeeze.

"Ahhh! It's going to kill me!" Cyrus screamed as he bashed his club into the serpent's pearly white underbelly.

Tristam wasted no time in using his machete to wildly hack at its body. Unfortunately, the snake's scaly armor was much too strong for the dulling blade to penetrate. Chance tried launching a number of arrows at the creature's eyes but couldn't seem to find his mark as it swayed back and forth with the speed of a lightning bolt. If something didn't give, all hope would soon be lost.

It was at this point when Devin decided to do something that he should have done all along. Flipping the silver switch on his dagger, he raced forward like the wind. With no time to think, he thrust his blade out in front of him and depressed the lever. In an instant, a bolt of white energy burst forth from its tip and blasted right through the serpent's scales, sending shattered, smoldering vertebrae to fly through the air like shrapnel while simultaneously ripping its spine clean in half. The creature instantly loosened its grip on Cyrus and sent him crumpling to the ground like a loose sack of potatoes. It then began to hiss and writhe about wildly in erratic spasms of anger and pain. As the last of its crimson life force spewed violently onto the ground below, its body went limp, and it collapsed with a thud.

Almost immediately, Aydin and the others rushed to Cyrus' side. Moaning and groaning in pain, he tried his best to stand up but found that he couldn't.

Gritting his teeth, he forced himself up on one elbow and said, "I think… my ribs… are broken." His voice faltered, and he abruptly fell back to the ground, heaving and wheezing in agony.

Tristam crouched down beside his old friend and did his best to comfort him. "Don't speak, and try not to move. It'll only make things worse." Glancing back at the others, he shouted out, "We have to get him medical attention quick! There's no way he can continue on in this kind of shape."

"No, there isn't," Aydin said as he slowly stroked the curls in his beard. "We have no other choice but to get him back to Iron Cove, as Starview is too great a distance. I'm sure that Sarina's mother can help him – her abilities as a healer are unparalleled."

Sarina voiced her agreement, "I have no doubt that she can. If we can get him on my horse, one of us can use the other to guide him quickly and safely back to the village."

"I should be the one to take him," Tristam said while rolling up his cloak and placing it under Cyrus' head. "I know this country better than anyone here, and I'm also the fastest rider. He'll have the best chance of survival with me by his side."

Aydin nodded. "Unfortunately, for all of us, I'm inclined to think that you're right." He paused briefly and sighed. "We'll just have to figure out a way to make do without you."

As time was of the essence, everyone pitched in where they could to help. Alexis dressed Cyrus' wounds with a healing salve that Aydin had brought along for the journey, while Sarina used a handful of medicinal herbs and a canteen of water to whip up a potent concoction that would help ease his pain and suffering. After the women were finished, Chance and Devin assisted Tristam in lifting Cyrus' huge frame off of the ground and onto Valoria's back. A short while later, the two men were fully prepared to make the return journey to Iron Cove.

"Go with Godspeed, Tristam!" Aydin called out as they began to ride away.

Abruptly swinging his horse around, Tristam gazed down at Devin and then at the dagger that hung loosely by his side. Glancing back up at Aydin, he shouted out, "We'll be fine! I think it is you who will need God's help!" Then, with a final shake of his head, he whipped his horse back around and began riding east.

As the two men disappeared from sight, Chance quietly remarked, "I guess it's just us now."

Coming up from behind, Sarina wrapped a slender arm around his waist and leaned in on his shoulder. "Everything will be okay, Chance. I just know it."

Glancing down at Sarina with a half-smile, Chance noticed that the sea-green streaks in her eyes were glowing with a faint luminescence. Bending down, he gently kissed her forehead.

Meanwhile, Aydin walked up beside Devin and placed a hand on his shoulder. "You did well, Devin. If you hadn't reacted when you did, Cyrus would surely be dead right now."

Devin, not quite knowing how he should respond, somberly nodded his head and cast his gaze towards the ground. He may have saved Cyrus' life, but that didn't change the fact that his plan to retrieve the orb had put everyone he knew in mortal danger.

Shortly thereafter, the remaining members of the group picked up where they left off and began trekking towards the cliffsides in the west. Unfortunately, the next hour or so was marked by a pervasive heaviness that hung in the air like a thick, dark cloud. Everyone knew that they had lost two of the most capable members of their party, and subsequently, the future was beginning to look and feel uncertain.

Aydin, normally the optimistic voice of reason, was unusually somber and quiet; Alexis, already burdened down with the knowledge that she might be on the verge of returning to a life of bondage, went out of her way to keep her distance from the others; and to top things off, both Chance and Devin were sulking and brooding at the back of the line, as they each felt that they were somehow responsible for the current, sorry state of affairs. If it hadn't been for Sarina's sudden burst of confidence and the infectious energy that accompanied it, they might have given up on the quest completely.

Unlike her companions, Sarina was riding high on a positive wave of emotion. Shortly after Tristam rode away with Cyrus at his side, her spirit had unexpectedly been overcome with a deep and abiding sense of peace and purpose. Though there was nothing about it that made any logical sense, she knew the feeling well. It often came along when things seemed bleak and hopeless, working as a light to guide her way through dark times. Having learned long ago to trust her gut feelings, she knew deep inside that everything was, somehow, going to work out. So, holding this knowledge close to her heart, she tirelessly worked to lift everyone's spirits and keep them pressing forward.

The day meandered on in this manner until, finally, the party reached the edge of the valley, where a series of tall, rocky cliffsides loomed high into the sky above them. The companions, each feeling relieved to be nearing the end of their side quest, opted to take a short break. Even though it was only mid-afternoon, the day's unfortunate events had drained most of their energy, and a short period of rest and recuperation was much needed.

After everyone had found a comfortable spot to settle into, Aydin decided to spend some time examining Devin's map a little more closely. By gauging the distance they had traveled from Roaring River Falls, he was able to get a better idea of their approximate location. Setting the map to the side, he took a few minutes to survey the landscape to the south and then to the north. At this point, the others had become curious about what he was up to and began to gaze in his direction questioningly.

Taking notice, he spoke up, "According to the map, the chamber should be hidden somewhere in this general vicinity. However, it appears that we may need to split up if we hope to find it before sundown."

Upon hearing this, Chance decided to stand up and give his input, "I agree, but don't you think that one of us should probably stay behind and set up camp – you know, just in case the sun sets before we find the orb?"

"My thoughts, exactly," Aydin said with a light chuckle. "As it turns out, I've already located the perfect spot to build a campfire." He pointed to a spacious recess in the cliffside just a few yards away. Both Chance and Devin grinned at this, as they already knew that there was no way on earth that Aydin was going to volunteer to hike a single step further.

"Okay, it's settled then," Chance said. "I'll travel south with Devin, and the girls will travel north."

"Hold on! Wait just a minute!" Sarina cut in as she lifted herself from the ground. "You're traveling with me, Chance, and I'm not taking no for an answer."

"Come on, Sarina! Why do you have to be like that?!" Chance sharply retorted. "I've barely spent any time at all with Devin since we started this journey, and besides, you'll do fine without me. It's not like we'll have to travel very far."

Sitting just a few feet away, Devin began to feel awkward and uncomfortable. Glancing over at Alexis, he watched as she rolled her eyes. *Apparently, she thinks this is as ridiculous as I do.*

Chapter 29

He then decided to speak up, "It's cool, Chance. I'll search for the chamber with Alexis." He glanced back in her direction. "That is, if that's okay with you?"

Alexis nodded and replied with a smile, "I'd like that very much."

Clearing his throat, Aydin said, "Now that we have *that* settled, I'd find it very helpful if all of you would help me gather some fuel for the fire before you leave."

Chance shook his head and sighed. He knew he had been beat, and there was no use in trying to fight it. Turning to walk away, he motioned for the others to follow. "I think I spotted an area on the way here where we'll have the most luck finding wood."

For the next half hour or so, the companions collected anything they could find that would burn for a sustained period of time. Unfortunately, they were forced to make do with dead shrubbery and scattered brushwood, which meant that they ended up having to gather at least three to four times as much as they normally would have just to build a modest campfire. After they were finished and Aydin seemed satisfied, they split into two groups and went their separate ways. Chance and Sarina traveled north while Devin and Alexis headed south.

Fortunately, Devin and Alexis didn't have to search for very long to find the hidden chamber. As fate would have it, they happened upon a shallow cave that was just a mile or so away from the campsite. When Devin stepped inside, he immediately spotted a tall steel door just a few yards away at the back of the cavern that was identical to the one at the entrance of the survival-chamber.

"Well, that was easy," he remarked as he paced forward.

"I agree," Alexis replied. "Almost too easy."

He nodded his head. "Either we got really lucky, or Aydin is just that good with a map."

Alexis giggled at this. "Considering how things have been working out here lately, I'm beginning to doubt that luck had anything to do with it."

Devin's features were suddenly overcome with a look of concern. "Do you think we should go back and get the others? I'm sure they'd love to see this."

"I don't think that's necessary, Devin. We'd just be wasting more time. If they really want to see it, they can take a look at it later."

His features softened, and he smiled. "I suppose you're right." Then, reaching into his pack, he dug out his security clearance card. "My father told me that I'd have to use this card to get inside."

Alexis seemed puzzled.

"Just watch."

Lifting the security card, he waved it in front of a small, rectangular panel that was located just to the right of the door. A few seconds passed, and nothing happened. Trying once more, he waved it in front of the panel again. Still, nothing happened.

"Um… Are you doing something wrong?" Alexis asked nervously.

"No, not at all," Devin replied, a hint of worry in his tone. "But I don't understand why it's not working."

"Maybe this isn't the chamber we're supposed to be looking for?"

"It has to be!" he responded in frustration. "I mean, what else could it be? Something's not right." His features were vexed with concern. Once again, he waved his card over the panel and, once again, got the same results.

There was a brief moment of silence, and then Alexis suddenly had an idea. "Try using your dagger! If it's anything like my mother's, you should be able to blast a hole right through the door."

Devin hesitated briefly before replying, "Okay, but won't we be taking a chance on damaging whatever is hidden inside?"

"Maybe, but do we really have a choice?"

With a shake of his head, he unsheathed his dagger and flipped the silver switch. "I think we should probably stand back."

"Agreed."

After they walked back to the entrance of the cavern, Devin turned around, lifted his dagger into the air, and aimed it directly at the center of the door. "Okay… Here goes nothing."

As he depressed the lever, the blade lit up in a flash of brilliant white. A split second later, a burst of energy blasted from its tip. As the beam made impact with the door, the entire cavern lit up in electric blue and roared in a thunderous explosion. Almost instantly, a slew of rocks and debris began to crumble and crash down from the ceiling. Devin and Alexis ducked reflexively and darted out into the open as quickly as their legs would carry them.

After they had put a safe distance between themselves and the crumbling cavern, they both turned around, huffing and puffing, and watched as the dust and smoke began to clear from the air. Fortunately, it appeared that the cave was still intact, more or less. Aside from a few large boulders that partially blocked the entrance, it looked as if they could still get back inside.

"Phew… That was a close one!" Devin exclaimed. "Let's never do that again!"

"Agreed!" Alexis nervously replied as she wiped a patch of sweat from her forehead.

"Shall we take a look?"

Glancing back towards the entrance, she nodded.

After removing some of the rocks that blocked their way, they entered the cavern and found a blackened, smoldering hole where the steel door had once been standing. Just beyond it was a small chamber that was now dimly lit by the daylight that filtered in through the cavern entrance. Cautiously stepping inside, they spotted the only item of interest in the entire room, a small, rectangular silver chest that had been positioned against the back wall.

"That has to be it!" Devin said excitedly.

Alexis' gaze traveled over the smoky, twisted metallic fragments that were strewn across the floor. "Hopefully, we'll have better luck with it than we did the door."

As Devin approached the container, he was overcome with a mild fit of giddy anticipation. Inspecting it further, he spotted a round black button upon its surface and thought, *That's probably how you get it open.*

Bending down, he took a deep breath and pressed the button. With a click and a pop, the lid swung open, revealing a perfect blue crystalline orb that was just about the size of a baseball. As he gazed down at it, he noticed a soft glow emanating from its center. Lying beside it were three finely cut, ruby-like gems that were nearly identical to the one Alexis had loaned him the night before.

Chapter 29

Alexis suddenly gasped, "I can't believe it! A Goddess Stone!"

"And three more energy crystals!" Devin added as he glanced up with a grin. "Alexis, I think we did it!"

With rapidly beating hearts and unbridled excitement, they scooped up the treasures and carefully stored them in Devin's pack. As soon as they were finished, they made their way out of the cavern and hurried back to meet with the others at the campsite.

Chapter 30

Sarina's Diary
Wednesday, October 6th, 2354 – Evening

Dear Diary,

I can't believe that I'm about to write this, but Chance was right – I misjudged Devin. Over the past few days, I've seen a side of him that I would have never believed he possessed. He not only displayed true courage and heart in the face of danger when he destroyed the disgusting river wyrm that nearly killed Cyrus, but he also risked his life to save my own, and now I feel ashamed.

It all happened earlier today, shortly after we were forced to retreat from a snowstorm that unexpectedly blew in from the north. We had been hiking west along Star Road for the better part of the morning when we finally came to the edge of the valley, where the trail began to ascend rapidly into the jagged mountains beyond. According to both Aydin and Alexis, it was the only viable way to reach Starview. As we started up the path, I felt a chill sense of unease – something deep inside my soul was warning me that we were headed into danger – however, having no other choice, I clung to Chance and continued to press forward.

After traveling up the pass for an hour or so, a line of dark clouds began to amass directly overhead. As the last trace of blue sky disappeared, the temperature began to plummet. It didn't seem like much time had passed before snowflakes were fluttering down all around us. We continued to journey on, thinking that the snowfall might let up, but the further we traveled, the worse things got. Before long, the wind was whipping around us in strong gusts, and the snowfall, which had started out light enough, had become a raging blizzard. It was at this point that we were forced to take shelter beneath an outcropping of rocks in a nearby cliffside.

Regardless of the fact that we didn't have the luxury of choosing the most ideal location to take cover, we somehow managed to stumble upon an area that shielded us from the heaviest part of the snow. There also happened to be a thick copse of pine trees and tall bushes growing just to the north of the inlet that blocked a great deal of the wind. For a few brief moments, it seemed as though we were safe and secure, and then the unthinkable happened.

First, we heard a low growl directly in front of us, and then, in an instant, an enormous bear with gleaming red eyes and a coat of icy blue came crashing through the thicket. I had never been so frightened in my entire life. With no time to think, we all scattered to the left and to the right. Unfortunately, the hunger in his eyes was directed at me.

As I scurried through the snow, which came halfway up my legs, the ice bear quickly closed the distance between us, and then, just as it was at my heels, I tripped and stumbled into a snow drift, kicking and screaming. However, in that very moment, Devin came up from behind and lunged at it with his dagger. With a heavy growl, the beast whipped around and violently knocked him on his back.

Completely immobilized with fear, all I could do was look on in horror, as it truly seemed like Devin was done for. But then, just when it appeared that all hope was lost, Chance loosed an arrow that buried itself right in the center of the creature's chest. Almost instantly, it sprang up on its hind legs and let out a deafening roar that bounced off the cliffsides. Then, falling on all fours, it tore down the pass in a frenzy.

Chapter 30

With tears streaming down my cheeks, I lifted myself from the snow and gazed back at both of my heroes who were rushing to my side.

Soon afterwards, we were all huddled together again beneath the outcropping of rocks, hoping and praying that the blizzard would soon let up. When it finally did, Aydin sent Chance and Devin off to search for a better spot to make camp. Fortunately, for all of us, they were able to locate a small cavern just a few miles up the trail, which is where we are now.

I can honestly say that spending the night in a cave off of Starview Pass right after a snowstorm was the last thing I thought we'd be doing when this journey first began. Though I've experienced some harsh wintry days in my life, none of them ever came close to what I'm going through right now. The rocky floor we are being forced to sleep on is making it nearly impossible to get comfortable, and the night air that continually drifts in through the entrance cuts like a knife and chills to the bone.

Back home, I could always hide away from the snow and the cold and warm myself by the glow of a roaring fire in the comfort of my own living room, but here, within the confines of this dark cavern, the only source of heat is a smoky campfire that is barely large enough to keep us from freezing to death. Still, regardless of how bad things may seem, I'm finding that I'm no longer scared. When I gaze over at the love of my life and our strange new friend from the ancient past, I find that hope is once again restored to my heart.

Chapter 31

Fervor of the Faithful

Her glory lights the way
For those who seek her face.
Her favor always shines
On those who know their place.

Her passion is a flame
To set the soul afire.
With fervency of faith,
We live for her desire.

Her strength will never fail.
Her plans will never falter.
Soon, the world around us
Will bow before her altar.

Her truth, a sacred fire
To set the heart aflame.
With fervency of faith,
We live to praise her name.

Her wisdom will prevail.
Her word is always right.
A star within the darkness,
Kanthis is our light.

With fervor we shall rise,
Shining like the sun,
Our mission never ending

Chapter 31

'Til all the world is won.

As the last line of the chorus rang out across the stone walls of the great hall, the high priest, a plump, balding man, clean shaven and adorned in a ceremonial robe of midnight blue, lifted himself from his seat of honor at the edge of the dais and shuffled over to stand in front of an ornate golden altar that had been erected against the back wall of the temple. Turning to face the congregation, he lifted his hands and beckoned for everyone to rise. Above him, the dim gray light of a wintry day filtered in through a round stained glass window that depicted a conical tower floating among wispy white clouds in a crystal blue sky.

With a loud, clear voice, he began to pray, "Kanthis eternal, as we conclude this time of worship, we once again dedicate our lives to the propagation of your glorious cause. We humbly ask that you would go with us as we leave the warmth and safety of your sanctuary behind. Please guide us as we endeavor to do the work you have set before us. May we always bring honor and veneration to your beautiful name, and may your grace and favor forever smile upon those you find faithful." He paused briefly and then finished with, "So let it be done."

In unison, the congregation repeated the last line, "So let it be done."

Almost immediately, the large crowd that had gathered in Starview Temple for the midweek service began to disperse and go their separate ways, with the exception of one. Standing alone near the front of the sanctuary, a tall, proud woman, adorned in a luxurious silken gown of magenta and wearing a circlet of burnished gold upon her head, gazed down woefully at the empty seat beside her. With long, wavy light-brown hair, a tanned complexion, and hazel-brown eyes, she looked like a fully matured version of the daughter who was causing her so much sorrow and distress, the daughter who had been missing for well over a month.

With a slow shake of her head, she whispered under her breath, "Alexis, how could you do this to me?"

Just then, she felt a soft hand upon her shoulder. "Lady Zandria, is there anything I can assist you with? It pains me to see you burdened like this."

Looking up, Zandria's features hardened, and she shot the high priest a piercing glare. "Don't speak to me of pain, Nigel! You know nothing of it! All day and all night you bide your time in this dusty temple, playing the role of Kanthis' chief caregiver. You traipse around in your silken robes, dining on rich foods and drinking the finest of wines, all while never lifting a finger to do more than point out the flaws of others. Tell me! What is it that you know of pain?!"

Swiftly bowing his head, the high priest replied in a trembling voice, "I'm so sorry, my lady. I meant no offense, truly."

Zandria's features softened, just slightly. Reaching out, she placed a long, slender hand on his shoulder and offered a mocking placation, "Of course you didn't, Nigel. How could you?" She moved her hand to his cheek and gently lifted his head. "Matters such as these are well beyond your station, are they not? It's not your fault that you can't understand." She sighed. "It is I who should apologize. I should have remembered your place. Now, please, leave me be!"

The high priest humbly bowed and apologized, "Of course, my lady. Please forgive my reckless intrusion."

Turning around, he scurried away to the privacy of his personal chambers.

A short while later, Zandria was comfortably seated in the back of a horse-drawn carriage that was just rounding a corner and nearing the giant, three-story stone mansion that she had lived in all her life, the illustrious Volkov Manor. As the carriage slowly came to a stop, she breathed a heavy sigh of relief. It felt good to be back in a place that still made sense – it felt good to be home.

However, upon exiting the vehicle, she could immediately sense that something was off. Glancing to her left, she observed that the chief overseer of her estate Bernard Higgins, a tall, ruggedly handsome man with a stern demeanor, and a handful of his servants were all standing in the snow near the garden wall. Kneeling before them was a man clothed in the expensive garb of a merchant, who appeared to be gagged and bound in chains.

"Lady Zandria, I hope all went well with the midweek service!" Bernard called out as he paced forward to greet her.

With a slight shiver, she replied, "I suppose it went about as well as can be expected. At least the choir didn't… disappoint." Her words faltered as she began to stare questioningly at the servants and the prisoner lined up in front of the garden wall. Returning her attention to the overseer, she said in a much more serious tone, "There better be a good reason for this, Bernard. I'm tired, I'm cold, and it's snowing out here. You already know how I feel about being bothered before or after midweek services."

The overseer nodded shortly and said, "I do apologize for the inconvenience, my lady, but I can assure you that this truly is a matter of the utmost importance." He then pointed back at the man bound in chains. "This *merchant* was apprehended by my servants shortly after he was caught withholding a portion of the monthly tribute required from all those who do business in the region."

Zandria cocked her head and looked the prisoner up and down, a cold, crooked smile traced across her pouty lips. "I assume he has a good explanation for his insolence, does he not?"

"I'm afraid he doesn't, my lady," Bernard replied with a slight shake of his head. "To make matters worse, I was informed by two of my contemporaries that this same man was spotted on multiple occasions spending his tribute money on loose women and cheap brew at the Moonglow. Apparently, when he's had too much to drink, he falls into a nasty habit of spreading lies about Kanthis and those who dedicate their lives to her service."

A flash of anger flitted across Zandria's eyes but dissipated just as quickly. With a cool and collected tone, she said, "Is that so? How intriguing." She laughed shortly and turned to face the overseer. "Well, it seems to me that this poor lost soul is in desperate need of justice. Please see to it that he is properly *attended* to. I will meet with him in the council chamber after I've taken some time to rest."

Bernard bowed his head. "It will be done as you wish." Turning to walk away, he shouted for his servants to escort the prisoner to a holding cell.

Shortly afterwards, Zandria retreated indoors to the warmth and comfort of her bedroom, which was located on the top floor of the mansion. First, she took a moment to stoke the fire burning in the hearth, and then she sauntered over to a small silver chest sitting atop a stone pedestal that was positioned near her silken canopy bed. Gently lifting the lid, she retrieved a flawless red crystalline sphere from within and held it out in the palms of her hands. As she gazed deeply into the faint light that softly emanated from its core, she sent up a silent prayer for strength and guidance. When she finished, she carefully placed the orb back in the chest and proceeded to undress herself. She then climbed into her cozy bed and drifted off to sleep.

It was late in the afternoon when the sound of the temple bell tolling in the distance stirred her from her nap. Feeling rested and refreshed, she crawled out of bed and mentally prepared herself for the confrontation that would soon take place. After retrieving a long black robe from her closet and adorning her head with a thin golden circlet, she traipsed over to a mahogany chest of drawers and picked up a matching golden chain link belt that had been lying on its surface. She held it out, dangling in front of her, and admired it before fastening it around her waist. Next, she opened the top drawer and removed one of her most valued possessions, The Blade of Kanthis. Swiftly drawing it from its gilded sheath, she watched as the reflection of tiny flickering flames danced across its mirrored surface. She then sheathed it and fastened it to her belt.

After freshening up her makeup in front of a tall wall mirror, she solemnly stared at her reflection. She was confident, she was prepared, but she was still missing one thing. Turning away, she strolled over to the pedestal with the silver chest and retrieved the Goddess Stone.

As she held it up and gazed into its quiet light, she thought to herself, *Now, you're ready,* and then placed it in a pocket within her robe.

Chapter 31

A short while later, she entered the council chamber and seated herself in a solitary, cushioned high-back chair that was positioned next to a stone pedestal at the far end of the long rectangular room. The two walls adjacent to her were lined with similar, smaller chairs, and a wide space carpeted with a red woolen rug opened up between them.

In the center of the chamber, a metal chandelier, lined with burning candles, hung down from the ceiling, its flickering light illuminating a handful of rich tapestries that lined the room's stone walls. One featured an artistic depiction of the floating tower, another portrayed a serpent wrapped around the blade of a silver broad sword, and the remaining two were interwoven with pictures of the region's most dangerous creatures, the fearsome ice bear and the cunning pumara.

A few silent moments passed, and then the oaken double doors at the front of the chamber swung open. Bernard marched through the entryway along with two of his servants, who were dragging the prisoner, still gagged and bound, between them. As they approached, Zandria removed the crystal orb from her pocket and carefully positioned it in the center of a small red velvet pillow that sat atop the pedestal beside her.

When the group reached the center of the chamber, she raised an outstretched hand and said, "That's far enough. Bring me the prisoner, Bernard."

"Of course, my lady," he replied as he grabbed hold of a chain and yanked the merchant forward. He then led him to a spot just few feet away from where Zandria was sitting.

"Remove his gag. I want to hear what he has to say for himself."

Bernard nodded and proceeded to untie the filthy rag. As soon as he was finished, he forcefully pushed the man, who was sputtering and gasping for air, to his knees. "You will show the Lady Zandria some respect!"

A faint hint of a crooked smile formed on Zandria's lips as she gazed down at the aging merchant and watched him struggle to regain his composure. He had wispy gray hair, brown eyes, and a scruffy, patchy beard. Aside from the fancy clothes he was wearing, there was nothing to distinguish him from any other run-of-the-mill plebeian residing in Starview.

After he finally caught his breath, she began her line of questioning, "I assume you know why you've been brought before me, do you not?"

"I... I do," the man answered with a raspy stutter.

"And what exactly is that reason, merchant?"

Glancing up with a toothy smile, he spit at her feet.

Zandria instantly shot out of her seat. "You impudent fool! Do you know who you kneel before?!"

"Of course... I do." The old merchant wheezed and coughed. "You're... Zandria Volkov... the biggest, spoiled rotten –"

His words were cut short by the back of Bernard's hand. "You will not speak to the Lady Zandria in such a manner, you pathetic wretch!"

"Tell me your name, merchant! Or do you have one?" Zandria smiled sardonically.

Huffing and puffing, he lifted his head and spit again.

This time, it was Zandria who reached down and slapped him.

Bernard swiftly spoke in his stead, "His name is Daryl Stonehill, my lady. He came here from the village of Harstad Hollow."

"Harstad Hollow, the great cesspool of the south." She smirked. "I should have known." Returning to her seat, she glared down at the prisoner with cold, penetrating eyes. "Replace his gag. I've heard enough."

The overseer nodded his head and removed the filthy rag from his pocket.

As soon as the gag had been replaced, Zandria carefully removed the crystalline orb from its resting place. Holding it in one hand, she stood up and slowly approached the prisoner. Then, reaching out, she placed her other hand on his forehead and began to pronounce a judgment, "I, Zandria Volkov, chosen guardian of the Goddess Stone, now declare Daryl Stonehill of Harstad Hollow to be a blasphemer, a dissident, and a heretic. With great fervency, I call upon the power of Kanthis divine to meet him with the justice he duly deserves."

In an instant, the orb lit up in a searing flash of red. As Zandria applied pressure to the man's forehead, his body began to tremble and shake. Suddenly, his eyes widened in shock and horror, and then, without so much as a whimper, he crumpled to the floor, lifeless and limp.

Beaming with terrible satisfaction, she lowered her hand and shouted out, "Remove this fool from my chamber! Take him to the garden and bury him with the compost!"

"Yes, my lady. It will be done according to your desire." Bernard bowed shortly. "Kanthis be praised."

"Kanthis be praised," Zandria returned as she sat back down.

Chapter 31

The overseer and his two servants then promptly lifted the body from the floor and began carrying it away. However, just as they reached the oaken doors, Zandria called out, "Bernard, send me Kysa when you see her. There's an important matter that we need to discuss."

Bernard quickly nodded. "Yes, my lady. I'll send her right away."

A short while later, Kysa, dressed in riding clothes, entered the council chamber and approached her master, who was leaning over on a closed fist and tapping her nails with impatience.

"My lady, I was told that you wanted to see me," Kysa said as she humbly kneeled down.

"Yes." Zandria abruptly straightened up. "According to the letter you brought me, Drake Thorne and his prisoners were supposed to arrive in Starview over a week ago, were they not?"

"That is correct," Kysa softly replied.

"And one of those prisoners was my daughter, was it not?"

"Yes, my lady. She could be none other than Alexis. She was even wearing the Kanthisian pendant that was gifted to her as a child. Of course, we immediately removed it from her person, just as you directed."

"That is very fortunate," Zandria quietly remarked, half to herself. Then, looking down at her servant, she spoke again, this time more directly, "Stand up, Kysa. You have proven yourself to be a loyal servant, someone I feel I can trust."

Kysa nervously lifted herself up.

"I want you to choose two companions from the town guard and ride out to find Drake Thorne. I feel in my heart that something is terribly amiss. He should have been here by now."

Kysa nodded her head. "As you wish, my lady. I will make preparations to leave right away."

"Of course you will," Zandria returned with a short laugh. "And you will not come back to me empty-handed, will you?"

"I will not."

Zandria gazed back at her servant with cruel eyes. "Good. Then I believe our business here is finished."

"Yes… Of course," Kysa fumbled as she gave a short bow. "Kanthis be praised!"

"Kanthis be praised, indeed," Zandria returned coolly. "Now, go!"

Kysa swiftly turned away and headed towards the chamber exit.

Chapter 32

Crystal Vision

It was sometime after midnight when Aydin took one last pull from his hand-carved pipe and sent a wispy cloud of pine-scented smoke to drift across the dark, rocky ceiling of the cavern. After lifting himself from the cold, stony floor, he shuffled over to the others who were lying in a circle around the small campfire. He sighed and softly shook his head as he thought about what he had to do next. He knew that sleep hadn't come easy for his young companions, who weren't used to camping out in such harsh conditions, and he hated to rob them of their much-needed rest. However, an unexpected development had drastically changed their situation, and time was of the essence. So, without another thought, he made his way around the circle and gently shook each of them awake, one by one.

As everyone sat up yawning and stretching, he began to speak, "I realize that no one wants to hear this right now, but we need to get back on the trail as quickly as possible."

Each of the companions glared back at him in annoyance and alarm.

Stifling a yawn, Alexis was the first to respond, "I don't understand what you mean, Aydin. Starview is barely a day's journey from here. Why the sudden sense of urgency?"

Aydin sighed and shook his head. "Two weeks ago, an old associate of mine, Draken Hawthorne, contacted me telepathically. He had been trying to tell me that I needed to be on the lookout for some sort of excitement that was stirring in Darkovia, however, before he could fully explain himself, our communication was abruptly cut off. Well, shortly after you all fell asleep, we managed to reestablish contact."

A sudden hush fell over the group, and they all began to listen intently, especially Devin, who had never before had any kind of experience with this sort of thing.

Aydin continued, "Apparently, Draken had been forced to cut our communication short and flee into the woods behind his house when a band of armed Darkovian guardsmen showed up unexpectedly at his front door with an order for his arrest. As it turned out, he was to be brought before the Darkovian High Council in Gordana for the crime of creating civil unrest, which is just a fancy way of saying that he had been caught freely speaking his mind in public about certain ideas that the council considered to be divisive and controversial.

After narrowly escaping imprisonment, he fled into hiding. During this time, he learned that a mysterious man traveling with an entourage of strangely-clad warriors had appeared in Gordana bearing news that the time of the goddess was quickly approaching. The man, proclaiming himself to be an oracle Kanthis, had met with Amaru Sidero, a wealthy and influential member of the Darkovian High Council, and convinced him to finance and commission a group of dignitaries along with a portion of the city guard and a few dozen mercenaries to retrieve the Goddess Stones and bring them to the floating tower."

Aydin stroked the curls in his beard as he took a brief moment to gather his thoughts. The small group stayed silent and continued to listen intently.

"The long and the short of it all is that those same dignitaries are due to arrive in Starview any day now, and we have very little time to spare if we hope to get our hands on the second orb before they do." Aydin paused reflectively and then added, "If we fail in this, I fear we may find ourselves faced with more trouble than we're prepared to handle."

Devin suddenly spoke up, "I don't mean to interrupt, Aydin, but there's something about what you just said that really concerns me. In my father's final message, he mentioned that a number of other survival-chambers, like the one I was in, had been constructed for the highest-ranking officials of the military to use in the event of a nuclear catastrophe. You don't suppose that the sudden appearance of this mysterious oracle and his strange entourage could somehow be related, do you?"

Alexis cut in, "I don't know about that, Devin. My great-great-grandfather was also visited by a Kanthisian oracle, and that was nearly 120 years ago. According to what you told us, the survival-chambers weren't scheduled to open up until after 300 years had passed. It seems to me that the timelines don't add up."

Devin cocked his head and squinted his eyes in consternation. "I suppose you might be right, Alexis. Who knows? Maybe I'm just being paranoid. But, still, something about all of this seems really odd to me. Do you really think that it's just a coincidence that the Darkovians made the decision to retrieve the Goddess Stones at around the exact same time that I woke up? And how do they even know where to look for them?"

Chance abruptly chimed in, "He has a point, Alexis. It does seem kind of strange, almost a little too strange to write off as just a random coincidence." He turned towards Sarina to get her opinion, but she seemed to be just as perplexed by the matter as he was.

Meanwhile, Aydin stood still, silently gazing at the companions with a pensive look upon his face. Finally, he said, "I, too, find the synchronicity of the events to be of a peculiar nature. However, I doubt that we will get our answers tonight. For the time being, we should focus our efforts on retrieving the remaining orbs before the Darkovians do, and that means we need to leave this place as quickly as possible."

With little room left for further debate and discussion, the companions did their best to shake off their weariness and began making preparations to trek out into the cold dark of night. A short while later, they left the warmth and safety of the cavern behind and began hiking in a straight line up the snow-covered mountain pass. Fortunately, the light of the waning gibbous moon was more than sufficient to illuminate the surrounding landscape, and a lantern was not needed.

At first, it seemed like they were making good time. The heavy snow that covered the pass was starting to thin out, and their speed of travel was slowly but surely increasing. Alexis even suggested that there was a chance that they might make it to Starview before sunrise. The thought of getting out of the frigid air and sleeping in a soft bed in the comfort of a warm lodge filled each of them with a renewed drive and desire to continue pressing forward.

A little more time passed, and then, out of nowhere, Sarina let out a choking gasp and came to an abrupt stop. The others, startled by the unexpected outburst, ceased their forward march and swiftly glanced in her direction. Upon doing so, they noticed that the sea-green streaks in her eyes were glowing with a fiery intensity.

Chapter 32

Suddenly, she cried out, "We have to turn back! We have to get off of this pass!"

Chance immediately rushed forward and put his arm around her. "Sarina, what's wrong? What do you mean?"

With a trembling, shaking voice, she replied, "I'm... I'm not sure. All I know is that there's danger ahead of us. I can feel it in every fiber of my being."

Just then, Alexis came up beside her and placed a hand on her shoulder. "Sarina, I believe you. Is there anything else you can see?"

Sarina, now shivering from the cold, shook her head.

Alexis quickly glanced over at Devin. "Can you bring me one of the extra energy crystals we found?"

"Of course! Just give me a second to dig it out of my pack!"

After locating one, he jogged back towards the women and handed it to Alexis.

"Here, try holding this close to your heart," Alexis directed as she handed the finely-cut gem to Sarina. "In Starview, there are people with similar gifts. Over the years, they learned that they could increase the potency of their abilities by drawing upon the power stored within Kanthisian power gems."

Sarina glanced back at Alexis curiously but held the gem close to her heart just the same. All of a sudden, she felt a pulse of warm energy flow out of the crystal and course all throughout her body. In an instant, her eyes began to glow with an intense luminosity she had never before experienced. A moment later, her eyes shut, and her mind was overtaken by a vision that was more lucid than any dream she could ever remember having.

As she gazed inward, she saw a woman riding atop a black spiral-horn beside two men outfitted in crude plate armor who were traveling on similar horses. The woman had brown skin, curly black hair, and fierce green eyes resembling those of a cat. She was dressed in plain riding clothes that consisted of light brown trousers, a loose-fitting, cream-colored top, travel-worn boots, and a brown hooded cloak. On her head, she wore a silver circlet featuring a single white jewel that glinted in the moonlight. Sarina immediately recognized her face. It was the same woman she had overheard speaking with the slaver shortly before she, Cyrus, and Tristam came together to rescue Chance, Devin, and Alexis.

With a gasp, her eyes popped open, and she dropped the crystal. "It's the same woman I saw at Drake Thorne's camp! I think her name was Kysa. She's heading this way with two others."

Alexis' eyes widened in alarm. "I know that woman! This can only mean one thing: she's been sent by my mother to find me!" Spinning around to face the others, she said, "Kysa is an expert assassin, and she's extremely dangerous. We have to get out of here, now!"

Aydin abruptly spoke up, "Where do you suggest we go?"

Alexis thought for a moment then replied, "There's a narrow mountain trail on the south side of the pass that shouldn't be too far from here. If we hurry, we can scale it and find safety. It's highly unlikely that anyone riding a horse would ever be foolish enough to try following us."

With a short nod, Aydin said, "Okay, then. Lead the way!"

Chapter 32

Alexis raced towards the front of the line and began marching forward. Aydin and Devin quickly fell in line behind her. Sarina, still standing near Chance at the back of the line, leaned over and retrieved the energy crystal from the snow. Briefly holding it up in the moonlight, she marveled at its appearance, and then, stuffing it into a pocket within her cloak, she took Chance's hand and hurried forward to catch up with the others.

Fortunately, the group didn't have to travel for very long before Alexis spotted the beginning of a steep trail that wound its way into the mountain ridge beyond. Turning to face her companions, she hollered back, "This is it! Follow me and try your best not to slip and fall!"

The companions tightened the straps on their packs and began to slowly hike up the steep, slippery slope. Fortunately, the snow wasn't as deep as it had been further down the pass, which made it somewhat easier for the travelers to find their footing. Aydin was the only one who seemed to struggle, but Devin stayed by his side and helped him every step of the way. Alexis continued to cautiously lead the group forward until, finally, the trail ended in a mountain hollow that ran south and then sharply curved back towards the west.

Coming to an abrupt halt, she turned to face the companions and said, "If I'm not mistaken, I believe this path will lead us into the Pine Hills region. If we keep traveling west, we'll eventually end up nearing the southern outskirts of Starview."

Chance suddenly popped in, "Where we'll finally get to sleep in a real bed," and lightly chuckled.

Alexis didn't return his laughter but, instead, grew quiet and pensive. After a brief moment, she glanced around at the companions and said, "I'm afraid warm beds are going to have to wait. It won't take Kysa and company very long to spot our footprints in the snow. As soon as they do, they'll start tracking us. After that, it'll only be a matter of time before every road leading in and out of Starview is covered and watched." As soon as the words left her mouth, she could sense that everyone's spirits had been dampened.

"The good news is there's an old hunting cabin on my family's land. It's rarely ever used, and there's little to no chance at all that anyone will come looking for us there."

This seemed to perk everyone up a bit.

She then added, "If we can continue marching west for the remainder of the night, we should reach the southern outskirts of Starview by sunrise. My family home is located there, and the cabin is just a few miles further south." She glanced around at everyone and waited for their thoughts.

Aydin spoke up, "Though I'll freely admit that I was looking forward to a hot meal and a warm bed, anything is better than spending another night out in these cold, foreboding mountains. So, by all means, lead the way!"

Alexis smiled with a nod and then, pulling her cloak around her tightly, swung around and began marching forward.

Fortunately, the remainder of the trip flew by without incident. The jagged cliffs eventually softened and gave way to the Pine Hills region, which, as its name implied, consisted mainly of low rolling hills topped by small groves of pine trees. As such, it wasn't especially difficult to traverse. Also, the snow, which was knee deep back at the cavern, had started to dissipate. By the time the companions finally reached the old hunting cabin on Alexis' land, it barely covered the ground. If the weather remained calm and clear, it would be gone by the end of the day.

Momentarily stopping to gaze upon the squat, single-story structure built entirely out of hewn wood, Alexis smiled. She had done it. She had led everyone to safety without getting caught. In that moment, she felt that Oren would be proud of her. However, as her mind raced forward, her smile began to fade. Deep down inside, she knew that the worst was yet to come. Turning to face her companions, she waved a hand and ushered them inside.

Chapter 33

Devin's Logbook

Entry 8:

If I hadn't seen it with my own eyes, I don't think I would have ever believed it. Of course, if someone would have come to me the morning after Erick's big party and told me that I was going to go to work and destroy the world with an energy drink, I wouldn't have believed that either. Now that I think about it, maybe someone did... Maybe it was that old hobo at the hoverbus landing with the cardboard sign that said something about the end being near? Maybe he knew something that I didn't, and he was trying to warn me? But that just sounds crazy, right? Or does it?

I honestly don't know what to think anymore. After all, what I witnessed tonight was also crazy, something that, before today, I would have never even thought possible. But, still, I watched it happen with my very own eyes, and the others saw it as well.

It all started when Alexis approached me and asked if she could have her energy crystal back. Considering that it was never really mine to begin with, I didn't think twice about returning it to her. After removing it from my dagger and replacing it with one of the extras we found in the orb chamber, I gave it back. She immediately attached it to her necklace and explained to me that it carried a lot of sentimental value, as it was given to her by Oren on her twelfth birthday. When she finished, she called for everyone to gather around.

I don't think there was anything that could have prepared me for what happened next. Stepping a few feet away from the table, she glanced back at all of us with a nervous smile and held the crystal up to her chest. As she did so, the yellow rings around her irises began to glow, and then, in a flash, she vanished into thin air!

I was so startled by it that I literally fell out of my chair! After picking myself up from the floor, I cautiously peered around in every direction and tried to wrap my head around what had just happened. I noticed that Chance, Sarina, and Aydin were all doing the same. It was obvious that they were just as dumbstruck and bewildered as I was.

After a minute or two had passed, she suddenly reappeared. It was plain to see that she was trying her best not to burst out in a fit of laughter. However, in stark contrast, we weren't in the least bit amused, as we were still trying to recover from the initial shock of it all.

Upon taking notice, she quickly apologized and then, after we all calmed down, explained to us that her ability to disappear was one of the primary reasons she felt so compelled to run away from home in the first place. Apparently, she had managed to keep her gift a secret for many years, but as time went by, she grew careless and got caught while trying to use it to sneak out of the mansion after dark.

Soon after she was found out, her mother began devising a whole slew of clever plans and devious schemes to enhance her power and grow her personal wealth by utilizing her daughter's rare gift. Needless to say, from that day forward, there was rarely a minute that passed by in which Alexis' every move wasn't closely watched and scrutinized. The only time she ever felt free was when she was spending time with her tutor and mentor, Oren Mendel, who would eventually lend a hand in arranging her escape.

Chapter 33

Shortly after she finished her story, she laid out a plan to retrieve the second orb and rescue Oren, which, of course, involved using her ability to disappear. First, she would sneak into her mother's mansion and steal both the orb and the keys to Oren's prison cell. Next, she would use the keys to free Oren. And, finally, if she didn't run into any trouble, she would meet us back here at the cabin. It was as simple as that.

Chance and I tried to convince her to let us come along, thinking that she might have need of my dagger and his bow, but she insisted that we'd only get in the way. I have to admit that, after seeing her vanish, it was kind of hard to argue with her.

That all took place earlier this evening, and it's been about an hour or so since she left for the mansion. Since then, we've just been hanging out here at the cabin while patiently waiting for her to return. Thankfully, it's warm and comfortable in here, which is actually saying a lot.

After the past week, it almost feels like we're living in luxury. I mean, this place has everything a person could need for an extended camping trip: a wood stove, cookware, a table and chairs, and four cots piled high with thick blankets. There's even a water well out back. I imagine a person could survive for many years out here if he or she had to.

At the moment, Aydin is helping Sarina prepare a rabbit that Chance hunted down earlier this evening, and Chance is out back filling our canteens with water from the well, which is a really good thing since we were dangerously close to running out of food and water. As for me, well, I'm just sitting here by myself, contemplating the future.

Truth be told, my mind is still reeling from everything that I witnessed earlier. I already knew that the energy crystals were powerful, but I never dreamed they were capable of making someone completely disappear. Even though I personally witnessed Sarina use one to turn her premonition into a prophetic vision, I somehow feel like this is on a whole other level.

It's a lot to wrap my head around. In the world I grew up in, supernatural powers and paranormal abilities were the stuff of fairy tales and fiction, but now they're a very real part of everyday life. I mean, Sarina can sense future events with pinpoint accuracy, Aydin can communicate telepathically, and Alexis can make herself disappear – and that's just what I've seen in my own small group. According to what they tell me, there are people all over the world who've been gifted with similar talents and abilities.

It really makes me wonder what else is out there that we haven't come across yet. Honestly, when I think about it, it's kind of scary. What if there are people who can call fire and lightning down from a crystal clear sky? Or what if there are people who can read minds? There might even be someone running around out there who can kill with just the touch of a finger! At this point, nothing would surprise me.

On a final note, I really hope that Alexis gets back to us safely. If something goes wrong and she loses the second orb, I have no idea what we'll do. It genuinely feels like the whole future is hanging by a thread right now.

Chapter 34

Frantic Flight

The companions had just laid down and closed their eyes when a series of loud knocks shook and rattled the old cabin door.

Jolting straight up, Devin burst out, "That must be Alexis!"

Chance immediately sprang out of his cot and unfastened the latch. As he pulled the door open, Alexis pushed her way inside, huffing and puffing.

"We have to get out of here!" she frantically panted. "They'll be on us any minute!"

"What do you mean!?" Aydin asked in a startled tone as he sat up and put his feet on the floor. "Where is Oren?"

Alexis shook her head rapidly as she tried to hold back her tears.

"What happened?" Aydin pressed further.

A few seconds of silence passed, and she somberly replied, "He's dead." Her gaze fell to the floor.

"Dead?!" Aydin seemed visibly shaken. "But how!?"

"There's no time to explain. We have to leave – now!"

No one needed any more convincing that the situation was serious. Chance hurried over to the wood stove and doused the glowing coals with a bucket of water while the others began to hurriedly pack their things. Within minutes, they were all rushing out the door right behind Alexis, who immediately began to lead them west.

At a pace that was somewhere between a brisk walk and a steady jog, Alexis plowed forward through a line of trees and into the shadowy hills beyond. The others, who were running on nothing but fear-induced adrenaline, did their absolute best to keep up but still struggled with the unfamiliar terrain. As they ascended the first hill, the faint, muffled shouts of their pursuers could be heard drifting through the forest somewhere in the distance behind them.

All night long, they rapidly scrambled over wooded hillsides and clambered down treacherous slopes that, slowly but surely, decreased in size and frequency as Alexis skillfully led them down the mountainside. Eventually, the hills disappeared completely, and a wide stretch of open grassland spread out before them. Still refusing to stop, she continued to goad everyone forward like their lives depended on it.

As they dashed across the plain, the last of the stars disappeared, and the night sky around them began to lighten. Soon, the black of night was completely replaced by the pale blue hues of early morning. Ahead of them, the long, sweeping shadows of the mountain range began to recede, and in front of them, the faint outline of a large settlement could just be seen emerging on the edge of the horizon.

Alexis suddenly called out, "The town of Mysa lies straight ahead!" and picked up the pace. "We'll find safety and refuge there! We have to keep moving!"

Being in no position to argue, the sleep-deprived travelers summoned the last of their inner resolve and continued to push forward, all the while hoping and praying that their strength wouldn't give out. By the time they finally drew near to the outskirts of Mysa, the sun had risen well above the mountains, and everyone, including Alexis, felt as if they were on the verge of passing out from sheer exhaustion.

Turning back towards the glade, Alexis listened as she stared into the distance, and after several moments of sheer silence, she was convinced that she and her new friends had lost their pursuers sometime in the night. Breathing out a heavy sigh of relief, she called for everyone to bivouac beneath a small grove of elms growing nearby.

After taking some time to catch her breath and stretch out her sore leg muscles, she brushed a few tangled strands of hair away from her face and glanced over at the others, who, with the exception of Aydin, were all sprawled out and lying flat on their backs in the shade. A faint smile traced across her lips.

Lifting herself from the ground, she spoke up, "I know we haven't had a minute to rest since last night, but we won't be doing ourselves any favors if we fall asleep out here. I'm sure we can find comfortable lodging in town, as the people here are used to catering to the traveling merchants who pass through on their way north or south."

"Did you have a particular place in mind?" Aydin inquired.

"No," she replied. "I just know that we'll be safe here. Oren always spoke highly of this place." With what felt like a knot in her throat, she continued, "He told me that he had friends and family here who wouldn't hesitate to lend a helping hand if I ever found myself in trouble."

"That's good to know," Aydin said with a slow nod. "And I assume you'll tell us exactly what kind of *trouble* we're in once we find lodging?"

Alexis gazed sullenly at the grassland to the east and nodded her head. A tear streamed down her cheek.

A short while later, the weary group entered the town and found themselves trudging down a crowded thoroughfare that was hustling and bustling with traveling merchants and street vendors who relentlessly called out their wares to the passing foot traffic. The small shops and stalls that lined the crumbling cobblestone avenue were constructed mostly from hewn timbers and coarse stones and, subsequently, weren't much to look at. However, in stark contrast, a large, two-story structure with white paneled walls and a peaked roof stood proudly at the end of the block. As the companions drew closer, they spotted an ornate wooden sign swinging in the breeze beside the front door. It had the words *The Saucy Survivor* painted across its surface.

Stopping, Alexis pointed and said, "Maybe we should try this place? It looks like it might be a lodge."

"It could be, but it could also be just another fancy pub," Chance said as he let out a huge yawn. "I spotted a number of them on our way here."

Sarina interjected, "Well, it doesn't hurt to look. I swear if we don't find something soon, I'm going to fall asleep right where I'm standing."

"You and me both," Devin agreed as he stretched out his arms and rocked back and forth on his feet. "I thought my first venture into Iron Woods was bad, but this was just completely over-the-top."

Chance grinned at Devin and silently nodded his head in understanding.

A brief moment or two passed by with the young companions gazing around tiredly at their surroundings and then back again at each other. Meanwhile, Aydin, who was standing just a few feet away, silently observed as his fellow travel mates fumbled around in some kind a of strange, indecisive stupor, his annoyance growing with each passing second.

Finally, he decided to interrupt, "Well, I'm not exactly sure what we hope to accomplish by standing out here and gawking in the middle of the street like a bunch of fools, but if this place does turn out to be a lodge, then I say the sooner we check in, the better." With a frustrated shake of his head, he swiftly turned away and began trekking in the direction of the building.

Breathing out a quiet sigh, Alexis shrugged her shoulders and fell in line behind him. Chance, Sarina, and Devin swiftly followed suit.

As Aydin pulled the large oaken door open with a tug, the mouth-watering aroma of steamed veggies and roasting meat hit him square in the nose, and almost immediately, his stomach began to rumble. Stepping through the doorway, he motioned for the others to join him.

As soon as they were all inside, a short, balding man with a thick brown mustache and a bulging belly that protruded over his belt stepped out from behind a polished wooden counter and exclaimed, "Welcome, friends! Come on in and make yourselves at home!" With a short wave of his hands, he beckoned them forward.

Aydin nodded with a grin and said, "Thank you very much, friend, but we were actually hoping to find lodging for the next day or so. You wouldn't happen to be in that business, would you?"

Returning Aydin's nod, the man replied, "I see, I see… Well, actually, I'm not officially in the lodging business, nor do I care to be." He paused and briefly glanced at the dining room behind him. "This happens to be The Saucy Survivor, the most famous restaurant in all of Mysa. Perhaps you've heard of it?"

Aydin shook his head politely.

"Well, okay, then. I'm just going to have to assume that you're not from around here." He huffed and squinted his eyes. "To answer your question, I do happen to have a spare room upstairs that I've been known to rent out from time to time – that is, for the right price."

Clasping his hands behind his back, he gazed over Aydin's shoulder at the scrubby, travel-worn group that had followed him inside. After sniffing the air a couple of times, he abruptly changed his tone, "On second thought, maybe you'd be better off trying The Pickled Onion Inn on the other side of town? I think you'll find the company there much more to your liking."

Stepping forward, Alexis cut in, "Listen, Mr?

"It's Mr. Ainsworth, young lady," the man replied.

"Okay. Listen, Mr. Ainsworth. We've been traveling all night long, and we're very, very tired. I realize that we probably don't look like the kind of patrons you're accustomed to dealing with, but I promise you that we didn't come here to start trouble. We just need a room for a night or two, that's all."

Reaching down into her cloak, she produced a small leather pouch and then, opening it, poured out a handful of shiny lavender-colored pearls into her outstretched palm. "Will these change your mind?"

With his hands still clasped tightly behind his back, the owner of the restaurant casually leaned over and examined the pearls more closely. As he did so, his face lit up with a bright smile. Abruptly straightening back up, he called out, "Mariza, I need you in the dining room, on the double!"

A muffled shout came from somewhere in the back, "I'll be right there, Mr. Ainsworth! Give me just a minute to stir the beets!"

A moment later, an energetic young woman, wearing a black dress and a long white apron, appeared from around a nearby corner. She had beaming brown eyes and tousled brown hair that was put up in a bun. As Alexis watched her approach, she felt like there was something familiar about her but couldn't quite put her finger on what it was.

The owner of the restaurant held out his hand and introduced her, "This is Mariza Romera, the culinary genius behind our world-famous cuisine. If you need anything while you're here, don't hesitate to let her know."

Mariza curtsied and smiled.

He continued, "Mariza, please show our guests to the spare room upstairs and see to it that their needs are properly attended to." He then turned towards the other and said, "After you've rested, don't hesitate to join us in the dining room for a hot meal. I believe that baked turkle is on the menu tonight. Is that right?" He glanced back questioningly at the young woman.

Mariza nodded and cheerfully replied, "Yes. The hunters brought a bunch of them in just last night. They'll be served with a side of roasted radishes and cabbage stew."

Devin suddenly nudged Chance and whispered, "What the heck is a turkle?!"

Chance leaned over and quietly whispered back, "It's a rare bird that lives in these parts. It's actually pretty good stuff if you can stomach looking at its curvy claws and lizard-like tail."

Devin's eyes widened in horror.

Chapter 34

Chance winked. "Trust me, you'll like it!"

Meanwhile, Alexis handed Mr. Ainsworth the lavender pearls and politely thanked him for his offer of hospitality. She and the others then proceeded to follow Mariza into the dining room and up a long flight of stairs at the back of the building. When they arrived at the top, they stepped into a carpeted hallway that stretched the full length of the restaurant. On each side, a number of doors opened up that led into bedrooms and sitting areas. With a polite smile, she directed them to the last door on the right.

As she stepped inside behind them, her cheery disposition morphed into one of frustration. "This place is an absolute mess!" Glancing around, she spotted three piles of dirty blankets lying on the floor and a bunch of loose papers scattered across the desk. "I can't believe he'd rent this room out in this kind of shape." Then, turning to the group, she apologized, "I'm so sorry about this. I'll send someone to tidy it up right away. I'll also have one of the cooks bring up a few of the spare cots." With a short nod, she promptly swung around and exited the room.

As soon as the scattered items were picked up and the cots were laid out with fresh, clean blankets, the travel-weary group wasted no time in putting them to good use. In a matter of minutes, they all drifted off to sleep.

It was sometime early in the evening when Alexis wearily opened her eyes. Glancing around, she noticed that everyone was still sleeping. In the background, the scraping and clanking of silverware and the faint chatter of hungry diners drifted up the stairs. After rubbing the sleep out of her eyes, she swung her legs over the side of her cot and stretched out her arms. She then stood up and wrapped her cloak tightly around her shoulders.

I really ought to check out our situation, she thought to herself as she held out her pendant necklace and gazed into the energy crystal. Pulling it tightly to her chest, she concentrated her focus and, in a flash, disappeared.

After cautiously exiting the room and quietly descending the stairs at the end of the hall, she softly stepped into the soft golden glow of lantern light that filled the rustic dining room and took a minute to observe her surroundings. It seemed that Mr. Ainsworth had a packed house. Glancing around, she noticed that many of the restaurant's patrons were dressed in expensive Darkovian robes. The sight brought back memories of the many luncheons and official dinners she had been forced to attend while growing up and caused her to curl her lips derisively.

As her gaze continued to drift over the crowd, it suddenly froze in place, and her heart skipped a beat. It was Kysa! She was sitting at a table near the fireplace on the far wall, sipping on a mug of beer and silently surveying the crowd with her cat-like green eyes. Sitting directly across from her were two guardsmen from Starview.

Alexis' thoughts began to race forward in a panic, *They're here looking for us. I just know it!* Abruptly turning around, she silently ascended the stairs. A half a minute later, she was back in the bedroom and stirring everyone awake.

"What's going on?" Devin wearily asked as he lazily pushed himself up on his elbows.

"Shhh!" came Alexis' sharp reply. She then turned towards everyone and, in a low tone of voice, said, "I don't think we can stay here much longer."

Chapter 34

They all glared back at her in shock and frustration.

"What do you mean, Alexis?" Sarina asked in fright as she pulled a lock of tousled hair away from her eyes.

"Kysa and two guardsmen from Starview are down in the dining room as we speak. I don't think they know we're here, otherwise, they'd have already captured us, but it's just a matter of time."

"This is grave news, indeed," Aydin said quietly as he lifted himself up from the bed and stretched. He then shuffled over to a small round table in a corner of the room and sat down. "Alexis, you do realize that, if they come up here, we'll be forced to fight?"

Alexis took a deep breath and nodded her head.

He then glanced over at the others and said, "We should probably pack our things. It appears that we may have another long night ahead of us." Turning back towards Alexis, he motioned for her to sit beside him. "I think now would be a good time to let us know what's going on, don't you?"

With a sigh, she nodded and sauntered over to the table. Everyone grew quiet.

After sitting down and glancing around at everyone, she began, "As you all know, I broke into my mother's mansion last night. I had my crystal activated, and I knew exactly where to go and what needed to be done." She whispered, "It should have been a breeze."

In a louder voice, she continued, "Once I made my way into my mother's personal chambers, I proceeded to take what I came for." She casually shrugged. "There really wasn't much to it." Standing up, she paced over to her pack that was lying next to her cot. Then, opening it up, she reached down and pulled out a perfectly round red crystalline sphere that glowed faintly in the shadowy room.

Devin gasped, "The second orb! You got it! I was so worried that you didn't, but I was afraid to ask – I mean considering… our circumstances… and all." His words began to falter as he noticed the darts coming from Sarina's eyes that reminded him of the same look that Rita gave him on the day that he walked into work for the last time.

Alexis sighed and nodded her head shortly as she set the orb on the floor beside her. She reached into her pack again and, this time, pulled out a dagger in a gilded sheath. As she drew the blade and held it into the light, everyone's eyes widened in astonishment. It was nearly identical to Devin's!

"I even took The Blade of Kanthis," Alexis said with a slight grin as she slipped it back into its sheath. She then returned it to her pack and picked up the orb. After standing up, she paced over to Devin and handed it to him. With a look that was dead serious, she gazed deeply into his eyes. "Keep it safe, Devin. It was paid for with a heavy price."

As Devin listened, he lowered his head and nodded solemnly.

Turning back to face the others, she proceeded to finish her story, "After I got back downstairs, I only had one thing left to accomplish – I needed to sneak into the chief overseer's room and steal the spare set of keys to the dungeon. It really should have been an easy task, a simple in-and-out affair. However, just as I entered his darkened bedroom, he swung around a corner and crashed straight into me!

We both toppled to the floor in alarm. Then, jerking straight up, he glanced around wildly, searching for the source of his obstruction, but he couldn't see me, as I was still invisible. Leaping to my feet, I darted across the room and yanked the spare keys to the dungeon off of a brass hook that was bolted into the wall by his dresser. He must have heard the keys jingle because he immediately lifted himself from the floor and charged at me. I swiftly jumped on his bed and sprang down to the floor behind him as soon as he got close.

As he chased the sound of my footsteps out of the bedroom and across the foyer, he began to shout out that there was an intruder, and within seconds, the sounds of feet hitting the floor and doors being thrust open filled the air. All I could do was sprint straight out the front door.

With no time to think, I scrambled for the backyard, where the dungeon is located. Activating my mother's blade, I turned and fired it at a large cedar growing near the stables. I figured the distraction might draw everyone off of me.

Fortunately, it worked. As the tree exploded in a ball of flames, everyone raced toward the stables, including the night guard who was watching over the entrance to the underground dungeon. I immediately took advantage of the situation and infiltrated his abandoned post. After rapidly descending a long flight of stairs, I rushed down the main corridor, checking each cell until I found Oren's."

As Alexis talked, tears were streaming down her cheeks. Not knowing how to console her, Sarina reached over and grabbed her hand. Squeezing it tightly, Alexis continued, "He looked so awful. Those monsters were starving and torturing him, like he was nothing! I temporarily deactivated my crystal and used the keys to open his cell. When he saw me appear, our eyes met, and we both began to weep. I braved a smile, and with what strength he had left, he helped me to assist him off of the dirty floor.

Unfortunately, he was in terrible shape, and we weren't able to make it down the corridor very quickly. As we passed by the other cells, the other prisoners began to holler and raise a loud ruckus, begging me to free them as well."

At this, Alexis stopped speaking and gazed up at the ceiling woefully. Lowering her gaze, she said, "I really should have known better. There was no way we were going to make it out of there without drawing attention to ourselves."

She sighed. "Needless to say, it wasn't long until we heard a set of footsteps coming down the stairs. At first, I thought it was the night guard, however, it was actually worse. It was my mother. When she spotted me, her face lit up with the most wicked, cruel expression I think I've ever seen in my life. I can't even find the right words to describe it. I almost forgot that we were standing in front of her because, at the time, all I could see was some sort of dark demon. I've never been more afraid.

Holding a crossbow directly out in front of her, she slowly stepped forward. In that moment, my fears of never really being loved by her, my suspicion of her hate for me and who I'd become, and my belief that she saw me as nothing more than a tool for her personal use were all completely justified. I just knew it was over for us.

When she got about halfway down the corridor, she came to an abrupt stop and gazed straight into my eyes. Then, in the coldest tone I'd ever heard her use, she said, "You're dead to me." A split second later, she pulled the trigger. Oren simultaneously threw himself in front of me, and the bolt struck him right in the center of his chest.

My heart stopped, and I started to scream in rage. I quickly drew my mother's blade and pointed it directly at her.

However, just as I was getting ready to depress the lever, I heard Oren's raspy, dying voice, 'Don't do it, Alexis. You're not like her.'

I instantly felt my heart break into a million pieces. Clutching my pendant to my chest, I vanished and bolted forward, knocking my mother flat on her back as I passed her by. Then, as quickly as my legs would carry me, I sprang up the stairs and fled the estate, still hearing the angry, stone-cold screams of my name traveling across the distance behind me."

For a brief moment, everyone in the room stayed silent and all was quiet, save for the faint sounds that drifted in from the dining room downstairs.

Devin was the first to speak up, "I'm so sorry, Alexis. I had no idea –" His words were suddenly interrupted by a light tapping on the bedroom door.

Everyone instantly jerked their gaze around.

A light tap, tap, tap came again and then a soft voice, "It's me, Mariza. Please open up. We need to talk."

Chance abruptly leaned over and retrieved a long hunting knife from his pack. He then marched over to the door and cracked it open an inch or so. Seeing that it was only Mariza, he pulled it open the rest of the way.

"What do you need?" Chance asked as he gazed down warily at her.

"I'm so sorry to bother all of you like this, but there's something important that we need to discuss. Can I come in?" She looked up at him pleadingly.

Turning around, he saw Aydin nod his head. He then ushered her forward with his hand.

Stepping into the middle of the room, Mariza immediately directed her attention towards Alexis, who had sat back down at the table in the corner. "I know this may sound kind of strange, but I think we know each other."

Alexis glanced back curiously and replied, "Actually, I don't think it's strange at all. It seems like I know you from somewhere as well."

"It's true," Mariza replied as she nodded her head. "I believe we used to play together when we were children."

Alexis' eyes suddenly lit up. "Wait! I think I remember now! You're Mari! You used to come and visit me with your parents during the summer. They were friends with my tutor Oren."

Mariza lit up and nodded her head excitedly. "And you're Lexi!"

Alexis giggled as she stood up from the table. "I can't believe it! It's been so long. You look so different now!"

"You do too!" Mariza said with a smile. "I guess we're all grown up now, huh?"

Alexis stepped forward and embraced her old friend warmly.

As soon as she finished, a look of worry swept across Mariza's features. "The reason I came up here is because there are three people downstairs who are looking for you, and they don't seem like the friendly type." She reached into her apron and produced a parchment. "They've been showing this around to our patrons and asking about your whereabouts." She held up a well-drawn sketch of Alexis.

Alexis' eyes widened in panic. The others began to stir around uncomfortably as well.

Mariza quickly grabbed her old friend's hand. "Don't worry! I told them that I would have a look around upstairs to see if Mr. Ainsworth had rented out a room to anyone fitting your description, but I never had any intention of giving you away."

Alexis breathed out a heavy sigh of relief. "Thank you so much, Mari! You have no idea how much that means to me. But why are you helping us?"

"Because that's what friends do for each other," Mariza replied as she leaned over and embraced Alexis once again. Straightening back up, she added, "Isn't that what Oren taught us?"

Alexis smiled and nodded her head. A tear streamed down her cheek. Deep down, she wanted to tell her friend about what had happened to Oren but figured that it wasn't the time nor the place.

Mariza continued, "Listen, I don't know why they're after you, but I know that it can't be for any reason that's good. We need to get you out of here before Mr. Ainsworth finds out about them." She paused and sighed. "I hate to say this, but if there's one thing you can count on, it's the fact that he loves his money. I have no doubt that he'll give you up for the right price."

"So what do you suggest we do?" Alexis asked as she glanced at the open doorway behind her friends.

"Well, I can send them on their way when I go back downstairs, but if they decide to come back in the morning, my hands are tied, as Mr. Ainsworth will be here."

Aydin suddenly cut in, "Then we have no choice but to leave tonight."

Alexis glanced back at Aydin and nodded her head in agreement. Then, turning back to her friend, she said, "Okay, we'll make preparations to leave as soon as everyone has gone home."

Mariza nodded. "I'll bring up some food to take with you when you go." She then glanced back at the door and said, "I hate to cut this short, but I'd better get back downstairs before they start getting suspicious." Looking back at Alexis, she smiled and added, "It's so good to see you again! I only wish it wasn't like this." With a short wave, she promptly turned away and exited the room.

Afterwards, the group used what little time they had left to pack their things and clean up their mess. Shortly after the last of the guests left for the night, Mariza appeared at their door with three loaves of bread, two blocks of cheese, and a bag of leftover turkle. She then led them down the stairs, through the dining room, and into the kitchen, where a back door opened up to an alleyway behind the restaurant. After giving them directions on how to safely get out of town without being seen, she bid them a safe journey. The companions then turned towards the south and began trekking off into the dark of night.

Chapter 35

Devin's Logbook

Entry 9:

 Unfortunately, I don't have a lot of time to write, as we're getting ready to pack up camp and leave again, but I wanted to make a quick note of everything that's happened so far.

 After leaving The Saucy Survivor behind, we fled Mysa and journeyed south across the plains. Aside from the small stretches of woodland that we were occasionally forced to cut across, travel was fairly swift and uncomplicated. During this time, my mind began to wander back to the events that had taken place earlier in the evening, and I began to mentally recount Alexis' story. Even though I hated the fact that her mentor had been killed, I couldn't help but feel a strong sense of relief in knowing that she was able to steal the second orb and get away with it. The truth of the matter is that, up until the moment she pulled it out of her backpack, I had been living in a perpetual state of fear and anxiety. When she finally held it up for all of us to see, it felt like there was hope again.

 I guess, for me, completing this mission isn't just about destroying the tower and saving the world from enslavement, it's something that I feel I have to do to make up for who I once was and for what I did to humanity. If I don't succeed, I'm not sure that I'll be able to live with myself. No matter how I look at it, failure just isn't an option.

 Anyway, by the time the morning sun came into view, we had put quite a few miles between us and our pursuers. We briefly stopped for a rest but then quickly decided that it would be in our best interest to continue pushing forward; the further away we were from Kysa and her men, the better.

A few more hours passed, and then Aydin and Chance spotted a shady patch of land that was partially encompassed by tall, billowy pines growing near the base of a cliff to our east. After taking some time to scope it out a little more thoroughly, they decided that it would be a good spot to make camp. They were both of the opinion that it would be much safer to rest during the day and travel during the evening and at night, as there would be less risk of us getting spotted from a distance.

As soon as we finished unpacking, we each took turns keeping watch so that everyone would have a chance to sleep. To say that it was a long, rough day would be an understatement. Nonetheless, we managed to pull through it.

It's now early evening, and we just finished eating the leftover turkle that Mariza sent with us. Chance wasn't lying when he said it was an ugly bird. As I picked one up by its leathery tail and held it up to my lips, I found myself gagging in revulsion. The others all giggled as they watched me struggle to take my first bite. I'm not sure if it was just because I was really hungry, but it turned out to be some of the best meat I've ever tasted, even better than Sarina's fried pumara sausage – although I'd never tell her that. My only complaint was that there wasn't more.

While we ate, Aydin took some time to study my map and then plotted out a route that takes us in the direction of the final orb. The good news is that there's a chance that we'll reach it within the day. The bad news is that the route takes us back into the mountains. I really can't say that I'm looking forward to another risky midnight climb. At this point, the only thing keeping me going is knowing that this part of the mission is nearly over.

It's funny, but every time I think that I've just about reached my physical limits, I end up having to push myself a little bit further – I'd be lying if I said that it didn't get old. However, these difficult times have taught me something that I never would have learned had I not been forced to go through them: when push comes to shove, I truly do possess the inner strength and determination needed to continue pressing on. I just wish I would have figured this out before I lost everything that ever meant anything to me, while my parents were still alive to see it.

Chapter 36

The Goddess Revealed

Devin's hand trembled as he nervously lifted his security clearance card and waved it across the small silver panel that was located next to the tall steel door. Almost instantly, the air was filled with the muffled sounds of gears churning and grinding against each other. A few seconds passed, and the door, which was embedded in a steep cliffside, began to slowly creak open, making a series of loud scraping noises as it bumped and slid across the rocky surface beneath it. Devin quietly held his breath as he watched, hoping and praying that the ancient retraction mechanisms wouldn't give out. A brief but tense moment passed, and then, with one final rickety, jarring motion, the door jerked open completely, revealing a small, darkened room beyond.

Turning around, he breathed out a huge sigh of relief and grinned at his companions, who were all looking on in amazement. "Well, at least it worked this time."

Alexis, recalling their chaotic first attempt at accessing an orb chamber, lightly giggled and said, "I never doubted that it would – not even for a second."

Devin chuckled as he slowly shook his head. "Well, that makes one of us." He then swung back around and stepped inside. With a short wave of his hand, he beckoned for the others to follow.

The gray morning light streamed in through the open doorway and faintly illuminated the back of the chamber, where a small dust-covered silver chest sat against the wall. Devin quickly paced forward to open it while the others followed closely behind him. As soon as the last member of the group stepped through the entryway, the door swiftly slid shut, leaving everyone standing in pitch-black darkness. A series of gasps swept across the room.

"Whoa!" Chance exclaimed. "This can't be good!"

Devin quickly intervened. "Everyone stay calm. It's okay, I think." He then leaned over and felt around for the button that opened the chest. "I'm pretty sure that we can use my card to open the door back up."

With a pop and a click, the lid swung open, and instantaneously, the back of the chamber was filled with a faint golden glow. Lying in the center of the chest was a flawless yellow crystal orb. Carefully picking it up, Devin held it out for everyone to see, its dim light revealing a look of relief upon his face. After laying it on the floor next to his feet, he proceeded to remove the other two orbs from his backpack and set them down beside it. The combined illumination of the blue, red, and yellow orbs created enough light for everyone to see each other's faces, if only faintly.

Turning towards Chance, he said, "Well, it looks like we finally did it."

"Yes, we did," Chance returned with a proud grin. "I always knew that we would." He then chuckled lightly. "It's been one heck of a journey, hasn't it?"

"It really has," Devin replied as he ran his fingers back through his tousled hair. "I'm amazed that we actually made it this far." He gazed down thoughtfully at the orbs lying beside him.

At this, Aydin quietly spoke up, "Unfortunately, I'm afraid that the worst is still ahead of us."

The look of relief on Devin's face quickly dissipated. "You know, I think you're right, and honestly, I'm worried that we might not even succeed. I mean, what are we supposed to do next – just walk into the floating tower and destroy it? Could it really be that easy?"

Aydin shook his head and lightly shrugged his shoulders. "I don't claim to know what lies beyond the horizon, Devin, but I do know that we have to complete this mission. The future of humanity depends on it."

The chamber grew quiet as everyone stood perfectly still in a circle and solemnly gazed down at the glowing orbs.

After a moment, Alexis broke the silence, "It's hard to believe that the fate of the entire world is sitting on the floor right here in front of us. It's kind of scary and surreal at the same time."

Sarina slowly nodded her head. "It really is. Though I'm ashamed to say this, it wasn't too long ago when I didn't believe that any of this could even be true." She stared down at the floor and sighed.

Looking back up, she brushed a lock of hair away from her face and turned towards Devin. "I've been meaning to tell you this for a while, and I suppose now is the perfect time." She briefly hesitated and then looked him straight in the eyes. "I want you to know that I was wrong about you. When we first met, I thought your story was crazy, and I was convinced that you were nothing but trouble, and because of this, I never gave you a fair chance. Maybe it doesn't mean a whole lot at this point, but I'm really sorry for that. I just thought that you should know."

Devin shrugged. "It's okay, Sarina. I really don't blame you for treating me the way you did. Let's be honest, I didn't exactly give you any good reasons to treat me differently. After that debacle back in Iron Woods, I'm surprised that we're even friends." He briefly glanced over at Chance, who closed his eyes and shook his head in embarrassment.

Returning his attention to Sarina, he continued, "I have something I want to say to you as well." He then peered around at everyone in the room. "As a matter of fact, I have something that I want to say to all of you. I want you all to know that I wouldn't have been able to do any of this without your help. The truth of the matter is that, if it hadn't been for your friendship and support, I probably wouldn't have made it past the front gates of Iron Cove, let alone this far. I owe each of you more than I can ever hope to repay."

The companions grew serious and quiet as he slowly gazed around at each of them with a look of humble gratitude.

After an elongated and slightly awkward moment of silence, Chance rolled his eyes and blurted out, "So is this when we're supposed to give each other a big group hug and, maybe, sing a song?"

Sarina swiftly jerked her head around and stung him with an icy glare.

Devin, thinking that it was probably a good time to wrap things up, shuffled over to the door and used his security clearance card to reopen it. He then proceeded to gather up the orbs and carefully place them in his pack while everyone else made their way outside. As soon as he finished, he joined them.

After eating a quick meal of bread and cheese, the companions, weary and worn out from having been up all night, reluctantly strapped on their backpacks and began hiking south across a narrow, rocky valley that was centered between two steep mountain ridges that rose up on both its eastern and western sides. In an effort to put as much distance between themselves and anyone who might potentially be searching for the orbs, they decided to continue traveling for the rest of the day. It was nearly sunset when they finally stumbled upon a well-hidden cove that was suitable for making camp.

The next day, they awoke before dawn and resumed their southward march. By the time the sun was beginning to rise, they rounded a series of steep cliffs and caught their first glimpse of the western sky spreading out before them. It wouldn't be much longer until they were completely out of the mountains.

As Devin took a moment to gaze into the distance, his jaw dropped open in stunned disbelief. Silhouetted against the sky, a large, island-like chunk of earth with an enormous conical tower rising up from its center could be seen slowly gliding towards a wide stretch of tangled forest growing up along the edge of the jagged, uneven horizon. It was so much larger and more imposing than it had been on the night that he caught his first glimpse of it back in Iron Cove. Skillfully constructed from cement, steel, and glass and equipped, from top to bottom, with gun turrets, battlements, and hover-landings, it rose up from the center of the floating island like a giant alien fortress. At the tower's peak, a massive barrel of a cannon could be seen stretching out from a metallic dome that glinted in the morning sunlight.

Eyes wide open in astonishment, he thought to himself, *That has to be the weapon my father was talking about!*

Suddenly, Chance appeared by his side. "Is everything okay?"

With a face as pale as a ghost, Devin glanced back at his friend and shook his head nervously.

Chapter 36

Reaching over, Chance firmly gripped his shoulder. "It's gonna be alright, man. We've got this. I'm not sure what's going through your head right now, but if you can, just try to remember that you're not alone – we're in this together."

Devin breathed out a heavy sigh of relief and nodded. "Thanks, Chance. I really needed to hear that."

At that moment, Aydin came up and stood beside them. "Well, it appears that we're finally nearing the journey's end." Stretching out his arm, he pointed towards the horizon. "The massive forest you see in the distance is all that remains of Highland City. If you look closely, you can still make out the vine-covered remains of the city's tallest structures rising up near its center. The floating tower has been drifting in wide circles around this general area for the last 300 years."

Upon hearing this, Sarina and Alexis sauntered forward to get a better view of the landscape. For a brief moment, they all gazed upon the ancient ruins and the tower that was slowly drifting by with an uncanny mix of fear and fascination.

As Devin's eyes slowly traveled across the broken horizon, he felt his heart sink into his stomach. Spread out before him lay the hopes, dreams, loves, and aspirations of nearly a million people, all reduced to ashes and dust in a single day, and all that remained to remember them by was a messy stretch of tangled forest and an airborne weapon of mass destruction. The awful sight caused a wave of self-loathing and hatred to permeate the depths of his soul, and he silently began to wonder if he would ever find forgiveness. With a woeful shake of his head, he cast his gaze to the ground and turned away.

Chapter 36

A short while later, the party resumed their descent to the bottom of the slope and then began journeying south alongside the mountain range. It only took another twenty minutes or so for them to spot a wide chasm opening up in the ground in the distance. As they drew closer, it became clear that the chasm was actually a gigantic, rocky crater. It didn't take any of them long to come to the conclusion that they had found the area where the tower first rose from the ground.

Suddenly, Chance shouted out, "Everyone, look!" and pointed towards a nearby cliffside to the east.

As the companions gazed in the direction that he was pointing, they spotted a tall, metal door in the side of the cliff that was identical to the others they had previously encountered.

Devin swiftly spoke up, "I bet that's the entrance to the tower!" He then turned to face the others. "I hope you're all ready for this."

"We're ready, Devin," Sarina replied with a reassuring smile. "Lead the way."

It wasn't long until they were all standing in front of a metal door that was identical to the one they had encountered the day before. As Devin passed his security clearance card in front of the small metal panel next to it, the door slid open without a single hiccup. Instantly, everyone, with the exception of Devin, grew wide-eyed with wonder as they peered down a long corridor that was lit from above with glowing ceiling panels. The bright white light produced by the panels illuminated a number of thick wires and small electrical boxes that ran along the smooth cement walls. Each side of the floor, which had been painted royal blue, was also lined with long yellow strip lights.

"This is absolutely incredible," Chance said as he excitedly gazed down the passageway.

"I think it's absolutely scary," Sarina said as her eyes darted back and forth between the strange lights and electrical devices that she had never seen before.

"Well, this is the world I came from," Devin replied as he stepped inside. "You might want to prepare yourselves though – I have a pretty good feeling that you haven't seen anything yet."

"I can't wait," Alexis said as she gazed forward in anticipation.

Meanwhile, Aydin stood by quietly and thoughtfully stroked the curls in his beard as he took everything in.

As soon as everyone stepped through the entryway, the door slid shut behind them with a loud whoosh. At that point, everything was dead silent, save for a faint hum of electricity that seemed to emanate from somewhere behind the walls. Devin quickly led the group down the long corridor, which began to rapidly descend underground right after they rounded a sharp curve at its far end. At the bottom of the descent, a doorway opened up on its right-hand side. Hanging on the back wall adjacent to it was a large white sign with the words *ATC Launching Bay* printed across it's surface in bold red letters.

"*ATC* stands for aerial transport craft," Devin remarked as he approached the doorway. "How do you all feel about flying?" He turned around with a pert grin and winked.

"Flying?" Chance asked as he glanced back incredulously. "As in flying like a bird?"

"Yep!" Devin replied with a light chuckle. "I mean, how else did you think we were going to get in the tower?"

The companions all stared back at him in wide-eyed astonishment.

As they passed through the doorway, a large, rectangular room opened up before them that was lined with computer stations, electrical generators, and life-support systems. In between these were a number of doors that seemingly led into offices and other parts of the underground facility. However, it was the silver bullet-shaped vehicle sitting at the far end of the room that immediately caught Devin's attention. Positioned in front of a long, dark tunnel, it reminded him of the rail car that took him to the survival-chamber shortly after his incident at the military complex.

"I could be wrong, but I believe that's our ride," Devin said as he began leading the group towards the vehicle. While they strolled along, he casually glanced around at the various electronic devices and gadgets that lined the walls, and for a brief moment, it almost felt like he was back in his old reality. Meanwhile, the sight of the ancient technology had rendered the rest of the companions speechless.

Upon arriving at the ATC, he strolled up to it and waved his card in front of a small circular panel next to the door. It slid open instantly, revealing three black leather-cushioned bench seats. Breathing out a heavy sigh or relief, he turned towards the others and stretched out a hand to usher them forward. "Okay, everyone, climb on in. Just leave me a place at the front. I imagine I'll have to use my card to activate the vehicle."

The companions glanced at each other nervously as they removed their packs and piled them in the back. Then, one by one, they climbed inside and sat down. After they were all seated, they glanced around at the plush leather interior of the strange space-age vehicle in a state of wonderment and awe. Meanwhile, Devin climbed into his seat and proceeded to wave his security card in front of a touchscreen display that was centered in the dashboard beneath the tinted window at the front of the vehicle. A small beep instantly rang out, and the screen lit up in a flash of blue.

Suddenly, an automated female voice came across the interior speakers: "Welcome aboard, Mr. Skye. Please select your destination."

Everyone suddenly gasped and glanced around anxiously in an attempt to locate the source of the voice.

Upon witnessing their reaction, Devin couldn't help but grin and chuckle. Turning to face them, he said, "Don't worry. It's not a real person. It's just a digital recording."

Chance immediately shot back, "What kind of madness is this?!"

Devin just shook his head with a grin and turned back around. Glancing at the touchscreen, he noticed that there was only one destination option: *New Scandinavia Sky Guard Aerial Assault Tower 1*.

Well, I guess that has to be it, he thought to himself. Then, with a gentle touch, he made his selection.

Once again, the automated voice came over the interior speakers: "Destination: New Scandinavia Sky Guard Aerial Assault Tower One. Estimated time of arrival: approximately one minute. Enjoy your trip!"

As soon as the message ended, the craft slowly lifted from the floor and began drifting towards the dark tunnel. The companions tensed up and kept their eyes glued to the front window as it began to accelerate. Then, suddenly, without warning, the vehicle shot forward like a rocket, thrusting everyone against the back of their seats. Both Alexis and Sarina let out high-pitched screams as their eyes began to glow fiercely, while Chance and Aydin gripped the edges of their seats for dear life. A split-second later, they were bolting towards a round patch of daylight that flooded into the tunnel from an opening directly in front of them, but before they could even begin to process their thoughts, they burst through the exit and shot across the rocky crater that they had spotted earlier in the morning. The next thing they knew, they were soaring upwards into a wide expanse of open blue sky.

As the group frantically gazed out the window, the floating tower appeared in the distance, steadily expanding in size as they quickly approached it. In less than a minute, the tower overtook their entire field of vision, and the craft began to rapidly decelerate. A few seconds later, they found themselves hovering over a circular landing pad that was located just a short trek from the tower's front entrance.

As the vehicle lightly touched down, the automated female voice came across the speakers: "You have arrived at your destination," and the door slid open with a loud whoosh. In the background, the sound of the rushing wind could be heard as it swept through the trees that sparsely populated the rocky surface of the floating island.

Turning away from the front window, Devin glanced back at his passengers, who were nothing short of stupefied. Even the normally calm and reserved Aydin seemed beside himself.

Subsequently, it was Aydin who first decided to speak up, "I don't even know what to say right now, Devin. What on earth just happened? And how in blazes does any of this even work?!" He glanced around at the interior of the vehicle in a bewildered daze.

Devin laughed and said, "Aydin, I'm not going to lie to you. This kind of travel was advanced even during my time." He briefly paused. "To be perfectly honest, this is the first time I've ever experienced anything quite like it. It was pretty cool though, right?"

Aydin stared back at him as if he had completely lost his mind.

After stepping out of the craft, the companions took a moment to observe their strange, new surroundings. If the tower was an imposing sight from a distance, it was downright terrifying up close. As they strained their necks to gaze upwards, they began to feel imbalanced, and their legs started to shake and wobble beneath them. The morning sunlight glinted off of the mirrored windows that climbed the full length of the structure, and every few yards or so, massive gun turrets and large battlements opened up in every conceivable direction. There were also huge platforms that stretched away from the tower every two to three stories that indicated the entrances to various landing docks and cargo loading bays. At the very top of the fortress, the long barrel of a mega cannon could be seen pointing towards the west.

The island itself was mostly barren, with the exception of an occasional large boulder or copse of trees that served to break up the rock-strewn landscape. Beyond its edges, the sky opened up and stretched out to the furthest horizons. To the north, the faint, dark outline of the Darkovian woodlands could be seen rising up and stretching out into the distance; to the east, Iron Cove Valley could be seen centered in a huge ring of jagged mountains and, beyond it, the thin silver line of a gigantic, distant lake; to the south, a series of wide open plains and rolling hills stretched forth until they faded into a hazy line of browns and greens; and finally, to the west, a huge, tangled forest, beginning with the ruins of Highland City, could be seen stretching out for as far as the eye could see.

Suddenly, Alexis spoke up, "It's easy to see how my ancestors were so easily convinced that this was Kanthis' palace. I don't believe there's anything quite like it in all of the known world."

Aydin, who had been staring up at the tower in awe and wonder, immediately chimed in, "It's also easy to see how the ancients were able to destroy the entire planet with such ease. The complex architecture and craftsmanship I see in this structure alone is nothing short of mind-boggling. I can only imagine what their weapons must have been like." Lowering his gaze, he turned to face Devin and stared at him with newfound curiosity.

"It truly was a different kind of world, guys," Devin replied as he began pacing towards the tall metal door at the front of the building. "And I'll be more than happy to tell you all about it as soon as we stop this tower from destroying the world we currently live in."

All of a sudden, Chance called out, "Wait! We can't go in yet. It's Sarina. I think she's having another premonition!"

Turning to face Sarina, the others noticed that her eyes were closed, and she was holding her energy crystal up to her chest. After a brief moment, she opened them.

"What did you see?" Chance hurriedly asked as he rushed to her side.

Chapter 36

With her blue-green eyes wide open and still glowing, she nervously shook her head and said, "I'm... I'm not quite sure." She glanced up and down at the tower with a look of worry. "I know this is going to sound crazy, but I saw something horrible and terrifying waiting for us somewhere within the tower. It was like nothing I've ever seen before, like some kind of gruesome mutant or deformed monster." Her body began to quiver as she placed a trembling hand over her racing heart.

Devin quickly responded, "That sounds like one of the genetically enhanced soldiers that my father warned me about. They're powerful creatures who are half-human and half-machine."

Chance's big green eyes grew wide with shock. "Half-human, half-machine?! What kind of unholy madness is this?!"

A wave of fear and panic immediately swept over the entire party.

Devin quickly threw his hands up and tried to calm everyone down. "It's okay, guys. They can't be activated without the orbs. Sarina must have had a glimpse of what will happen if we fail." He shook his head and sighed. "As long as we don't fail, there's nothing to worry about."

Sarina instantly shot him a piercing glare that caused him to doubt himself.

"Look, I don't like this any more than any of you do. All I can say is the sooner we get inside and finish this, the sooner our lives can go back to normal." Devin slowly lowered his hands. "This is why it's so important that we complete the mission. If we don't destroy the orbs and this tower, I can guarantee you that genetically enhanced cyborgs will be the least of our concerns."

Upon hearing this, everyone seemed to calm down a bit, except for Sarina, whose eyes still hadn't stopped glowing.

With a heavy sigh, Devin finished, "I don't know what else I can say, guys. You're just gonna have to trust me." He then turned away and resumed trekking towards the front entrance.

A few minutes later, the companions were all gathered around a tall, steel door that had the words *New Scandinavia Sky Guard Aerial Assault Tower 1* painted across its surface in bold black letters. Outside of that, the door was nearly identical to every other door the group had come across. Taking a deep breath, Devin removed his security clearance card and proceeded to open it up. As the huge door slid open, a huge, well-lit corridor opened up before them.

Stepping inside, Devin took a moment to peer down the long passageway. Every few yards or so, he noticed that the corridor had been reinforced with huge steel beams that ran up and down each side of the gray walls. In between these, a number of other steel doors and glass windows could be seen on both the left and right-hand sides. The paneled ceiling featured two long rows of white tube lights that ran its entire length, and the floor was tiled in smooth, polished gray stone. It appeared that the passage ended in a huge open chamber, where an enormous metallic column could be seen rising up from the center of the floor. He suddenly shivered as a series of chills ran up and down his arms.

Everyone remained cautiously quiet as they followed him down the long passageway. Upon approaching the first glass window on the left-hand side, they took a minute to peer inside. What they saw shocked them. Staged in three wide rows were a series of glass boxes that looked like coffins. Each of them contained a sleeping body.

Devin quietly remarked, "Those are survival-chambers. They're nearly identical to the one I used to survive the Great Firefall. The people you see lying inside them are the cyborgs that my father warned me about – I think." He briefly paused in thought and then shuddered. "We need to find the self-destruct mechanism, and we need to do it fast."

"I couldn't agree more," Aydin said as he opened up Devin's map and began studying it. "According to the map, the self-destruct mechanism is located just below this floor in the center of the tower. It appears that there's a stairway leading to it on the other side of the chamber just ahead."

With that, the companions resumed their trek towards the center of the tower. After passing by two more windows and around ten more doors, they stepped into a wide circular space that spread out and opened up all the way to the very top of the tower. Each ascending floor featured a well-lit balcony that wrapped around the entirety of the central chamber, and beyond these, various entryways, both large and small, opened up and branched off in every direction. In the center of the room, an enormous metallic column traveled all the way up to the mega cannon. The sight was both magnificent and terrible to look upon.

As Chance gazed upward, he shook his head in wonder and said, "Not once in my life did I ever imagine that I would see anything like this." He then slowly lowered his gaze and turned to face Devin. "This is quite possibly the most amazing thing that I've ever laid eyes on, and I think I might be starting to understand your world a little better now." He shook his head again and lightly chuckled. "Well, at the very least, I can see why you've had such a tough time adjusting."

Devin cracked a grin and nodded. "I don't expect you to fully understand this, but at this point, I'm seriously beginning to think that we might have been a little too advanced for our own good."

Aydin, who had been looking down at the map, cut in, "It appears that the stairwell is located on the far wall behind the column."

"Well, what are we waiting for?" Devin said with a grin. "Let's finish this." He then turned away and began to pace across the chamber. The others quickly followed from behind.

As they were drawing near the metal column, a bright flash of light suddenly came from behind. Stopping dead in their tracks, they swung around and spotted a strange cloud of glittering, sparkling light hovering in front of the chamber entryway. As they gazed at it, the sparkles began to materialize into the shape of a human. A few seconds later, they faded, and standing in their place was a tall, dark, and handsome man with wavy brown hair that was styled and perfectly parted on one side. He was dressed in an expensive-looking black knit sweater that was complimented by a pair of gray dress slacks and black leather shoes. Devin immediately recognized his face, and for a moment, all he could do was stare back in disbelief. It was Mateo Florez, Channel 12's top field reporter.

"Well, well, well, what do we have here?" Mateo asked as he glared at the party through piercing brown eyes. "If it isn't my old friend, Mr. Devin Patrick Sky." He shook his head and smirked. "I've got to be honest, you're absolutely the last person I ever thought I'd see again." He laughed sardonically.

Devin immediately shot back, "How on earth did you get in here, and how is it that you're still alive?!"

"Oh, Devin," he said with a laugh. "How little you know." He grinned and nodded shortly. "I never actually went away." He then glanced at the others, who were looking on with a mix of fear, shock, and confusion. "And who are your little friends?"

"That's none of your business, man! Answer the question!"

Mateo shook his head and began to pace forward. "Well, I live here, Devin. Don't you know?" He hesitated briefly. "I guess that's not quite right. I don't *actually* live here. I prefer to spend most of my time on my ship, but I do check in on this place from time to time." He then came to an abrupt stop and waved a hand towards the room. "So how do you like the goddess' palace?"

Devin swiftly threw his hand out in front of him. "Don't you dare take a single step further! How do you know about the goddess?"

At this, Mateo crossed his arms and began to laugh heartily. "How do I know about the goddess, you ask? That's easy, buddy. I made her up." Shaking his head, he fell into another fit of laughter.

Alexis, feeling completely enraged, suddenly shouted out, "Made her up!? What do you mean you made her up?!"

"Oh, you poor thing," Mateo returned with mock sympathy. "I know who you are. You're Zandria Volkov's daughter. Believe it or not, I've been keeping an eye on you for quite some time." He briefly paused in thought as he lifted a hand up to stroke his chin. "In ways, you remind me so much of your great-great grandfather. Why, you even look like him!"

He smirked. "Unfortunately, you lack his dedication and zeal for Kanthis, a trait that I find most disconcerting."

Devin quickly interrupted, "Answer her question, Mateo. I think we deserve to know what's going on here."

"Okay, but first, why don't you tell me what you're doing here?" Mateo looked Devin dead in the eyes. "It wouldn't possibly have something to do with three lovely orbs, would it?"

Devin just stared back silently.

"Of course it does!" Mateo laughed. "I actually dropped in because I thought that, maybe, Colonel Gundersen and his men had decided to stop by for a surprise visit."

"Colonel Gundersen?!" Devin's eyes widened and his jaw dropped. "*The* Colonel Gundersen?!

"Yes, Devin. There's only one. He's been scouring the countryside in an effort to retrieve the orbs for me." Mateo began strolling forward once again. "But you have them, don't you? I mean, why else would you be up here?" He then stopped and threw his hand out, palm facing forward. "Wait! Don't answer that! Let me try to guess. It was your father who put you up to this, wasn't it? I always suspected that he was behind their disappearance." Mateo shook his head with a twisted grin and resumed walking.

Devin glanced at his companions nervously. "How do you know my father!?"

"I'm tired of answering questions, you little punk. Hand over the orbs – now!"

"Never!" Devin shouted back defiantly.

Suddenly, Mateo's eyes grew wild with rage, and he dashed forward at full speed.

Chapter 36

With no time to think, Devin unsheathed his dagger, flipped the switch, and fired it at his would-be attacker.

As the energy bolt made impact with Mateo, his eyes lit up in a flash of red, and he began to laugh maniacally. "Your silly energy weapons are useless against me, boy!" All of a sudden, he stopped running and tore his sweater clean off his back. It appeared that his entire body was pulsating with some kind of strange kinetic energy. He then screamed out in a rage and threw his hands up in the air as his skin took on a scaly, almost reptile-like quality. Glaring back at the companions, his eyes began to glow with a deep red light. As he lowered his hands, they noticed that long, razor-sharp claws were protruding from the tips of each of his fingers.

"What on earth is it?!" Chance exclaimed as he quickly unslung his bow and nocked an arrow.

Devin shouted back, "I think he's an alien!"

Mateo screamed out, "You're all fools! Those orbs don't belong to you. They never have. They were created by my race a very long time ago, and we want them back!" He began to dash in their direction.

Alexis suddenly grabbed hold of her pendant and disappeared. Racing forward at breakneck speed, she met him halfway and thrust The Blade of Kanthis straight into his gut. Momentarily fazed, he swiped a clawed hand in front of him and knocked her flat on her back.

He then screamed out, "You can't kill me!" and began laughing as he continued to race forward.

"Chance, you have to do something!" Sarina yelled as she drew her hunting knife.

"Yes, please do!" Aydin said as he reached into his cloak and produced a small glass vile that was filled with a venomous acid.

Chance stood perfectly still and breathed in deeply as he steadied his aim. Just as Mateo was nearly upon them, he let the arrow fly. Almost instantly, it buried itself right in the center of his left eye.

Mateo immediately let out a deafening roar that reverberated up and down the tower and fell to the floor clawing and scraping at his face. Without a second of hesitation, the group raced forward and lunged at him with their daggers and knives. Aydin uncorked his bottle and flung the acid straight into the creatures eyes. As the blades punctured his vital organs and the acid sizzled upon his face, he let out a choking gasp, and his body went completely limp.

For a moment, all that could be heard was the labored breathing of the companions as they slowly picked themselves up and gazed down at the strange, reptilian creature that lay crumpled on the floor before them.

For the first time since entering the tower, the sea-green streaks in Sarina's eyes stopped glowing. Glancing over at Devin, she said, "This is the reason why I've never ignored a premonition."

Devin slowly nodded his head and woefully cast his gaze to the floor.

At that moment, Alexis reappeared. Covered in blood and limping, she sauntered towards the group. "Well, I suppose that's the end of Kanthis."

"Indeed it is," Aydin said as a trace of a smile formed above his curly beard.

"And I say good riddance!" Chance blurted out as he strapped his bow back on his back.

Looking back at Sarina, Devin finally spoke up, "I'm so sorry, Sarina. I never should have doubted you."

"It's okay, Devin," she said with a warm smile. "I never should have doubted you either. I guess we're even now, huh?"

Devin returned her smile. "I guess we are."

As soon as everyone had taken a moment to rest and regain their composure, they strapped on their backpacks and resumed their trek towards the staircase. It seemed that the worst was behind them, and the only thing left to do was to destroy the floating tower.

As Devin followed his companions towards the stairs at the back of the chamber, he suddenly began to feel woozy and lightheaded. Stopping in mid-step, he said, "Hey, guys. I don't feel so well." However, to his complete surprise and dismay, they kept marching forward as if they hadn't heard him. As he watched them walk away, a wave of dizziness swept over him that nearly caused him to collapse. Once again, he tried to get their attention, only this time he shouted, "Hey! Wait! Where are you going?!"

All of a sudden, the strength in his legs gave out, and he felt himself topple forward. Just as he came face-to-face with the floor, everything around him faded to pitch-black.

Chapter 37

Anamnesis

The sound of muffled voices could be faintly heard as Devin slowly came back to consciousness. Laying perfectly still with his eyes closed, he passively listened to the voices and thought to himself, *Everything must be okay now. I bet they managed to destroy the tower while I was passed out*.

Feeling a slight chill, he reached down and gripped the edge of his warm blanket. With a short tug, he pulled it up to his neck and breathed out a quiet sigh. *Ah, that's so much better*.

All of a sudden, he could clearly hear the voice of an older man, "Madeleine, I think he's waking up!"

A few seconds later, the soft voice of a woman rang out in response, "What did you say, Cedric? I didn't hear you."

"Honey, I said that he's waking up! Hurry up and get in here!"

A moment later, Devin could hear the man and woman talking just a few feet away from him. As the sleepy fog began to dissipate from his mind, he slowly forced his eyes open. Standing at the foot of his bed was a middle-aged man and a beautiful woman. The man had shaggy brown hair and a well-trimmed mustache and beard. The woman had long blonde hair and stunning blue eyes.

Who are these people? he thought to himself as he twisted his head to look around. Sitting on a small wooden nightstand next to the bed was a picture of a young man standing beside the same two people who were currently in the room. The young man was dressed in a blue cap and graduation gown and was holding up a diploma in his left hand. Standing near the picture was a small lamp, and lying beside it was a brown leather wallet.

Where am I? he suddenly thought as he began to panic and nervously glance back and forth at the strangers.

"Greyson! You're finally awake!" the woman said, as she rushed to his side with a big, bright smile.

Devin lifted his head and said, "Who the heck is Greyson?! And where's Chance, Sarina, and the others!?"

The woman's eyes suddenly widened in panic. "Honey, you're Greyson. Don't you know who you are? Are you feeling okay?"

"What are you talking about?" Devin frantically asked as he quickly sprang to his elbows and glanced all around. The room he was in was sparsely furnished with a cushy brown chair, a computer desk, and a bookshelf that appeared to be loaded with science fiction and fantasy novels. To his right, he noticed a large window that appeared to be looking out on a black sky full of stars, and hanging on the wall beside it was a poster of the solar system. "Where am I?"

"It's okay, Madeleine," the older man softly replied. "There's no need to worry. This is absolutely normal. I did the same thing when I was his age."

As Devin's eyes shot around the room, he suddenly began to feel as if everything around him was somehow strangely familiar, but for the life of him, he couldn't pinpoint why. All of a sudden, he reached up and felt something wrapped around his head. Grabbing hold of it, he lifted it up and held it out in front of him. It was a strange metallic headband that featured a series of blue, red, and yellow blinking lights and a small display panel, which was currently blank.

"What is this?" he asked as he held it out to the man and woman.

"That's our family legacy, Greyson," the man said with a smile. "You just went back in time 700 years, in a manner of speaking. Are you starting to remember yet?" He glanced back inquisitively.

Devin stared back at the man curiously and rapidly shook his head.

"Cedric, don't you still have that bottle of Neurolight that we picked up back on Mars?" Madeleine asked as she softly traced her fingers through Devin's tousled hair.

"I believe I do. I think it's on the top shelf of the medicine cabinet," Cedric replied. "That'll probably help."

Madeleine quickly paced out of the bedroom and then, after a few minutes, returned with a measuring cup and a bottle of medicine. "Here, take this, sweetie," she said as she handed him a light dose. "This should do the trick."

Reaching up, Devin retrieved the cup and gazed at it precariously.

"It's okay, Greyson," she said. "It won't hurt you, I promise." She smiled warmly.

Devin thought that there was something strangely reassuring about her smile, and after a hesitant moment of deliberation, he brought the cup up to his lips and swallowed its contents in a single gulp.

Looking down, Cedric grinned. "Son, we'll be right back. There's something that I want to give you, a graduation gift, if you will." He and his wife then turned around and strolled out of the bedroom.

A few minutes passed as Devin glanced around curiously at the room, and then, out of nowhere, a plethora of memories came rushing back to him. It almost felt as if someone had flipped a light switch on in his mind.

Oh, my lord! I'm Greyson Cedric Skye! he thought to himself as his eyes widened in surprise. *And that entire thing I just experienced was nothing more than a simulation!* His jaw dropped open as he picked up the picture beside his bed. *These people are my parents.* He lightly shook his head and smiled.

At that moment, his parents came sauntering back into the bedroom. His dad carried with him something that was all too familiar, a beautiful dagger that featured a mirrored blade, a black leather-grip handle, and a beautiful bluish-green jewel set in the center of the crossguard.

As they approached the bed, his father said, "Son, this is also part of our legacy, and now that you've graduated high school and are getting ready to go off to college, I want you to have it." With a tear in his eye, he handed him the blade. "We both want you to know that we're proud of you."

Suddenly, his smiling mother pulled a hand out from behind her back and held out a beautiful brown leather-bound journal. "As I'm sure you already know, keeping a journal has been a Skye family tradition for the last 700 years. I hope you like it." She then handed him the journal and leaned over to kiss his forehead. "We love you, son, and we believe you're going to do great things."

"I love you too," Greyson returned with a smile. "I have every intention of making both of you proud."

His dad's face lit up in a big smile. "You already have."

"Honey, I imagine he's probably ready for some real sleep," Madeleine said as she turned to face her husband.

"Let's give him some privacy now. I'm sure he has a lot to think about."

Cedric grinned and nodded, and then they both turned away and shuffled out of the room.

A short while later, Greyson found himself at his computer desk examining the ancient blade that had been in his family for 700 years. After setting it down, he picked up his brand new leather-bound journal and quickly flipped through its blank pages. He then laid it in front of him and grabbed a pencil. Opening it up to page one, he began to write:

In just a few days, our ship will be arriving on planet Earth, and shortly after that, I'll begin attending Starview University. It feels so strange to be sitting here and writing like this, considering that, in the past, I never felt in the least bit inclined to keep a journal. However, after having experienced my ancestor's life via a computerized simulation, I almost feel as if he's become a part of me. His thoughts were my thoughts, and in a way, his experiences were also mine. Throughout his life, he faithfully kept a journal, and subsequently, I plan on doing the same. All that aside, I really don't feel like being the first person in my family to overturn 700 years of tradition.

I'm not sure what the future holds for me, but after today, I feel a thousand times more prepared to handle it. In the past, my plans for college involved women and a whole lot of partying, but after what I just went through, I think I'd be better off if I focused my attention on doing something slightly more productive.

On that note, the first thing I'm going to do is get out of this bedroom and spend some quality time with my parents.

Chapter 37

If there's one thing I learned from Devin's life, it's that you don't know what you have until it's gone...

www.ingramcontent.com/pod-product-compliance
Lightning Source LLC
Chambersburg PA
CBHW030553260626
47157CB00006B/2298